M000014645

CARROLL & GRAF

SECRETS & SCENTS

SECRETS
— & —
SCENTS

ANONYMOUS

CARROLL & GRAF PUBLISHERS, INC.
NEW YORK

This collection copyright © 1997 by Carroll & Graf Publishers, Inc.

First Carroll & Graf edition of *Three Times a Woman* 1983
First Carroll & Graf edition of *Secret Lives* 1983

Carroll & Graf Publishers, Inc.
19 West 21st St., Suite 601
New York, NY 10010-6805

ISBN: 0-7867-0499-3

Manufactured in the United States of America

Contents

SECRETS & SCENTS

THREE TIMES
A WOMAN

(Grushenka)

CHAPTER I.

Katerina walked in great dismay through one of the unpaved streets in the Northerly quarter of Moscow. She had much reason to be uneasy and in bad humour. Here it was spring; soon the whole household would be moved to the country and she had not yet been able to fulfill the command of her mistress, the young and capricious Princess Nelidowa Sokolow. At first the Princess Nelidowa had only mentioned her request casually, as something she would like to have. But lately she had demanded, nay commanded. The young Princess had become very irritable. She was always on the go, never at rest, not even for a reassuring prayer.

It was not for Katerina to question the orders of her mistress. She was the housekeeper, an old and trusted serf, hardened by rough work, now burdened with the weight of running the huge household, to which the young and pleasure seeking Madame gave never a thought. She had been trained since her early youth to follow orders and to do so promptly. Katerina was not in dismay because she was

5

afraid she would be punished. She was not in fear of the lash. No, it was not that. She simply wanted to do her duty and her duty was to satisfy her Lady.

What Princess Nelidowa wanted was this: a serf-girl, who had exactly her own measurements, who duplicated exactly her own figure. It may seem strange that Nelidowa should have had such a desire, but it was not. It must be imagined through what nerve-racking torture, (so she thought at least) Nelidowa had to go standing as a model for hours and hours in her boudoir, while the tailor, the chemise-maker, the bodice-maker, the shoe-maker, the coiffeur and all the other untold clothiers tinkered around her body.

Of course, it is every woman's delight to adorn herself, to choose and to invent what is most becoming to her. But Nelidowa was suddenly in a hurry. In a hurry to live, to enjoy herself, to play the lady, to be everywhere, to be seen, and last but not least, to be adored. To be adored and envied by women, meant clothes and more clothes. And that meant to have to stand still and suffer, to be touched all over by the dirty hands of the dress-makers. The Princess despised the dress-makers as she did all other working people and treated them haughtily and unjustly. She disliked the smell of them, but she had to bear it in order to look lovely and rich.

Rich! That was the word which sang always in the ears of the newly wed Princess. Rich, mighty, a figure at the court, a mistress of many souls. Of course there was a price to be paid for it, a price with disgusting features. This price was that she had to be the wife of Alexey Sokolow. She hated it, but what could she do? It was a bargain she could not confide to her most intimate friends. She was always conscious why she had to endure it, but had not thought yet how she might get round it.

For Nelidowa had been terribly poor. So poor that in the convent where she had been brought up, she had not been given enough to eat. The nuns had used her as a kitchen maid and on the great holidays, when all the other aristocratic girls donated candles to the Saints as big as a log, she could not even buy a little waxen stick. Her father had been a great general, a superb aristocrat, her mother a Tartar Princess. But when her father, in one of his usual drinking spells, had fallen into the Volga and drowned, his family was left without a penny. Ill-meaning relatives scattered his brood, as they called it, into institutions and charity houses.

Grown to be twenty, and without any desire to become a nun, an old and half blind aunt in a little city had taken her in. There she was chained to a cranky invalid who gave her the switch once in a while, which it was then the mode to use even for educated girls as long as they were not married. Therefore, it was like a miracle when the match with the mighty Alexey Sokolow was suddenly in the air. It was a fata morgana, not to be trusted, and when it finally became true, Nelidowa had to pinch herself many times to make sure she was not dreaming.

This match had been made, after the fashion of the times, by correspondence. Now, in the little city where Nelidowa then lived, was a fickle young man, son of the Military commander of the district. He fell so violently in love with Nelidowa that he told his father—and told him with passion—that he was going to marry the girl of his love, although she was poor and socially a nobody. The father, as it goes in the world, did not want to consent. The best thing therefore, so it seemed to him, would be to remove the girl from the sight of his son and the best way to remove her was to marry her off. Being a school chum of the mighty Prince Alexey Sokolow, and having corresponded with him for many years, he now sent him such showers of praise about the virtue and charm of Nelidowa, that he succeeded in getting the old bachelor engaged to the girl by mail.

There was no doubt that Nelidowa would grasp this opportunity with all her ten nimble fingers. Ex-Governor Prince Alexey Sokolow, was known throughout the country as one of the richest landowners, a figure at court, a political factor and as a host who gave elegant parties. One of the grandees of his time, he had inherited his fortunes and tripled them by bold strokes which often bordered on robbery. That he was thirty-five years her senior did not disturb Nelidowa. It all meant he one great windfall of luck for her. But that he consented to marry her made her wonder very much.

It cannot be said whether Sokolow would have been able to get one of the rich ladies of the court as a wife, but it is sure that he had his special reasons for making the abrupt decision to marry the unknown girl. These reasons were not that she was an aristocratic girl and the daughter of an old friend of his. No, the real reason was that Sokolow wanted to do some spite work to his relatives. They were already counting on his death, had already figured out what they would inherit from him, would in fact have liked to poison him. Now let them wail! He would marry this girl who was young and healthy, marry her and have children and the whole chorus of loving relatives would have to go away empty handed.

When this clever idea entered his head, he acted with his usual abruptness. Nobody should know beforehand. He simply wrote a letter to Nelidowa, without any explanations or previous correspondence, to the effect that he had heard from his old friend that she was a marriageable person, that enclosed were 5000 rubles for her dowry, that the ring he was sending had been worn by his mother, that the carriage sent to her door was hers, and that he expected her without fail by return post. But he advised her to travel by easy stages, so that she should not be tired at the wedding ceremonies, which would take place as soon as she arrived in Moscow.

There was the handsome carriage with a huge coachman and two footmen at her door, there was 5000 rubles—Nelidowa had never in her life seen so much money—there was the ring with a ruby, thick as a pigeon's egg, there was the confirmation of the Military Commander that all this was his work. Well, Nelidowa jumped into the carriage and did not travel in easy stages but in such haste, that the coachman often had to change his poor horses. Nelidowa didn't get tired at all. She was so excited that she did not feel the lack of sleep or food. She was in a trance.

She did not even lose this state of excitement when she saw the bridegroom. No poet could have made him into a desirable lover. He was in his middle fifties, short, brutal and bald, with a large belly, which protruded from underneath his hairy chest. Only when Nelidowa found herself with him in bed, did she realize the disgusting reality—but that must be told later on.

This was the reason why the young Princess plunged herself with such vigour into all and every kind of amusement and social debauchery. She had to make up for the past and she had to make the most of her bargain. Therefore, during the second season of her life in Moscow, she left no stone unturned if it meant any pleasure for herself. She treated her servants with reckless brutality, she became nervous, irritable and restless and was ceaselessly thinking of means to make everything as easy for herself as possible. She had decided that she did not want to try on her own clothes, but that a substitute should be found. That is how Katerina got her order to find and buy the duplicate of Madame.

Katerina had tried to fill this order for quite a while, that is, since after Madame had gotten many headaches trying on the last fall styles. But so far Katerina had been unsuccessful. Not that the Princess had such an extraordinary figure. But those tramps, those peasant slave girls all had such miserable bodies; sturdy undercarriages, broad backs, large hips, terribly thick bottoms and legs. On the other hand, Nelidowa had very full, oval, pointed breasts, carried over an amazingly subtle waist. She had very well formed, straight legs and small, aristocratic hands and feet.

Nobody knew these differences better than the old housekeeper, because she herself had taken the measurements of Nelidowa's body. The "little mother," as her household serfs called her, had stood quite still as Katerina took her height, the measurements of her bust—above, over and below the full breast—of the waist-line, the hips, the bottom, the thighs and the calves, the length of the arms and the legs. Nelidowa had stood quite still and had smiled, thinking it was the last time that she would have to do the trying-on herself.

Katerina had taken these measurements in her own way. She could not read or write, she could not handle the tape measure as those silly talking French clothiers did so skilfully. Therefore, she took ribbons of all colors, every time another color for another measurement, and cut them exactly to the right length. She was able to remember without fail which color represented, for example, the wrist or the ankle measurement, because this fat and slightly grey and ignorant peasant woman had a better sense of recollection than any of the caste of learned and educated men. These colored ribbons were then carefully sewn together so that they made a long string in the order in which Katerina was taking her measurements. In this way, a practical yardstick of Nelidowa's proportions was procured.

How often she had tried in vain! First she had gone around to the households of other Grandees and after a friendly chat with the Major Domo or with the head-housekeeper, she had looked the serf girls over, because it was always possible to buy a certain girl if no special reasons kept her in the household, such as the master liking her best as a bed companion. But not even among the ladies' maids and linen girls who were supposed to be of the finer kind, could she find any who came near her measurements. Then she had gone to the serf markets, which were held from time to time to make exchanges of serfs in the different houses of the aristocracy. After that, she had visited what one could call dealers; certain persons who had once been major domos and were liberated for one reason or another, and who make a scanty commission in buying and selling serfs, mostly young, good looking girls who were traded to the many whore houses which at that time started to flourish in Moscow, a fashion lately imported from Paris. In this way, Katerina had been hunting the whole winter, and while she found here and there a girl who came near the requirements, she had been told to bring a girl who would fit exactly. But how to get her?

This all was on Katerina's mind on that April afternoon

(it must have been, approximately, in the year 1728) while she was on her way to a private dealer in the poor quarters of the North of Moscow. The sudden haste which crept up in her made her do something that was extraordinary for her. She hailed one of the droskis which hung around a street corner, one of those dilapidated one-horse-carriages, which were not promising as to safe arrival at one's destination. The half drunken driver sullenly started with her, after she had made a hard bargain for the fare. Soon she found herself in babbling conversation with the driver, who was her equal in being unable to keep his mouth shut, and who scratched his long hair when his ill-fed and tired horse stumbled over the rough cobblestones. Because it was not Katerina's way to keep anything to herself, the driver knew very soon that she was out to buy a serf girl for her Princess and mistress. Here he saw a chance for himself and told Katerina that a cousin of his, who had seen better days, was going to sell two of her girls, young and sturdy, and very obedient workers. But Katerina did not want to listen. She was determined to go to her destination and there they went. The driver was paid, and his remark that he would wait until his client got through with her business, received no answer.

Katerina was expected at the house of Ivan Drakeshkow, because she had sent him a message that she would look over his girls before they were offered at auction. She was greeted with dignity and almost reverence. A buyer with money is always welcome. Ivan Drakeshkow lived in a small, one story house, surrounded by an untidy little garden, where some chickens were busy looking for prey after the rain. Ivan had bought the property when he was an ebony cutter, a successful craftsman in his line, and during this time, he had married the parlour maid of a Grandduchess, who had given the girl her liberty and a dowry. But Ivan had contracted an eye trouble which left him almost blind, and his wife, once good hearted and gay, had become a sour old witch who bossed him meicilessly. In fact it was she who started the trade in serfs and she earned just enough for food and fire-wood but never enough for a bottle of hard liquor, for which Ivan craved in vain. "Who does not work shall not drink," was her motto, and she forced her good-for-nothing husband to wash the dishes.

Katerina was offered, with too much politeness, a huge and comfortable armchair. She was treated with tea from the ever boiling samovar. She was drawn into long conversation about the Czar and her master. But she was in haste, uneasy, and wanted to see the girls. Madame Drakeshkow saw that the business had to be started right away.

"You see," she said to Katerina, "I will have for the auction more than twenty girls, but they are not all here yet. The later they come to me the less I have to feed the slobs. So if you don't find what you are looking for, just keep in touch with me and I am absolutely sure I can serve you. There is nobody who knows so well all the serf girls in town." (She had only seven at present and did not expect to have more for her auction, which Katerina knew very well.)

She got up and went towards the bed room next door to fetch the girls and presently came back with them, because the girls had been waiting to be called.

"Open up those curtains and get light in the room," she called to her husband, who did obediently as told. After that he sat in a dark corner, looking at the wall. It was because of his eyes that the room was always kept in semi-darkness.

Katerina looked the seven girls over. They stood motionless in a row, in short Russian blouses and cheap, wide, woolen skirts; stockingless and in bare feet. Four of them Katerina dismissed right away, while Madame Drakeshkow praised eagerly the beauty and health of them all. The four, who were much too small or too tall, were very reluctantly sent away by Madame Drakeshkow, who was consoled by the demand of Katerina that the three remaining ones should take off their clothes. Buyers usually scrutinized the naked bodies minutely before purchase.

The stripping was quickly done. The blouses had to be unbuttoned, the skirts to be unhooked and the girls were nude. They now eyed Katerina, because she might become their future mistress, and although they discovered from her costume and bearing that she herself was only a serf, it was evident that she must be in an important position since she was delegated to buy new servants.

Katerina viewed the nude forms. Two of the girls were impossible at a glance. One had very small, almost boyish breasts and of course the wide hips which were so common. The other one had such thick thighs and so broad a bottom, that she might already have had a couple of children. Katerina disregarded them entirely and though they stayed in the room, it was only because it had been forgotten to send them away Katerina now motioned the last girl nearer to the window and took out, to the amazement of Madame Drakeshkow, the above mentioned multicolored ribbons. With some misgivings she started with the height, (which was correct) came to the bust, where more than the thickness of two fingers was missing and gave it up when the hips proved more than a hand's breadth too large. With a sigh, she put her ribbon back in her sack and moved without speaking to the exit-door. She paid no attention to the rain of words by the utterly bewildered Madame Drakeshkow, who had not understood what she had been about. To measure a servant girl! Who had ever heard of such folly? But Katerina was already on the street with the look of a beaten dog in her eyes, undecided what to do next.

The droshki driver, warmed meanwhile by a drink from a nearby public house, saluted her cheerfully and coaxed her to hire him again. He hoped that her eminence had completed her mission perfectly and that he could drive her home in roaring speed. Katerina let him know that she had been unsuccessful and that by the name of her personal Saint, she would have to give up. Then the befuddled driver remembered that she wanted to buy some girls, and anew praised the goods which his cousin wanted to dispose of. He'd drive her over quickly and—

Katerina looked at the sun. It was still early. One unsuccessful try more or less did not matter and she climbed back into the carriage, which answered with a sigh, bending to her weight.

We soon see Katerina heavily breathing while climbing up a creaking and steep staircase to the cousin's attic. It turned out that this cousin, a thin spinster of about fifty years, was handling an embroidery business on a small scale; that she had two girls working for her; and that she wanted to give up her enterprise and leave Moscow in order to stay with relatives in the South. Lacking money for the long trip, the sale of the two girls should provide the means. Katerina was led into the adjoining room, a large, very light attic room, bare of any furniture except a work table crowded with materials of all kinds.

On a bench before this table, bent over their work, sat two girls. The cousin commanded them to rise and it was then that Katerina uttered a cry of amazement. One of the girls was an exact duplicate of her Princess; at least her face and features were so perfectly like those of her mistress that Katerina first feared a spook might have tricked her. Still, the face did not matter at all. It was only the right contours of the body which were sought. The height was right, the form seemed so, and Katerina hastily demanded that this dark haired girl with the shinning blue eyes be stripped. The other girl was a short, flat nosed, sturdy creature and Katerina disregarded her. Not so the cousin. She made it quite clear that she would not sell one girl alone; it must be both or neither. Katerina mumbled that all that could be arranged, just let her see the dark one.

The girls, who had no previous knowledge that their madame wanted to get rid of them, flushed slightly, looked at each other and at the cousin, and stood sheepishly. The cousin slapped the dark girl and demanded to know whether she had become deaf and when she wanted to start to take her clothes off. With excited fingers, the buttons of the blouse opened; then came a bodice of common linen, strapped and fastened with many ribbons, and from underneath a rough chemise stood out two full and hard breasts with deep red nipples.

Katerina, the never smiling, grinned. It was the kind of bust she was looking for. The wide skirt of flowered and cheap material fell to the floor and a pair of wide trousers, reaching to the ankles, came to view. A bush of thick black hair protruded through the open slit of the drawers, which was there for the sake of commodity. (The women of that time attended to their natural functions through the gap of their trousers, which they opened up while sitting down for the necessity.)

Soon shirt and drawers were also removed and Katerina eyed her find with growing satisfaction. She went around and around the nude girl. The waistline was perfect; the legs full and female but subtle and the flesh of the ass seemed to be even softer than that of her mistress. To find out, she came close to the girl and felt her body. She was content. This was not the usual peasant type. This was not a tough and common brat. This girl had the form of an aristocrat, a form which must be like that of her "little mother."

Katerina remembered her measurements, took out her ribbons and began her comparisons. Well, the height was almost perfect, a little too tall, but she could tolerate that small difference. The length of the back, the breasts, the waistline, the thickness of the thighs were right or what one might call right. Even the wrists and the ankles fitted. It turned out that the length of the legs, measured from the slit to the floor, was a trifle too long, but Katerina had already resolved that this girl was to be bought.

When the last measurement was taken and Katerina, kneeling on the floor, had touched the pussy, the girl had drawn slightly and irritatedly back. For the rest, she had behaved quietly and with that absence of shamefulness or shyness characteristic of other serf girls. These girls did not know of the existence of anything like shame. From early youth on their bodies were at the disposal of their masters and their secret parts were no more theirs than their hands or faces.

17

The bargaining started. Katerina wanted to buy only the dark girl and she did not want to pay more than 50 rubels; the blonde imp was not wanted; her master owned 100,000 souls and did not need any more. The cousin shrieked that then he did not need to buy the dark girl either. While Katerina zealously defended the money of her master, the blonde girl leaned against the table and the nude dark one stood motionless with hanging arms in the middle of the room, as if she had nothing to do with the affair. The driver here and there interjected an appeasing word from the door, where he loitered as a witness who is waiting for a handsome commission. The cousin was thin and hard. Katerina was eager to buy and after a battle, the old housekeeper's hand went into the bodice which covered her enormous bosom and brought to light an ugly leather purse, from which she paid the cousin 90 rubels in glittering gold. She had gotten the price down from the demanded hundred, but she had to take both girls.

No, she was not sending a carriage for them. She was going to take both with her. She was afraid she might lose her precious discovery. They would start immediately. The girls had nothing to pack. They had no belongings except some woolen kerchiefs and the like, which were quickly made into a bundle. After the dark girl was hurriedly dressed again, Katerina took a quick leave with her purchase, though not without assuring the cousin anew that the price paid had been outrageous. The cousin made the sign of the cross over her former serfs. They in turn, automatically and without feeling, kissed the hem of her dress and soon the three women sat in the carriage. The driver was paid a little distance from Sokolow's house and received what he demanded. It is quite sure that with this money and the commission from his cousin, he was senselessly drunk for several days.

Starting towards the palace, Katerina asked the dark girl what her name was. "Grushenka," answered the girl, readily. That was the first word she spoke after she had become one of the uncounted souls of Prince Alexey Sokolow. She did not know then the name of her new master.

CHAPTER II.

It must be remembered that our story takes place shortly after the death of Peter the Great and that the revolutionizing changes he had made during his violent dictatorship came at this time to their first blossom. Peter the Great had done away with the seclusion of women who had lived before then in the oriental life of the harem. He had forced them into society, where they were at first so awkward that he got them drunk in order to loosen them up. He had lifted the Bojars, the aristocratic caste, to an elevated position by forcing the working class into unheard of servitude and submission. He had, by the most cruel tortures, in which he participated personally, built up a social order in which might was God and the serf a slave. He had forced Western culture upon his Bojars and one of his orders had been that they should build themselves great castles and houses.

Alexey Sokolow was only a score of years the junior of this great ruler. While eager to take all the advantages which were offered to his class, he had enough cunning to see that it was wiser to stay away from the inner court circle, where the greatest generals or officials were uncertain when they would find themselves on the rack or the wheel and eventually beheaded. Sokolow had therefore established his city life in Moscow instead of St. Petersburg and here in Moscow, he had erected the magnificent palace which can be seen to this day.

Katerina dismissed the droshki a few blocks away, so as not to be seen by other servants riding in a hired carriage, and led the two bewildered serf girls to the huge arch of the main entrance guarded by two soldiers with muskets, high tin helmets and high boots. They paid no attention to the three women who quickly entered the archway and were admitted to the inner courtyard.

Flowers, lampoons, grass, even bushes covered the tremendous square of the inner court and tables. Tables, chairs and benches stood about in great disorder. This courtyard was normally a barren place of cobblestones, but the Princess had given an entertainment the night before for which the flowers and grass had been raised in hothouses in the country.

Katerina gave her wards no time to look or to think. She hurried them through the court and down a stone staircase to the basement, which consisted of endless halls and rooms and kitchens. Here Katerina left the blonde girl with a woman who seemed to be an overseer of this underground labyrinth. She then took Grushenka by the hand and marched on with her. This time she led her up a small and winding wooden staircase, which ended at the second floor. Thick Turkish carpets covered the light hallway and Grushenka soon saw a room which she was going to know very thoroughly afterwards. It was the try-on-room of the Princess, fitted with a big oak table in the middle of the room and huge chestnut closets and presses along the walls between which mirrors of all kinds and dimensions were installed.

On a curt order from Katerina the girl took all her clothes off, and entirely nude, was dragged by the old housekeeper through other rooms, which were magnificently adorned with silks and brocades. Through the half open door of her mistress's boudoir. Katerina led the substitute of madame, in her excitement not waiting for permission to enter.

The Princess was sitting before a mirror at her toilet table. Boris, the coiffeur, was busy curling her long dark brown hair. A young serf girl, sobbing apparently from a recent thrashing, knelt on the floor and put rouge on her mistress's toe-nails. In the corner, near a window, sat "Fraulein," an elderly spinster who had been a German governess in different houses of the great, and who was now reading aloud in a dry and monotonous voice some French poetry. The Princess listened with slight understanding or interest. The French poet had worked into his fable all kinds of persons from the Greek and Latin mythology, which meant nothing to the capricious listener. But when he described how the enormous shaft of Mars was pushed into the grotto of Venus, that called for noticeable attention.

In her mirror Princess Nelidowa had seen Katerina appearing with Grushenka and waved angrily not to be disturbed. So Grushenka had an opportunity to study the group just described. The Princess wore only a short batiste chemise which left her more or less uncovered. She did not mind that Boris, clad in the formal house uniform of the Sokolows with a long pig-tail at his back, could see her nudity, because he was only a serf. He had been sent to Dresden some years ago to learn the art of hairdressing

23

Grushenka

with a very famous master in the Saxonian capital. Sokolow
had intended to rent him out to one of the ladies' hairdressing parlours recently opened in Moscow, but the Princess
had taken the clever fellow into her private service. He
was responsible for her many tufts and locks worn in the
day time and for her powdered wigs decorated with precious stones which went with the evening gowns.

When the reading of the poem had ceased, Katerina
could restrain herself no longer. "I have her! I have her!"
she cried and dragged Grushenka closer to the Princess. "I
found a substitute who fits perfectly and she is ours now!"

"I know you could have found her sooner." said
Nelidowa, maliciousiy. "But you'll be forgiven since you
dug her up at last. Now show me, does she really have the
measurements or are you lying to me?" She rose hastily
from her stool, so that poor Boris was in danger of burning
her with his hot irons.

"She really and truly fits." answered Katerina. "Here,
I'll show you." and she took out the multicolored ribbons
to prove the fact. But Nelidowa was not interested in that.
With sharp eyes she scrutinized Grushenka's body and she
was not dissatisfied.

"So! That is how I look. A full pair of good breasts,
aren't they? But mine are better!"—and taking out without
concern her own breasts from her thin shirt and holding
them close to Grushenka's she started a minute comparison—
"Mine are oval and that is rare, but this slob's are round.
Look at her nipples! How big and common!"—and she
tickled with her own nipples those of the girl.

Now it is true, there was a slight difference, but hardly
noticeable. Nelidowa then took hold of Grushenka's waist
with both hands and did not handle her too tenderly.

"I always said," the mistress continued, "That I have

24

an excellent waist-line and here one can see it. Among all the court ladies, not one can compare with me.''

That it was not her own waist-line she admired but that of her new slave girl did not come to her mind. She proceeded to the thighs which she pinched, surprised by Grushenka's very soft flesh. "My legs," she commented, displaying now her own thighs and squeezing them a bit, "are sturdier than those of this little bitch, but we'll take the softness out of her." With mock laughter she commanded Grushenka to turn around.

Nelidowa as well as Grushenka had a remarkably well modeled back; round female shoulders, soft and full lines down to the bottom, small and well rounded hips. Only Grushenka's buttocks were too small, almost boyish and went too evenly and straight to the thighs. Her legs and feet were normal and straight and could have been used by artists as models.

"Now!" laughed the Princess. "This is the first time that I see my own back and truly I like it. Isn't it fine that this tramp should have just my back. Next time my father confessor demands that I inflict some lashes on my own poor back I can take hers as my substitute and I can be generous with the number of blows I give myself." To demonstrate this splendid idea, she gave a goodly pinch to Grushenka's flesh below the right shoulder blade. Grushenka twisted her mouth a bit but stood motionless and without a cry. She was confused by what was happening and would have stood a greater shock without moving.

The witnesses of this scene, especially Katerina, were astonished by the similarity between these two women as they stood close together. It was astounding to see that not only the figures, but the features and faces of both were so much alike that one could have sworn they were twin sisters. Nature sometimes plays tricks of that kind. Grushenka was younger; she had a whiter skin; she blushed at present in her excitement and looked fresher. Also her flesh was softer and a bit more female than that of Nelidowa and she had a timid bearing and was not so self contained as the Princess. Otherwise, they were strangely alike, though no one would have dared to tell this to the Princess.

"I am pleased with you, and I'll present you with my new prayer book with the pictures of the Saints in it which you admired the other day. It's yours. Go and get it." Katerina with a deep curtsy kissed her mitress's hand, overjoyed that she had at last satisfied her. She was taking the girl out of the room when she was stopped by a last word of her mistress, who watched the nude form depart.

"By the way, Katerina, have all the hair under her arms and on her dirty cunt removed so that she doesn't infect my garments. And have her spotlessly washed and powdered. You know how filthy these pigs are." Katerina assured her she would have the girl taken care of.

Katerina had Grushenka take her clothes over her arm and went with her again to the basement. She knew that both girls had to be taken in as new serfs and she took care of the requirements usual on such occasions in her efficient way.

Grushenka and the other girl sat a few minutes later before a huge cleanly washed table. Soon plates with food, brought quickly by other serf girls, piled up before them. A new serf was always fed to the utmost by the new master and the girls were hardly able to do justice to the resources of the kitchen of Prince Sokolow. Their former diet as supplied by the stingy cousin had consisted of coarse bread, onions and rice and many of the dishes which now stood before them were utterly unknown to them. They ate all they could but had to give up when a big apple pudding proved too much for their filled stomachs.

Grushenka had been sitting nude through the meal. When they had eaten, the blonde girl was asked to take her clothes off. They were then requested by the woman in charge of the basement to throw their clothes into the big stove of the kitchen, where they soon burned away. A great master would not allow a servant to wear clothes another master had previously given him and also it was well known that clothes often brought the germs of disease into a house. Pest and small pox were flourishing and no precaution against these scourges of the time could be omitted. After this the girls were brought over to the servants bath, where a few bath-girls waited for them. They were soaped all over with a stinging soap and afterwards put in two wooden tubs with very hot water so that their skin became red as boiled lobsters. They were then pushed into the steam room which was in charge of a one armed invalid, a former soldier and bodyguard of the Prince. He did not look at the girls. He merely coughed and muttered vile and disgrunted words, because his body and mind were unbalanced.

Grushenka sat in the large, bare room with its wet brick walls and steaming boilers and began for the first time to give herself an accounting of the last few hours. From the poor rooms of the morose and thin cousin, she had been brought to the fairy palace of a Prince. For what, she could not understand. And while she wiped away the pearls of water which collected on her bust and belly, she whispered to her companion, "What do they want of me? What do you think they want?" But the blonde one whispered back that it would be ten thousand times better than before and that Prince Sokolow—they had learned the name from the

27

girls who had previously served them—had so many thousands of serfs that if they managed rightly, they certainly would have the time of their lives. So far it was too good for words: a dinner of abundance, a real bath as it was given only to fine people; even a steam-room for the servants! Who would have dreamt of that?

Presently they were called out of the steam-room, their skin loosened by the heat, and were given a very cold washing with clean water which was poured on them from buckets. They shivered and screamed trying to avoid the gushes but it was quickly over. Then they were rubbed with thick towels and dried thoroughly.

Katerina now took hold of them again to bring them to their quarters. The male servants lived in the stables or over the stables. The women had their quarters in the loft of the main house which was under the supervision of an elderly serf woman. Breathing heavily, Katerina led the way up the back stairs, scolding herself inwardly for going so seldom to the loft. (She herself had a chamber in the basement.) Her old knees resented the many hundred steps.

The upper floor of the palace contained many rooms and large halls in some of which were rows of wooden beds and board closets for clothing and linen. The woman in charge rose out of a half slumber to meet Katerina's unexpected visit and showed the girls to two unoccupied beds at the end of one of the halls. She left, upon Katerina's command to fetch some linen and garments for the newcomers and Katerina, catching her breath again, turned to the girls.

"I did not look you over before buying you," she said to the blonde and stocky girl. "It was my duty, but I hope you are clean and will not bring sickness to the house. Let me look you over now." The blonde girl grinned, knowing she was healthy as a bear and that her brown skin did not easily take infection. Katerina started her inspection in a matter of fact way. She opened the girl's mouth and looked over the teeth, which were sharp as those of an animal. She fingered the small breasts. (The girl was not more than seventeen years old.) She looked over the flesh of the belly, the legs, the back, under the arms and finally had the girl lie down over the bed and with her legs spread open. She opened the lips of the cunt and felt with one finger for the virgin membrane which was still in place. Katerina understood these things. She had helped many women in child bed and had acted as midwife when any of the women of the household gave birth. She did not disregard the ass hole, which might indicate a sickness of the stomach—but the girl was in good shape and underwent these operations with the stubborn submissiveness of the Russian serf.

Katerina then addressed the girls with a little speech as was usual on such occasions. She pointed out that as they had eaten today, so would they continue to eat, that they would be clothed and housed in splendid manner and that they were to be proud to be the servants of the noble Prince Sokolow. On the other hand they were required to be extremely obedient and industrious and to do their best for their new master. If they failed in that, they would be punished heavily and so it would be to their own good to submit to rules and orders.

To make this clear to them, and to inaugurate them into the household, she would now give them a light and friendly whipping, hoping she would never again have the necessity to do so. She then ordered Grushenka, to whom this address was mostly delivered, to lie on the bed in order to receive the strokes. Meanwhile the woman

29

had come back with blankets and linen and hearing Katerina's words, brought from the middle of the hall, two buckets in which fresh switches were kept in salt water.

Grushenka laid down on the bed on her stomach and buried her head in her hands. Often as she had been submitted to bodily chastisement, she could not endure it. She trembled, and kept her legs close together in nervous tension. But that was not to Katerina's liking, who saw it as an act of revolt. Roughly she pulled apart the girls legs, shouting at her to loosen up the muscles and to be still or she would give her the much more painful leather whip.

"Didn't you hear what the Princess said?" she added. "We'll take the softness out of you, you yellow dog." and she started to prepare the fine bottom for the punishment by squeezing hard the full flesh, even pulling the hair of the Mount of Venus, which protruded between the legs. Katerina now had evil eyes, her mouth was tightly shut and the nostrils of her nose moved greedily. Such a little imp of a serf, making a fuss because she was to get the switch! Grushenka groaned and tried to stop quivering, but she was so frightened she could hardly control herself. Katerina took a switch from the servant woman and ordered the blonde girl who watched the proceedings without emotion, to count aloud to twenty-five.

The first blow went over the right side of the bottom and it was a heavy stroke, because Katerina was angry and was a muscular peasant woman. Grushenka cried out and bent her body up as if she wanted to rise but put herself again in position. The second blow and the next few went over the same thigh, where a crimson pattern appeared in sharp contrast to the whiteness of the rest of the body. Katerina proceeded to the other thigh which was next to her, and laid blow after blow with great firmness on the skin.

Grushenka screamed and shook her body, but she did not move away and always got back into position. She had received almost twenty-five blows. Katerina had several times changed the switches which broke into pieces. When Katerina applied the last strokes to the insides of the legs which had not been hit before, it was too much for Grushenka. She rolled over to the wall and held both hands to her bottom pleading for mercy and protesting she could not stand it. But Katerina was not willing to give way to a young and obstinate serf girl. Therefore, with an energy and brutality which one would not have suspected in this fat and greyish housekeeper, she forced Grushenka to the middle of the bed, laying her on her back with her arms folded under her head and spread the girls legs open with rude force. "If your ass can't stand it," she shouted at the frightened girl, "then your front can have it and don't dare to move, because if you do, I'll have some stable men put you on the rack and give you the cow-hide and we'll see how you'll like that."

She began with fierce strokes to whip the inside and the front of the thighs. Grushenka was so thoroughly paralyzed and frightened that she did not dare to close her legs or to protect herself with her hands, although she moved instinctively to do so. She received about ten strokes in this way and although Katerina avoided striking the open cunt, for Grushenka it was an agony which seemed endless.

Finally it was over. Katerina's eyes remained fixed on the growth of hair around the cunt and on the slit itself. She had forgotten to find out whether this girl was virgin or not and she stooped without ceremony to make the examination. As soon as she touched the lips of the pussy, Grushenka became convulsive, partly because she expected more painful punishment, partly because she was sensitive at that spot. Katerina pushed her down and shoved her finger into the hole and found the resistance of the membrane. (The cousin must have had her girls under close observation, because these hussies usually liked nothing better than to fuck.)

Grushenka was still a virgin and as far as Katerina was concerned, she should remain so. She had forgotten her own youth and the thrill she used to get out of a good poke, and kept her girls under very strict watch. She was through with Grushenka now and ordered her to get up and looked with disdain at the crying, twitching face. What a soft girl, who could not stand such a little punishment!

Without much enthusiasm, she turned to the blonde creature. She ordered her to lie on her back and to move her legs up so that her feet touched her shoulders. The blonde did so without hesitation. She had a thick skin and a whipping more or less did not matter much in her young life. Katerina felt the flesh of the firm ass which was in this position put conveniently at her disposal. She was hardly able to squeeze the bottom because the flesh was so hard that it did not move under her fingers. She gave the girl some twenty strokes, not so severe as those she had given Grushenka, and the blonde one counted the strokes herself in a subdued but clear voice. It was one of those quick and unexciting beatings which mean nothing because the beating party is not much concerned with the job and the receiving party is more annoyed than hurt. When it was over the blonde one rubbed her ass and that was all.

Katerina had both girls kiss the end of the switch which she held in her hands, then ordered them to go to bed and stay there until they were called the next day to their respective duties. The blonde was to join the sewing crew, because she was handy with the needle after her education by the cousin and Katerina herself would take care of Grushenka.

Both girls crept dully between the sheets, Grushenka sobbing, and the other one quite content.

"What do they want of me?" sobbed Grushenka. "What can they want? . . . ." until she fell asleep.

CHAPTER III.

The next morning, quite early, Grushenka who had slept soundly in a bed that seemed to her the best she had ever had, was awakened by noisy shouting. With wondering eyes she looked about her. A hundred girls and women seemed to enliven the big loft, yawning, shouting, babbling and laughing in a confusion of washing and teasing and dressing and admonishments to hurry up. Actually, there were only sixty-three servant girls housed here, ranging in age from fifteen to about thirty-five. Younger and older women were not kept in the city palace.

The girls put on all kinds of dresses, according to their duties; the kitchen maids dark woolen garments; the linen and silver maids, a white uniform-like costume; the sewing squad, flowery cashmeres. The personal chamber and bedmaids of the Princess, about eight or ten, and the special favorites of the Prince, slept near the apartments of their masters. Some privileged elderly women and cooks had quarters in the basement.

Soon they were all sitting on long benches in a big hall

near the kitchen in the basement and steaming soups and white bread were devoured in great quantities. Katerina always saw to it that the servants got plenty to eat. Not that she was concerned with their likes and desires. She simply wanted to keep them content and healty, to enable them to perform their duties to the last ounce. Katerina was quite a fanatic on this point and any shirker could be sure of the whip, if not of a harder punishment.

After breakfast, Grushenka received the short order to go to the bathroom. She could not imagine why. She never before had been allowed more than one bath in a month; bathing was expensive because it meant fire-wood. Yet, now she was bathed and scrubbed thoroughly. Furthermore, the bath-girls were told to clean her up every day right after the breakfast and to see to it that she was spotless or else they would be sorry. The bath-girls took no chances and they scrubbed and rubbed and cleaned her everywhere and anywhere. Grushenka then was told to take her clothes over her arm and to wait in the try-on room for Katerina. There she sat now, on an oaken trunk, full of precious silks and embroideries, shivering after the bath, her clothes clutched to her body. Many maids passed through the room, walking here and there, sometimes giving her a friendly nod, mostly not taking notice of her.

Presently Katerina appeared and seeing Grushenka, she went to a closet and got a box of powder and a big powder-puff. She proceeded to teach her how to powder her whole body, omitting no part. Then she suddenly remembered the shaving business. She sent for Boris, who was soon there with his outfit of razors and soap. "You heard what her Highness said, yesterday," she addressed the barber. "Shave cleanly her hair under the arms and between the legs. But don't cut her. We paid a big price for the bitch.''

Boris made Grushenka hold both her arms straight up and soaped and shaved her under the arms, quite cleverly and quickly. He then glanced over to see if Katerina was still there. He had never before shaved a girl's cunt and wanted to have some fun with it. But Katerina stood solidly there, leaning on an oaken stick and she looked sternly at Boris, who quickly avoided her eyes.

Grushenka was now laid on a table with her legs apart. Katerina saw that the marks of the switch were clearly visible in red-violet welts. "She has a softer skin than all of them." thought the old housekeeper, but not with pity, rather with a resolution that she would thrash the girl oftener in order to get her used to it.

Grushenka was trembling nervously as Boris, with his scissors, cut the long curls from her Mount of Venus and below. He then soaped her with his brush, not sparing the lips of the cunt, and finally expanded the skin with two fingers on his left hand. There followed the soft grating of the knife, that cut the hair closely to the white flesh. He started to put his fingers between the lips of the slit as if to extend the skin better, but Katerina tapped sharply with her stick and he thought better of it. A wet towel was now applied and the job was done.

Open lay Grushenka's cunt. The fine red lips were slightly apart. Rather long lips with the entrance hole settled down quite low, right in the neighborhood of the ass hole, which was small and well contracted. Boris, now in possession of a throbbing erection, was mad to make use of this delectable shaven pussy. He even would have liked to suck it a bit, to tickle and taste its naked contours with his tongue. But Katerina sent him scooting and he was forced to find solace with less alluring material. There were many girls about who were enamoured of his sturdy prick and he quickly managed to find a dark corner and a soft hole in which to get rid of his load.

Katerina called out to the sewing rooms next door that a couple of dressing girls should come in. She now had Grushenka dressed up in one of the Princess' outfits to see whether she would really do as a model for the new summer wardrobe. Long silk stockings were applied, a chemise with golden threads was put on her. Long trousers, fitted and closed with ribbons on the ankles, came next. A crimson bodice without stays was tied on. (Stays were worn in Western Europe at that time, but not in Russia, where the elegnt women liked to show their breasts with the nipples sticking out above their dresses.) A tunic, which took the place of the skirt and blouse, then was hooked and buttoned and over this fell a long loose cloak, leaving the arms underneath bare. During this procedure all the girls of the tailoring and sewing departments had left their work and watched eagerly. When Grushenka was ready and was told to walk up and down the large room, turning and displaying the costume and herself, the watchers clapped their hands and stamped their feet. "That is our Princess!" they cried, "Just like her! Can you imagine?" Katerina heard this outburst with satisfaction. Yes, she had found the clothes-horse for her mistress.

Grushenka was instructed that she was to be used from now on as the fitting model for her Highness. Then and there started for Grushenka a long period of waiting and dreaming, dreaming and waiting until some dress-maker would come around and fit some garments on her, turning her around and around, trying on, admiring his own craftsmanship, or cursing the sewing girls who had done a bad job. These try-ons were at first very displeasing to Grushenka, because all these workers, men and women, some of them serfs, some of them free people, who called themselves artists, touched her body all over and took many liberties with her. This was all the more so because she was such a perfect counterfeit of her Madame, before whom these men crawled on their bellies.

It was thus fine fun for them to paw her breasts, to pinch her nipples and to play around quite abundantly with her pussy. This last Grushenka hated especially and she tried to shove them away, only to be stuck painfully with a needle in the buttocks or in the breast. So she got used to it, especially when she found that when she resisted she was plagued much more, but if she kept still, the men were not so insistent. It usually went along this way: A little tailor's helper, who had the order to try something on her, would put his finger in her cunt and would say, "Fine morning, your Highness. How did you like the prick of the Prince last night?" and laughing at his own joke, would begin his work.

Months went by this way, first in the palace in Moscow, then at one of the great estates in the country; months of dreaming and waiting. Of course, Grushenka, meanwhile, got well acquainted with the great household. She listened to the gossip about the brutal and drunken Prince, whom the Princess hated, but played up to; of the young lover the Princess had taken; of the way she had her bedmaids make love to her to satisfy her everlasting cravings. But Grushenka heard these tales without taking notice and nobody seemed to take much notice of her. It was hard to say of what she was thinking, maybe of the clouds which passed along or of a bird in the big tree outside the window.

Then came the day which changed her whole life. The

Princess had been out to a party and it had turned out badly. Even her lover had neglected her, nay, had flirted openly with a rival. The Princess had drunk too much, had had an argument with another lady and her husband, the Prince, furious with such misbehavior had slapped her face violently while driving her home. Nelidowa was wild. She accused everybody but herself. She let the whip fly freely on the backs of the girls who undressed her and still was not able to ease her rage. When she saw her brocade gown with the silver stripes lying on the floor, she suddenly remembered that Grushenka had modeled it for her approval that same afternoon. In her crazed state, she imagined that this gown and thus the girl who had displayed it, were responsible for her misadventures.

It was two o'clock at night and Grushenka was fast asleep, when she was dragged naked from her bed. Drunk with sleepiness and knowing of no fault she had committed, the girl was taken before her mistress. The Princess, now in bed, accused her in the vilest terms of having induced her to wear an unbecoming dress and ordered one of her chamber maids to lash Grushenka over her bare back with the leather whip which lay always ready for this purpose on the toilet table. Another maid stepped in front of Grushenka, turning her back toward her, took the arms of the frightened girl over her shoulders and bent forward so that Grushenka lost her foothold on the floor and lay helplessly on the back of the chamber maid.

The whipping started at once. The strokes cut whistling through the air. The shoulders, the back, the behind were hit and hit by a rain of blows. Grushenka did not know that the whipping girl applied the punishment with great craftmanship, cracking the whip loudly but taking care that the lash cut the flesh as little as possible, for this girl was angry at her Madame and sorry for the innocent victim. In spite of this fact, Grushenka underwent awful pain and screamed and kicked her legs as well as she could. The Princess lay in her bed, her teeth bared in rage, her fingers with their long nails held in the form of claws as if she wanted to scratch the flesh off the girl's bones.

Although not told so, the whipping girl finally ceased beating as if she were exhausted from swinging the lash and Nelidowa did not command her to go on because she felt suddenly sick from the liquor she had drunk. Grushenka was now lowered to the floor and putting both her hands to her aching ass she walked straddle legged from the room. At this moment the eyes of the Princess fixed on Grushenka's slit, which having been shaven as usual was entirely open to sight. The Princess stared hard at this slit because it was formed differently than her own and while the girl was supposed to have a body similar to hers, the cunt certainly was an exception.

Nelidowa did not say a word about this dissimilarity, but she kept the thought in her mind. There had been an instance, when something seemingly had been wrong with her own pussy and she could not make out what it was.

There happened to be in Moscow at that time a Spaniard, an adventurer who lived by his wits, a chevalier no doubt, but a shady character and fortune seeker. He was permitted to mix in society because he represented the higher and so much admired Western culture. Also because he could tell such elegantly slippery stories and all kinds of gossip from the bed-chambers of the well known gentlemen and ladies in Paris, London and Vienna. This lady-charmer, with his glittering eyes and short black mustache, (he had no long beard as the good Russians wore) had the reputation of kissing a lady's cunt, an act which was unthinkable to a Russian Nobleman and a fashion which had been brought lately from Italy to Paris, so it was said. Nelidowa had made up her mind to capture this gentleman for that very purpose. She had managed to sit next to him at the gambling table one evening and had stacked a pile of gold rubles on his side. These she then tipped over with her elbow in his direction. The gold which she showered towards him she did not reclaim.

Of course, the gentleman made use of this opportunity and later in the night walked with her through the park, where they sat down on a bench. His words had flown in a stream of romance and he had admired her beautiful feet which aroused his passion to such a degree that he just had to kiss them. He had started with the feet and had gone tenderly up the calves and landed on the thighs, which he kissed fervently. Nelidowa, apparently overcome by his ardour, had bent back, opening ever so lightly and with apprehension her well-shaped legs so that the slit in her trousers permitted any intrusion which might be wanted. The chevalier had then spread open this slit with his aristocratic fingers, pressed many kisses on the small part of the belly and approached by degrees the pussy. He had furthermore sucked with his lips the flesh close to the very entrance. Then suddenly, he had stopped. He pressed a quick kiss on the slit and went up abruptly, without doing the very thing for which she had prepared so carefully.

That evening when she came home Nelidowa had investigated before a mirror to learn what was wrong with her grotto. Yes, the lips of her cunt were thick and flappy and left the entrance which they were supposed to close, quite open. But had not all married women such cunts and what

was the matter with hers? At any rate that night Nelidowa
had one of her bed girls suck her cunt for hours and when
the girl got tired and did not rub the tickler with her tongue
strongly and quickly enough, her mistress promised her the
whip if she did not suck more effectively.

How was it that Grushenka had a nicer cunt than she
herself? How was it that her own pussy was not good
enough for this coundrel and cheat of a Spanish adventurer?
One afternoon, when Nelidowa lay idly on her couch, she
made up her mind to find out and forthwith sent for
Grushenka. She made the girl take her clothes off and was
glad to see the blue and red stripes which the whip had
left, especially on one side of the body where the end of
the strap had cut the flesh. She asked Grushenka to come
very close to her, straddle legged, so that she could
inspect the girl's pussy. Of course the slit was very finely
made; the Princess had to tell herself that in spite of the
anger she felt. The lips were thin and rosy and cut the oval
of the Venus hill in an even curve which did not stick out
and puff up like her own. She made Grushenka hold the
cunt open with her fingers. The slit was shallow and of a
bright red and the vagina had its opening near a small hole
on the lowest part of the body between the legs. With her
eyes on the girl's spot, but without fingering her, Nelidowa
started to question her.

"When were you fucked last?" she began. Grushenka
hardly understood the meaning of the question. But the
Princess insisted, "How long ago is it, since you were
poked by a prick?" Now Grushenka knew what was meant
and answered quite firmly, "No man has ever touched me,
your Highness. I am a virgin." "Oh!" thought the Princess,
"Of course when I was still with the nuns my pussy was
probably like hers, but since that old bastard (by which she

43

meant of course the Prince) every so often puts his damned machine in my hole. . . ." But aloud she said with laughter, "I'll fix you up my child and that right now. Never fucked! Still a pimply virgin, eh? You lie down here now and we'll soon attend to you."

She got up from the couch with some spirit. She enjoyed this splendid idea. It would pass the time piquantly. Who to get for the job? Oh, yes, there was her riding groom, that broad-shouldered fellow with the big bush of tousled hair. His blondness would make a good match for Grushenka's deep black hair. Nelidowa had looked sometimes with longing at Ivan (she had a habit of calling all male servants Ivan) and had more than once glanced over his muscular arms and legs and rested her eyes on his trousers. She would have tried him herself, but she had no desire for the brand of brutal male love which her husband supplied. However, this was just the right man to rape that stupid lump on the couch.

Ivan had been loading hay. When he came in, in linen trousers and an open shirt, hay was still clinging to his hair and clothes and he brought with him the smell of the stable. Meanwhile the five or six chambermaids who were always around their mistress, had not been idle. They enjoyed in advance, like madame, the spectacle which was coming. They had put a pillow under Grushenka's bottom, with much giggling they had smeared some salve in her gap, they had put their fingers in her hole, and pitied her in mock tones, that she was going to be torn. Grushenka lay very still, her hands clasped to her face, uneasy and wondering. Perhaps she had dreamt during the past months of the lover to whom she wanted to give herself. Perhaps she had made him a romantic hero, some man from the moon. Yet here she lay waiting to be ravished by a stable boy.

"Ivan," said the Princess, "I have called you because this poor girl complained to me that no man ever made love to her and that her virginity is itching her terribly. I chose you to give her the fuck of her life. Go on my boy and make a poor longing virgin happy. Get your tool out and screw the bitch."

Ivan looked bewildered from his mistress to the nude form on the couch and again from one to the other. He fingered his hands before his body as though he were holding a cap and turning it uneasily around. He did not move. Was it a trap or was it serious? The Princess was becoming impatient.

"Get your trousers down and fuck! Don't you hear?" she shouted at him.

Ivan mechanically opened up his trousers. They fell to his feet and he pulled his shirt up over his navel. The eyes of all the girls, except Grushenka's, stared at his big dark brown balls and an equally dark brown, big tool which hung its head listlessly and unfit for work.

"Now go over and kiss your bride." continued the mistress, leaning on the toilet table and rubbing her own cunt with the palm of her hand, being a bit excited. Slowly, Ivan moved to the couch, then with a determination to go ahead, he took Grushenka's hands from her face, bent over her and kissed her on the mouth. The chamber maids applauded. But Grushenka lay so lifeless that Ivan lost pluck again. He fidgeted, looked at the naked girl and at the others and did nothing more. His prick was still in its flabby condition. It was again the Princess who had to bring the proceedings to life.

"Lay on top of her, you stupid ass!" she cried. "And you," pointing to one of her girls, "You, give that prick of his a good finger feeling or suck him prettily so that he gets stiff, the big swine."

As ordered, so was it done. Ivan, hindered in his movements by the trousers around his ankles, laid himself on top of Grushenka and a bed maid, obeying the order she had received, caressed his tool with apt fingers. Another girl, quite voluntarily attracted by his firm bare ass, started to squeeze it a little and playfully inserted a finger in his ass hole. Ivan was a tough and sturdy stableman, so no wonder that his prick began to swell and grow under such treatment. And suddenly he began to enjoy the job to which he had been assigned.

His prick became a stiff lance. His muscular behind started uneasy and nervous movements and he tried to rub his shaft on Grushenka's belly. But it was kept firm in the hand of the bedmaid, who was not willing to let go of such a nice plaything.

Grushenka kept her legs close and pressed her knees so tightly together that they hurt, but Ivan struggled to get between. He moved a bit, got his strong hand between her thighs and with a sudden jerk, lifted her right leg high up, almost to her shoulder. He now got between her legs with his own and his prick rested firmly on top of her cunt. The resistance of the girl had made him hot, but what followed made his prick almost burst.

The moment the prick touched her, Grushenka lost her apathy and with a wild scream, started to fight. Ivan had his arms around her, the left one over her right shoulder, the right one in the middle of her back. The tight grasp and the weight of him could not be shaken off. But Grushenka could move her ass and her legs and she made amble use of these when the dangerous shaft came in contact with her love-nest. The Princess, who would have killed any serf not performing her orders, was highly delighted to see this struggle and slipped her hand under her chemise to give her itching tickler a soft caress with her fingers.

Ivan tried to find his way. He moved his right hand under the buttocks of the struggling girl. He lifted his own behind and tried by crafty pushes to find the entrance, but now the girl who had previously caressed his ass, again came to his help. She went around the couch and caught Grushenka's other knee which she forced up against Grushenka's shoulder and moved it so that the virginal love-hole lay unprotected and open. The other girl again got hold of the prick and directed its head to the rosy entrance. "Now!" shouted all the watchers, and Ivan well understanding that he was at last in position, lowered his weapon with force. Pressing with his right hand against the girl's bottom, with one firm and slow stroke, he thrust the prick into the cunt up to the hilt. Grushenka let out a terrible cry. After that she lay still as a corpse. Ivan moved back and forth several times until passionately groaning, he felt he could not hold it any longer. He spent; raptuously, grimly, abundantly sending his fluid into her. His muscles relaxed; breathing heavily he lay on her, stupidly exhausted.

The Princess was furious, her maids disappointed. They had hoped to see a good, long fucking match, but it was over before it really started and all there was now were two motionless bodies on top of each other. Certainly there was nothing thrilling in that. "Get out! You brute!" commanded the Princess. "Get back to your stable and stay there. You serfs are even too stupid to fuck." But she looked with interest at his still stiff prick, which he now slipped slowly out of the pussy, covered with blood. Ivan collected his pants, dropped his head and left the room like a beaten man.

He did not dare to look up or to glance at Grushenka. She lay with a pale face like a corpse on the couch, the middle of her body still raised by the pillow under her, the blood trickling out of her wound besmearing her thighs and the pillow. She had fainted and one could see that she was quite ill. With dismay the Princess had had her carried up to her room.

What sort of girl was this—who could not even stand a poke? That was what she said to a lady at afternoon tea as she was relating the story and added that the silly peasants were too stupid for words. The lady was not of that opinion. She answered that she often arranged a party for some of her hand-maids and serf-men and that they put on very exciting shows, enjoying their fucking in all three ways. She promised to invite Nelidowa as spectator to such a party and the Princess graciously accepted.

Meanwhile, Grushenka was in her bed, taken care of by Katerina. Katerina was afraid this episode might lead to pregnancy, and though she knew how to handle an abortion, she was afraid Grushenka's figure might change and Grushenka had become very useful. The scenes the Princess used to make because of her try-ons had been avoided since Grushenka took her place as a model. Therefore Grushenka had been washed and cleaned and in spite of her protests a hot irrigation had been made with water into which Katerina had put a powder. Next a cold wet towel was put between her legs. It did not ease the pain in her torn cunt. She still had to overcome the shock which the rape had effected. She was allowed to stay in bed all the next day by the old housekeeper, who muttered, "What a soft girl! What a soft girl!"

CHAPTER IV.

The weeks after her rape were perhaps the happiest of Grushenka's youth. At least she looked her best and became a ravishing beauty. She was awakened. Her days of dreaming were over and gave place to a lively vivacity and an ever good mood. Many times, full of hell, she played little pranks on the other girls and the tailor folks and was sometimes punished by having to stand in a dark corner or with a few strokes from the whip. They were not severe punishments. The girl had such an air of good hearted spirits and happiness about her that no one became really angry with her. The reasons for her change were as follows:

A few days after losing her maidenhood, she had had to show her mistress a new costume, a light blue, fluffy affair with many ribbons and laces. The Princess had liked it, and incidentally had ordered the girl to show her cunt. She wanted to see what changes had come from the fucking. Grushenka lifted the costume carefully in front, another girl spread the slit of her trousers open while the Princess took a good look. There was no change. Nelidowa was thinking that one poke might not effect a great change, but that if that pussy before her eyes should be used often, the rosy and thin lips would certainly become thick and vulgar. Hence the order to Katerina that Grushenka was to be poked daily and that Katerina should supply various men in order that the business be attended to properly.

Katerina disliked this new order, for which she could not imagine the reason, but what could she do? She moved Grushenka's bed to a separate room in the basement and after dinner, gave the girl her instructions. First she gave her a salve and ordered her to smear it every day after dinner into her tube. This salve was to kill the sperm. The irrigations, to be taken afterwards, would make doubly sure that she should not get an enlarged belly.

Presently she sent a stable boy to the girl's room, a redhaired, freckled, undersized man, who grinned with delight. The love-making of the servants was controlled, but once in a while they were allowed to do some fucking. It was not half enough and they always craved for the opportunity. Very often there was a love match between two serfs and they were sometimes allowed to marry, receiving from the master a shack and a bit of land that they had to till in addition to the land of the owner of the estate. More often, when some girl got pregnant, the master commanded one of his men to marry her.

It was always a feast to be allowed to fuck and it was usually done in the hay of the stables or somewhere in the fields. A good party in a bed and an order to give her the limit was a pleasure! When the news came to the stable, the men threw dice for the trick and the red-head was much envied when he won.

Grushenka was sitting uneasily on her bed; she held one hand over her breasts, the other one clutched her thin dress in front. With a pitiful voice she begged him not to take her, to spare her. The shock from Ivan's handling was still in her bones. But the red-head had other ideas. He threw his wooden slippers into the air, slipped out of his shirt and trousers, and assured the frightened girl that it should be as if it were his wedding night and that he would not need any help like Ivan. Nay, he'd do the job alone and quite thoroughly. As he stood before her, naked, his prick ready for the anticipated pleasure, she did not know what to do. She kneeled before him and implored him to let her be, but he instead took hold of her hair and pressed her face against his testicles and laughed aloud when she tried to struggle away. Then he lifted her bodily up and threw her on the bed.

"For the quick poke in the woods," he said, "It's all right with clothes on, but I'll have you nude, my little bride. It's so much nicer."

He started to loosen the hooks of her skirt and to tear it off her. Grushenka felt that resistance would not do and that her garments would be torn, and that meant the whip, so she unbuttoned her blouse herself and got rid of her trousers, while her lover-by command lauded her change of mind. When they lay belly on belly, Grushenka again begged and prayed. She was very beautiful and the red-head had no reason to hurt her. He promised to be careful and explained to her, being a nice chap, that it would not cause her any pain, that she would, in fact, like it and that if she followed his suggestions, they could both enjoy it profoundly.

The frightened girl promised to do all he said and he proceeded with great care. He tickled her pussy with the point of his shaft for a while and then inserted it by degrees, moving always a bit back and shuffling it in again, each time more, until his hair rubbed closely against her well shaven Mount of Venus. He then inquired whether it had hurt and Grushenka answered in a soft, wondering voice, "Just a bit. Oh! Be careful."

But it had not hurt her at all, it was just a funny feeling, not exactly exciting, but almost pleasing. He told her to move her ass slowly up and down, which she did, while he lay stiff and strong, until he started himself to heave and to push, finally forgetting himself and fucking quite to his heart's content. Grushenka did not answer his strokes, she was still afraid that it might hurt her again. But she held her arms close to his back and when he finally came, she pressed her cunt firmly against his belly and felt something like satisfaction when his hot scum spread into her insides.

He had not had enough. He stayed in her bed joking with her. He played around with her breasts and her cunt, laughed to see that she was shaved and pinched her bottom, good-heartedly. She discovered with amazement that he got stiff again and she did not fight him off when he put his prick in anew; a prick which was not so strong and terrible now as it had been before. This time her fright was gone. She wondered: "So that is what they call fucking." She thought, "Really, it's not so bad." Still she did not get a thrill out of it, although it felt rather pleasant.

This time he had to work harder to get the load out of his balls. She assisted him very little, although she caressed his back with her hand shyly, and tried to make her cunt as small as possible, so that the slippery machine down there could get as much friction as possible. After he had come, she started to move and to heave. She wanted something more now herself, but he slipped his tired love shaft out of her. She was tired and slept so soundly that they had a hard time getting her up next morning.

Every night after dinner, a man came to fuck her. Sometimes they were elderly and brutal and did not undress, just laid her over the bed and fucked and gave her a slap on the behind and disappeared. Sometimes, they were mere boys, who were shy and Grushenka had a great time teasing them and working them up and finally seducing them many times so that they walked from the room with weak knees.

Grushenka learned to love it. She could not say when she came for the first time, but after it had happened, she succeeded in getting the supreme thrill with every man; half a dozen times if she liked her partner. She learned how to make love and soon became a passionate lover. The male servants in the house who had tried her out, praised her with glittering eyes. What a girl! What a figure! What a piece of ass! A volcano!

These were fine weeks, weeks of thrills, weeks during which her body filled out and her mind became clear, weeks without dreams, full of reality. She looked at other girls with searching curiosity. She learned from them about their love affairs, she studied her mistress with appraising eyes. Couldn't she manage to get a nice boy as a husband and a little house with some acres and have children too? Why not? She learned who was influencing the master and the mistress, she made plans, she laid eyes on one of the best body servants of the Prince and though she never spoke with him or had intercourse with him, she believed she had fallen in love with him. All that ended of a sudden, and it was again her mistress who affected the change, her mistress who was by right and law Grushenka's destiny.

Nelidowa used to start many things, give many orders, and forget about them again. Her mind wandered. Everything that did not pertain to her lover (of whom we will have to speak later) was done in a haphazard way. But Nelidowa remembered one night when she came from the bedroom of her husband, after working over his prick for some time, that Grushenka had been her means for finding out how a cunt would change by fucking; so she sent for her.

Grushenka had had a quick and meaningless poke from an elderly man that night about an hour before, and was still awake when the hand-maid of Nelidowa came for her. She put a bed sheet around her shoulders and walked nude and bare footed to her Highness's bedchamber. (It must be remembered that all people, high or low, male or female, slept without nightshirts at that time, and it is said that Marie Antoinette, some fifty years later, was the first one to create the mode). Nelidowa had just washed her pussy and sat naked before her toilet table, while one of her maids braided her long black hair into pigtails.

Nelidowa was in a good mood and told Grushenka to wait until her hair was done. In a few minutes, she took the nude girl on her lap. She inquired whether Grushenka had been poked daily, whether the pricks had been big and long, whether she had learned to fuck properly and whether she liked it. Grushenka answered automatically, "Yes," to every question. Then Nelidowa gently opened the girl's legs and examined her pussy.

There was no change to be seen. The little love nest was tender and innocent, as though it had never held big male machines. The lips were perhaps more red, and fuller, but still firmly closed and thin. The Princess opened them and fingered the girl, who quivered under this caress. The Princess moved her more towards her knees, opened her own legs a little and wondered at her own cunt, which was wide open with thick flappy lips. Apparently it was not fucking but the hand of nature which had made the difference between their cunts.

Everything seemed to go well and the Princess was about to send her double to bed again, but in her dissatisfaction with the imperfect loving she had received from her husband, she felt induced to play more with Grushenka's cunt. Her finger started to rub it more insistently, she fingered also the ass hole, and then went back to the pussy. Grushenka leaned closely on the shoulder of her mistress, put one arm around her and with her free hand, caressed Nelidowa's full breasts and nipples. She sighed slightly and prepared to come, wiggling her bottom as well as possible in this sitting position.

Just when Grushenka began to feel fine, the Princess got vexed that the girl should get a kick out of it, while she herself felt only that her cunt was bothering her. With her old meanness, she pinched Grushenka's pussy with her sharp finger nails, hurting the tender inner parts of the lips terribly. Startled and with a cry Grushenka leapt from the woman's lap holding the injured spot with her hands, instinctively ducking away from her mistress.

Nelidowa, upset by the girl's screams, her nerves offended, said the guilty one had to be punished. As she reached for a leather slipper, her eyes had a gruesome expression. She scolded the girl and made her lie down over her lap. Cracking slaps fell on Grushenka's backside and thighs, the pain shot in lightning heat with each stroke through her body. The slipper was merciless. Grushenka wiggled and kicked, cried and screamed, then subdued her cries to sobs. Her buttocks, her legs felt as if a red hot iron was being applied.

The struggling ass before her eyes did not leave the

Princess without feeling. She started to feel rather good, nay she felt keenly that her cunt got hot, and she acted accordingly. She let Grushenka fall to the carpet, then took hold of her head and forced it between her own opened legs. One of her hand-maids, seeing what was going on, rushed behind her mistress, embraced her breasts and coming with her arms from behind, drew her gently back, thus placing her in a position in which to enjoy herself.

Grushenka did not know what to do. She had, of course, heard that the Princess was sucked off by her bed-maids and she knew that some servant girls were supposed to do the same to each other. Lady's Love was at that time more common than it is today. It was an art practised with great finesse in the harems, and the Russian household was still very much like a harem.

Grushenka did not know exactly what was expected of her; no one had taught her these things. She was half suffocated by the passionate pressure with which the Princess forced her face against her open hole. She kissed or tried to kiss the hair around the entrance but kept her tongue in her mouth and only her lips rubbed and brushed over the battlefield. Nelidowa took that as obstinate resistance. She let her go and pushed her away with a firm kick of her bare feet. One of her bed-maids immediately took Grushenka's place (the girl said later she had done so to avert murder, so wild were the eyes of her mistress) and with apt and learned strokes of her tongue she brought the passionate young Princess to fulfillment. She came, groaning and moaning, cursing and mixing into the words tender expressions which were meant for her lover. Finally she closed her eyes and hung exhausted in the arms of the serf girl who held her. The bed-maids carried her to her bed and put her softly between the sheets. Grushenka slipped out of the room, hoping all would be forgotten the next day. She made up her mind to ask one of the girls how to satisfy the mistress in case she again should be called to this duty.

The next afternoon it was clear that Nelidowa had not forgotten. Katerina was ordered to appear with Grushenka. The Princess instructed briefly and without explanation, "Give that girl fifty lashes with the cowhide and do it yourself and don't let her be fucked from now on."

Katerina closed her lips tight. If she followed her mistress's order, the girl would be dead by sunset. She never could stand it. Men died with less than that number of blows. She led the trembling and loudly sobbing girl to the basement, where in a far corner a room for the punishment of the serfs was equipped with instruments of torture. Katerina led her to the whipping block and Grushenka, her eyes full of tears, stripped without resistance and laid herself over the saddle-like middle of the block. Katerina chained her arms and feet to rings. Then she questioned the frightened girl and Grushenka, her head hanging to the floor, related the happenings of the night before.

Katerina was thinking hard while she fingered the different whips to find one of lighter weight. She looked at the white body, stripped for punishment and at the whip and threw the whip away. "Listen!" she said. "One should not trust such a bitch as you are, but I will spare you if you can keep your mouth shut. Right after this you will go to bed and stay there for two days and be sick, and you'll tell everybody that I put a wet linen over you, so as not to blister your skin. If you do as I say, you'll get off lightly, because you did not know better and it was not your fault." Whereupon Katerina hit her several times with her hard hand over the ass which did not hurt less than the slipper the night before. "And one thing more. You are going to learn how to suck perfectly so that you know better next time. Understand?"

Katerina had something on her mind when she made this decision. Nelidowa was using up her maids in quick order and Katrina had always to supply new ones. The Princess, cruel and beastly as she could be (like many people who come from nothing into power) was equally good-hearted and carelessly friendly when she was in a good mood. None of her personal maids liked to stay long with her. The small leather whip with the golden handle was always too near and the moods of the mistress changed too quickly. The way to get away from her was to get married. They sometimes asked her for it outright and got what they wanted, including the men they had picked for themselves. Sometimes they did what they could to get pregnant and then they were scolded or even put for a few days in a dark room with water and bread. They were never severely punished (oriental women have a religious respect for a pregnant woman) and in the end were usually supplied with a husband. Then it was up to Katerina to find another maid; handsome, with a good figure, well trained in washing and clothing the mistress, alert, keen and also a good Lesbian.

The handmaids lived in one big room where, when not busy they waited the call of the Princess. They passed their time telling lewd stories, playing with each other, indulging in sucking parties. They were ready for that always, because they wore only light Russian blouses with such a low neck that half of the breast was exposed and wide skirts with no other garments below. Bending down and pulling the skirt up offered the necessary position for the whip and lying down and pulling the skirt up made ready for a little play with the tongue.

After Grushenka had spent two lonesome days in bed, she was turned over to an efficient instructress of cunt lapping. Three or four young girls, not more than seventeen years of age were broken in by this woman, who was above thirty and understood her job well. The girls had to give each other a sucking, and then they had to show their ability to the teacher by working on her pussy. If it had not been for the fact that this teacher always had a switch in her hand, which she used when she was not satisfied, Grushenka would have enjoyed these instructions.

When she was put before the pussy of a young blonde girl and told to lick first around the lips, then to enter the vagina at the bottom and finally to concentrate on the clitoris, she liked it and was herself tickled by the movements of her tongue. Perhaps this was because this girl was very responsive, quivering with delight and passion under the tender tongue treatment. Grushenka also enjoyed it hugely when one of the girls got hold of her own pussy and she responded with such delight that the teacher had the execution stopped before she came. Grushenka did not mind. When her turn came to lick the cunt of this woman, she slipped unnoticed a finger on her own spot, and while rubbing herself to a climax, she gave the woman so amazingly strong a tongue licking that the elderly then prophesied that she, Grushenka, would become a famous lover. Most of the peasants learn in time to satisfy even a refined lady's love, but they did so automatically; the vigor and that fluidom of love which cannot be described was missing.

Grushenka was no more to be touched by men. The little divertisement she had while learning to be a Lady's Lover ceased quickly also. She was at a loss what to do to satisfy the passion which she had developed. Should she take a secret lover as many other girls did? There was the danger of being found out and having her bones broken on the rack. Should she start an affair with another girl? That again would lead to some terrible punishment. She tried her own finger, even stole a candle and played with herself in bed. It was not good, in fact she felt unhappy the next day and cried without reason. But while so far her life had been like that of most of the other girls, a new and exciting chapter was to begin for her.

CHAPTER V.

When Nelidowa went to bed for the first time with Alexey Sokolow she understood of a sudden what her marriage would cost her. She had known that His Highness, the Ex-Governor, her exhalted Prince-husband, was wealthy and she would have social position and power. But there, lying next to her like an orang-outang was the ugly body of the man who was now by right and law her master, mentally and physically. He was bald but had plenty of wooly hair around the lower part of his head, growing into a long thick beard reaching to his chest which was covered with thick black hair. His chest was enormously broad, his arms short and muscular with broad short hands, and he had an enormous belly with a tissue of muscles all around the waist line. His skin was dark, his thighs almost brown. He had small piercing suspecting eyes and a big mouth with the lower lip especially thick and sensual. His prick was short and thick and his balls betrayed at a glance that they held plenty of ammunition and loved the shooting game.

During the long stupendous wedding with a thousand new faces congratulating her, everybody bowing deeply before the Prince, who was in a jovial mood, she had been thrilled. He had seemed handsome clad in a brilliant blue uniform studded with glittering medals and buttons of real gold and with a snow white wig with a long pigtail, which had dangled frivolously over the gold collar of his costume. He had worn high patent leather boots and rings with dazzling stones. It was thus that Nelidowa, the bride, had first seen her new spouse. She had been startled to fright when the cannons bellowed on their arrival at the palace and was moved to tears when the Arch-Bishop (think of it, a real Arch-Bishop performing the ceremony, and in her home town, not even the lowest monk would listen to her confession) spoke the blessings for them. She had drunk it into herself, blinded with the splendor, and had made all kinds of good promises to herself. She had been in a trance, had kissed her new hand-maids and assured them heaven on earth when they undressed her late at night, and she had gone to her new husband (according to his orders quite nude) intending to thank and thank him, to tell him that she was going to be his chattel and his faithful wife. But when she lay next to him, when she observed how this Prince of the costly uniform had changed into an abhorrent brute, she had not been able to say a word.

Prince Alexey Sokolow did not expect a word from her. He had never thought of a woman as a human being but as his property. He owned many and kept dozens of serf girls always near his bedroom. He had them follow him on his voyages. He had had them since his father first ordered him to fuck a girl when he was sixteen years of age. He never had an affair with a society girl, because she was somebody else's property. While he made many daring business ventures and acquired the estates of many men convicted for political or other reasons during his two score years as governor, women were something not to be taken illegally. If you liked a bitch, you could buy her; there was always a price which could be met.

During his trips to Western Europe, he had learned that there were harlots, whom one could buy for an hour or a day. He even brought to Russia with him some wenches who did a nice job in bed. It seemed money wasted, however, because his own slave girls could do as well and even better. They were harder, had no moods and were easily put in their places when they did not behave properly.

Alexey had no special love habits. He did not know about the refinements of copulation; he just wanted a good fuck. He wanted to put it in to his own satisfaction, regardless of the pleasure of his partner, and was satisfied when the ass moved up and down against him. That is, it had been so when he was younger and had not yet acquired his belly. Now he would not have been able to touch the spot with his machine had he laid himself on top of a girl. With his growing belly he had discovered a better position; the girl had to kneel straddle-legged over him and move up and down while he lay still, moving only the muscles of his enormous buttocks alternately. He also managed to give his shaft a to-and-fro movement without lifting his ass from the linen, because the muscles were well developed around his sex-organs.

He did not explain much of this to his bride. She really was stunning looking and he was well satisfied with this new acquirement to his bed assortment. He had not married her for love, and if she had not pleased him he would have fucked her once or twice (he liked to take maidenheads) and then probably forgotten her. But she was a good morsel and he was going to use her. He broke her in without further ado. He felt her over with his thick hands, he rudely forced his finger into her pussy, he pulled her on top of him, he spanked her bottom a bit, in short he first took possession of her with his hands.

Nelidowa tried to make it easy for herself by kissing him on the cheeks (with closed eyes) by snuggling against him (to her own disgust) and by not struggling when she felt his big finger enter her hole. Then, with a jerk, holding her with his hands at the waist-line, he sat her with his powerful arms on top of his testicles. Nelidowa knew well what it was all about; a married girl friend had told her, so she understood that Master Prick, now cornered between her Venus Hill and the steep wall of his belly, had to go into the cage and she knew that it would hurt her. But she was not only required to stand for it, she had to put it in herself; she had, with her own weight, to tear that little piece of skin which is precious only to virgins. She did not have the nerve. She stared with fixed eyes at the brute who was lying below her, a few hours ago still an utter stranger and now entitled to defile her.

"Put it in and sit on it and fuck." yelled Alexey to her. Poor Nelidowa. She took that hard instrument, so broad but still not so long, in her nimble fingers. She moved it towards the entrance and nervously lowered her bottom. But things needed a more vigorous handling. Alexey was prepared for that. He did not like to induce a woman to do this or that; he did not like to fumble. He had taken more virgins than one since his belly had grown. He had expected even more resistance from his bride and the usual preparation had been made.

He struck a little gong on his night table. Three servant girls rushed in. Before Nelidowa knew it, two had gotten hold of her with an expert grip: one hand went underneath each knee, took hold of it and stretching the leg as far from the middle of the body as possible, the other hands grabbed her shoulder. She was lifted up a bit and lowered down carefully. Meanwhile the third girl took the tail of her master with one hand, opened up with apt fingers the unused cunt, and saw to it that both met in the right way. She then commanded: PUSH, and both women, holding the Princess, gave a satisfactory pressure to her shoulders. Satisfactory, because Master Prick was in and had pierced the little membrane.

Nelidowa howled, the Prince moved his bottom, the girls let go of her knees and took hold of her waist and shoulders and moved her up and down. It took about five minutes for the Prince to come.

The Princess received a washing and the master was likewise cleaned up from the blood. She had to lie down again along side of her master. "You'll learn." he said. "And now we'll show you how the next part has to be done." He bedded her head on his hairy chest, put her hand on his machine and told her to massage it tenderly. As she did so he groaned and snorted, his fat hand on her small bottom. It pleased him that her ass was small and her thighs straight and slim; when the girls were fleshy it was hard for him to bury his prick deep into their cunts.

After a while he was stiff again. The gong sounded a snappy order, and a serf-girl ready for work, entered the room. She knew what to do. She mounted the master, so that her face was towards his feet and her back towards his belly. He put some more pillows under his head and managed to bend forward enough so that he could reach the behind of the girl, who was riding him with slow firm motions up and down. He lay perfectly still, his hand playing with her behind, and he found her ass hole and squeezed his finger in just as he came. After that he lay quietly and had himself washed with a wet towel.

He explained to his new wife that fuck number one was to be given with full front view; fuck number two reversed. He said that she was to come three times a week, that she was to learn her technique quickly and that she could now go back to her own bed-chamber, because he wanted to sleep. No good night, no caresses, no good word for her. But also no bad word. He was instituting a routine which was kept from then on.

It was strictly kept because he liked her better than his slave girls and she soon learned how to squeeze out his prick properly with her pussy. Also it must be remembered that he paid more for her upkeep than for that of his other female retinue. Nelidowa did not mind the prick so much; she simply closed her eyes and managed to come and to get a thrill. What she could not stand was the play of his strong hands over her body before every jump, expecially between the first and the second fucking, when he wanted to heat himself up again. At this time, he hurt her quite often. He fussed around with her breasts, pinched the nipples and laughed when she tried to avoid him. When he toyed with her love nest, he did not begin with any gentle play around the entrance, warm up the tickler and then intrude into the tube. No, he just pushed his finger rudely in as deep as he could, crooked it and rubbed it. It always gave her pain and a shock. But she did not complain and even gave him gentle words and told him how happy she was. It was the price demanded of her and she gave it.

The rest of their personal relations were also regulated by rules. They ate apart, except when they had guests. They went to all social affairs together and he liked to show her off and sent her for such occasions, jewelry from the seemingly endless store of his iron chest. He spoke politely to her, in few words, and never told her about his own affairs. For example, she did not know that he had big estates in the South, until they travelled over them. He confided his affairs only to an old trusted man servant and to very few of his friends. He was a man of few words, used to command and he exercised his will with great determination.

Nelidowa had to find her life with her women friends. She chatted with her bed-maids and amused herself as she could with anything that was proper and becoming for the wife of a great Prince. He never beat her, as many husbands did their wives and he never lost his temper. He had resorted to the lash only a few times in his life, sending the culprit to the stable master for the punishment. However, when he was seriously dissatisfied, he would have the guilty person stand while he smacked the face a few times.

He did this to his wife on occasions when her giddiness had aroused the mockery of other society people and he had heard of it. When he heard that she was beating her maids or had them beaten, he discussed it briefly with her. He said that she had the right to do so, but that if one of the servants should become seriously ill or die on account of the punishment, he would then inflict the same torture on her. "They are My property," he added, "As well as you are." That closed the incident because he remembered that his mother had whipped her maids also.

He had expected to have a child from the Princess; he wanted an heir to cheat his relatives. She remained barren. He had a few virgins come from one of his estates, fucked them and held them under strict watch, so that they could not sleep with other men. Out of four girls, two became

69

pregnant. Therefore it was Nelidowa, not he, who was at fault. But he decided not to take another wife. Not because he could not have gotten rid of her or because he loved her, but that it was not so important after all. She was there and she could remain there.

After the first year of her marriage, feeling secure now as a Princess and a powerful man's wife, Nelidowa was ripe to take a lover. He must be distinctly different from her husband, a bit exotic, maybe a Frenchman. As it turned out, he was a Pole. Gustavus Swanderson, he made known, was his name. He came from Warsaw, where his father had a string of disorderly houses. Gustavus, who then bore the name of Boris, managed, during a raid on his father's establishments, to get hold of some gold which the old man kept hidden. With this, he travelled to Sweden, changed his name, bought the patent of an officer and played the nice chap for the ladies. He was decidedly romantic, with a wealth of brown hair, elegant in his movements, enterprising, and not altogether a bad boy. His hobby was drawing and his satirical sketches of society people were quite the thing. He started to learn architecture, first just to play with it, but later became interested and took part in the erection of some military buildings and forts. When Peter the Great was already quite elderly, he came to Russia and offered his services as builder. Peter, though not much impressed with him, sent him to Moscow where a big bridge was under construction and here he began to be a slight success in his line.

When he met Nelidowa he was around thirty years of age, ten years her senior. He was different from the other men; his skin was white, he was not hairy, his hands were fine, almost feminine and tender. He kept himself clean and modish and his laughter was of a romantic sadness.

Nelidowa selected him for herself at first sight. The man had very little choice as to whether he wanted her or not. He had to conquer her because she wanted him. Oh, she fixed it in a very romantic way. Poems fluttered through the air; secret words passed, only understood by the conspirators. Nelidowa played her part wonderfully, with tears and resistance and with faked fainting spells.

She won him and she was very satisfied. He was so tender, so full of caresses, so loving, so romantic and when, after long kissing and playing and toying, she finally felt his hot rod enter her hungry crevice, she nearly fainted with delight. Of course, when he built lovely castles in the air about elopement and how they would live in Paris as happy as doves, she listened like a happy but already grown up child to a smartly told fairy tale. While she avoided saying "No", in her heart she never considered him more than a lover. Something necessary to a woman's life, but not to be mixed up with the reality of a Princess.

On the other hand, this reality bothered her three times a week when she walked nude, except for blue slippers, through different rooms to the bed of a big brute who offended her body and for whom she was nothing but an instrument for prick-massage. She could not pretend she had a head-ache or did not feel well, because if she did, her husband would send a servant with a brief méssage that he was not fucking her head but her cunt. As long as she did not have her monthly, she had to appear. No pity from that quarter and no excuse accepted.

Another incident occured which proved to be annoying. Gustavus fell in love with her and the longer the liason lasted the more enamoured he became. With this his jealousy developed, and while the brutal and elderly Prince in his strength entertained no slightest thought that his wife might be unfaithful, Gustavus, in his tender and weak constitution, was crazed with jealousy. She had once described to him in what way she had to fuck her husband and though this was still early in their affair, he was near to assassinating his rival. Lately he had pestered her to refuse to play the dutiful wife and in passionate words had threatened to take the life of the Prince and even hers. She told him she would do as he wished and, lying, said she did not go to her husband since at present he had a passion for one of the serf girls. Gustavus did not believe her fully and they had many scenes. She did not want to give up her lover. She could not stay away from her master. She had to think her way out.

Suddenly she was struck with an idea: didn't they tell her that Grushenka looked just like her, not only in figure but in face also? It was whispered that they were like twins, that nobody could really say who was who. If that was true then Grushenka could take her place in the bed-chamber of her spouse. This thought was so daring, so exciting, that she had to go to work right away. She commanded Grushenka to her presence and had herself and the girl clothed in dresses exactly similar and their hair done in the same way. She then had one of her maids ask other servants from the basement which of the two was the Princess. The servants looked uneasy, afraid to make a mistake. They tried to avoid a direct answer and finally pointed at random, missing the Princess as often as they chose her. That was fine! All that was now needed was for the Princess to teach Grushenka exactly how to behave with the master.

She dismissed all the servants including her hand maids, locked herself in her bedroom with Grushenka and made her kneel down and swear solemnly never to betray her. She confided her plan to the girl and rehearsed to the smallest detail the way the fucking parties took place. When Grushenka undressed, an obstacle appeared: Grushenka was clean shaven around the pussy. There was nothing to do but to wait until the hair had grown. So it was decided. During this time, for many an afternoon, Grushenka was told how she would have to behave during the coming fucking parties and Nelidowa, during this period, observed herself in all details when she was with her mate. She was sure of success. The bed room of the Prince was lit by a single large candle which stood in a corner far from the bed and there was a small candle in front of the Ikon. This small illumination would not have permitted him to find out the difference between Nelidowa and Grushenka even if they had not been so much alike.

Another remark must be made concerning these confidential rehearsals between the young women. They began to like each other. The Princess had never thought of Grushenka before except as a low and silly serf girl. Now she wanted something from her. She ordered her, of course, to take her place. Grushenka could tell the master and the catastrophe arising from such a mishap would have been unthinkably awful! Therefore the Princess became kind to the girl, chatted with her and tried to discover her character. She was captivated with Grushenka's simple charm and faith. On the other hand, Grushenka now learned that the Princess was unhappy, uncertain of herself, that she had had a hard youth, that she longed for kindness and that her nervous and brutal behaviour did not arise from coldness, but from unawareness. Grushenka became a hand-maid of her mistress, was always around her, was her confident in her love matters and her companion during the long hours of the dragging days. The whip was never applied to her, she was not scolded, and she slept next to her mistress's room and became something like a little sister.

When Grushenka's hair had grown, (they examined it daily) the day came when a male servant announced that his Highness expected the visit of her Highness. Grushenka put on the blue slippers and both women walked through the several rooms to the master's chamber. Grushenka entered while Nelidowa, with beating heart, peeped through a crack of the door. The Prince had come from a card game where he had been drinking and felt tired and a little lascivious. Grushenka held his stub in her hand, worked it firmly, mounted the horse and worked his machine into her tube. For quite a time he could not come on account of the liquor he had drunk but she came herself once or twice (she had not fucked for ever so long) until he groaned and moved his ass and was through. He was through for the night and sent her away with a slap on the behind.

Nelidowa took Grushenka with her to her bed. She was excited, joyously excited, while Grushenka was very calm. She had done the whole job without hesitation. She wanted to help her mistress. That was her duty; for the rest, she was not concerned. Nelidowa hugged and kissed the girl and aroused by the fucking she had seen, had two hand maids come in to give herself and her friend (as she said now for the first time) a good sucking.

So it was that Grushenka became the master's wife as far as his bed was concerned. The first few times Nelidowa went with her to the door and peeped. After that she remained in the bed until Grushenka returned and a few weeks later was no longer concerned about the mater. When the servant came to announce that his master's prick was ready (that was the sense of the message) Nelidowa would say she'd come right away, and Grushenka who lay on the bed in the next room, got up, went to the Prince, fucked, washed her pussy and went back to sleep.

Until that time Nelidowa had satisfied the whims of her mate in spite of her repulsion. She now found her satisfaction under the pushing of Gustavus' considerate shaft while Grushenka had to look forward to the short but thick prick of her master. Grushenka had never known fine people, so the rudeness of the Prince did not shock her. On the contrary his brutal force and immense vitality captured her and made her forget the repulsion which his belly might have inspired. She loved his scepter. She began not only to massage it, but to caress it, to kiss it and she soon began to suck him. He thought first that she wanted a gift from him, perhaps one of his estates or a will made out in her favor. But when no such demands came, he felt with pleasure what a passionate, refined and loving wife he had.

Grushenka had a much easier time with him than Nelidowa used to have. The Princess always used to aggressively try to stop him from taking hold of her body with his hands, but now the Prince was stiff before Grushenka was in bed and she sat on him before he could annoy her with his hands. Besides, she fucked with so much passion that she did not mind when he squeezed her nipples while his machine was in her pussy. During the intermission, he lauded her with teasing words about her newly found temperament but hardly touched her, waiting until she would take hold of his prick again. She sometimes lay between his legs, raising his big behind with a pillow, and licked his dark brown balls with intense ardor, the hard strong smell of his balls and the odor of his rim was a sensation to her nostrils. She quivered all over and got immensely excited and worked herself up by pressing her legs close together. She did not want to follow his orders to come up and mount him; she wanted to make him come with her lips, to drink the liquid, but he never let her.

Sometimes Nelidowa would watch this scene out of curiosity, jealous that the girl enjoyed it so much. Afterwards she would pinch her and scold her about something and then again she would kiss the girl's mouth, lick her lips and teeth, because she felt the contamination of the sex excitement which had gotten hold of Grushenka. Sometimes she would decide to go to her husband herself, but at the last moment she would change her mind, and go to her lover. If he were not in the neighborhood, she would have one of her maids satisfy her caprice.

All went well except for some small incidents. For example, the master would tell Grushenka something he wanted done the next day and she, not familiar with the people concerned or with the facts, would have a hard time remembering exactly what he had said. Or the Princess would be asleep when she came from the master's bedroom and she would lie awake the whole night so as not to forget. At other times, Grushenka would have a rash or pimples on her face which Nelidowa did not have, and she would be much afraid of detection in spite of the subdued light in his bedchamber.

Nelidowa told her lover the huge joke she had played on her mate and smuggled him into her own bed room and prepared with care the comedy of watching the fucking party of her husband with Grushenka. When Gustavus arrived, she presented Grushenka to him and made him compare them to find out who was who. To her great satisfaction, he was not for a moment in doubt although they wore no clothes. The reason for his quick judgement was that Nelidowa alone spoke, while Grushenka kept silent with a smile on her lips. She wanted to please Gustavus of whom she had heard so much; she had a romantic affection for him through Nelidowa.

Grushenka liked Gustavus as soon as she laid eyes on him. He was so gracious in his movements, his bearing was elegant, his hands were white, fine and well taken care of, in great contrast to those of the Russian men. He was eager to point out differences between the two: a little mole underneath the shoulder blade, the different shape of the bust, the flavor of the hair. Of course "his love" was more beautiful. Though this pleased her, Nelidowa had to show him that she was the mistress and Grushenka the slave. First she told him what a pig Grushenka was for liking the prick of the Prince and sucking him off, then she turned Grushenka around and around, exposing her in every fashion. Finally she pinched the girl and suggested that Grushenka prove her art by kissing his shaft, but Gustavus, ashamed of all this play, refused.

Just then a message came from the Prince, who expected the Princess. Grushenka moved her hand over her bust and belly as if she were stroking her skin, she lightly rubbed her pussy with her fingers and opened the lips a few times just to have everything ready. She then stepped into the little blue slippers and went towards the bedroom of the Prince-husband. Nelidowa and Gustavus followed. Tip-toeing quietly, they took posts at the crack of the door.

Grushenka, well aware of the watchers and annoyed by the humiliation to which Nelidowa had submitted her, did not follow the usual behavior. The lovers at the door could see the Prince on a bed with light blue silk covers, resting on his back, his fingers playing a happy rhythm on the bed sheet, his lips sensually pursed; the picture of a man who knows that he will be taken care of shortly. The door through which the lovers peeped was toward the foot of the bed, and his monstrous hairy body and big belly were plainly visible.

Grushenka leaned over and took in her left hand the big balls, caressing them while reaching underneath them and playing with her finger in his rim. Meanwhile her right hand held his prick, which she massaged. The prick was half asleep but with a good inclination to wake up. The gentle treatment soon made the machine stiff. Grushenka did not kiss it; she pointed maliciously with her tongue in its direction and smacked her lips, but she did not embrace the shaft with them.

Instead, she mounted. The lovers could clearly see how she held the prick with two fingers of her right hand, how she opened her cunt with the left hand, and how Master Priapus slowly poked his nose into her love-nest. Grushenka bent forward, and giving over her splendid breasts to his grasping hands, made a few firm and deep up and down movements.

Then of a sudden, she bent back. Opening her knees as wide as possible, getting a deep hold of his machine with her cunt, she leaned so far back that her elbows almost touched her own heels. Of course the fat master was unable to reach any part of her body in this position, and groaning with excitement, he swore at her to bend forward. He used all the curse words he knew and his short arms waved with helpless strokes through the air. It was a funny picture; the riding girls with a determination on her face to squeeze his prick out with her cunt, and the pinioned monster who had to submit to his excitement, though mad to reach her. It was so funny a picture that Nelidowa and Gustavus could not restrain their giggles. Until this had happened, they had stood close together, Nelidowa holding his prick while his fingers fondled her love nest. When Grushenka had engulfed the Prince's shaft, they had keenly felt their own sex excitement.

The Prince was startled. Who was at the door? He moved and was about to throw his fair rider off to investigate. Grushenka, sensing the danger, threw herself forward and pressing him into the cushions with her weight, began to love up his face and head with kisses and the caresses of her hands. This brought about his crisis. He came with all his force and was unable to do anything but squirt his sperm into her. Thus the lovers had time to escape. Of course, the second party when Grushenka was riding the other way around, could not be observed by them, but, as by that time Nelidowa was already squirming under the pressure of her beloved "soldier" perhaps it did not matter much.

CHAPTER VI.

When Prince Sokolow was on one of his estates, the Princess usually contrived to have Gustavus as house guest with them. The Prince was usually building and constructing and Gustavus had become his architect. Therefore there was no reason for misconstruing his presence. The Princess went to her lover's room as soon as Grushenka was with her husband. Great precaution was taken to prevent detection, lest their idyll be destroyed. But in Moscow it was very dangerous to smuggle Gustavus nightly into the palace, so he took a suite not far from the Sokolows, and Nelidowa stole out of the house at night by a small back door and visited him. That is what she had done one night, the dramatic events of which will now be told.

The Prince and Princess had been to a ball. They came home together, she gaily talking; he as usual, saying little. He told her to come to him as soon as she was ready. Entering her room, the Princess called Grushenka and while she changed from her ball gown to a simple street dress, not forgetting to put some perfume under her arms

81

and between her legs, Grushenka left for the bedroom of the Prince. Soon afterwards, Nelidowa departed from the palace.

The first encounter between Grushenka and the Prince took place as usual. Grushenka was a bit lazy and tired that day. In fact she had been sleeping before the couple came back from the ball. But she Frenched him all right and rode his prick afterwards, quite a long ride this time because both of them seemed, somehow, without desire. Having accomplished her aim, she stretched herself alongside of him and started mechanically to play with his testicles preparing for the second encounter.

The Prince began, in a muttering way, a conversation. "How did you like the diamond necklace which the Countess of Kolpack was wearing tonight?" he asked.

"Ah! Splendid!" replied Grushenka indifferently.

"Do you intend to go to the tea-party of Countess Kolpack?" continued the man.

"Maybe I will. Maybe I won't," Grushenka said, trying to imitate the nonchalant ways of her mistress and getting intensely interested in her master's balls. But to her great surprise and fright, the Prince sat suddenly upright, but his one hand on her throat and with the other seized her hair.

"Who is the Countess Kolpack?" he shouted. "Who is she? Who is she?" Such a countess, in fact, did not exist.

"Well, well—" was all Grushenka could mutter under his grip. She felt the game was up. She felt that the question had been a trap. She knew everything was lost. It was. One of his man-servants had told all to the Prince, who had investigated carefully and learned everything, even knew that at this very minute his cheating wife was in the arms of her lover. But he wanted to make sure. He wanted the facts first hand.

"Who are you? Don't lie!" he cried into Grushenka's face, lessening his grip to give her an opportunity to speak.

"Who am I—" stuttered the frightened serf-girl. "Well, don't you know your own wife? Have you lost your mind? God forgive me!" and she crossed her heart in great anguish.

The gong sounded. The servant, prepared in advance, came in. Grushenka was seated on a chair. The Spanish shoes were brought in and put on her feet. The wooden edges of this instrument, invented during the Inquisition, pressed painfully against the flesh and bones of her nude feet even before the servant started to turn the screws. The Prince stopped him. He addressed her, almost formally, asking her again to confess who she was. She kept her mouth shut. She bit her lips. A motion from the Prince and the servant made the first turn. Her feet went numb. The second turn—the pain shot up her body. Screaming, she twisted in her chair, trying to liberate herself. She was mad with fright and pain, even though the wood had actually not yet cut her skin.

Then she gave in. She promised to confess everything; the screw was unloosened, so was her tongue. In a stream of tears, she confessed. When she came to the end, she threw herself at the Prince's feet and begged for mercy, not for herself, but for her poor mistress. He just frowned at her incoherent utterances. He told the servants to lead her away as arranged in advance.

She was taken howling and screaming to the torture chamber in the basement. Large torches were lighted. She was put on a chair with two arms but no back. Her arms, from the elbows to the wrists, were fastened to the arms of the chair; a leather strap secured her tightly to the corners of the seat. After the two male serfs had done this job, they were uncertain what to do next. They felt her all over, had their jokes with her and discussed whether they should put their pricks in her mouth.

While Grushenka had been in the service of her mistress and taken her place with the master, none of the serfs dared to touch her. But now she seemed doomed. Why shouldn't these servants make her suck them off before her bones were broken on the rack? For that was, in their opinion, the least the master would do. Uncertain as the whole affair was, however, they decided to nap until further orders were forthcoming, and they stretched themselves on the floor in a half sleep.

Grushenka looked around. She had plenty of time to observe the gruesome room. Next to her stood a chair similar to the one she was strapped to. All kinds of handles and machinery were underneath the seat, but she could not make out what they were for. In the middle of the room was the flogging block over which she had been laid by Katerina, the most used instrument in the room, a kind of saddle on four legs , with rings and ropes on it to tie the delinquent in the most receptive position. One wall was covered with all kinds of beating instruments: knouts, leather straps, whips and the like. On the next wall were the racks; ladder-like frames against which the culprit was fastened, while light and heavy bats stood around with which legs or arms could be broken. Chains and hanging racks, on which the man or woman to be punished was hung in such a way that the arms were twisted backward, completed the outfit of the room, a replica of which existed in the houses of all the masters of that time.

While Grushenka observed all these terrors, Prince Sokolow acted according to his plan. He dressed in a

Russian blouse and high boots. He had his servants pack his trunks. He then went down to the back entrance through which Nelidowa was to come home. He took a low stool and sat down, watching the door. He sat thus for many hours, motionless, staring at the door, not closing or even blinking an eye. Dawn came, and with it Nelidowa. She entered with light steps in a happy and satisfied mood after a good fucking party with her lover. As soon as she closed the door, the short and tremendously strong Prince sprang at her, lifted her high in the air and flung her over his shoulder, her head and the upper part of her body dangling on his back. She uttered a piercing cry. She struggled to liberate herself, not knowing who had seized her. He carried her swiftly to the chamber where Grushenka sat.

"Tear the clothes from her body and strap her to that chair!" he commanded the serfs, throwing her in their direction. The Prince sat down on a low bench and waited for his order to be carried out. This was not very easy, for Nelidowa put up a terrific battle. She swore at the servants, she hit with her fists, she bit, she kicked—all to no avail. Her clothes were torn from her body, one man holding her hands against her back, while the other one removed one garment after the other. First came the skirt, then the trousers and the stockings. As soon as the lower part of her body was naked, one slave put his head between her legs. Holding her feet, he raised himself up and stood straight, so that she hung on his back, her spot right on his neck. The other man took a short knife, cut open her sleeves from the writ to the shoulders, then did likewise to her blouse and chemise.

She was nude. They fastened her on the chair the same way they had Grushenka, and one of the men, with a bow, announced to the Prince that they were finished. The Prince ordered them from the room.

Nelidowa understood the situation perfectly by this time. But with a haughty air she demanded that she be set free immediately, shouting that he had no right to punish her like that squealing brat, that serf girl next to her; that it was his fault and not her's that she had deceived him, because he was a brute, a monster with whom no decent woman would sleep. She told him that he was repulsive to her, that she despised him, that if she had not found this substitute she would have left him openly,—and so on. In her rage she made a full confession about her love for Gustavus and that she was going to marry him as soon as she was rid of her tormenter.

The Prince did not reply. He inspected the nude women, amazed at their likeness. He felt no pity in his heart, not for them and not for himself. He knew her confession without having to listen to it. It was true! She had deceived him. Everybody but he had known it a long time. She had defied him doubly; put a serf girl in his bed while she fucked with her lover. A hugh joke on himself. It had to be punished thoroughly.

He first went behind Grushenka's chair. He turned a handle. The seat on which the girl was sitting lowered itself down. Through holes in the seat came wooden nails, the points sticking upwards. Grushenka felt them pierce the flesh of her buttocks. At the same time the arms of the chair gave way while she tried frantically to get a hold of them. The braces of the arms fitted into tubes and she could not hold her weight on them. Her feet did not reach the floor, she sat on the nails and her own weight was driving them slowly and with increasing pain into her tender flesh. The Prince stepped behind the chair of his wife and unloosened here also the bolts which held the seat and the arms. After that he went with slow steps to the wall and took down a short leather strap and turned to his wife.

"I should burn your cunt which betrayed me and your mouth which just now besmirched me, with hot irons to mark you forever," he said in a low voice. "I will not do so. Not because I love or pity you, but because I understand that you are branded for life with a more terrible stigma. You are a low creature, not born to be a Princess. It was my error that I took you and I beg you to forgive me—" He made a low bow while she sneered at him— "but you must be punished in order to know who the master is." Those were his only words to his wife and were the last he ever spoke to her.

With firm strong lashes of his muscular arms, he now began to whip her. He started with her back, laying stroke after stroke from her shoulders down to the lowest part of her body. The lashes hissed through the air. Nelidowa yelled and cried. She was unable to hold still. The points of the nails tore her bottom and cut the flesh more and more when she twisted around under each stroke. Her back, of which she was so proud, was covered with welts, but the Prince was not yet satisfied. He now began in front, hit her feet, her legs, stood before her on an angle and hit into the full length her thighs. He beat her belly and—without fury or hurry—finished up by laying cutting lashes over her breasts. He stopped only after he found her whole body was a mass of bruises.

Nelidowa did not cease to yell and cry and Grushenka mingled her own outcries with those of her mistress, not only because the nails bit into her bottom, but also out of compassion. She expected the same treatment but Sokolow resolved otherwise. He threw the whip away, came very close to her, looked into her fear-stricken eyes, and said, "You did wrong. I am your master. You should have told me the first time."—and he gave her two good smacks in the face as he would have done to a servant who had forgotten something. He left the room and slammed the door behind him.

There the two women sat on the nails, not knowing what the future had in store. Nelidowa cursed Grushenka and promised to roast her to death as soon as she could lay hands on her. She howled in her pain and tried to faint. Grushenka wept softly and avoided moving her body to lessen the pain from the nails. The torches burnt slowly down. The room became dark. The sobbing and wailing cut through the dark silence.

The Prince ordered a carriage. He went to Gustavus' house. He was bent on action. He aroused a sleeping servant, pushed him aside, strode into Gustavus' bed room, which was already filled with the first morning light, and awakened the soundly sleeping Adonis with a punch in the face. Gustavus jumped out of his bed. The Prince pointed a pistol at the naked form of his rival. He demanded: "No words are necessary between us. If you want to say a prayer, I will give you the time for it."

Gustavus was wide awake. He was a squeamish Adonis, but he saw there was no escape. He stood upright, folded his arms over his chest and faced the stocky man in front of him. His white, slender body was motionless. The Prince took careful aim and shot him through the heart. Leaving, he tossed a purse of gold to the scared man-servant who cowered in the hall.

"Here," shouted the Prince, "Take that money and see

to it that your master gets a decent funeral. Harlequins like him might not leave even enough money for that."

His next stop was at the main police station. He aroused the drowsing lieutenant in charge and reported with sharp words: "I am Prince Alexey Sokolow. I just killed with one shot Gustavus Swanderson. He was the lover of my wife. The whole city will confirm that, I am sure. The police will not prosecute me or I will chase my dogs at their throats. You know that! Report my word to the policemaster anyway. I leave for France today. I expect to have the policemaster as my guest when I come back. Report that to him. I will first call on the Czar in Petersburg to get leave of absence from him. (Here the voice of the Prince became threatening and the lieutenant understood him perfectly well.) If the policemaster wants to do anything about this affair, have him send a report to the Czar." With that he strode out of the room

Next he drove to his nephew, a lieutenant in a cavalry regiment. The orderly did not want to let the Prince enter his superior's apartment, but when he mentioned his name the soldier stood back in awe. Sokolow opened the curtains of the bedroom and the sun disclosed the sleeping lieutenant in close embrace with a girl. She woke up first and was a sight. Her make-up was smeared over her face by the night's love making, her bust was drooping, her legs were bent. She was a little Jewish whore who slept with the lieutenant for a few copecas. He loved his prick but he had no money to buy himself a good looking sleeping partner. He was a lighthearted boy of twenty-five, slightly dumb, good looking and with a fine physique. He was deeply in debt. His rich uncle had never given him a cent or lent him his influence, because Sokolow disliked him as he did the rest of his family. But he was his nearest kin and had to be treated differently now.

Disregarding the bitch in the bed and all questions and objections of the aroused lieutenant, the Prince forced him to dress and accompany him, while the girl settled back under the covers with a yawn. The Prince drove with his nephew, who was very startled by the intrusion, to the house of his lawyer. He rang the bell and sent the sleepy servant upstairs to demand that the lawyer get dressed and come down at once. They sat in the coach, waiting. The uncle perfectly calm in his manner, drumming with his fingers; the nephew nervously apprehensive, trying in vain to learn what it was all about. Finally the lawyer joined them and they drove back to the palace. Prince Sokolow took them to his library, put paper and ink before the lawyer and dictated a complete power of attorney in favor of his nephew, instituting him as master of his whole estate until this granted power should be revoked. He demanded certain moneys sent to his banker in Paris; made a codicil to his will, dividing his estate and leaving the greater part to his nephew, who did not trust his ears. After that he dictated to the lawyer the summary of a divorce action against his wife, claiming infidelity and disowning her entirely. Then he ordered vodka and tea, walked with firm steps from one corner of the room to the other and explained to his amazed audience exactly what had happened.

He told his nephew that he hoped that in the future he would not sleep with such awful harlots, especially since he would find such a fine assortment of Russian girls available on his estates and would not need to soil his body on low whores. He dismissed both men, ordering his nephew to take leave of his regiment, to straighten out his small affairs and to return immediately to take charge. So and so much had to be earned by the estate during a year and if he should find on his return that things were not in shape, he would disown him again. The men left the lieutenant with a startled feeling of joy in his heart.

Two travelling carriages were now made ready for departure. The Prince went down to the basement where a crowd of women were in a flutter. They all knew what had happened. Grushenka had fainted, but Nelidowa was still wailing as she hung broken in the chair. The Prince sent for her hand maids. He had both women unstrapped and brought up to Nelidowa's room. Grushenka was revived and sent to her bed. The Prince ordered Nelidowa dressed. When they tried to put the chemise and the trousers on her, she screamed in pain because her lacerated body could not endure the touch of the linen. Nevertheless they put a dress on her and did it quickly because the staring look of the Prince made them hurry.

When Nelidowa was ready, they carried her to one of the carriages. The Prince ordered three of his most trusted men to enter the carriage also. He told them they were to drive her home to her aunt's, not to stop on the way, and to feed her in the coach.

"Let her shit in her trousers," he added, "but don't let her leave the carriage for a second. She is your captive and if you don't follow orders, I shall have you killed."

The carriage drove on. It is not said what became of Nelidowa, nor do we know what became of the Prince, except that his divorce was granted and that he returned to his estate, as the records of his divorce trial prove.

CHAPTER VII.

Leo Kirilowicz Sokolow, the nephew, left the palace drunk with happiness. He, the unimportant little lieutenant, indebted, bound by the discipline of his regiment, short of everything that makes life wonderful for a young man, had suddenly become rich. Yes, he was independent, the master of a hundred thousand, maybe even a million souls. How should he know how many? He was a man now who would sit in council, be courted by the ladies, govern a huge estate. Of course his power was only temporary, only for the time Uncle Alexey was in Western Europe. But who could tell, the old bugger might die soon. In all events let the present be the present!

Things went so swiftly for this young man on this day that it is hard to detail even a part of them. Paul, the orderly, was kissed by his young master on both cheeks. The Jewish whore was pulled out of the bed by one leg, while Leo laughed like mad, and, after she had covered her meagre body with her rags and was leaving the barely furnished room, she felt something strike her on the back and fall to the floor. An oath on her lips, she picked it up automatically. It was a purse full of rubles, the total wealth Leo commanded before his uncle got him out of bed. The whore fled from the room clutching her unexpected wages of sin to her stomach and followed by the hilarious laughter of the young man.

In turn, the adjutant of the regiment, the captain and the colonel were notified of his resignation. Comrades were invited to a drinking bout at the palace that same evening. His scanty belongings were shipped over to the magnificent home of the Sokolows.

The new master started immediately to learn about his new household by questioning the various head servants. He sought advice on the administration of his estates by conferring with lawyers and men holding public office. He even sent messengers to all the head administrators in the provinces, mostly trusted serfs, inviting them to a conference on some future date. In short he plunged headlong into the task of his new responsibilities.

During the banquet that night he got so drunk that four men had to carry him to his bed where he collapsed unconscious. The palace itself would have been under great peril of demolishment by his no less sober friends had not one of them suggested a visit to a famous whore house.

When Leo awoke late the next day, his trusted orderly was at hand to nurse his tremendous headache with ice and herring. All the wealth in the world was then of no meaning to our Leo whose rebellious stomach chained him to his bedchamber. But early the next morning found him in the saddle on the back of one of the magnificent horses of his uncle's stables and he rode around inspecting his land. As he rode he began to collect his mental balance. The whole story of his young aunt and her substitute was certainly the best stroke of luck that ever could have happened, but it was not yet quite clear to him how it had all come about. Hence his order when he came back to the palace that he wanted to dine that night "en deux" with Grushenka, and that she was to be clothed exactly like his aunt would have been for a great evening party.

Grushenka, after she had been lifted out of the nail chair, had been cared for by the other serf girls. They put sour cream on her offended behind, gave her cold water to drink and she fell into a feverish slumber which after a while became sound sleep. In fact, just as the above mentioned order was given she was getting out of bed and her buttocks, although still covered with scratches and red puncture marks, did not hurt anymore. She felt fit except for the anguish of wondering about what further punishment awaited her. She learned with great concern the fate of Nelidowa and Gustavus and the sudden departure of the old Prince. The message from her new master and the description of him—a nice young chap with a pointed black mustache, fresh eyes and a leaning toward drunkeness— was the sole theme of the conversation between her and the other maids.

Early in the afternoon they started to prepare Grushenka, putting on her the finest silk shirt of the Princess, a pair of laced trousers, silk stockings, high gilded shoes and an evening gown of light blue-silver brocade which left the breasts bare up to the nipples. Boris put on her with much earnestness and care a formal white wig with many ringlets. Her fingers and toe nails were perfectly manicured. A mild perfume was sprayed on her. Everyone of the handmaids did her best to make Grushenka as beautiful as possible as though she were a bride prepared for her wedding night.

There was much speculation but very little doubt that the young master would fuck her. All the maidens in the house were eager to know about that and wished that they themselves might some fine day be the bed-fellow of the new Prince.

Grushenka entered the dining room flushed with embarrassment. Scores of candles were throwing a glittering light from reflecting Venetian chandeliers. Four men servants stood like soldiers ready for service. The major domo, in spotless uniform, waited by the door. The new master arrived with quick steps for the good reason that he was hungry. He wore a soft shirt, a pair of house pants and slippers but he had put on the coat of his formal evening uniform on which he had pinned many medals from the box of his uncle. Checkered like his uniform was his state of mind and his behavior. He bowed low and formally to the girl, who responded with a deep curtsey. He gave her his arm and conducted her with grace to her seat, but remarked, while carefully moving her chair underneath her behind: "You have a fine pair of breasts."

During the first course, he studied her carefully, comparing her with his aunt, whom he had seen only a few times and being really uncertain whether it was his aunt or not, especially when he saw how well Grushenka handled fork and knife. She was afraid to make a move and hardly able to eat, but she was graceful by nature. He opened the conversation: "May I inquire, my Princess," said he, and not in a mocking tone, "how you rested last night and how you feel today?"

Grushenka glanced at him and her full blue eyes had a begging expression. "Forgive me your Highness." she said. "that I dare to eat in your presence and that I sit at your table, but your orders—" and she stopped. But he did not pay any attention to her words and went on in the same formal manner: "Did my cherised Princess have a nice walk today and are you satisfied with all the service given to you? If there is anything you wish, please be good enough to tell me."

"My only wish is to please my master." was Grushenka's answer.

"Well now, you can do so." he said. "Tell me exactly the story of how you and Aunt Nelidowa put it over the old bugger. I haven't yet understood how it really happened. Of course you know the whole city is enjoying the story immensely. You see he's the meanest and shrewdest old swine there ever was and I ought to make a statue in honour of both you women. Hurrah!"—he concluded his little speech—"Let's drink to the health of Uncle Alexey."

He lifted a glass of champagne toward her, drank it himself to the last drop and made her do the same. Grushenka, who had never before drunk a drop of wine or liquor, very soon began to feel happy and gay. Giggling she told him the whole story of the bed fraud until she came to the terrible end with it's punishment. This she merely mentioned. Meanwhile they had a real Russian dinner from caviar to goose, from goose through roast beef to pies and fruits. They ate and drank constantly while the Prince asked the most intimate questions about the illustrious prick of his relative and the girl told him with utter frankness every detail of it. She knew no shame or reservation and her words were to the point.

When the meal was over he conducted her most formally to the drawing room. The conversation went on while they sat alone in the big room and it occured to Leo for the first time, that he was now the master, that he could take everyone of these girls and handle her the way he saw fit. He learned of the way Nelidowa used to hit and pinch her girls, he heard of the torture chamber, of the rules of the house, of the gossip, of the wishes of his male and female serfs and he began to understand their absolute submissiveness. Not that Prince Leo had not known all these things, but he had known them only from afar. Now they came clearly to his mind from the chattering talk of this, his slave girl who was a bit tipsy but not drunk.

She began to get drowsy; it was time to go to bed. Leo again conducted her on his arm, this time to the bed chamber of the Princess where the chamber maids still lingered, curious to hear from Grushenka how the evening had passed. Leo saw with pleasure all these young creatures of whom he could make good use from now on. Knowing they were his property, he did not bother about a close inspection. He had heard so much about his aunt and of the perfect bodily likeness between her and Grushenka, that he was curious to see with his own eyes what his aunt looked like. Therefore he sat down in a low chair in a corner and gave the order to the girls that Grushenka should play the part of Nelidowa and behave exactly as though she were the Princess going to bed. The girls were also to conduct themselves as usual.

The girls giggled and started the little show. They helped Grushenka out of the gown. Grushenka stood before the mirror. She made graceful movements with her arms, caressed her breasts lovingly, rubbed her pussy playfully with the palm of her hand and said cooingly, "Oh, Gustavus! If I had you here now."—a remark which Nelidowa had made quite often to her own pussy and which usually was the sign for the serving girls that some sucking would be in store. Grushenka sat down. One girl kneeled before her and slowly removed her shoes and stockings. Another one took her wig off, loosened the long black hair and began to braid it. Grushenka meanwhile gave an account of the evening, an imaginary ball: finding herself the most beautiful woman present, telling about men who made longing eyes at her or others who seemed to have good balls in their trousers—all in the manner of Nelidowa. She even took the whip and lightly hit a servant girl over the legs, complaining she had handled her hair too roughly. Finally she got up from the chair, went to the middle of the room, and with feminine gestures, removed the little shirt she was wearing. Still rubbing her body voluptuously, she proceeded towards the bed.

Young Leo had been sitting motionless except for his big tool, which had lifted its head slowly. The half nude girl at the toilet table was good bait for Master Prick who sensed that a little hook up would not be amiss. He rose and stopped Grushenka; he looked her over closely and appraisingly. He let her turn around and as his eyes slid down over the beautiful back, he discovered the red marks on her bottom. This brought back to his mind that she was his property and subject to his bidding. He laid his hands on her, felt her all over and started to deliberate what to do with her.

His desire grew with every second. He pinched her cheeks and then opening her lips with two fingers he said, "Well, this mouth has been used alternately by my stinking uncle and my cheating aunt. Now as much as I like to get sucked off, I would not put my prick where other people have had theirs. When I know somebody has had a girl before me, I will not fuck her. You may ask my comrades if that isn't so. Of course,"—he added—"I have fucked many whores, and so far as I remember, never a virgin, but then if I don't know who had the bitches before me, it doesn't matter. Funny, isn't it?''

None of the girls in the room understood him, but many men are the same way. Yet he somewhat resented his own peculiarity, especially when he took her full bust in his hands and played with it. Of course he did not stop there. Soon his finger was in the slit and he was excited when the girl became responsive to his fingering and moved her ass around. In fact she put her arms around his neck and pressed herself to him, moving her thighs between his, and was gratified to feel his machine in proper condition. But just because she apparently wanted him, cooled him off and he let her go with the crisp order, "March to bed!" He did not want to fuck the bed companion of his uncle whom he detested. He would pick one of the hand maidens and have a good party.

Grushenka turned away from him and went to the bed and putting one knee on it and was just about to slip underneath the sheets. His glance had followed her and became focused on her bare bottom. His testicals signalled an idea to his head. "Stop!" he commanded. "Kneel with both knees on the bed and bend forward."

Grushenka did as bidden, fearfully wondering why she should be beaten now, which was what she expected. But she learned something else very soon. He came over to her, opened up the rim of her behind and fingering the ass hole asked her, "Did my uncle use this way also?"—a question the girl denied with an astonished "Oh, no, no!" She had never heard of such a thing.

Leo, however, had wanted just this thing for a long time. The cheap whores and little tarts he could afford had always refused that very thing, but some of his brother officers had bragged about it. Here was his opportunity. This ass was his. He could use it as he pleased.

"That's fine!" he exclaimed. "There goes another virginity of yours. Hurrah, for ass-fucking!"

With that he opened his trousers and took his prick out, much to the satisfaction of his tool which had felt for the past few minutes eager to come out of its narrow jail of tight trousers; and much to the satisfaction of the onlooking maids, because he had a good big and long instrument. No doubt he would be the right master for their wet pussies—although they would be terrified to get pushed in the back entrance with such a big shaft. Some of them actually moved their hands over their behinds, as if protecting their rear passage. But Grushenka crouched on her hands and knees on the bed, like a dog, pressing her thighs together in a shiver. Leo came close to her, demanded that she lie down on her elbows. When she started to lie down flat on her belly, he lifted up her bottom and spread her knees apart, so that nothing should stop an easy access.

"One of you girls." the young man ordered, and he was quite excited anticipating this erotic venture which was new to him—"One of you girls, put it in for me, but in the back hole, if you don't want to feel the whip."

Grushenka felt a hand open up her rim and the point of the prick touched her ass hole. She held herself motionless, but contracted the muscles of her rear entrance involuntarily and when the Prince began to push he could not enter. He tried in vain to gain an entrance and was answered by Grushenka with little cries of pain. While it did not really hurt, she anticipated that it would. The whole room became excited with this ass rape and the watching girls were in a state of tearful pity and sexual stimulation. Young Leo became impatient.

"Wait a minute, your Highness," said the girl who had tried to put his prick into Grushenka's ass. "I know how to do it."

She arose quickly and got a jar of salve from the toilet table. The Prince, looking down, saw her lovingly smear a white ointment on his machine. Then he saw how the girl annointed the little contracted hole of Grushenka all around on the outside. After that her finger began carefully to enter the ass hole, going in and out, taking more salve to smooth the way for the trip. The young fellow got awfully hot seeing the ass of the girl get fingered before his eyes and hardly could wait until his time came to shoot.

Grushenka had a curious sensation. While the feeling of the finger playing in her ass hole was not particularly agreeable, she felt at the same time the sensation of getting hot in her love nest and because nobody else caressed her hungry little clitoris, she brought her own finger to the spot and pressed the rhythm of a melody to it, while the flesh of her loins and her thighs trembled with a thrill. This curious feeling was subdued very quickly by an unpleasant pain. Something very big moved into her ass and filled her insides completely. Because of the salve, the hard, long shaft entered her without any resistance to speak of.

The man was fucking her in the ass, pushing with mighty strokes, not considering her reactions, just pushing and pushing. His hands grasped her strongly about the hips, they pulled her bottom towards his thighs leaving her free only to swing out for a new push. With the boiling heat in his loins, he forgot himself more and more. The standing position became uncomfortable, it was too much of a strain on his legs. He threw the whole weight of his body on her, flattened her out on her stomach and lay on her back, squeezing her full breasts. Her feet and her head were in the air over the sides of the bed. He was working on her furiously and the pressure in her ass hole became awful. The buttons of his uniform and the medals scratched the skin off her back; her head was swimming. She started to fuck with her bottom against him, giving him response as well as she could, not because she felt wanton, but to make him come more quickly.

She succeeded finally. He shot with might, flooding her insides and groaning. After that he lay still, wondering whether he had made a fool of himself. But when he slipped his tool out of its warm embrace and turned around, he found one of the girls ready with a bowl of water with which she cleaned him devotedly. He realized he was the master and could use these girls according to his moods. Tired and lazy, but smiling with satisfaction, he gathered himself together and got off the bed. He gave Grushenka a good slap on her bare bottom and retired to his room with the remark, "You aren't such a bad ass after all."

The girls now started to wipe Grushenka's bottom clean, while they discussed the event. So that was the way they were going to be taken! They uneasily rubbed their behinds, feeling frightened and excited, because the passion in the Prince's loins had left an impression on their minds. Grushenka stretched herself on the bed of the Princess and turned around to try to sleep. She felt sore and empty and unsatisfied. She did not say a word. She did not want to hear a word.

During the next few days of getting acquainted with his duties, the Prince decided the question of the females in his household. The former bed-fellows of the old Prince were sent away to the different estates from which they came. They had been his uncle's private prick massaging machines and Leo detested the old man so much that he had no desire to be his successor in this respect. The personal maids of the Princess were commanded to constitute his personal harem. He had seen that evening that they were all hand picked. He resolved to try them out one after the other, to keep whom he liked and to replace the rest.

The next evening he sent his orderly to bring one of them to his bed. This sturdy Cossack went into the room where the girls were sleeping and tapped the first one on the shoulder. Naked as she was, she followed him, and thinking uneasily of her ass, she took with her the white salve which she picked up while crossing the bed room of her former mistress. She was a big blonde whose flesh had excited Nelidowa to many a good pinch. Her arms, legs, even her belly still had some blue and green spots on them. She crept docilely into the bed and started to fondle and kiss Leo. He fingered her pussy and found it good and large. But in spite of that she was healthy, fresh, laughing and eager and he liked her. He got on top of her and gave her an amazingly good poke right in the cunt. This delighted her immensely and she gave herself to him whole heartedly. They repeated this procedure a number of times and it must be said that the young Prince never again fucked a girl in the ass.

The girls were most happy about it and discussed it at great length. As he did not take a special fancy to any one of them he had a group of most ambitious bed-fellows competing for his favor. They liked him and all spoke well of him, because he was a nice chap and kept them well satisfied. The only other thing worth mentioning was that he could not pass any young and good looking woman without stopping to give her a good feeling, especially to make the acquaintance of her cunt. But this little habit is understandable as for so many years he had had to restrain this natural impulse that now he could hardly be blamed for his self indulgence.

Grushenka had been one of Nelidowa's hand-maids and was therefore now assigned to the Prince's personal staff. There she remained for over six months. He never touched her again or spoke with her again. She tried several times to induce him to take notice of her, once even went into his bed room claiming he had sent for her. But he would have none of her.

It was of more importance that Grushenka, during this period of idleness, began to learn to read and write. Serfs were not permitted this privilege and for that very reason they made it their business, whenever they could, to learn their "A-B-C's." Grushenka soon could read simple stories. In fact, she—and with her the other girls—got their first contact with the outer world by stealing from Prince Leo the current gazettes and magazines which were delivered to him.

CHAPTER VIII.

The hot summer days had gone by. The huge oak and maple trees on the lawn of the Sokolow country estate turned from deep green to yellow. Fall was approaching and with it the whole household would return to Moscow.

Every year at that time, Madame Sophia Schukow made her appearance. She came in her own small coach with two horses, followed by a big rented carriage with four horses and nobody in it. This carriage was to be filled. Madame Sophia was buying girls from all over the country for her famous establishment in Moscow. This year she needed at least six new girls and her stop was at Sokolow's where she could hope to pick up the majority of them.

The business of renting out serf girls to whore houses had become so prevalent that a few special laws existed about it. For example: what was to be done if one of the girls became syphilitic? She was not suitable at that time and she was of no use to her owner or to the whore house. Therefore the law provided that she was to be sent to Siberia, the cost to be divided by the owner and the Madame. Or what price was to be paid when a girl should run away? The girls were not sold, but rented out; quarterly instalments had to be sent to the owner, ranging from five to thirty rubles and after a year or two, the girl had to be returned.

Madame Sophia was a thin, agile person with a never ending flow of words. She talked so much that customers of her house quickly made their choice of the girl they wanted in order to get away from her. She was very elegant, treated her girls with candied words and most brutal beatings and was very successful in her trade.

Sophia's visit to the summer palace was of special concern to Katerina, for whom she brought many little gifts, from French candies to Viennese stays, and whom she did not leave for a minute during her stay. Katerina looked forward to these visits because Sophia told the gossip about the fine men of Moscow, men whom she watched during their intercourse with her girls, and knew more about than their own wives. During the eating hours Sophia looked over the crop of serf girls at the palace. She did not make her choice quickly. She picked her prey with sharp eyes and watched for a few days before the bargaining began. Katerina was not easily persuaded to let a girl go, but in the end she always succumbed to Sophia's clever tongue.

There were three girls Sophia wanted. Then by accident, she met Grushenka. She had not seen her before because the bed-fellows of the Prince had their own quarters and their own meals. Sophia made up her mind that, cost what it might, she was going to get Grushenka, even if she should have to go on her knees before the young Prince, who was taken up by hunting parties, riding, and cursing his farmer serfs. She broached the subject to Katerina and was astonished to find no resistance.

Katerina knew very well that the Prince made no use of Grushenka and Grushenka was a sore spot on Katerina's mind. It was on her account that the old and rightful owner of the estate was now away from the holy ground of Russia and that this young ne'er-do-well, his nephew, was in charge. She therefore promised her help and took the matter up with Prince Leo, who after a moments thought consented. When his uncle came back it might be an unpleasant reminder to find the substitute of his former wife still there. While he did not know whether it would be wise to sell Grushenka outright, to rent her to a whore house for a couple of years was a very good way out.

Hence Grushenka was looked over by Sophia, who indulged in a stream of praise about her beauty and who secretly congratulated herself on her find. What a tid-bit for her customers, to be told that they could fuck a girl who had played the part of the Princess Sokolow! Before Grushenka knew what it was all about she was sitting in the large carriage with three other girls, being driven drowsily over rough country roads leading apparently nowhere.

After many night stops the four girls were put up in a public house, a station where express horses were changed, while Sophia went for a few days to a nearby estate to do more of her shopping. The girls were in charge of the big coachman, a drunken and brazen fellow who was told to exercise his whip on them in case they should not behave. That they might try to run away did not occur to Sophia, who had told them a thousand alluring stories of the wonderful gowns they were to wear, of the many rich lovers they were going to have, of the food served on silver platters and so on.

The other girls believed her and praised their luck that they could get away from the hard work in the household and be "Ladies" on their own. Not so Grushenka. She knew what was coming, she had heard enough stories of girls who had been mistreated in whore houses, of sickness and abuse. The moral element of the matter did not enter her mind. To her it was perfectly right that her owner should use her body to gain money. But having had it easy in Sokolow's house, she nourished the idea of making a get-away. Of course she knew that if she was caught the hot branding iron would be the least of her punishments, yet she could not help thinking and planning.

The girls stayed two or three days in the public house; sleeping in the mornings as long as they wanted, taking walks over the fields, sitting about in the one big guest room which the place offered for travellers. All kinds of people passed through the road-house. Farmers driving their cattle, officials in exprress coaches, tradesmen and monks. The girls looked at them with lazy eyes; they were not interested in getting acquainted with them or having affairs with them; soon there would be a stream of pricks to be satisfied, to be caressed.

One night, Sophia having not yet returned, a fine carriage drove into the yard. The youngish aristocratic men sat in the cushions. They did not leave the carriage, but admonished the coachman to change the horses quickly because they wanted to reach another road-house that night. Grushenka lingered around the yard, avoiding the heavy atmosphere of the crowded guest room. She walked slowly over to the carriage. Her face and figure, not clearly visible in the twilight and the light from the coach lanterns, intrigued one of the men, the smaller of the two.

"Will the young lady" he said to her, "charm two hurried travellers with a friendly good evening?" and he tipped his hat in a respectful manner. He was not sure who Grushenka might be. She had a fine dress on, one of Nelidowa's travelling dresses, which Katerina had given her because she had no use for Nelidowa's things anymore, and she had a fine bearing and presence. But why should an aristocratic girl stay in such a second rate road-house over night? That was usually not done. Grushenka went leisurely to the coach, leaned over the low door and slowly looked the men over.

The smaller fellow spoke again, this time more enthusiastically because of the girl's beauty. "If we can do anything for you, my Lady, let your word be a command. Be sure that my friend and I will do anything we can for such a lovely Lady as you are." He gave his friend a slight poke in the side, indicating that he should help along the same line. But this young man was absorbed in his own thoughts.

He had not paid much attention to the girl and seemed a bit annoyed that his companion was trying to sail into an adventure. He was dressed, like his friend, in a wide travelling cloak. His white neck cloth of fine silk shone in the flickering light of the yard. He had a most distinguished face, bold blue eyes, an aristocratic nose and a clean cut, full mouth, sensual but displaying the force of self restraint. He hardly glanced toward Grushenka; his eyes eagerly followed the doings of his coachman and of the stable men. He looked like a conspirator who wants to reach the place of action on time. Grushenka liked him at first sight. In fact, she felt so attracted to him that she resented his passivity towards her. But the eagerness of his companion spun the conversation one step further.

"I cannot imagine, Madamoiselle, that you would stay here over night by your own wish, when twenty verst from here is the famous X.......... Inn, where all comfort is rendered to travellers. Has your carriage broken down, or is there any other reason why you cannot move on?"

Grushenka rested her eyes fully on the speaker. If he would give her a lift she would be in Moscow before that fool of a coachman would have notified Madame Sophia and before that time she was quite sure no attempt would be made to follow her. The little fellow, aware of her deliberations, continued his efforts. "We certainly would be delighted to take you along to Moscow, or even to Petersburgh, where too we are going, if you. . . ." and he stopped.

Grushenka decided her fate. She would do it! Run away! She leaned into the carriage and whispered, "You see that big oak tree down the road? I will wait there for you. If your carriage stops, I shall be glad to accept your invitation and you won't be sorry—" she added with a faint smile. After that she went to the appointed place with quick steps, without looking back. She was very excited. Would they pick her up, or not?

The handsome man turned to his smaller companion and reminded him that they were in a hurry and not interested in girls at that moment. The other one retorted that there was never a time that one should not pay attention to the weaker sex and when they came to the oak tree, the coachman stopped. Grushenka slipped in. She was seated between the men on the broad back seat of the carriage. The little fellow very formally began the introduction. "My name is Fladilow Szerementon." he said. "This is

Mihail Stieven. We travel on a government commission of which we won't speak. We're bound for Petersburgh, as I said before."

Grushenka nodded and was satisfied that this time Mihail took full notice of her, making a little bow and trying to distinguish her features in the soft moonlight. She answered, "I also am on a trip whose object I won't mention. I'm on my way to Moscow and am very grateful that you gentlemen can take me along. You will permit me not to give you my right name. Call me Mary, which is one of my names. I cannot expect that you take me to Moscow for nothing and I will do right by both of you, if you so desire. In fact I have to ask you to pay for my lodging at the Inn and it will be cheaper for you if I share a room with you. You will ask me why I am so outspoken in all this." she added and turned to Mihail. "But I see your thoughts are far away and I will spare you the trouble of finding out all about me and of courting me I am easy and willing." She took a hand of each of her travelling companions and leaned full back in the seat giving both a warm pressure with the sides of her body.

"You have very fine hands, anyway." said Mihail, taken by surprise by this unusual little oration. "You certainly are not a girl used to work. We will not pry into your secrets and will see to your comfort—although I am annoyed with that little man on your other side, who can never let the women alone. Beware of him!" he added with a smile.

"Then to our good friendship." answered the girl. She turned lightly around to Fladilow and gave him a little kiss. This done, she turned to Mihail, put her hand behind his head and as well as the swaggering coach would permit, she kissed him on the lips.

113

During this kiss something happened which once in a while does take place. Grushenka fell violently in love with Mihail. It went through her body like an electric shock. She looked at him with glaring eyes, she could not help feeling his body, she caressed his face, she pressed herself towards him, she was so attracted by him that she travelled along the road in a trance. She felt light and happy as though suddenly cured after a great illness. She behaved like a young girl who has been, against her will, very virtuous for many months and is suddenly close to a man who electrifies her.

She forced Mihail to put his arms around her, she leaned her head on his chest, she looked longingly at the moon. She had her hands on his thighs, but did not dare to come near his prick, which she felt was not averse to the young woman making love to him. At the same time she did not forget the other companion whose good graces had put her in this position and who had to be taken into the bargain. Her free hand, therefore, was in his lap, playing with his shaft which became slowly but surely alert.

Grushenka remembered this poetic drive through the moonlight her whole life. Her first love, her first adventure, something she had done of her own free will. The softness of the drowsy waggling of the coach, the giggling of her enamoured mind, the stillness of the wide country! Mihail was pleased but still a bit suspicious as to where this adventure with a mysterious girl would lead. Fladilow was also satisfied, for even though a good poke might not be in store for him, he at least had fixed it up for his friend and superior and that would be a feather in his cap.

The lights of the inn came in sight. They had arrived for their night's rest. Mihail took a big private room, ordered the deeply bowing inn keeper to serve a hearty meal, and

Fladilow, seeing that Grushenka was taken up so much with his boss, asked the Inn keeper whether he could not send another girl as a fourth guest to the repast. The inn keeper, with a twinkle in his eye, swore that he had a most beautiful girl at hand for the comfort of his guests and that he would send her right to them.

The light of the flickering candles shone over the mixed company: the young and aristocratic men in shirt sleeves, hungry, dusty and behaving most informally, as two young fellows will do when they are not in the company of ladies; the wayside whore, rustic, healthy and plump, eager to get as much money out of her prey as possible, and Grushenka, in the stylish dress of a Lady acting refined and using every opportunity to please Mihail towards whom she shot ardent glances. Both men were most attentive to her, treating the little whore scantily and the latter could not make out what it was all about. She got really jealous of Grushenka, who seemed to take both men away from her and whom she could not classify. She tried her best to get the men for herself. Under ordinary circumstances Grushenka probably would have kept still and would have let things take their course but in her happy mood of being out of her serfdom, at least for the moment, and being near to the man who seemed the dream lover of her past years, she developed a cheeriness which led to a silent battle between the two females.

Meanwhile the men ate with hearty appetite and Fladilow encouraged Grushenka whenever he saw an opportunity. Not so Mihail, especially not after the dinner, when Grushenka sat down on his lap and started to smother him with kisses. She took possession of him and although he was enchanted by her charms, he felt that she became too "sticky," too close to him. Before the real love-making between them started, he was already wondering how he could get rid of her with grace. Fladilow loitered around the room, kept the country vixen at her distance and took another room next to the one they were in, where he intended to have a quick party with the little whore in order to fall easily to sleep. They had a long trip ahead of them the next morning and it was getting late.

But his eyes were longing for Grushenka and the little whore did not miss that. Feeling that she could not triumph mentally over her rival, she tried physically. Without a word she took her blouse off and slipped the ribbons of her shirt over her shoulders. Turning towards both men, she displayed two big and well made breasts with full red nipples. "Here," she said, "that's the reason why men call me in and why no traveller passing this inn forgets to send for me. Let that bloodless young woman (pointing to Grushenka) show what she has to say to that! I bet her poor cushions fall down to her belly, or she would not hide them so carefully." and she swung herself proudly from her hips. Fladilow got angry and was about to scold the girl for this sudden aggression against Grushenka when Mihail intervened in a way which Fladilow did not understand.

"Well," he said quietly to Grushenka, who was most intimately ruffling his hair, "Well, my dear, what do you say to this challenge?"

Grushenka looked for a moment questioningly into his eyes. She rose from his lap. With quiet motions she took her clothes off, all of them, as if her old mistress had given her the order. She crossed her hands behind her neck and stood before the men in devoted dignity. There was not a lascivious motion or thought in her and the raptuous beauty of her body made the men stare in adoration. All four were silent until the whore broke out in an angry speech.

"Look at that fuck hole of hers!" she cried. "I bet many hundred men—" But she could not finish the sentence. Fladilow rushed up to her and closed her mouth with a rude push of his hand. "Get out of here!" he shouted at her. "Get out and stay out." and with that he threw her bodily out of the door, half nude as she was. He flung her blouse and other belongings after her and topped it with a silver ruble, which she caught with alertness while her scornful words bellowed through the hall way. Fladilow grinned with delight. He always liked cursing whores.

He re-entered the room. He bade the two, "Good night and a good time" and his longing eyes were fixed on Grushenka, who had meanwhile ascended the big bed. "It was a bargain for both of us." said Mihail. "This young lady is coming to see you very soon, I assure you. Don't fall asleep too quickly."

What was in Mihail's mind was that by dividing the young girl between his friend and himself, he was getting rid of all obligations and there would be no fear that this creature should have any claims on him. He went leisurely to bed, tinkering around with his port-manteau, washing up and showing that he was in no hurry whatsoever. Meanwhile Grushenka lay in bed with closed eyes, telling herself the most ardent love words she knew, but not moving her lips. It is not impossible that she mixed silent prayers with her longings for him.

Mihail came to bed finally. He laid himself next to her, put his arms around her and seemed to express with his movements, "All right, now let's have it." He expected that she would kiss and fondle him, he would not have been surprised if she had manhandled him. The contrary was the case. She hardly stirred. Of course she rested close to him, touching his body with hers, but nothing more than that. He turned towards her, he rubbed his shaft against her flesh and became stiff, which was natural for a young fellow with such a beautiful creature at his side. He mounted her and he worked away on her. She pressed him in her arms, close—so close. She encircled him with her legs, raised her thighs so high that her heels pressed tightly on his bottom.

But she did not respond to his love making. She was as if in a trance, unable to move, overcome in a passive rapture—but he did not know anything about that. She did not give him any pleasure and he was disappointed and came. What a silly girl! First to act like a lovelorn cat and then, when it came to the point, a creature without any feelings. Well, Fladilow should at least see for himself what a poor bed-fellow he had picked up on the roadside. When Mihail was through, he told her in decisive words to take care of his friend. She got up like a sleep-walker. She stopped in a corner of the room over a night pot, washed her pussy, peed a little, and disappeared into Fladilow's room.

Fladilow was eager to explain to her that since she loved his friend, he was too much of a gentleman to touch her unless she wanted it, but she read between the lines that he was quite hungry for her. Grushenka wanted to talk with Fladilow about his friend, she wanted to know everything about him, but there was still too much of the serf in her to let her thoughts get into her mouth. She was ordered to relieve the young fellow of his passion and she proceeded to do so. She remembered how she had done this with Prince Sokolow and she did her job in the same fashion. Without much ado she pulled the sheets away from him, bent over him and began to caress, then to suck his prick. He lay still on his back, moving his behind now and then until he became very excited. She then mounted him, inserted his member with apt fingers into her pussy and started an expert ride on top of him. In fact she herself now became hot. Her loins quivered, she bent over to feel his hands on her globes, she expertly contracted her hole, sucking his shaft with her cunt to the best of her ability. Thus she gave him one of those extraordinary good fucks which the old man Sokolow had so admired. When she felt that he came, she bit him on the shoulder and panting with passion, let herself come to the climax just as he was spending. But she lay only for a few minutes on his chest, then left him with a gracious and silent movement of her slender body.

"What a creature! What a wonderful fuck—" thought Fladilow before he fell asleep. What great praise he would get from his friend the next day! And Morpheus visited a very satisfied young man a few minutes later.

Mihail was already asleep when Grushenka returned. She hardly dared to go back into the bed alongside of him. But he did not wake up, he did not stir. Sleep was far away from Gushenka's eyes. She lay awake, glaring through the darkness of the room at the man next to her, at her beloved, the one and only. She did not cry because fate would take him away from her the next day, she just prayed for him, she was ready to give her life for him, she adored him and she was happy until the early morning hours closed her eyes for a short rest.

It was a grey morning of drizzling rain and they were three tired and moody travellers. They spoke very little. The horses made haste to reach the next stable while the coachman uttered faint curses and did not bother to wipe the rain drops from his wet face. They ate hurried meals by the wayside and the spirit of adventure and sentiment of the previous night was forgotten.

When Grushenka left them for a moment in an inn, Fladilow wanted to collect the laurels for the night before. Winking with his eyes after the disappearing girl, he commented on her unusual love making qualities. He was surprised at the answer he received and could no more understand his friend than the other one could get the meaning of his words. "Lousy!" remarked Mihail. "Just Lousy! Take a piece of timber and screw a hole in it and you'd get a better reaction. Isn't it so?" Which left them both puzzled, especially when Fladilow swore that since that Swedish girl in Stockholm, of whom he had spoken so often before to his friend, since her, he had not had such a wonderful time, except with Grushenka. To which Mihail just answered, "Pooh!" and the matter was dropped.

The sleepless night, the sure separation from her idol, probably forever, the uncertainty of her future, made Grushenka sad and monosyllabic. They reached the towers of Moscow after dark, passing the gates without molestation after Mihail had presented his pass. The clattering and rumbling coach entered the ill lit streets of the poor quarters. Grushenka begged to be permitted to take leave. The men wondered what this well dressed beauty might want in this squalid section of the city but they stopped the carriage assuring her that if they could do anything for her at any time they were at her service.

It was Mihail who got out of the coach first and helped her descend, quite politely now, because he was satisfied that she could not be a future impediment to him. Grushenka bowed low over his hand and kissed it. He drew his hand back, as if an iron had burnt it. He kissed the girl on both cheeks and felt a sudden attachment to this mysterious beauty. Grushenka clasped Fladilow's hand with a hearty shake and before they finally parted she felt Mihail press something into her hand. ''Pass-word to the gates of heaven and hell!'' he cried, merrily—and the coach drove on at a quick pace.

Grushenka stood on the side walk. It was dark all around. She was alone, very alone. In her hand were a few gold pieces. When she discovered them she started to cry softly. He had paid her! What a shame! What a disgrace! But she did not follow her first impulse to throw the money into the muddy street, no, with a second thought she clasped it securely in her hand. It would be a life saver, a life saver.

She collected her senses. If she was caught here in the street by a gendarme or by the watchman who cried out the hours during his rounds, she would be brought to the next police station and the game would be up. A night prowler on the streets would not be left alone unless he had a pass from his master or a very clear excuse. She knew the neighborhood well enough and started a hasty run along the houses, keeping in the shadow, through gardens and side streets, until she came to an old and dilapidated two storey house. The big front door was closed and she did not bother to ring the bell or call for the janitor. She moved around the building to a back entrance which was open and ascended a creaking wooden stair, dimly lit by small oil lamps. On the top floor she stopped and knocked on one of the many doors which were around this landing. First she knocked faintly, then more boldly with great fear in her heart that her only girl friend Martha might not live here any more. She had not seen her since she had gone to the Sokolows, in fact had never had the opportunity to tell her about her change in life. What would happen to her now if she could not find shelter with Martha?

Finally there was a faint rustle inside and a terrified small voice asked who was outside. "Grushenka." answered the girl, her heart leaping with joy. "Grushenka, you little dove!" . . . and soon the girls lay in each others arms, kissing each other's cheeks and crying on each other's breast to celebrate their having found each other again.

CHAPTER IX.

Martha's history can be told very briefly, a story of which there are so many similar ones. Born out of wedlock of a mother who was a rich and independant farmer's daughter who had been driven from home when she was heavy with child, Martha had been given in servitude to a modiste. This modiste, Mademoiselle Laura Cameron, kept a fashionable hat and gown store in one of the few elegant thoroughfares of Moscow. Martha was not yet 14 years of age when she became a servant of this sweet, lisping but keenly selfish woman who exercised parental rights over the little girl and abused her with hard work and harsh treatment. In exchange she paid her small wages which Martha had to deliver to her mother who received the money by making her signature on a slip of paper. This signature consisted of three crosses, because mother and daughter could not read or write.

Martha's mother refused some offers to sell the girl as a serf. She had taken a room in the poorer quarters and done such odd jobs as a woman could find, barely enough to keep them alive. Worried and exhausted by hardship she had finally consented to die, leaving her little girl to shift alone.

Martha did not dare to tell this to her employer, because she feared that she would make a real serf out of her right away, taking her into her house where she kept a few girls already. She received the small wages and signed with the crosses as if her mother was still alive. This and many more things she told to Grushenka, who in turn related her story. Of course this all took several days, rather nights, because Martha went to her work early and came home at sunset. Meanwhile Grushenka stayed in the poor room, sleeping in the big bed and not going out for fear she should be picked up by the police or by the searchers of Sophia. However, with the gold pieces which Mihail had left in Grushenka's little hand, they had a wonderful time together, eating and drinking what money could buy.

But it was apparent that this could not go on forever, so they decided that Martha should tell her mistress that a cousin of hers had arrived in the city and desired to enter her services. Moved by Martha's raving description, Madame Laura consented to take a look at Grushenka and thus they went one fine morning to the store of this commanding lady. Martha had bought Grushenka some clothes such as a farm girl might wear when she came to the city; a multi-colored blouse, a pleated skirt, a kerchief to be wound around the head, all very becoming to Grushenka, who much to her advantage, displayed the tan on her cheeks which the country life on Sokolow's estate had left there.

Martha, stout and stocky, with a round good hearted face, certainly not pretty, but young and unspoiled, hesitated several times on the way. Of course she had given her girl friend a description of Madame Laura and her establishment and of course Grushenka had seen hard treatment in her almost twenty years of serfdom and did not expect to be treated with kid gloves. But had not Martha given too good an account of that which would be in store for Grushenka? To ease her mind she told Grushenka frankly that she had suppressed many unpleasant features which the work for Madame Laura would carry with it. Grushenka, however, had decided to go through with it. What could she do? There were no labor markets where jobs could be found. Labor was conducted by the members of a family in small enterprises; the bigger ones bought serfs. Some trades requiring craftmanship such as carpentry or pottery, hired workers but only through their own guilds. Furthermore, if Grushenka should really have the luck to be hired by Madame Laura, could not she and Martha live together and continue those heavenly nights, during which Grushenka could rave about her Mihail? Work and mistreatment? Was Grushenka not used to that since early childhood?

Martha made the sign of the cross and they entered Madame Laura's. Through a gilded door covered with fresh garlands of flowers they came into a huge sales room with low ceiling and elegant furniture. Grushenka's eye, trained through her work as clothes horse for the Princess, detected with pleasure the trick array of woman's styles, expensive materials, good craftmanship—this must be a store for the very rich! Crossing the room, they entered the second salesroom consisting of a small hallway which parted half a dozen private rooms equipped with huge mirrors, easy chairs and couches. Of course there were no customers at this early morning hour but a few attractive girls were busy cleaning and dusting. The third room on the ground floor was Madame's sumptuously furnished private office.

Madame Laura was not yet in, in fact she would not come before noon and Grushenka went with Martha to the sewing room on the next floor. Fifteen or more girls already sat at their work, sewing, cutting and trying on the hats, gowns, dresses and underwear created under the supervision of two elderly expert modistes. Martha joined the workers while Grushenka sat modestly on a chair and watched, eager to do this kind of work so pleasing to her female instinct for beautifying. At last one of the girls came from down stairs notifying Martha and Grushenka that they were wanted by the mistress.

Madame Laura received the girls with her sweetest smile, complimenting them on being two such lovely cousins. She scrutinized Grushenka with sharp eyes, asking her whether she had learned sewing with "her dear mother" and asking many questions about hers and Martha's home village, but not waiting for any answers. Everything seemed to go well as the girls shamefully stuttered a few words but did not dare to glance at each other. But Madame Laura's keen sense of people, which had brought her her clientele and fortune, suspected that something was wrong. For example, where did this girl, supposed to come from the country, get those silk stockings and those shoes? Then she detected the well manicured and soft hands which surely were not those of a tramp from a village.

Madame Laura moved around to her desk chair of rosewood with brass heads on the arms. She had Martha close the door and put Grushenka in the full light opposite herself. She concentrated her attention all the more on this newcomer because the girl seemed to be unusually well made, obliging, and certainly a business proposition if rightly developed. She wanted to see more of her and demanded that Grushenka take her kerchief and blouse off, under the pretext of finding out whether she might be suitable as a model. Grushenka did as she was told without hesitation, thus adding a new proof that she was not a dumb country girl. In fact Grushenka discarded her skirt and drawers also and Madame Laura had difficulty in suppressing her wholesome admiration: a perfect shape, straight legs, soft but firm flesh, a morsel for the appetite of the most refined taste of any man.

Madame Laura was a connoiseur. Procuring was her most important magnet for securing a clientele and she made ample use of it. Who was this girl? Of a sudden she changed her tactics, the smile faded, and Martha was in for it! First Madame Laura asked her sharply to tell the truth. But fat little Martha stuck to her story, stuck to it even when Madame Laura's hand, manipulated on Martha's behind, caused her to emit many "Oh's" and "Ah's." In Madame Laura's hand was a long needle which Grushenka detected as she stood helplessly aside in her nakedness.

After that, Madame Laura began to use stronger means: she opened Martha's blouse, took the girl's left breast from underneath the shirt and squeezing the breast firmly, pointed the needle directly at the nipple. Both girls watched the point of the needle anxiously and as Martha still held to her story, the sharp steel was pricked slowly into her flesh. Martha tried to suppress a howl as a big drop of blood ran slowly down over the milk white globe, but clung doggedly to her former assertion. Her face was twisted, tears streamed down her cheeks, but she did not dare to tear herself loose and run away. Impatiently Laura rose, took a short leather whip from her desk and demanded that the girl bend over. She tore her drawers down and as Martha's fat behind lay bare, demanded that she tell the truth or be whipped until her flesh was cut to the bone.

Before Madame Laura could lay the first smarting blow on the wide target, Grushenka threw herself between her and Martha, exclaiming that she would tell the truth, because she could not watch her friend suffer on her behalf. She then related her whole story to the silently listening Madame Laura, who knew that now she learned the true facts. Here was business for her! But she did not say a word of what was on her mind when Grushenka finally fell at her feet and threw herself at her mercy, imploring her to take her into her services. Instead Madame Laura behaved like a fury and answered that it was an outrage that this run-away slave girl wanted to make her a partner in her crime, reminding her that any person giving shelter or food to a run-away serf was liable to be sent to Siberia.

Martha, who had tried to stop Grushenka and had implored her to let her have her punishment, had to be dealt with first. Laura, who did not want to impair the working value of the girl, gave her six lusty strokes on the bare bottom and sent her away. Martha kissed the hem of her mistress's gown and went weeping back to her work, sending a last pitiful glance at Grushenka who lay sullenly on the floor. Madame Laura speedily got her up, though not without letting her have some lashes from the biting whip. She then led her to one of the empty dressing rooms, locking it resolutely from the outside. While Grushenka, helplessly crying, nude, awaited an uncertain fate between the four partitions of the small dressing room, Madame Laura wrote with her own hand a falsified billet-doux which she sent away with one of her delivery girls.

As the hours passed, Grushenka stopped crying, having

given in to her fate. Probably she would be branded now. They would brand her on the forehead if they sent her away to Siberia, but if Sophia decided to take her into the whorehouse she would have her branded between the legs or on the shoulder blade so as not to mar her face. They would lash her, put her on the rack, maybe break her bones. . . . she must wait. She had done wrong. She should not have run away.

She lay motionless on the couch. She heard through the thin partition that the establishment of Madame Laura had become lively. Deprived of her clothes, she got slowly up from the couch and started to move around in the small dark room. Some light filtered in through cracks in the walls, which she soon found to come from the booths which adjoined hers. She peeked through the crevices and discovered that she had a view into the dressing rooms on either side. With the fear of her own fate in her heart, she began watching the happenings alongside of her.

In the booth on her right side sat an elderly gentleman, very correctly dressed in a long black coat, playing with his three cornered hat. Apparently, he waited for something. The rings on his fingers glittered with precious stones.

Grushenka turned to the other wall. A stony old woman sat in an easy chair. She was dressed in flashy colors; laces, ribbons and feathers hanging all around her as if she were a young chicken. She supported herself with an oak staff, but despite her old age and her crazy dress, her bearing was impressive and commanding. Next to her sat a nondescript woman companion, while Madame Laura and one of her models tried to sell her a hat. A pile of lovely hat creations lay on the couch and on the chairs. The model and Madame took new ones from white and cream-colored boxes and described their beauty with sweet smiles and sentimental words, but the customer would not be satisfied. As a matter of fact, the old hawk rejected the idea of buying with the outspoken words which one would have expected in the mouth of an army sergeant. Madame, in turn, poked the model in the ribs and in the back, and although the girl preserved her frozen smile, there was no doubt that Madame's finger held a needle which drove her saleslady to every possible effort to make the old lady buy. No such luck! She got up, remarking that nothing charming enough could be found to adorn her old wrinkled face, and shuffled out of the room. After Madame had bowed her out, she turned around and hit the model soundly in the face, leaving her to repack the expensive hats. The girl was accustomed to such happenings. She wiped her face with the back of her hand and went slowly but dutifully on with her work.

Grushenka turned back to the peep hole in the other wall and as she expected, found Madame and the gentleman in animated conversation. It seemed that the gentleman had just paid a bill to Madame, probably for clothes his wife had ordered and still had something on his mind. Madame knew very well what it was, but made a little play so as not to recognize his wishes too quickly. The gentleman, leaning from one foot to the other and stroking his mustache, finally said that he would like to see some styles, if Madame had a few models who could show him her newest creations. Madame smilingly asked whether he wanted to see the same models as the last time and whether it was not a good idea to show him her new line of underwear. The gentleman hastened to answer that the models the other day had been very lovely indeed, but that he would not mind seeing some others—all very lovely and very obliging, he was sure, if they worked for the famous Madame Laura—and that underwear was quite to his liking. Madame responded that she would show him a few models, that he should act as Paris did with the Greek Goddesses but—and Madame looked down at her hands which played with a few gold pieces. The gentleman smiled, assured her that the delicacy with which she handled the matter could not be surpassed by the most refined French woman, a compliment which Madame ate up eagerly, and he slipped her some more gold rubles.

Madame Laura left him to get her girls. The gentleman took off his long formal coat displaying a waistcoat with silver buckles matching exactly his shoe buckles. No doubt this was a dandy. His white wig with pigtail was immaculate, his black breeches and stockings of finest silk. He sat down on the couch and loosened up the top button of his trousers, underneath his vest, with the beaming face of a man who knows that he will be taken care of.

Presently Madame came back leading a flock of her models, good-looking girls with all kinds of figures, from the tiny blonde to the statuesque brunette. The girls wore all types of underwear but were uniform in one respect: they wore no stays, but small bodices, which hardly covered the lower half of their breasts and left the nipples free. They had on embroidered shirts and long lace trousers, reaching to the ankles. While they walked around in a circle, through the open slits of their pantaloons one could get a glimpse of blonde, brown, or dark hair, an effect arranged that way by Madame, who understood showmanship.

The girls hardly looked in the direction of the man; they did not want to attract his attention because they knew that he would pick out one of them for his purposes. He had them go around a few times, smacking his lips and looking them over very carefully. At last he pointed at two of them, both of them small girls without very good figures, at least in the judgment of the watching Grushenka. Madame dismissed the other girls, who left the room with an expression of relief and taking the two who remained into a corner, she whispered a harsh command. The girls looked at her anxiously but seemed unmoved by what she said to them. Turning to the gentleman Madame Laura remarked that he had chosen two very obliging girls but should he have any complaint, she had a well-working leather whip which would change the mind of any stubborn little brat. Then with a majestic nod, she left him.

The girls sat down on the couch on each side of him, put their arms around him and cuddled themselves against him with a faint "Hello, uncle." He in turn put his arms around their backs, grabbed their breasts and was pleased with their behavior. "Now girls," he started "first of all close the slit of your trousers and don't let that nasty hair peek out there. Sure, I believe that you have little pissholes down there, but who wants to get busy with such dirty little places?"

The girls lapped over the sides of their drawers, closing the openings, and continued their dalliance. Cuddling him, one of the girl's hands passed the front of his trousers and he took hold of it and indicated that it was to open up his breeches. Fumbling around with the buttons, the girls opened up the breeches and took his instrument out. It did not look too enticing to Grushenka. It was red, half stiff, of a flabby fullness.

"Kiss me," said the gentleman to the other girl, "and put your tongue nicely into my mouth." He then kissed her mouth, sucking it and glueing his mouth so hard to hers that she became breathless and red in the face. "Oh!"

he interrupted his kissing, "play better with your tongue, you little imp."—and Grushenka could see how the blond girl made every effort to satisfy him. But she didn't succeed entirely.

He let her go and started the same procedure with the brunette who was obediently holding his prick in her fingers. "Let's see whether you're any better than she is." She was. She had a broader tongue and rubbed it slowly and more firmly against his teeth and his tongue. He grunted with pleasure. His sex feeling was swelling, but not his prick, which remained in its flabby state. It should be taken care of now, he decided.

He arose and crossed to the huge standing mirror which covered one side of the booth for the try-ons of the female customers. He threw one pillow in front of him, another one behind him. Standing sideways before the looking glass, he told the girls to kneel down on these pillows. Of course Madame had told them what to do and after they were on their knees, they pulled his trousers down to his ankles, rolled his grey silken shirt up underneath the vest and got busy. The little blonde one had Master Prick before her. She took it in her right hand, put the left hand under the balls (they were quite small) and began to run her tongue over his belly, up and down the inside of the thighs, over the prick and balls. Finally she slipped the point of the penis into her mouth and started, with easy movements, to slide her lips up and down his machine, a machine by the way which still was not stiff.

Meanwhile the brunette had opened the cleft of his ass with her fingers and pressing her face firmly towards the cheeks of his behind, began to tickle the rim with her able tongue. Grushenka admired her work in that respect. She even rubbed her own little pussy a bit, imagining that this good little worker was doing the same service to her lovenest. The gentleman stood straddle-legged, his hands on the heads of the girls, admiring the picture of this group in the looking glass.

He again became dissatisfied with the blonde. "Not that way, you little bitch," said he. "Take just the end of the prick between your lips and tickle my little piss-hole with your tongue." Which was duly executed.

Many minutes passed, both girls breathing heavily from their work, while he did not seem to be much affected. The brunette had already taken several intermissions in order to give her tongue a rest when suddenly he turned around, now giving her his prick to suck. The blonde stared for a moment at the ass which was presented to her. Apparently she had never rimmed a man before. But then a certain determination came to her face as if she was saying to herself, "What's the use? We've got to dip in."

She first rubbed the rim with her fingers to wipe off the moisture which her brunette co-worker had left there, then stretched her tongue wide out, as if to loosen it, which tickled Grushenka so that she almost laughed. The girl then buried her face in the rim and Grushenka could see by the side of her neck that she was licking. Immediately the gentleman demanded more vigor. She leaned back for a moment, glanced in the mirror and seemed to have an idea. She took hold of him again but seemingly with such passion that he was turned out of his position, almost facing away from the mirror. Of course he grumbled and said that she needed plenty of love education and that he would mention her to Madame. But she pressed her face to one of his cheeks, opened his rim with the fingers of her left hand, and began to tickle his ass hole with the little finger of her right hand, which she quickly had wet beforehand.

The result was excellent. The gentleman started groaning in praise of her ability, congratulated her on her expert tongue and worked himself up to a heat. "Lick my ass-hole, lick my ass-hole, you little bitch! Oh, that's good, that's excellent! Why didn't you do it before, you little cocksucker. . . ." and so on, while the blonde girl with a mixture of pride that she was cheating him and fear that he might find her out, played with her little finger on his black hole, even entering it a bit here and there.

Meanwhile the brunette had sucked and sucked and she felt that he now was coming. Not that he got stiff, but the nerves and muscles of his love-machine twisted and jerked and—there it was—his sperm flooded out. Not in a hot thick spray, but just barely trickling out. It was not the first prick which the brunette had sucked off, in fact the Frenching business was the specialty of Madame Laura's establishment and all her girls were experts. Therefore the brunette did not mind drinking his juice, at the same time squeezing his shaft and embracing his balls tightly in order to clean him out thoroughly.

"Very good," he murmured, pushing the girls away "Very good."

"Just stay where you are for a moment." said the brunette. She got a bowl of water and a towel and did an expert job of cleaning, front and back, quite a lesson for Grushenka, who had never done this before herself. The girls now arranged his trousers properly, even brushed him up, although there was not the faintest dust on his clothes, helped him into his long coat and gave him, like good servant girls, his three-cornered hat with the feathers on it. He spoke good-heartedly with them, scolding the blonde for having teased him at first, saying that he should tell Madame. But it was all done jokingly and Grushenka could see that a very proper and well pleased gentleman left the booth with important steps such as were becoming to an elderly man of standing. Before he left he gave each girl some money.

He had hardly gone, the girls were just adjusting themselves before the mirror, when Madame Laura rushed in. "Turn over the money!" she shouted and extended her hand. "Turn it over and back to your work or I'll speed you up." To Grushenka's surprise, both girls gave up the money without protest. Madame Laura counted it carefully and was satisfied; for this visitor paid well. She pinched the cheeks of the girls and added smilingly, "A funny bird, isn't he? Can't possibly get stiff and yet loves his prick. You got rid of him quickly, though. The last time the girls had an awful job until the old fool was able to come." And she shuffled her chickens out of the room.

This whole scene had been a revelation to Grushenka. Madame Laura apparently had a side line to her dress business, a side line which attracted many customers and which she handled quite openly. The idea shot through her head that her girl friend Martha might be used for such purposes also, but then, in spite of her own predicament, she had to laugh at the thought that fat little Martha with her freshly upturned nose could be a love-maker to refined people. Of course Martha was only a sewing girl—when she stopped on the street before she brought Grushenka to Madame Laura, it must have been because she was afraid that Grushenka would be used as a "model"—and Grushenka was fully aware again of the danger she was in. Would Madame Laura send for the police, would she be turned over to Sophia's house? But just then she heard bustling in the other compartment and went back to her look-out.

She discovered a couple shopping for a dress, a long green and fluffy evening gown which they had just bought. The woman, who held the dress in her hand and was giving orders how to change it to her liking, was about forty years of age, petite, but with an inclination to be fat. Her arms and legs, which seemed always agile, were short, round and unattractive, her swelling bossom, the upper part of which looked out of a rich afternoon gown, showed a red-brown skin. Her deep black eyes were sharp and unkind, while her lips, always pursed to an affected smile, tried to hide her true nature. She was accompanied by her husband, a husky fellow of her own age, broad-shouldered, dumb and hen-pecked. He repeated everything she said with a silly horse laugh of his own invention and seemed without a will of his own, which he probably did not need, being tied to such a mate.

A heated discussion was under way. Madame Laura excitedly praised the value of the gown, while the woman demanded a bargain in consideration of the fact that it was her first purchase in Madame's famous dress house. When a moderate sum was finally agreed upon, the woman looked around towards the models and declared herself satisfied if a certain model would bring the dress to her house that evening. The girl she pointed out was a tall, full-built brunette. Her unusually white skin attracted Grushenka's admiration. Madame Laura looked at this girl for a moment and hesitated, but then, with a bow, declared that the girl would be at her Ladyship's house and at her service that evening. The husband paid, with a silly laugh and a remark of his own, "A woman must always have it her own way." The tall girl's eyes followed the departing customers with a sheepish look.

"Are you all right, or are you still unwell?" demanded Madame Laura. The girl lifted up her dress, murmuring an indignant "Oh!" and opening the slit of her drawers, put her fingers into her cunt from which she took a piece of cotton. It seemed clean. Madame took a small piece of white cloth, wrapped it around her finger and inserted the finger deep into the girl's vagina. Upon taking it out again, no blood could be seen.

"You fake!" shouted Madame Laura. "Half of the time you tell me you have your menstruation and the other half of the time that you're just getting it. Backing out all the time, eh? And you have a stronger ass than any other girl here. You little liar! How long ago was it anyway, since you got your last whipping?"

"The week after Easter," answered the girl meekly.

"Well," retorted her mistress, "you should get a good whipping for lying to me now but instead you'll go over to those people tonight and you'll do whatever they want—I don't know them yet—and if that Madame is satisfied with you, I'll let you go this time. But if I hear that you have not been perfect, I won't waste my time and my strength on your behind again, which is much too tough for my leather whip anyway, but I'll send you over to the police and let you have twenty-five lashes with the knout. That will cure your laziness, you tramp."

(It must be inserted here for the understanding of the modern reader, that in Russia, servants were sent with a letter and a small fee to the nearest police station, where the requested punishment was inflicted, usually the knout over the back or over the behind. The servant then brought back to his master a receipt for the money and a short account of the punishment inflicted. This custom prevailed even in the larger cities until the end of the 19th century).

"What do you think this couple want a girl for?" asked one of the girls as they cleared the place up. The question remained unanswered.

Grushenka moved about in the semi-darkness of her cage. She didn't dare to cry out for help; she was hungry and thirsty. She rememebered that the other booth had some water on a corner table. She groped around, found a similar table and a silver bowl with water in it. She drank in big gulps and returned to the couch. The minutes were creeping. She heard voices and laughter in the booths next to hers, but she did not care to peek. Then, to get her mind off her own anguish, she went back to one of the peep-holes.

The scene was worthy of her attention. The woman customer in the room presented an odd appearance. She was about thirty years of age and seemed to be more bony than muscular. She wore a riding costume with straight lines, closely fitted on the neck and wrists. She had very intelligent eyes, a hard mouth, and no color on her cheeks which gave her an unattractive appearance. She had secured a lovely model from Madame Laura and had certainly paid enough for the right to amuse herself with her. The model was a natural blonde of medium height with full breasts and an innocent look in her face. She was quite feminine and although twenty years old, appeared almost childlike. The woman was busy taking off her bodice. She took the soft, milk-white breasts in her bony hands and admired the small nipples. Rubbing them against her cheek and sucking them playfully, she mumbled, "You're a good girl. Aren't you? You would not allow those brutes, those men, to touch you. Would you?"

"Oh, no, never!" answered the girl. "Never. I only

wait on ladies and Madame Laura would not even allow a man to look at me.''

"Yes, such soft breasts, such small nipples, untouched, lovely child", continued the customer. Becoming more emotional and kneeling down before the girl, she undid her long drawers and took them off her with a caressing gentleness unexpected in a woman with such large hands and feet. She then proceeded to rub her cheeks against the Mount of Venus, going up and down the sides of the girl with tender strokes of her hands.

The girl looked into the mirror, unconcerned with what the woman did to her. She teased her breasts a bit, arranged a curl which had left its place and moistened her lips with her tongue to make them look fresh and jolly. She opened her legs mechanically when the woman inserted the index finger of her right hand into her vagina and began to kiss her belly and the blonde curly hair around her pussy and gave in readily when the woman moved her over to the couch. There she stretched herself out, rolled and tucked a pillow under her head, let one leg fall down on the floor and bent herself in such a way that her open slit lay on the edge of the couch readily willing to take what was coming.

The woman now began systematically to French her, interrupting her tongue-play over and between the lips of the pussy with many poetic little outcries, as if she had found a preciously chiselled piece of jewelry. But the owner of this little masterpiece of nature did not seem to be impressed. In fact when her customer pressed her mouth vigorously to the cunt and started to suck with great force at the same time taking firm hold of the behind and pressing it forward against her strongly working tongue, the blonde rubbed her nose and smoothed her hair as if she

140

was not even present at the treat which was being given to her love parts. Of course, now and then remembering what it was all about, she put her hand on the head of the Lesbian worker, moved her ass around in slow convulsions and ejected deep groans. But getting bored with her own behavior, she quickly forgot to participate.

Grushenka was baffled at this coldness or rather insensibility of the blonde and sympathized with the excited woman who now pressed her knees hard together, wiggled her behind in the air, got red in the face and began to sweat in her tight fitting garments. Finally she groaned and the blonde, taking this as a sign that the climax was near, made a last effort and fucked the sucking mouth with simulated sighs of lust.

The woman customer got to her feet, her whole face wet, probably from her own saliva, while the blonde lazily brought some water and a towel and cleaned the moist and perspiring face. Her customer no longer found her the peak of loveliness. "Well, that's that!" she said. "You lousy slut, lying on your back for everybody who pays the price. Brats like you should be whipped daily for an hour, until they give up their brazen lives and refuse to open their legs for everybody and anybody. You're a God damned fucking cunt, that's what you are and not worth the bread you eat. Oh, well, what's the use anyway, you do it for money and here is some" and she put some money underneath a pillow, apparently as far away as possible, so as not to touch even the skin of the girl's hand. "There! You fat pig!" and she rushed out of the room.

The words had struck home to the blonde and as she wiped her own pussy dry after the wet attack, she looked her figure over in the mirror with a scrutinizing vanity. However, Madame Laura rushed in, went straight to the pillow and got the money. "Aha!" thought Grushenka, "Madame is watching also, probably from the other side of the booth."

Madame Laura was not very satisfied with the amount she found. "You really are getting lazier every day" she turned on the girl. "You have a new boy friend. Haven't you? And he probably fucks hell out of you. At least you could pretend better than you do. What will happen to your father and yourself if I stop paying him? You won't have a crumb of bread to eat. But maybe that will do you good, because you're getting fatter every day. Hurry up now and put some black underwear on and the white evening gown with the low neck. There are some customers in booth four. Go on now!"

There was nothing more to see in the other booth. Grushenka lay down again on her couch. The time passed. She dozed off until somebody unlocked her door and called her out. It was Martha, come to bring her back to Madame Laura's private room. Madame Laura now had a changed face. She was beaming and full of cordiality.

"My dear girl," she smiled, "I have been giving your case a thorough consideration and I agree that you were right to run away from Madame Sophia's service. I am going to help you and I have a great surprise in store for you. You dress now and go home for tonight with your dear friend Martha. Be here tomorrow at noon sharp and leave it to me. I'll see to it that you'll have a happy future. While I cannot allow myself to harbor a run-away, I'll have a magnificent place for you by tomorrow where you will live like a queen. Quite what you can expect, beautiful as you are. . ." and so on. Madame Laura even inquired whether they would have something really good to eat tonight or whether she should provide something and after the girls assured her they had all they needed, she presented Grushenka with a broad embroidered ribbon, fitting very well with the peasant dress she wore.

The girl friends curtsied and left the house. Grushenka related what she had seen, but it was no news to Martha who had heard of these things but who could not really understand their meaning because she was completely a virgin. But Grushenka lay sleepless and thinking for a long while that night. She mistrusted Madame Laura and would never go back to her. She would have to leave Martha also, without telling her where she was going. Madame Laura would probably hunt for her or send word to the police or to Sophia. Therefore Grushenka had to drop out of sight.

She did not know that Madame Laura had received an answer to her letter from an old gentleman who had written that he would be pleased to buy such a beauty from Madame Laura, but could not come before the next day at noon. He would be disappointed the next day at the noon hour and Martha would state as her explanation that Grushenka had disappeared, that she must have been picked up by the police. Madame Laura finally joined her in this belief, at least she was satisfied that Martha did not know about Grushenka's whereabouts. She was very sore about it, because she would have been able to get a good price for the sale of the girl. However, she did not want to investigate too much, because it was better not to mix into the affairs of a slave girl who had run away.

CHAPTER X.

Grushenka stretched herself in Martha's four posted bed. Martha had kissed her good-bye and left for work, admonishing her to be at Madame Laura's at noon. Grushenka slept and day dreamed. She got up lazily and put on her peasant dress, leaving her fine travelling dress in Martha's closet. She put all her money, except one ruble, on the mantel-piece, said a word of good-bye to her absent girl friend and left the house with slow steps.

She did not want to think of the future. She walked leisurely to the border of the city, went through the gate where some Cossacks loitered and found her way down to the Volga. She sat down on the bank of the river, let her eyes go over the wide plain and observed without much attention, the peasants harvesting the fields. The waters of the wide river flowed down in easy rhythm. Far away some boys and girls were swimming.

Grushenka dreamt as only a Russian peasant can dream, a thoughtless and wordless dream, uniting herself with the soil, becoming a part of it, losing the sense of place or time. When the sun dropped lower on the horizon, she got up and slowly returned to the city. She stopped in a public house where she ate a bowl of soup and some bread and cheese. The few customers and the inn-keeper, hardly noticed this peasant girl with her lovely face hidden beneath a kerchief. Back again on the street, she pulled herself up with an energetic nod of her head and walked with quick steps to Ladislaus Brenna's establishment. She had never been inside that place, but she knew all about it.

Ladislaus Brenna ran a famous bathing establishment for middle class people and Grushenka had made up her mind to become a bath attendant. She would have liked to get such a job with one of the new and elegant bath houses patronized by the fashionable world but she did not dare to do so as she might be found out. No one would look for her in Brenna's.

After she had opened the door, she stood immediately in the big bath hall for men. The hall took up the whole ground floor of the building. On a white, wooden floor stood forty to fifty wooden bath tubs in irregular arrangement. In these tubs the bather sat on a little bench, the water coming up to his neck. A few customers were bathing; others were reading, writing on little boards put over the tubs, playing board games with each other or just chatting.

Mr. Brenna sat on the opposite side of the room behind an elevated bar which was covered with all kinds of refreshments and drinks. Grushenka lost no time but went right over to him while the eyes of all the bathers and attendants followed her. She stated without shyness that she wanted to become one of his bath girls. Brenna looked sharply at her and ordered her to wait. He was a whale of a fellow, about forty-five years old. His hairy chest, open to view, and his wild black beard exaggerated his tousled appearance. Grushenka sat down on a wooden bench and looked around with curiosity. She had often heard Brenna's place discussed. It was supposed to be full of fun for it's visitors, men and women alike, but most housewives disapproved violently when they heard that their husbands or grown up sons frequented it.

Grushenka's attention was first directed towards the bath attendants, about ten girls, some sitting on a bench near the big open fire-place, others moving about the big room pursuing their duties. All the girls were nude except for wooden slippers and here and there a short apron or towel around the hips. Any kind of clothes would have been annoying in this air heavy with steam and dampness. They were all husky, rather good looking girls and seemed in good spirits and satisfied. They carried buckets of hot water to the occupied bath tubs pouring it in to keep the temperature even. They brought beer or tea or other refreshments to the men, laughed and joked with them and did not seem to mind when the men felt their breasts or their pussies. When one of the customers wanted to get out of his tub, they opened up the linen top, placed a foot stool and helped the man out. Then they followed him into one of the many cabinets which lined the walls. These cabinets had doors which closed behind the pairs and while Grushenka could not see, she could well imagine what happened inside them.

The last customer having left, the girls began to clean up while Brenna admonished them to take their time and do a thorough job. He had a gruff voice but underneath one could feel that he was a good sort. At last he turned to Grushenka and ordered her to follow him. They went upstairs, passing the women's bath hall on the second floor and passing the third floor where Brenna lived with his family. When they reached the attic, Brenna pushed open a door leading into an unoccupied room furnished with a large wooden bed, a washstand and two chairs.

"Well," he said, "I will look you over to see whether you are strong enough to carry the water and to give a massage. I could use a bitch like you, but you seem to be too weak. Show me what you got."

With that he went to the little window and looked out into the twilight. His huge frame in front of the window shut out almost all the light from the room. Grushenka quickly got rid of her clothes and stood nude in the middle of the room, waiting for him to pass judgement. She was now a bit nervous. What would happen to her if he did not employ her?

Brenna gazed for quite a while out into the sunset. Finally he turned around to her, moved away from the window and put her in a position where the slowly fading light fell directly on her. He was amazed at her fine figure, especially her full breasts attracted him. Her straight legs and firm thighs did not displease him. He felt the muscles of her arms, pinched her bottom and the flesh above the knees the way one feels the leg of a horse, while she contracted her muscles as well as she could in order to appear strong. He moved her around again, uncertain whether a girl with such a small waistline would be suited to his type of work, and fixed his eyes on her Venus Hill. Grushenka was a well built girl, above medium height, but before this giant of a man she felt rather small just when she wished to be big and strapping.

Without warning he threw her on the bed so that she lay, not lengthwise, but across the bed. He opened up his linen trousers and took out a mighty and hard blown-up prick. She had hardly time to be aware of what was coming when he bent forward, rested his weight on his hands next to her shoulders, and moved his prick towards her entrance. She lowered her hands to insert his shaft and was surprised at its huge dimensions; she could hardly span it with her hand. She wanted to insert it carefully, but before she had a chance he pushed it in with a mighty stroke. Grushenka answered with a heavy groan. Not that it really hurt her, but it filled her to the utmost and stretched her cunt to the limit.

It was a few days since she had had intercourse and the scenes she had watched at Madame Laura's had also served to stimulate her desire. Therefore this unexpected attack brought her to a fever heat. She raised her legs, which still hung on the floor, high above his massive back. She thrust herself against his prick with all her power, encircling his love-instrument with the full suction of her cunt. She crushed her fingers into his musclar arms and began to fuck him with everything in her.

She closed her eyes. All kinds of lascivious pictures when through her mind; she remembered the first time she had been flogged on the bare bottom when she was four- teen years old; she thought of the peasant who had raped her and of various men who had given her satisfaction; finally the angelic features of her Mihail stood out clearly, telling her in sweet words how much he adored her.

All this time she was working with strong pushes against those of her partner while she circled her bottom around the way belly dancers do. Gradually her whole body be- came more and more contorted until only her shoulders touched the bed as she strove to find the best position in which to fuck and to fuck. Her body was covered with sweat, her hair became loose and partially covered her face, her mouth twisted, her heels beat his back and his buttocks. At last with an outcry the great climax came. Then she lay motionless, heavily breathing, all muscles loose. Her bottom dropped and the prick fell out of its hot nest.

Brenna lay on his hands hardly moving; he was satisfied with the vitality which this girl displayed. So satisfied, in fact, that he was not ready to let her go right now, especially since his prick was still as swollen and red as it had been.

"Eh, little hussy," he interrupted her after-love dreams, "Don't stop now. My little fellow down there is still stiff and angry."

Grushenka opened her eyes to find herself staring into this gruff face surrounded with flowing black hair. An utterly strange face it was to her with black eyes, a short broad nose and full lascivious lips. Still, somehow, there was a sense of humour about it which took the sting out of its roughness. She gazed into this face and it came to her mind how much depended for her on satisfying this man. By her uncontrolled passion she had given him a wonderful time; now she would give him a still better time by her thorough knowledge of the art of fucking.

Dutifully she put her legs up on his back, this time moving them even higher, so that she almost touched his shoulders with her heels—whereby Master Prick slipped back of his own accord into his former kingdom.

She grasped his head with her hands and moved it down. His feet slid slowly backwards and he soon lay with his whole weight on her. She now lay on her back at full length and so had better means of wiggling her bottom under him. Then she arched herself under him and moving her right hand down, managed to get hold of his balls. She proceeded to caress and finger his testicles with soft strokes, at the same time tickling the inside of his ear with the little finger of her left hand.

He put his right hand under her small bottom—so large was this hand, that he was able to hold both cheeks with one clasp—and began in slow strokes to do his work. He pushed his scepter deep into her cunt so that it touched her womb, moved slowly back to the outer entrance and repeated this play in regular rhythm. She moved her behind in circles with her eyes wide open. She was aware of every move and this enabled her to give him her fullest cooperation. When he got really hot, however, he forgot himself entirely. He got back on his feet, standing close to the bed, and raised her behind up so that her head and shoulders hardly touched the linen. Holding her by her hips, he connected with her only by the contact between prick and pussy and he fucked her with all his might. She felt him come! She felt a hot flood of sperm shooting into her and strange to say, she came again.

As unexpectedly as he had attacked her, he now let her go and her behind fell to the edge of the bed. In a matter of fact way he put his still stiff prick back into his trousers. He took another look at her and liked her. Her feet touched the floor, her legs were still half open. One of her hands lay above her black haired pussy, the coral lips of which protruded, the other hand rested on her full breast. Her mouth was a bit open, her deep black eyelashes shadowed her steel-blue eyes, her hair hung around her face. The girl was so beautiful he felt like giving her another fuck. He bent down and felt again the soft flesh of her thighs. A bit weak, yes, but his guests would like this trollop.

"Wash up, and get ready for supper", he said with resolution. "I'll try you out. You might do."

He opened the door and called for Gargarina. The attic was the living quarters for all the girls employed in the house and they had come up in the meantime to dress. Presently Gargarina came in and was ordered by Brenna to break in the new girl to her job. He left without further explanation.

Gargarina was an older girl, about twenty-five years of age, tall, blonde and husky. She had a shirt on and was just about to button her long lacy drawers. She looked at Grushenka with a certain curiosity. Grushenka sat on the edge of the bed, weak but not exhausted, and scratched herself thoughtfully along the soft flesh of her belly and her thighs. Gargarina opened the conversation:

"Well, he looked you over, didn't he? He certainly has the best prick in the whole neighborhood and we ought to know. I can imagine how you feel. It's almost four years since I came here and he just killed me. After that, he told me that he could not use me. That's the way with most girls who apply for work here; he tries them all. We thought he would send you away too. You know, I just stayed on and came to work the next morning. He yelled at me to get out, but I know how it is with a stray dog. He just couldn't get rid of me and that was four years ago."

"I don't know what I would have done as I have no other place to go to either."

"Never mind that now. It's that way with most of us girls here except those of us who were brought by their parents. One of the girls was brought by her husband. He had been drafted for the army and where could the poor creature go until his seven years are over? She don't know whether he'll ever come back. He was last heard of in Siberia. He can't write, you see, and she can't read."

"Oh!" answered Grushenka with a flicker of pride, "I can read and write."

"That's fine!" retorted Gargarina kindly. "Then you'll be able to read us some stories out of books and write our love-letters for us. You will be quite a busy person with that. But now you'd better clean out your pussy—" and she looked at the sperm which ran out of the love-nest and wet Grushenka's legs—"because you couldn't serve down in the bath hall with a swollen belly."

She brought her a bowl of water and a towel. Grushenka sat down on the floor with the bowl, inserted a finger in her orifice, after she had wrapped the end of the towel around it, and rubbed herself, pissing at the same time. The hot gush of the piss and the rubbing of the vagina made her feel quite well and she enjoyed it. Gargarina, who was watching her, remarked. "Tomorrow, I'll show you a better way to get your pussy clean, down in the bathing hall. But now dress quickly, dinner will be ready in a minute."

When Grushenka came down to the dining room, she regretted that she had left her fine travelling dress at Martha's. All the other girls were dressed up fit to kill and her peasant dress looked rather out of place. There were twice as many girls as she had seen downstairs, the additional ones being those who served in the bath for women. They all sat around a long table. At one end Mr. Brenna presided, at the other end sat his wife. She was a very small, thin woman of over forty, with a sharp, pointed nose, and looked like a greedy and hardened spinster. But if she was that kind, she certainly did not take it out on the girls in regard to food. Two strapping maids served a rich meal, no less good and healthy than Katerina provided for her wards. The girls hurried through their meal, anxious to leave. In fact only two or three stayed home that night, the rest having rendezvous or visiting their folks. For police identification, each girl carried a permit issued by Brenna.

Grushenka chatted with the girls remaining in the attic. She learning that room and board was all Brenna paid for their services, but that they made many, and sometimes good tips. They all were satisfied and while they were rough and used strong words they seemed to get along in good-hearted comradeship. Grushenka went to bed early and heard the girls coming home during the night.

The next morning she was up many hours before being called to breakfast. Brenna's place opened up after noon, the first guests arriving only after two or three and the whole job was done by seven in the evening. The arrival of any customer was signalled by the young fellow in the door way, who incidentally had charge of the large stove in the basement, supplying the hot water, the heat in the wintertime and the steam for the steam room. He rapped with a stick against the door and when he rapped a few times that meant a man of money and a good tipper. All the men were more or less known to everyone.

Grushenka, taken in tow by Gargarina, lined up with the other girls near the entrance and solicited the entering man. It meant tips and the more customers a girl could get, so much the better for her. Sometimes the girls fought about the customers and that was the only thing Brenna would not stand for. He would beat them mercilessly with his fists and the girls were very much afraid of that for he would go into a rage and not take care where he hit them.

The first man who came in looked like a poet. He wore a long flowing necktie and was young and blonde. Gargarina told Grushenka not to try to attact his attention because he had a steady girl, a plump dark-haired creature with big soft breasts. This girl took him by the hand and led him into one of the cabinets where they remained for a long while. Gargarina explained to Grushenka that he was a writer on a gazette and came every afternoon to save the soul of the dark girl. However, his sermon always ended sexually.

After him came a wealthy coachman who kept many carriages and gave good tips. All the girls besieged him, but Gargarina and Grushenka had no luck. He was followed by a master baker who was Gargarina's steady customer and the two girls went with him into a cabinet. Gargarina explained that she had to break in the "new girl."

The baker was a sturdy, short man, with snow white hair, bristly and unkempt. As soon as the door was closed, Gargarina started to make love to him, but he would have nothing of it. The girls undressed him leisurely, taking off his coat, vest, trousers and shoes. He wore no stockings but a kind of undergarment of cheap cotton which he slipped off himself. Meanwhile he told them that he was damn tired. After getting through with his baking job, beginning at nine at night and finishing at three in the morning, his old lady had wakened and had forced him to give her three rides.

His prick vouched for this statement; it hung sadly downwards. In spite of his protest Gargarina insisted on giving him a massage and he lay down reluctantly on the massage table. Gargarina took a handful of liquid soap and began to knead his flesh. She told Grushenka to do the same and while she had one side of his behind and legs in operation, Grushenka started timidly with the other half. Seeing how hard her teacher worked, she put her whole weight into her hands and soon found herself sweating.

When his back was done and he was turned over, she avoided touching his testicles. This amused Gargarina, who taking the limp prick in her hand, asked Grushenka whether she would not kiss it a little and made a thousand jokes about a penis.

The baker paid no attention to this chatter. He got up from the table before they were really through with him, and walked over to a tub, which they filled with hot water. The linen was pulled over him, he leaned back and soon was soundly snoring. During the following hours, without waking him up, they kept pouring hot water into the tub, first carefully taking a bucket full of water out of it.

A few more men entered but other girls got hold of them. Then came a tall thin man whom none of the girls wanted. Grushenka held herself back instinctively. It was just her luck that he selected her. Gargarina stepped right up explaining that the new girl was under her supervision. As all three entered a cabinet together Gargarina whispered to her ward that this one was a pest.

He behaved in a very orderly way while they undressed him, told Grushenka that he was the scribe with the new judge, and that he came from Petersburg where it was the newest fad with the ladies to paint their nipples a deep red. After he was naked he embraced Grushenka, pulled her tightly to his lean body and running his long fingers up and down her spine, told her how beautiful she was and how soft her flesh felt. Meanwhile he pressed one of his thighs between hers and rubbed his prick against the soft flesh of her leg. Soon enough this love instrument became stiff and Grushenka felt that it was very thin and very long. He then proceeded to put one finger in Grushenka's cunt and began to frig her.

Gargarina had meanwhile gone behind him and embraced him from behind, rubbing her breasts on his back and her pussy on his behind. She leaned her head over one of his shoulders just as Grushenka did and both girls were almost mouth to mouth. Gargarina made faces indicating haste, but at first Grushenka did not mind his playing with her. He had apt fingers and always managed to tickle just the right spot. As she became more excited, she showed it on her face and her pussy got wet. Her ass came slowly into swing. The scribe had his other hand on her behind, but another idea struck him. He told her to take firm hold of him, and leaving one hand in her pussy, extended his other hand back until he found Gargarina's love nest and began to frig her also. Gargarina, who knew him already, fucked that finger right away as if she was terribly excited. At last he got tired of this playing around. He had another idea.

"Now, you both," he said, "lie down on the massage table, side by side, ass up, and I will give you a massage." The girls did so and he began to stroke and caress their behinds, making comparisons between Gargarina's full and motherly ass and Grushenka's boyish buttocks. He then went to the foot of the table and started to give both girls at the same time a rimming with his index fingers.

"Let him do it," whispered Gargarina, putting her arm around Grushenka's shoulders and taking her breast in her hand. "It won't hurt you"—for Gargarina already knew that they were in for a finger fuck in their ass holes. No sooner had the warning been given, than Grushenka felt him insert his long finger in her bottom hole and rub up and down, up and down.

Grushenka held still. Instead of hurting, it gave her the same feeling of longing which she had felt when Prince Leo had fucked her there. Gargarina began to wiggle around and to raise her bottom in fucking movements and Grushenka, becoming more excited, did likewise.

The thin scribe stood naked with his long prick in the air. With growing pleasure he watched the nicely moving buttocks, his disappearing and re-appearing fingers, the slightly opened ass holes, and the wide open lips of the cunts underneath. Gargarina heaved and groaned, raised herself straight up of a sudden and fell down motionless as if she had come. Grushenka repeated this fake, although she felt she would have come if she waited a bit longer. The customer let his fingers slide out and the girls sat up on the edge of the table, glad to get up from the hard boards. He stood before them and grinned, his dirty fingers outstretched before him.

"Now," he said, "after having massaged your cunts and your back holes, suck my fingers clean with your sweet lips and I'll give each of you one ruble."

"Nothing doing!" countered Gargarina. "Five rubles each and pay in advance. You forget that sometimes afterwards."

A long squabble began between the two, he protesting that a ruble was enough money to live a week on (which was true) and Gargarina declaring that the finger sucking was not their business. They finally settled it for three rubles each, but he was allowed to play with their back holes again. While he got the money from his trousers, Gargarina got hold of some towels and whispered to her friend to be quick with them later on.

The bargain paid for, they sat down on the edge of the table, raised their knees high up, put their feet on the table and opened up. From underneath, he again stuck both his index fingers into their ass holes and began the finger fucking anew, much to the satisfaction of his long, thin prick, which had shown an inclination to droop during the money quarrel, but which now raised its head proudly. Grushenka again felt her pussy getting wet and glanced at the play of flesh of Gargarina's strong thighs, she saw that her teacher apparently was also becoming heated up.

Meanwhile the scribe's mouth watered and he babbled on to the effect that their pretty lips would soon suck the fingers which were now playing in the dirty back alley. Finally he got through with their bottoms, took his fingers out and pointed them at the girl's mouths. Quick as lightning Gargarina grabbed his hand and cleaned his fingers off with her towel, despite his protest, and of course Grushenka quickly followed her example. Although he swore wickedly they then took his fingers in their mouths and sucked them.

Grushenka at first had a sickening feeling and would never have done it had not Gargarina set the example. But strangely enough, when the finger was moving back and forth in her mouth it aroused the same feeling of longing and desire as it had done before in her behind.

The scribe's face turned crimson and Grushenka's eyes, sliding down to his prick, saw how Gargarina had skilfully grasped his long tail between her feet. She was rubbing it gently in this manner. After a little while of this play, he came suddenly, shooting out a flood of white sperm in great gushes. He immediately took his fingers out of their mouths, took his prick in both hands and finished himself off, emptying his balls to the last drop.

No sooner was this done than he began again to talk about the money, which he demanded back, threatening to report them to Mr. Brenna for stealing. But the money had disappeared and Gargarina laughed at him. She had hidden it in her hair and took it out of there, to Grushenka's amazement, when she later gave her her share. After that, they laid him on the table and gave him a rough massage. He struggled and screamed under their hands—it was a little revenge on their part. When they had finally seated him in his tub, he read a big manuscript of legal matters and behaved very important. Then both girls went back to sit on the bench near the stove to await a new customer.

Gargarina advised her new girl friend that the scribe was as bad a customer as they were likely to get. He was hard to handle but had they not gotten ten times more money out of him than any other man would pay and wasn't that the main thing? Seeing that Grushenka rubbed her pussy with her palm, she laughed and remarked that they probably would still get plenty of good pokes before the day was over, because that was what most of the men did who came there.

She was right. The next man they had was a young stone mason and Grushenka soon felt the hard boards of the massage table under her back and shoulders while a young prick pumped away in her hole. Gargarina looked playfully on, teasing her breasts and behind with her expert fingers. After the mason they had an elderly inn keeper who wanted a ride, half of which was provided by Gargarina, while he sucked Grushenka's nipples, the other half by Grushenka's cunt, which did the job excellently, remembering its exercises over the fat Sokolow's love shaft. He proved a good tipper but had a distasteful habit; he smacked their behinds lustily with his fat hands and when Grushenka tried to avoid this, he gave her what he termed, "A little love spanking."

They had other men—all of them curious about Grushenka because she was a "new girl." But after a few weeks Grushenka became just one more of Mr. Brenna's attendants, and while she was pretty and a good love partner, she had days when she attended the men without any lovemakings, other days, of course, when she had to be of service several times. She did not mind it.

One fuck, however, she received daily and there was something curious about that. Each day since she had started to work for Mr. Brenna, as soon as the customers had gone, he walked up to her room and fucked her exactly as he had done the first time. In fact he became enamoured of her. He watched her constantly when she worked in the bath hall, until she sometimes felt uneasy of his lurid eyes always focussed on her spot. Brenna had never before had a favorite among his girls, and it became the gossip of the whole establishment that he had fallen for her. He did not interfere with her in any way; seldom spoke with her; let her take care of the customers; let her go out in the evenings; but always before dinner he followed her upstairs and poked her with his tremendous machine. She gave him her best. She took care of the customers in a more or less routine way, but she clung to his prick with all the vitality and sacrifice of her young cunt.

During this time she had many amusing evenings. The girls took her out to some parties, usually with young boy friends, sailors, students and the like. They would sit around in the dark public parks or on house stoops and occasionally in the rooms of the boys where they drank heavily of vodka, delivered enthusiastic orations about the rosy future, or were just busy love making. A young student, the son of poor parents, fell in love with Grushenka and she felt very flattered because he was so educated. He told her all about his studies and how they would marry when he made money and they could settle down. It was not a romance on her part, because she still dreamt only of her Mihail. Yet it was pleasant to be adored by such a clean boy. That was about all the feeling she got out of it, because he had big, red hands, was awkward and shy and did not even dare to kiss her. When she embraced him once, he got so terrified that he avoided her for days and then lectured her to the effect that only man and wife, being duly married, could kiss each other. He had only known what her occupation was and what her life had been so far!

Grushenka felt curiously happy. She had forgotten her fear of being detected by Madame Sophia, she had saved up a little money, tied in a kerchief. She bought fine material and made herself dresses and coats and skirts, she was on good footing with the other girls—nothing was lacking. But one evening the following occured.

As usual she lay across her bed and Mr. Brenna had his good love instrument in the right place and both were working away at their best when the door opened and Madame Brenna entered. She watched the scene for a moment without their having heard or seen her. Then she rushed forward, yelling and screaming and began to beat her unfaithful husband's huge back with her bare fists. Of course he let Grushenka go and turned around, his big yard sticking out accusingly. But the thin little Madame Brenna had not done with him yet. Yellow with rage, she showered him with blows, biting his hands, which he held out against her to shield himself, scratching his face and tearing his clothes. He could have knocked her down with a single stroke of his powerful arms, but he was so scared and in awe before his rightful wife that he took it all without protest. Finally she pushed him out of the door, kicking him down the stairs, all the while letting him know that she would not stand for his giving another girl what was rightfully coming to her.

After she had gone Grushenka remained in a daze on her bed. What would be her fate now? Would that woman kill her, would she beat her mercilessly, would she have to leave the house, would she be adrift again? She wondered and did not dare to dress to go down to dinner. Finally she heard steps at her door and when she sat up in bed, Madame Brenna came in. She was very calm now and almost friendly.

"It was not your fault," began Madame Brenna. "What could you do? You had to fuck him. I understand that. When his father gave me a job here some twenty years ago and the son started to fuck me, I couldn't object either. Then he married me. That big brute! But never let it happen again. Will you promise me that? Swear it to me!"—and Grushenka swore it.

"All right then, and if he tries again, you run away and come right down stairs. I'll fix him up. Understand? You'll not work for him again downstairs. You start tomorrow in the woman's department—and keep away from him or next time I'll break every bone in your body!"—and making a gesture showing that she would tear her to pieces, Madame Brenna left the room with resolute steps. She had more energy, thin and small as she was, then Grushenka had expected.

CHAPTER XI.

Grushenka was somewhat downcast with this verdict. It would have been better if she had received a good licking and had stayed in the men's department. First of all she liked men and not women, and secondly Madame Brenna was quite severe with her girls. She had mostly serf girls working for her and their backs, bottoms and thighs often showed signs of harsh treatment. What should Grushenka do—quit? Then what? She gave in and reported at the women's department the next noon. The equipment of this bathing hall was almost the same as that downstairs, except that on the floor and in the cabinets, were some runners and rugs. Madame Brenna sat behind an elevated desk where she sold tea and cakes instead of beer and vodka. But she did not stay behind her bar as her husband always did. No, she ran about all the time, seeing to it that cabinets were cleaned up after a customer left, chatting and gossiping with the women in the tubs and ceaselessly admonishing the girls to keep busy. With her commanding words, usually went a pinch on the arm or on the bottom.

The girls lined up at the door when a customer came in. Each tried to get as many as possible, because of the tips. The customers were of the same kind as the men, middle class women of all ages. Many came only for a hot bath because there were no bathing accommodations in the houses of the middle class of that time. Some of them wanted a massage and a rest and many of them, not having any serfs at home, wanted something more. But all of them used the attendant bath girls as their private property, as serfs, rented for a time and on whom they could let their fancy go as it would.

Grushenka realized this with her first customer. This patroness was a young girl of about Grushenka's age, whose father had recently made some money with a pottery business. While this father refused to allow his family an elegant household with servants and the luxury of the upper class, there was enough cash available for his daughter to behave the thorough snob outside her four walls. She was decked out in a cloak with golden threads woven into it, her shoes had big silver buckles and she looked like a real lady.

When she came in she eyed the ten girls who stood there naked and smiling. She took her lorgnette and slowly and carefully looked them over. Grushenka felt a chill when the eyes of this young girl wandered from her bust down to her belly and then down to her spot and over her legs. She was not so happy when she was selected. She did not know why, because this young girl had a harmless and friendly face, though around her mouth were lines of haughtiness and disgust.

She led her customer to a cabinet, closed the door and began devotedly to undress her. The girl stood perfectly still and did not make a move, not even opening a ribbon or slipping out of a single garment. Grushenka found it best to admire loudly all of her wearing apparel although she met only with the answer that it was very costly and that Grushenka should lay each piece out or hang it up with great care. The girl demanded her hair undone and braided, so that it should not get wet. Meanwhile, she sat before the mirror studying her face and her decidedly good figure.

After her hair was done, Grushenka asked whether she desired a massage and which way she wanted it. Instead of an answer, the girl turned around and began to study Grushenka's form and features. She became jealous of Grushenka's full and even bust, her subtle waist, her straight belly and good legs. Of a sudden, she put a finger into Grushenka's pussy, shoved it all the way in, and drawing her nearer asked:

"All men are crazy about your spot—aren't they?"

"Oh, no!" answered Grushenka instinctively. "Oh, no! Men usually don't like me."

"Not much, you liar," sneered the fair patroness and letting her finger slip out of the hole, she gave her a resounding slap on the thigh.

Grushenka drew back, holding her smarting spot with her hands and groaning, "Oh, Oh—please don't do that!"

"Why not? Why shouldn't I give you a sound spanking if I like to?" retorted the girl with a sneer. "Didn't I hire you for my pleasure? Since when can I not do with Madame Brenna's girls what I like? Shall I call her in and ask her?"

"Please don't call Madame Brenna," answered Grushenka timidly. "I'll do everything you want me to—but please don't hurt me. You don't need to pay me if you don't want to," she added.

167

"We'll see about that, you little serf girl," replied the customer. "Now come here and turn around and bend over—yes, so—that's all right. And don't dare to move away or I'll teach you!"

With that remark, she began to pinch Grushenka's bottom. First she took the flesh of the right cheek between the thumb and index finger, squeezed the soft flesh firmly and turned her hand around. Grushenka put her own hand to her mouth so as not to cry out aloud, for it hurt her terribly. She leaned forward, trembling in her legs. The girl watched with pleasure. The pinched spot first turned snow white and then deep red.

"Now you look all uneven," she remarked. "We can't stand for that—" and she pinched the left cheek of the ass in the same way. Not content with that, she attacked different points above and beneath the bruised area and admired her handiwork with laughter.

Grushenka suffered under each pinch as if fire burnt her backside. Between pinches, the girl reached through Grushenka's open legs and pulled the hair of her Venus Hill, not very hard, but hard enough to make her groan aloud. Meanwhile Grushenka had the feeling that she had to piss. But she was afraid to piss over the customer's hand—Madame Brenna's whip would have been the consequence. Then the girl got bored with her doings.

"Sorry," she said, "That we haven't a whip or a switch here. Otherwise I would erase the nice design which I made on your bottom." Grushenka straightened out and turned around. The girls eyes were fastened to her full breasts. "How I'd love to whip your breasts," she went on, "with a small leather strap, the one I have home for my lap dog. It would be a pleasure to see your breasts, of which you're so proud, prettily striped with the lash. You see I don't like to hit you with my hands because that hurts me and wouldn't go through your thick skin anyway, you slut.''

Nevertheless, she made Grushenka hold her breasts with both hands while she struck her a couple of times with bare hands. Grushenka was able to catch these slaps with her hands, but it stung her anyway not a little. This over, the girl demanded her satchel, out of which she took a large artificial penis. She laid herself on the massage table, opened up her legs, had Grushenka stand close to her, and gave her the phallus. Grushenka opened up the lips of the cunt with her left hand and with her right, she carefully sunk the artificial prick into the vulva.

The girl became very passionate. She put her right hand between Grushenka's thighs, near the cleft and clamped her hand into the flesh, sinking the nails into Grushenka's soft skin. At the same time, she held her left hand tight on her own well-formed bosom and worked her bottom against the prick in a quick rhythm. Grushenka duplicated this rhythm by easing the prick into the hole up and down. The girl heaved heavily, whispered the name of her imaginary lover and moved her bottom up higher and higher until when she reached her climax she rested only on her shoulders and on the soles of her feet. She fell back on the table and lay motionless while Grushenka removed the intruding shaft and cleaned the pussy with a wet towel. She was glad it was over, but that proved a mistake. As soon as the girl came to, she had another scheme.

"Give me the prick!" she commanded. "And you go down and give my sweet pussy a good licking and don't stop before I tell you. Understand? No, that's not the right spot. Stick out your tongue, you stupid fool! Deeper! Yes, that's it.''

Grushenka had her head buried between the thighs of this newly rich girl who revenged her own poor childhood with its many whippings and humiliations by taking it out on another girl. Grushenka had not practiced using the tip of her tongue for some time, and although she knew how she had formerly done it, she worked too quickly and pressed her mouth too hard into the open vulva, so that she soon was breathless and her tongue became sore.

The girl had crossed her legs behind Grushenka's neck and pressed her tightly against her pussy. She was not yet excited because she had just come under the pressure of Master Prick. This dildoe she held playfully in her hands, placing it between her breasts, tickling her nipples, finally kissing it all along the shaft and then inserting it into her mouth and sucking it with delight. She did not concentrate on the feelings of her pussy beyond the agreeable tickling which Grushenka's tongue play produced. Grushenka stopped for a moment, getting her breath and resting her tongue, and looking up saw the penis disappearing and re-appearing from the mouth. The fair sucker was not willing to let her have a rest and hit her on the back with the soles of her feet.

Grushenka resumed her occupation. This time she held the pussy open with her left hand and, coming from underneath, inserted the index finger of her right hand in the vulva and massaged the sheath all the way along until the womb seconded the efforts of her tongue to make the little love place spend. This method apparently met with the approval of the buttocks, because they started to move up and down, first slowly, then increasing their tempo to such a degree that Grushenka had a hard time keeping the tip of her tongue exactly at the right spot.

However, it was the desire of her patroness to prolong

the play. She twisted away, even took the priceless shaft out of her mouth and ordered Grushenka to stop. But Grushenka hung on. She kept her mouth close to the cunt and sucked with all her might. Finally the girl gave up fighting and came. She lay panting while Grushenka took a soft towel and rubbed her legs, belly, breast and arms removing the sweat and giving her at the same time a strengthening massage. Her customer had her eyes closed and seemed to sleep. Grushenka was about to leave, when the girl got up lazily, gave her a malicious look and started for the door. Grushenka thought she was going to the tub. Instead, the girl opened the door and motioned Madame Brenna, who, always on the watch, came swiftly inside.

"I always pay well and you know I never complain," said the girl, "but look at this serf girl here. She is so lazy that when I tell her to kiss me a little, she just gives me words. I don't care what you do about it, but you know there are the aristocratic bath halls where I should have gone in the first place. . . ."

"Is that so?" asked Madame Brenna with a grin and a severe look in the direction of Grushenka. "I'll wake the bitch up, if you permit. Come here Grushenka and lie over this chair. Yes, the bottom up."

Grushenka did as told. Her head hung down; her hands held the legs of the chair with an anxious grip; her poor behind was turned up. Madame Brenna took a towel, held it in water until it was soaking wet and put her left hand firmly on Grushenka's back. She saw the marks of the pinching and guessed the rest of the story, making up her mind to fake the beating. But Grushenka, trembling and weeping and protesting her innocence, now lost control of herself entirely. She not only felt like pissing, nay, she pissed! In a big stream the yellow liquid ran out of her pussy and over her thighs onto the carpet.

The girl laughed aloud. After the sadness and bad mood which had followed her two orgasms, she now felt delightfully happy. Madame Brenna, however, became really angry. The wet towel proved to be a more painful instrument than a switch or a leather strap. While the latter gave the kind of stinging cut suggested by its switching sound through the air, the wet towel gave only a thud when it hit, but it crushed the flesh, inflicting the pain of a contusion. Madame Brenna understood how to handle a wet towel on a naughty girl's bottom. She had perfected herself through over a score of years and Grushenka's behind was just another ass to her.

"Such a lousy girl, to piss on that good rug," she thought, and Grushenka's behind was soon purple red from the knees to the small of the back. She howled and squealed like a pig being killed. She tossed about in her awkward position, her tear-dimmed eyes fixed on her own knees which she saw underneath the chair seat. On her body, arched so that the behind was its highest point, the blows rained with awful strength—swap—swap—swap!

Madame Brenna did not count the strokes. Grushenka had roused her anger and she'd know when it was time to stop. The girl customer looked on, highly amused. While she still laughed about the peeing business, a gleam of perverted passion glowed in her eyes and a feeling of satisfaction crept through her loins. "Oh, if father would only buy some serf girls," she thought, "I'd beat them myself—but with a good leather whip, not with a wet towel." She herself had felt the switch and the strap not so many years ago when her father was still poor and she was the hired maid of a rich market woman. And how often the leather whip had cut her young breasts—and in recollection, she caressed her full bust with both hands, reassuring herself that those times were over forever.

Meanwhile Madame Brenna had finished her job and motioned her customer out of the cabinet and into a tub. Grushenka let herself fall from the chair and lying on her stomach felt her sore backside with careful fingers. This indulgence, however, was short lived. Madame Brenna soon was back again and made her clean up the room. Taking her roughly by the arm, she dried her face with a handkerchief and tied up her ruffled hair.

"Not another sob!" she said, "or I'll start again. Pull yourself together and go after your work. You see," she added maliciously, "that's what comes of getting the biggest man of the neighborhood to squeeze it into you; you can't even hold your water."

Grushenka subdued her sobs. Under Madame Brenna's orders, she carried hot water for re-filling the tubs, she cleaned out a tub and so on. While Grushenka's ass hung heavy with pain, she was given no time to sulk and mope.

Furthermore, she soon had to take care of a customer of another kind. A middle-aged woman of a motherly type selected her; a woman with kind eyes and ruddy complexion, more stout than fat, more big than tall. While she undressed her, Grushenka admired her firm flesh, her lage hard bust, her muscular legs. The woman stroked Grushenka's head, called her all kinds of sweet names, complimented her on her lovely features and body and did not seem the least bit jealous of her beauty. After she was naked, she asked Grushenka to wash her pussy. When this was duly done she said, "Now, my sweet darling, please be a dear and give me a long and good sucking. You see my old man hasn't touched me in over five years. I don't know whether he could find his way anymore, if he wanted to, and I can't help craving some excitement. You see every so often it tickles me down there and so I come here once a week and have my little hothouse regaled with the play of an apt tongue like yours, and remember, I enjoy it most when a girl is willing and beautiful as you are." With this, she moved Grushenka's head, carefully and with caresses, between her big thighs.

Grushenka started the job. She had plenty of operating field before her. The woman spread her big legs wide open; the small part of the belly, both sides of the cleft, the over-developed Venus Hill received soft kisses and slow ticklings with the tongue while Grushenka's well-formed hands gently took hold of the big buttocks. Grushenka took the large long lips of the grotto in her mouth alternately and sucked them, even biting them tenderly. Then she turned her efforts towards the main object, namely the large but juicy vagina.

The woman lay still except that her fingers tried to tickle Grushenka's ears, but Grushenka shook them off. When, however, the tongue nipped the clitoris, licked around it and pressed and massaged it with stronger strokes, the woman changed her behavior. She began to heave and to toss with passion and her sweet words turned into sharp curses. Grushenka could not make out what she whispered so hoarsely, but words like 'take your damned prick away' or 'you lousy old cock-sucker' turned up repeatedly in this randy monologue. When she finally came, the woman closed her strong legs behind Grushenka's head, drawing her so tightly towards her cunt as to almost suffocate her. Releasing her, she sat up on the table, scratched her fat belly thoughtfully and muttered more to herself than to Grushenka: "It's a shame for an old woman and a

mother of a grown up daughter—but what can you do?''
Soon she sat in her tub, a respectable elderly woman with
kind looks and refined behavior. Grushenka received a
good tip from her.

Grushenka was greeted with many sarcastic remarks
from the other customers and girls wherever she passed.
Her first patroness had told the story of her pissing on the
floor and all the women considered it a huge joke. This
same patroness annoyed and vexed her again when she
was through with her bath. After she had been dried, an
operation during which she found many faults with
Grushenka and during which she pinched her with her
sharp fingernails under the arms and in the sensitive flesh
of the breasts (of which she was jealous) she had another
one of her striking ideas.

"You little pisser! You know what you are good for? As
a piss-pot! Come, sit down on the floor and I will piss in
your mouth.''

Grushenka did not obey. She brought a piss-pot from
the corner and put it down. The girl clutched Grushenka's
hair around the pussy and raising her right hand threatened
to hit her. But Grushenka remained firm.

"I shall yell for Madame Brenna.'' she said and stood
her ground. The girl wavered.

"What else do you do,'' she retorted, "but eat cunts all
day long? Why should you, you of all people, refuse to
drink a little piss?'' Grushenka struggled free and went to
the other side of the massage table.

"I believe, Madame,'' she said, "that another girl will
serve you better than I can. May I call another one?'' The
girl shrugged her shoulders.

"No! No!'' she muttered and had herself dressed without another word. Ready to go, she took a ruble's worth of

coins out of her purse. Grushenka reached for it, but the girl had decided to give it to her in another manner.

"Wait," she said. "Lie down on the table and open up. I'll put it in your hole as a cork to stop the leak."

Grushenka did as she was told, hoping thus to get rid of her tormentor more quickly. She held her pussy as wide open as possible so as not to get hurt when the silver was slipped in. The girl, who already had her gloves on, opened the slit with two fingers and for a moment examined this finely made love nest. The lips were rosy and oval, the opening lay deeper than her own and in close neighborhood to the clearly visible back hole. The sheath seemed narrow and the tickler, being near the entrance, raised its head freshly. 'What a treasure of a cunt,' she thought, 'Really, I never would lick a pussy, but this one—'

Grushenka moved nervously; her tender parts lay open to the aggression of this patroness whom one could not trust. The girl slipped the coins in, first the small silver coins which had a higher value, then the big copper coins worth one or two kopekas. She had quite some fun when these pieces did not go in so easily, while Grushenka trembled anxiously, not hurt, but afraid of what still might come. Finished, the girl slapped her with her gloved hand over the open hole. Grushenka jerked her legs together and jumped from the table, while the girl laughingly remarked from the door: "Keep it there and you won't get broke."

During the many weeks Grushenka worked in the women's department, she found out that women are crueler and meaner than men. The women had no humor or fun on their minds; they wanted only to be satisfied, utterly selfishly. They complained without cause and having power over their attendants, they tormented and vexed them without reason and very often unexpectedly. They might be very nice and considerate to Grushenka and all of a sudden pinch her or call for Madame Brenna to punish her. They tipped not half as well as the men did and called attention to it heavily when they parted with a few kopekas. None of them ever kissed her pussy or made love to her, while many requested that she bring their elderly ticklers to the climax. Grushenka did not mind that. She soon learned to work her tongue over their bodies or their pussies in a routine way, hardly considering what she was doing and faking passion and eagerness when she felt that her patronesses were about to spend. But what got her nervous was that she never knew when Madame Brenna would find fault with her and punish her.

These punishments were of all kinds. Madame Brenna would whip her soles with a leather strap when she had not moved with enough alacrity; she would hit her breasts with a switch when a customer complained that she had admired herself in the mirror; she would tie stinging nettles on the inside of Grushenka's thighs or on her bare behind when she was tired or drowsy.

While none of the women customers made love to her, they always liked to rub their thick fingers in her sheath, not in a friendly and teasing way, but roughly, as if they wanted to enlarge her wonderfully small passage. Unconsciously, perhaps, they were envious because Grushenka had the narrowest hole of them all.

Grushenka thought that Madame Brenna kept after her more than after the other girls because she was still angry about her husband. That was wrong. But her conscience was soon especially uneasy and for a good reason. One evening when she had been in the woman's department only a few days and, through with work, had just reached her room, in came Mr. Brenna. As was his habit, without saying a word, he threw her over the bed and gave her one of his tremendous pokes. She did not dare to fight him or to yell for help. She just gave in, gasping. She did not enjoy his big shaft for she kept watching the door, dreadfully afraid that they might be detected.

The next day he came again and from then on every day. As things seemed to go smoothly Grushenka finally forgot her fear and concentrated again on his love power which filled her with hot chills and stimulated her to the climax of sacrificing passion. This went on for weeks and then, of course, one fine day Madame Brenna stood in the room again and the same scene as before repeated itself. Only this time, after having beaten up her husband, Madame Brenna gave Grushenka a murderous look, drove her husband out of the room, went herself, slammed the door behind her and locked and bolted the door from the outside.

For a moment Grushenka was horrified. She sat on the edge of the bed, paralyzed, unable to move or to think. Then an idea flashed through her brain, an idea that drove her to feverish activity. Flight! Away! As quickly as possible, as quick as lightning. She dressed, wrapped her clothes into a bundle and stuck the kerchief with her money into her bodice.

Flight! How to leave the room? The oak door did not budge. The lock was of forged iron. But there was the window! Through the window, over the window sill, along the house ledge into the open window of the next room. A dash through that room, flight down the stairs, out of the house, along the street, around the first corner, the second, the next.

Exhausted and with a beating heart, Grushenka leaned

178

against a house wall. Nobody had followed her. Still breathless, she forced herself to move on. The twilight turned to darkness. She reached Martha's house and the girl friends kissed each other tenderly and with tears. For a long time, neither spoke a word.

CHAPTER XII.

The stay with Martha was brief. The little money Grushenka had went quickly. Grushenka did not want to be a burden to her friend. She had to think of the future. She had found out from Martha that Mme. Laura once had a scheme to dispose of her and she resolved to try Mme. Laura again. Without telling Martha about it, she got ready one day at noontime and was soon sitting in Mme. Laura's private office.

Mme. Laura took little time to scold her for running away, but she asked Grushenka if she would this time accept what was provided for her. Grushenka consented meekly. Thinking it over, Mme. Laura dispatched a letter, this time to another gentleman. Grushenka sat in a corner of the office and waited. About an hour later Mme. Laura returned with a man about thirty years old. Dressed like a dandy, with a face like an Italian, his mustache was twirled up audaciously. He seemed coarse and vain and of a false hilarity. His hands were covered with dazzling diamonds.

"Here is a beautiful model of mine," Mme. Laura said,

pointing at Grushenka. "One of my serf-girls. I want to get rid of her because I promised a poor dear relative of mine her place. Now if she were just one of the usual run I would not have sent for you, but she is one of the finest and most beautiful creatures I have ever seen. As you are a connoisseur of women and always on the lookout for special beauties, I thought I had better send for you." She looked searchingly at the man. He twirled his mustache with affected fingers. He hardly looked in Grushenka's direction.

"One more or one less, it doesn't matter with us." He seemed bored.

"Come here, my dove," Mme. Laura made Grushenka get up and step forward. "Show yourself to the gentleman."

Grushenka stood before him, Mme. Laura tenderly stroking her hair and turning her slowly around. His face was expressionless. When Grushenka stood with her back towards him, she felt Mme. Laura slowly raising her dress, her petticoats, then flattening out her drawers so as to expose her behind. The gentleman seemed pleased. "Oh," he said, "you know my taste, don't you. Always give your customers what they ask for, eh? You know damn well that I like well formed, small behinds, not those big fat asses with their fat bolsters which are always in the way." And he laughed in falsetto.

When he heard that the price was only a hundred rubles, he took a handful of loose gold out of his pocket, threw ten pieces on the table with a move of his hand as if to say, "a hundred rubles—bah, what's that"—and Grushenka was sold. Needless to say, Mme. Laura made the money disappear, not with undue haste, oh no, but quick enough to be sure that she had gotten every bit of it.

At the door waited a princely carriage. The man got in

and had Grushenka sit down with him on the front seat. Grushenka wondered at a master driving through Moscow with a serf sitting next to him on the driver's seat of the carriage.

The answer to this came soon enough. Grushenka learned all about it while she had her first meal. Serge, that was his name, had been a serf himself. Now he was major domo to the old Prince Asantschejew—not only major domo but his jailor and tormentor. The old Prince was entirely at his mercy. He was kept a prisoner in his own bed, was not allowed to see any of his relatives or friends, was in fact held incommunicado. Serge had made himself master by trickery and sheer physical strength and had set himself up as tyrant over the wasted estate of the old Prince. He had forced his master to liberate him and in his last will to bequeath him a sizeable farm and some money. He had not dared to stipulate too large an amount for fear that after the death of the Prince the heirs and relatives would throw over the document and take their revenge on him. Therefore he kept the old man alive in order to steal as much cash as possible from the estate before his death.

Serge was an excellent administrator. By tolls and taxes he knew how to squeeze their last penny out of the farmer-serfs of the estate. But the household was run in a very disorderly manner, every servant doing just about what he wanted to do. The house, a tremendous castle, was unclean, the servants were dressed in rags, the horses were not cared for or properly fed, the whole little community of over fifty people lingered around without plan or discipline. Serge did not give a damn. He went about cursing and swearing, a short leather whip hanging from his belt always ready to strike—but only because he was concerned with his own comfort.

"What does he do with so many good looking girls?" asked Grushenka. "Well," they answered, and grinned, "You'll find that out in time."

After dinner and a bath, Grushenka was first of all able to save her own clothes. They were not burned as usual and she was happy, for she had bought them with her own money. The elderly housekeeper then said that she had to give her the usual thrashing, but Grushenka wiggled herself out of that too by flattering the woman, kissing the switch and just making her forget to use it on her. But now she was a serf-girl again. The price for her liberty was in the purse of Mme. Laura.

Serge forgot about Grushenka after her arrival and she behaved like all the other serfs in the house. When they heard him approaching a room—and he was usually shouting and yelling—they quickly fled before he could see them. She never saw the old Prince Asantschejew. Only two elderly women were allowed to enter his room, women trusted by Serge because they too had been taken care of in the Prince's will.

One day Serge missed one of his rings. He was in a rage. The ring seemed to have been stolen by one of the women (he kept no male serfs in the house and never had visitors). He ordered all the women into the biggest room of the basement and shouted that if the ring were not returned he'd kill every one of them to be sure that he didn't miss the thief. One of the girls suggested that she had seen the ring on a sideboard upstairs, and a few girls, including Grushenka, went to that room with him. There the ring was found.

But meanwhile Serge had laid his eyes on Grushenka. Grushenka was dressed in a blouse and petticoat without skirt or drawers. Her legs were bare and she wore wooden slippers. It was her working costume. As he looked at her, Serge's eyes sparkled.

"You are Mme. Laura's girl, aren't you?" he said, and he put one hand under her petticoat on her bare bottom, while his other hand stroked her thighs and the flesh of her belly but without touching her pussy. "Well, well, I forgot all about you. But no time is better than the present. Kneel straddle-legged on that easy chair and bend over, my chicken."

Grushenka did as she was told, put her knees on the arms of the wide easy chair and bent over a bit. She expected to get poked. The other girls watched him with malicious smiles. But Serge was not quite satisfied. He grabbed her by the neck and bent her forward until her head touched the seat of the chair, doubling her up to the utmost. One of the girls threw Grushenka's petticoats up and over her back, and Grushenka could see through her opened legs how Serge took his sizeable shaft out of his dirty linen trousers. She went with her right hand to her cunt, parted the lips with a quick move of the fingers and held it open awaiting the attack.

"A nice, clean ass," remarked Serge. "Sorry I forgot so long about it."

He moved forward, got hold of her loins, and glancing down, approached her with the tip of his shaft. Grushenka reached for his love-instrument, but he shouted for her to take her hand away. He then began to press his prick against her back-hole.

He was an ass-fucker by conviction and inclination. First of all he did not want his girls to become pregnant. Furthermore he found the back-hole smaller and tighter. Finally he did not want to give his girls a thrill; he liked to do his fucking himself and to spin out his amusement as long as possible without the help of his partner.

Thus the head of Serge's shaft now engaged in a struggle to enter Grushenka's small back-hole. He pressed, screwed and pushed. It pained her. Not that she was still a virgin back there. Prince Leo had initiated her ass hole, more than one finger had rubbed and entered it. Serge however did not use any ointment nor did he direct or help with his hand, and she groaned and sighed under his lengthy attack. He was expert in entering a back-hole. He knew that the muscle holding it tight was on top, and he massaged this muscle with his pressure. It gave way and his shaft entered in full.

After he had it all in he paused a moment, got himself into a comfortable position and began a slow fucking. Grushenka, glancing through her legs at his big brown hairy balls and the end of the appearing and disappearing shaft, wanted to help along and wiggled her bottom. But he slapped her on the thigh and commanded her to hold still. She felt his machine grow bigger and bigger, she felt like taking a good shit, she felt that empty longing in her cunt, while the minutes crept by. The other girls stood around and whispered.

Finally he came, not speeding up his movements at all and not withdrawing his prick afterwards. He just stood and waited until it became small and soft and slipped out by itself. Then he left the room without a word. He had hardly left when the girls burst into a babble of comment and hilarity. The remarks flew through the room:

"Well, another virginity and no blood shed. . ."

"I want to be Godmother in nine months."

"I always play with my finger, when he sticks it into my ass."

"He would not take me, my veranda protrudes too much"—displaying a very muscular and fat behind with such a tight cleft that the back-hole could not be seen.

"He usually lines three or four girls up in a row, has them bend down as you did just now, and goes from one hole to the other."

"Be careful not to wiggle your behind; when he comes too quickly, he'll beat you to a bloody mess."

"And don't put salve into your cleft. He wants to force the entrance and hates an easy hole."

"You'll be on his list from now on. I could see he liked your buttocks."

"Oh, if I only had a good prick—right now—for my little pussy!"

"Have yourself sent to the stable for a thrashing. The boys won't hurt you, but they'll fuck you all right."

"I can loan you my finger, if that will help you out."

"Why not take a candle?"

It was done as said. The girls were excited after seeing Grushenka get fucked. Serge never allowed them to go out of the house and they could hardly ever manage to get a prick in the right spot. The girl who was the leader of the chorus lay down on the couch. Another girl took a big candle from one of the side-brackets and filled the longing love-nest with intensive pushes. They had done this often before. They had found out who had the longest vagina, making a mark on the candle for each cunt, and they were clever in satisfying each other in this way.

Grushenka, who watched with interest as each girl took her turn to lie down on the couch, felt rather randy. In the group was a very young girl, not much more than fifteen or sixteen years old, very blonde and delicate. She would not let herself be pushed but she caressed the faces and breasts of those girls wiggling under the candle. Grushenka put her arm around her and whispered in her ear. "Will you do to me what I do to you—everything?"

The girl shyly nodded her consent. Grushenka laid her on the carpet, rolled her petticoats up and began to smother her soft belly with kisses. The girl was ticklish and giggled. Grushenka opened her young legs and buried her head between the girl's thighs. The pretty little pussy was still almost without hair. The girl was fighting against the intruder, not earnestly, yet struggling a bit, and this made Grushenka still more anxious to suck this cunt with all the ability she had acquired during her stay in Mme. Brenna's bath establishment.

The girl sighed and heaved and tossed about entwining herself with Grushenka's sucking mouth when the climax came. The girl was, in fact, a virgin and this was the first time she had ever come. She lay now without stirring, her lips slightly parted, smiling and exhausted.

Grushenka studied her with curious sympathy; she knew the girl would not reciprocate and she let it go at that. Her own pussy could get satisfied only late at night when she stroked herself with loving fingers, thinking of her beloved Mihail.

Serge did not put her on his special list. He was much to busy trying to make money and to pile it up in his private iron chest. He loved to drink and gamble with the stable boys and he did not often feel inclined to get rid of his sperm. Whenever he felt in the mood he grabbed a few of the girls who were around, discarded the ones with fat asses and poked the others after his fashion. But Grushenka was to come into contact with him in another way.

One afternoon, cleaning the dining room, she was carrying one of the chairs with the big princely crown burnt into its leather back. Serge, running hurriedly through the room, bumped a leg of the chair with his knee. It hurt him and the culprit had to be punished on the spot. The leather whip was unhooked from his belt. Grushenka had to bend forward, put both her hands between her knees and was told to press her knees tight together and not to move. He ripped her blouse over her head. With his left hand he took hold of her hair, wrapping it around his wrist and the whipping began.

He raised the whip and flourished it over her. The stroke fell over her nude shoulders and the pain was worse than she had anticipated. It took her breath away and made her gasp. She uttered a loud shriek, writhing and twisting her loins in agony. He went on whipping her slowly, so that she felt the full sting of every stroke. It was as if a red hot iron was being drawn across her back and shoulders. She winced and squirmed every time the leather thong bit into her quivering flesh. She hopped around the room with her legs closed tightly together but that didn't do her any good. It only made him lay the strokes on in such a way that the end of the strap curled around her body and bit into her breasts, thus doubling her agony. She was about to faint or throw herself on the floor regardless of the consequences when he stopped. He kicked her in the behind and warned her to be more careful the next time.

When Grushenka, weeping and groaning, came back to her senses the other girls had gone. In fact they had quickly stolen out of the room when he took hold of her, because Serge did not mind whipping half a dozen backs once the mood was on him. They came back now and put sour cream over the long red welts which covered her back, shoulders and one of her breasts. It took days before Grushenka felt normal again and had forgotten the pain; it took weeks before the welts had disappeared.

It was a long time before Grushenka again came face to face with Serge. This happened when he sent word to the old lazy housekeeper to send him the six girls who had the best breasts. The girls did not understand what he had in mind and were thoroughly frightened. But they had to go to him. Of course Grushenka was one of the girls, who, clothed only in petticoat and naked from the waistline up, went to his room. They stood inside the doorway and waited. Serge sat over a big accounting sheet writing figures and cursing. Finally he threw the quill away, took a pinch of snuff and looked the girls over.

They all had full hard breasts, with white or brown skin, rosy or dark nipples. He had his choice. He got up, felt them, tickled them, weighed their full flesh in his hands and pinched them. They wiggled a bit and giggled but were uneasy. Naturally he decided on Grushenka. She had the finest of them all, milk white, full but pointed and with rather large rosy berries. He told her to go and put her finest dress on; a skirt and blouse but no shirt underneath. Grushenka hurried off to do so.

When she came back she saw him busy with the other girls. They kneeled in a row on the couch, bottoms in the air, one of them intruded by Serge's prick but probably all of them already honored with a few pokes because they comforted their behinds with their fingers or were tickling their pussies. He soon took his machine out of the hole which engaged it and went to the next crevice. Grushenka took care not to make any noise and not to be noticed in the doorway. She had no desire to give her behind this treat.

After Serge had come with his present incumbent, he gave every girl a slap on the ass and chased them all from the room. He put his prick quietly back into his trousers without troubling to wash it after his trip into the dirt holes, and turned to Grushenka. He opened her blouse in front, took her breasts out and tried to arrange the blouse so that the bust protruded well out of it. But it couldn't be done. The blouse was too large and had too many pleats, so that no matter how arranged the material covered most of the bust. He ordered the housekeeper to appear and demanded that an elegant evening dress be made for Grushenka but so cut in front as to go below the bosom. He smiled knowingly when he gave this order.

A light blue brocade, embroidered with silver flowers, was found in one of the many chests. This was duly cut and sewn into a magnificent evening gown. Grushenka helped and supervised this work eagerly. She knew from Nelidowa's tailors what was becoming to her and how a dress had to be made, and she looked very stunning when she presented herself a few days later to Serge. A bristling line of style and elegance ran through the whole creation; leaning back on a train, tightened together in a wasp-waist flanked by the long sleeves which trailed down to the knees and crowned by the absolutely nude bust which stuck out almost with impudence. Add to this that Grushenka had colored her nipples with henna (as she had seen Nelidowa do); that she had her hair dressed in the high artificial style of the time and that she wore her most enchanting smile. Serge, the crude peasant and slave driver, could not help but admire and compliment her. Of course there was a great difference between Grushenka in a dirty working blouse, unkempt and half nude, and Grushenka fixed up as a great lady. More than satisfied Serge took her by the hand and led her to the room of the old Prince.

The old man shrank together and trembled fearfully when they entered the room and was about to hide under

the covers of his large bed. His long hair was snow white
and his white beard uncut. His small eyes were half closed,
the eyelids red with inflamation. His nose seemed small
and shrinking and the whole impression was of a Santa
Claus who had met with an accident and lay frozen in the
snow.

"Well here I bring you something fine," began Serge,
"something that you will like, something to play with.
And if you try to hide under the covers or to look away I
shall hit you, you scoundrel. Didn't you always like the
bitches with the big breasts, eh, when you were younger
and I had to clean your boots? Sorry you are too weak or
I'd make you clean mine now. Didn't I have to look on a
thousand times, in those old days, when you put your
pimply prick between their breasts—in those days when I
always had to select the big breasted ones for you? Well
you see I am kindly inclined now and bring you something to play with. Come on and feel it and suck it a little.
It will do you good, won't it?"

The real reason for Serge's behaviour was that he had
had enough of the old man. He wanted him to die but still
shrank from the deed of killing him outright. His plan was
to enervate the Prince still further. He hoped that the old
man, after not having seen a woman for so long a time,
would get excited and croak. Therefore he now pushed
Grushenka towards the bed and the old Prince, trying to
ward her off, could not help but touch her naked bust. This
not enough, Serge pushed her over so that her breast lay
on the Prince's face. But Serge saw that as long as he was
present fear would occupy the old man's mind more than
Grushenka's young bosom would excite him.

Sizing Grushenka up and finding her not dangerous,
Serge decided to leave the two alone. He directed Grushenka

to caress the old man's face every half-hour with her nipples, to let him play with her and to let him fuck her if he so desired. "After the abstinence of so many years he is entitled to a little pleasure," he remarked. With that he left them.

Grushenka sat modestly on the chair and watched the Prince. He lay still and stared stupidly into no-where. After a while she turned her eyes away from him, pitying him in her heart. She felt that he in turn was now scrutinizing her and before he could avoid it she caught a very keen and intelligent eye. So he was playing the old stupid man but was still very far from being demented! Finally he said in a low voice:

"You won't kill me, will you?"

"I'll pity you. I'll help you. I hate Serge"—was her answer. But they were both very careful not to say more; perhaps the serf who played the master was eavesdropping. After a while she got up and leaned over him as if to tease him with her breasts and whispered: "I have to do this, he might be looking through the keyhole."

The Prince played his part and stroked her bosom a bit. She noticed some books on the table and took one of them and began to read aloud. He was amazed that she could read and listened with interest to the story. But this interest grew to admiration when she inserted sentences into her monotonous readings which certainly were not printed in the book. For example, 'be very careful' or 'I must see you again' or 'make some plans of what to do' or 'when he comes back behave as though you never wanted to see me again' and so on.

When Serge came back to fetch Grushenka the old man complained in a stupidly wailing manner that she had gotten him hot and feverish, that he did not want to see her again, that she had disturbed him with her reading. Serge was pleased at this and felt especially gratified when Grushenka told him, after they had left the room, that the Prince was a delapidated old man, had no sense any more, and was certainly suffering from softening of the brain. Serge ordered her to make a daily visit to the Prince and annoy him more each time.

"Take his prick," he said, "or what is left of it, and rub it or suck it. Let him have a little excitement before he goes to hell—you are his serf anyway."

At present, however, Serye wanted his own excitement quelled and Grushenka looked too beautiful in her full dress not to make an excellent partner. Right then and there her head was buried in the cushions of a couch while a sharp pain in her back-hole announced that Serge was still able to raise Master Prick to action. When he had thrown the long train of her dress over her elevated bottom and found a pair of drawers in his way he ordered her never to wear drawers again. He also decided that hereafter he would fuck her each day when she came out of the Prince's room. The dress of an elegant lady had stimulated his low-born senses and he ordered his other favorites also to be fitted with fine gowns to be worn when they reported for his pleasure.

Meanwhile Grushenka had to bear the brunt of his desire and she did so with the resolution that her revenge would not be far off. She had her ass-hole fucked again and again and surprisingly she very soon found it was not so terrible after all. On the contrary she learned how to loosen the muscles, how to give herself easily, how to enjoy this reverse form of erotic excitement. Her only objection to her encounters with Serge was that he demanded she hold herself absolutely motionless no matter how aroused she became and how much she would have liked to answer his thrusts with wiggling pushes.

The liberation of the old Prince Asantschejew and the crushing of Serge came much more quickly than even Grushenka had hoped. She smuggled paper and pencil to the old Prince and, while she read to him, sitting so that a watcher from the key-hole could not see him, he wrote a letter. It took the old feeble man many days before the letter was ready and addressed. He had to hide the half-finished paper for days under his sheets, trembling for fear that he would be detected—and that would have meant a violent death from Serge's hand. Finally he slipped the finished document to Grushenka. It was addressed to a distant relative of his who had his castle in the city.

While Serge was in the house Grushenka, who had not confided in anyone, did not dare to carry the message herself to its destination. But one day when Serge drove away to watch the races she dressed hurriedly, ran out of the house, took a droshki and sped through the city. The relative was not at home, but his wife was. Grushenka forced her way through a chain of servants, came to the mistress, fell at her feet and poured out her story in great excitement. At the same time she delivered the letter.

At first the lady did not want to listen. Had not the old Prince sent them insulting letters some years ago asking them never to see him again nor to communicate with him again? Had not that dirty major domo refused her husband entrance to the house, acting upon orders from the old Prince? Had they not been shut out of his life entirely? How could he now expect to get help? But when Grushenka prayed hard to her she finally read the letter. She began thinking it over and had Grushenka repeat the story.

Then suddenly she understood; it became clear to her

that Prince Asantschejew was actually the captive of his
slave, that he had kept them away under the threat of
death, and that they had to act. But how? She broke out in
a flood of lamentations for with her husband away she did
not know what to do. Yet Grushenka was in a terrible
hurry. Action had to be taken before Serge came back, for
he would strangle the old man upon the first suspicion.
She suggested that they should get hold of some male
acquaintances of Madame, should get some men from the
police station, and—. But now Madame was calm again
and took charge. She selected a half dozen of her strongest
stable men and they drove at great speed to the castle of
the old Prince.

Serge had not yet returned. The old Prince, upon seeing
his relative, became hysterical, interrupting his joy with
shouts of fear. Serge, whom he called an almighty devil,
would kill them all, he proclaimed. His fear did not lessen
even when they brought Serge before him, chained and
shackled.

It had been an easy job. When he had re-entered the
house, the six men of Madame had fallen upon him and
subdued him in no time. A police-picket was sent for. In
the presence of the lieutenant, the old Prince made his
accusation against his serf and demanded that he be hanged.
And so they led Serge away.

The captain of the police decided not to string him up
but to send him to Siberia. But it never came to that.
Serge, who had been stunned in the beginning, had a
violent fit in the evening and tried to break loose. The
answer was the knout and the policeman who exercised the
whipping hit him so awkwardly that he broke his back.

Serge died during the night—this all can be read in the
old family papers of the family Asantschejew. There also

can be found that the old Prince gave Grushenka her freedom and a handsome dowry. He lived on for many months in peace and happiness. During this time Grushenka nursed him. After his death the relative who helped to free him inherited and lived in his castle—her name is reported as Countess Natalia Alexiejew. Grushenka stayed with the Countess Natalia until—well, the next chapter will tell you.

CHAPTER XIII.

Countess Natalia Alexiejew and her husband, the Count Vasilis, were Russian aristocrats of the old conservative order, a kind Grushenka had not yet met. They were religious, straight-forward, strict but just. They felt themselves the absolute owners of their serfs, but felt toward them more like a father or a mother than a master. Their day started early with a prayer meeting which was attended by the whole household, followed by breakfast at a long table, the masters presiding. If there was not a special party with guests, masters and servants ate at the same table and of the same dishes. After that, work was done.

Laziness or stupidity were at first treated with admonishing words. Only in rare and grave cases was the whip resorted to. The masters did not swing it themselves, however, but sent the culprit to the stable where an old and trusted coachman, named Joseph, laid the guilty one over a bundle of hay and administered the beating. Joseph was a Judas and beat them longer and harder than he was told to. The other serfs hated him. They took good care not to be remiss in their duties so as to stay clear of his fangs.

Furthermore, no erotic abuse took place in the household. The aristocratic couple shared the same bed throughout the year. The Count, who was past fifty, had lost his sexual aspirations, and the Countess, who was ten years his junior, was apparently satisfied with what he was able to let her have. She was nice and plump, with firm flesh and many pretty dimples. She had motherly ways, though always a bit preachy, and was beloved by all her servants.

A few weeks after the death of the old Prince she approached Grushenka and asked her what she intended to do. Did she want to leave her? Should she look around for a husband for her? Would she like to settle down on a little farm? What were her plans? Grushenka had no answer ready. After talking it over they decided that Grushenka should stay at the house for the present and the Countess put her in charge of the linen and silver room.

Grushenka now carried on her belt a chain with many big keys which opened drawers and chests. She was proud to take care of countless sets of linen, from the coarse and daily-used bed linen of the serfs to the finest table damask, and of hundreds of pieces of china and many valuable silver ornaments which were put on the table on special occasions only. She had ten girls working under her, cleaning, repairing and sewing the new linen which had been woven by another group of girls or by the peasant women on one of the estates.

Her pride made her ambitious to have the utensils entrusted to her always at their very best. This ambition did not meet completely with the zeal of the girls working for her, especially in the beginning when they started to clean up after the years of disorder that preceded the death of the old Prince. She began to admonish her girls with friendly words, but she was timid and they laughed behind her back. It took all her courage to pinch one or the other on the arm, and she felt that as soon as she turned around they made faces at her and giggled. At last she complained to the Countess who gave the matter serious thought. She advised her as follows:

"The trouble with peasants," said the Countess, "is that they won't hear with their ears until they have felt with their backs. It won't do for you to report them to me and for me to have them sent to the stable. They'll only pin on you the stigma of a traitor and they'll think you're afraid of them and will play you plenty of tricks. No—you will have to keep some good fresh switches in salt water in your working pantry. If you beat one or two of their backsides sore, they'll kiss the hem of your sleeves."

After this advice, Grushenka got the switches and gave the girls a warning, but she made very little headway. The girls joked about the switches and broke the stems in the middle when she was not looking. There was one in particular, a big fat girl, about thirty years of age. She had been married twice to farmers, both of whom had died, and had always returned to the inner circle of the household because she had been one of the last favorites of the deceased Prince. She used to call Grushenka "baby" and told stories about her married life which made the other girls stop working. She herself would do almost nothing in a day's time and when Grushenka pinched her in the arm, she would grin and say, "Why, dear, do that again, please. It feels nice."

She certainly did not feel it very much. She had a tough brown skin and the hard flesh of her peasant stock. Her overgrown, full breasts had first attracted the old Prince

when he saw her once swimming in the river of his estate.
She used to kneel down before him, put his penis between
her breasts, press them gently together and rub until she
felt his sperm flowing over her throat. She imagined that
she had superior rights to Grushenka, hence her heckling
and resistance. Therefore, when she aroused Grushenka's
temper again and again, the supervising girl finally lost her
patience and condemned her to twenty-five strokes over
the bare bottom with the switch. The girl arose unmoved,
took some hairpins out of her hair, and with them pinned
her skirt up over her back. With slow movements and
ceremony she removed her drawers, laid herself on the
floor bottom up, and said sarcastically, "Please hit me,
sweetheart. I like to have a hot ass."

Grushenka knelt with one knee on the back of the culprit
and put the bucket with the switches next to her on the
floor. In front of her was a tremendous ass; two big brown
globes, muscular and steel-hard. The girl held her thighs
closely together and strained her muscles in order to ward
off the strokes. She was not at all afraid, because Grushenka
was not very strong. Grushenka felt that if she did not beat
the culprit into submission she would lose the respect of all
her girls, and she pressed her lips together in anger.

"Open up your legs as wide as you can," she ordered,
curtly.

"Certainly, my dove," retorted the girl mockingly,
"anything to please my little pet." She spread her legs as
wide as she could and at the end of the cleft appeared a
great hole; a hair-infested cunt which seemed able to hold
a big stick. The thick flesh on the end of the cleft was not
muscular and the inside of the thighs next to the cunt
attracted Grushenka's eyes. She directed the switch at
those parts.

At first, being greatly excited herself, she laid the strokes weakly and swiftly. But when the girl did not seem to mind at all, even muttering flip remarks, she began to whip her with a force which she herself had not suspected she had. The flesh around the cunt became crimson; the first drops of blood appeared. The girl began to move uneasily. The ends of the switch were cutting the lower part of the lips of her pussy.

Soon the switch had broken to pieces. Grushenka picked a new one. Her hand got sore, but she did not mind. She was breathless, but she whipped and whipped, her eyes directed towards the end of the cleft and neglecting entirely the big, muscular thighs. Finally the girl felt the pain keenly. She had stood it at first to show up Grushenka and prove that she could not hurt her. But now the pain became too violent. She closed her legs. Grushenka, sensing victory and submission would not have it so. She shouted at her to open up again, and when the girl did not obey, she bent over in a rage and bit her viciously in one of the big buttocks. The girl groaned and cried out, but reluctantly opened her enormous thighs again. This was not enough for Grushenka who jerked them open as far as it was possible and resumed her whipping, until the girl prayed for mercy and to be forgiven.

Grushenka stopped beating, but she was not yet through with her. She told the girl not to move until she had washed her up herself. In the hollow of her hand, she took salt water from the bucket and rubbed it into the raw, beaten flesh. The sting of the cold salt water shot up the girl's back, and as she instinctively recoiled, Grushenka manhandled her spot, pinching her all around the pussy and pulling its hair severely. Finally she inserted her sharp nails into the lips of the lovenest and with a last pinch,

203

which made the culprit scream, let her go. After the girl rose, she gave Grushenka a strange look of mingled astonishment and devotion. She curtsied and kissed her sleeve, then went humbly to her work without wiping off the tears which trickled down her cheeks. From that day her girls looked up to Grushenka with respect, and some of them even told her how glad they were that Grushenka had punished that bitch, who had been so fresh.

Grushenka herself had undergone a change by this experience. She now looked at her ten girls as her property and she enjoyed feeling that she could do with them what she wanted. She felt a certain thrill when she pinched their bare arms. She did not hurry when she had them expose the inside of a thigh or even a breast, so that she could squeeze the flesh slowly between the knuckles of two fingers, pinch hard, and twist her hand around. When her victim yelled or did not hold still, she did it over and over again, and she was aware that she got a thrill out of it.

She took even more advantage of her girls and they did not dare complain to the Countess. Grushenka had no lover, and her pussy often felt randy. What had Nelidowa done with her girls? For what had those lazy bastards their tongues? Remembering her one-time mistress, Grushenka had these girls suck off her cunt. The fat girl, who had been her antagonist, became her favorite for this sport. She had a long, crafty tongue and used to alternate rimming and tickling of the spot without being told to do so. But if one of the younger girls did not satisfy her, she beat her with a clear conscience. She used to say to herself, "Who had pity on me when I was in the same position?"

All this was erased by an event. The Count and Countess gave a great party. Grushenka supervised the serf girls in the handling of the dishes at the big buffet overflowing with food. Of a sudden there stood next to her—she had not seen him approaching—her Mihail. He was attired in gala uniform, smart from foot to head, young, alert, and in the best of moods. Grushenka only saw the bold blue eyes which had captivated her so many months ago. She stared at him as if here were a ghost and finally, understanding that he was really there before her, a guest of the party, she uttered a faint cry and turned abruptly to run away. He seized her and drew her toward him.

"Hello Mary!"—that was the name she had given him when he and his friend had picked her up on the road—"Hello, you mysterious lady. Don't run away. I have been looking for you everywhere. If you knew how often we discussed you, my friend Fladilow and I—he is still in Petersburg. We even made bets as to who you were. Now again I can't tell. You don't seem to be a guest, you're not wearing an evening gown, and you certainly are not a servant." Grushenka wore a modish but simple grey silk gown and no wig.

"Let me go, let me go!" Tears dimmed Grushenka's eyes and she was all in a flutter.

At this moment the Countess passed and Mihail called her to his assistance.

"I can tell you all about my little brave friend," said the Countess. "She is a fine girl and very sweet too, isn't she?"

"We are old friends," continued Mihail with a twinkle of the eye, "but she does not like me any more. See, she wants to run away."

"Please don't tell him anything," pleaded Grushenka with her mistress. "If—well, then, I'll tell him everything myself,"—and she sighed so pathetically that they both laughed.

"All right," consented Mihail, "that will be much more to my liking."

Grushenka took him by the hand and led him out of the room, away from the glamor of the thousand candles and the laughter and merriment of the aristocratic party. She seated him in a dark corner of one of the many pantries, and while the servants passed the room busy with their work, she poured a torrent of words out to him. She made herself as humble and miserable as possible. She told him that she was only a serf girl; that when he and Fladilow had picked her up, she was running away in the stolen clothes of her mistress, that she was a low, dirty creature not worthy even to speak with him.

When she was through, she burst into a stream of tears, embraced him and kissed him and clung hysterically to his neck, telling him that she had been liberated and was free now to go wherever she wanted and she would never separate from him again. Mihail understood only one thing of all this: that she loved him and had ceaselessly dreamed about him. She was very beautiful and in her tears she looked to him like a Venus. She felt that she pleased him and suddenly became normal again, quite reasonable in fact. She chided herself on being stupid, tidied herself up and smiled at him with great charm. He kissed her without passion, rather in a brotherly manner, and teasingly asked her whether she would sleep with him again. He promised her to be more polite hereafter, and not to snore. Saying he would see her again very soon, he went back to the feast.

The information he received from the good-hearted Countess was quite contrary to what Grushenka had told him. Of course the Countess knew nothing about Grushenka's past; in her good-heartedness and naiveté, she had not even a suspicion of Grushenka's previous adventures. She supposed the girl to be still a virgin, probably born of as fine parents as a free girl, but forced to sell herself into serfdom to ward off poverty. In liberating the old Prince, she had certainly shown great intelligence and courage, for if Serge had detected the plot, he would have tortured her to death. Jokingly she asked Mihail not to fall in love with Grushenka because she was no match for him. That they might start an affair did not even enter her mind.

But of course, that was exactly what happened—and how happy Grushenka was! Mihail, under the pretext of paying his respects to the Countess, had made good his promise and seen her again, and they had set a rendezvous. Grushenka slipped secretly out of the palace that evening and they took a long drive in his carriage. They had no intercourse that time, but loved each other like two good healthy young people. The next time, however, she went to his quarters, and they were passionately entwined on his bed before they themselves were aware of it. Grushenka, who felt heavenly thrills pass through her body when he only touched her hands, gave him her young body with all the passion and strength she was able to muster. They loved and fucked and kissed each other until complete exhaustion overcame them. Mihail became almost more enamoured of her than she was of him. In fact, she soon became indispensable to him. They kept their meetings very secret and so enjoyed their happiness the more.

Summer was approaching. Mihail, whose full name was Mihail Stieven, had to go to one of the family estates which he administered for his father. He did not want to part from Grushenka. Naturally he conceived a bold plan to take her away with him as his mistress. Thus one morning the Countess received a very well composed letter from Grushenka who thanked her for her kindness and advised her that she had left for an unknown destination. The night before, Grushenka had smuggled all her belongings out of the palace and had left in a carriage with young Baron Stieven. They enjoyed all the happiness of an elopement.

The honeymoon in the country was too wonderful for words—at least Grushenka thought so as she silently said a prayer. In order to give her standing, Mihail had introduced her as his young wife and Grushenka was the "beloved Baroness" and "little mother" of her entourage. He should not have done that, as it turned out later on, but for the present his "young wife" had a rosy time.

Grushenka, in her profound happiness, treated all the servants with great modesty and care. She was good to everyone, visited sick peasant women, brought food to their children, and the only quarrel she might have had with her beloved man was that he complained that she was too lenient and that she spoiled everyone.

She certainly spoiled him with her love. Nightly she encircled his muscular, firm body with her slender form. She gave herself to him without holding back anything, thrilling him to the core with the passion of her love. Not that she ever kissed his always excited love-shaft; much as she wanted to, she did not want him to know that she understood anything about that kind of love-making. Not that she had caressed his balls or had even taken his privates in her soft hand. No, as soon as they lay naked in bed together, she beneath him, his tool would find the entrance by itself. But then she would practice her art— moving her buttocks in subtle circles, prolonging moments by forcing him to keep still when she felt that he was too near the climax, stroking his back with her hands and kissing his face and head over and over again.

Sometimes when he was already in bed and waiting for her impatiently, she would tease him, hiding her pussy and her breasts with her hands, beguiling him by shaking her hips. When she came too near the bed, he would pull her in and it would take no time until she felt his beloved prick in her burning love-nest.

She learned to ride a horse, they drove around in his carriage, they took long walks, they discussed heaven and earth together. His admiration for her intelligence, quick wit and sound judgment grew steadily. He promised himself never to part from this girl, and she was immeasureably happy to feel the grip she had on him. They avoided visiting their neighbors lest the aristocratic landowners should be insulted with her presence. So perfectly did they seem made for each other that the future looked as bright as the present. They never discussed Grushenka's past life; Mihail did not want to know where she came from nor what she had done. She, on the contrary, wanted to know everything about him and he had to tell her his life from childhood on.

One day, after many kisses and goodbyes, Mihail left her to see a neighbor with whom he had to discuss grain prices and other things relating to the account he would have to make to his father about the affairs of the estate. He had been gone a few hours when the carriage returned with his coachman bringing her the message that she was to take the carriage and meet him at a certain place where he would ride on horseback. Grushenka had been sitting under a big chestnut tree in the garden, busy with some embroidery. She got into the carriage in her simple house dress without bothering to change or to take a hat. The destination named by the coachman was on the estate and not very far off. The coach drove with speed over the rough country ways. A few times the coachman turned his round, kind face back to her with a look in his eyes which she understood only afterwards.

After covering a few miles they met a huge traveling coach. The coachman stopped, so did the traveling coach. Two men stepped quickly out, jumped at Grushenka, bound and gagged her, threw her into the traveling coach, and went off with her.

Grushenka was in a daze. Her own coachman, who naturally should have defended his mistress, had not even looked around. There was no doubt about it, this was a plot. Her abductors had put a kerchief over her head and resistance was impossible. The coach drove on for miles and miles. When the carriage stopped she was forced to get out, made to go up some stairs, bound to a chair, and then the kerchief was removed from her face.

She sat in a well-furnished room, apparently a room of an expensive inn. Her abductors left immediately, and she heard them report in the next room that she was safely delivered. Two elderly gentlemen, well-dressed aristocrats, one with snow white hair, entered. They looked sternly at her, especially the older one, who scrutinized her with hard, unkind looks.

"So this is the vixen who has bewitched him," he broke the silence. "Well, we'll attend to her"—and such anger was in his tone that the other interfered.

"We won't make any headway that way," he said. "Leave her to me and everything will come out all right." Then he addressed Grushenka, who sat anxious and fearful. "Are you the wife of Baron Mihail Stieven? When and where did you marry him?"

"Who are you?" responded Grushenka. "What right

have you to ask me—and I am not his wife anyway." She added this because she felt fear.

"Not his wife?" began the man again. "Well, aren't you living with him?"

"I love him and he loves me and we can do what we want to, can't we?"

"Now look here, young woman, this is a matter of grave concern. This man is Mihail's father. Rumors have come to him that his son married secretly. Of course, he was interested in who his daughter-in-law was. Information came to us easily from the serfs of the estate. It's not Mihail's estate, remember, but his father's, and that is why the coachman abducted you today. We have also checked up on your past. That was not hard either. The Countess suspected that it was you who had eloped with Mihail. The girls told us that you had been bought through Mme. Laura, who in turn brought us in touch with Martha. She knew all about you. You are nothing but a run-away serf from the Sokolow estate. You've tricked the unsuspecting Mihail who is only a boy. He would not have lived with you as his wife if he had known that you were only a run-away serf whom we shall turn over to the police. Now confess when and where he married you and what priest performed the ceremony. We have means to make you speak," he added threateningly.

Grushenka felt her hands get numb. She straightened herself up as well as she could and answered with dignity. She had never deceived her beloved Mihail, she had never married him, not even thought of it. He himself had given her a lift when she had fled from Mme. Sophia. She loved him dearly and knew very well that he was much too aristocratic and good for her. She was willing to become

211

the serf of Mihail's father of her own free will, if only he would allow her to live near her lover.

Her words came unexpectedly to the elderly gentlemen. They seemed to be true and her arguments had weight. The two men had a lengthy discussion in French, which Grushenka did not understand. Mihail's father still seemed incensed, but the other man was more friendly. He proved this by cutting the strings with which she was tied without warning her not to run away. Finally Mihail's father spoke to her.

"I have other plans for my son and I will not allow you ever to see him again. That is final and he will acquiesce to it, because he does what I say. You can choose your own fate. If you are willing to make a sacrifice and stay away from him, I will take care of you. If not, I'll turn you over to the authorities, to Mihail's and your own ruin. For his mistress and bed-fellow will be whipped naked in a public place. She will be branded with an iron and sent to Siberia, as is becoming to a serf who deserts his rightful master. Take your choice."

Grushenka cried. She cried for her lover. The men left her alone and locked the door. When the friend of Mihail's father came back to persuade her, he found that she had made her resolution. Of course she could not spoil the future career of Mihail. She was willing to give him up and when she was told that she could not even say good-bye to him, she acquiesced to that also. She was allowed to write him a letter and she put into her awkward hand-writing all the love and good wishes she had in her heart, telling him at the end that he should obey his father. Whether he ever received this letter is a question.

The men had supper with her in her room. She was unable to eat, but she managed to sit with them and to speak a little. They looked at her now with other eyes; they found her beautiful and enticing and the friend of Mihail's father remarked that he was punishing his son severely by taking such a lovely companion from him. But the old man remained firm and announced what her fate would be.

She had to leave Russia immediately. Traveling clothes would be provided for her, also her passport, and trusted servants would accompany her to the frontier. The Baron advised her to open a hairdressing salon or a gownshop with the ample money he would give her. Also that if she ever tried to get in touch with his son again, he would see to it that she'd die under the knout.

This was spoken by a man who had the power to do what he said and whose vengence would surely follow her if she broke faith. Grushenka understood this only too well. Fate had taken happiness from her. She had been born a serf; the mighty decided her fate and her tears were not a weapon with which to fight against their will.

CHAPTER XIV.

Grushenka's trip through Europe is a history in itself, and cannot be retold here. She was young and beautiful, but sad. She had an abundant amount of money, or so at least it seemed to herself. She gave the impression of one of those travelling Russians so well known at that time for their unlimited orgies. Instead of settling down somewhere, she moved restlessly on until she came to Rome. This city impressed her greatly with its splendor and gaiety. With the Russian ability for languages she learned to speak Italian easily. She mixed with all kinds of company; with artists and students; with kept women, and now and then even with society.

After she had gotten over the blow which had struck her she plunged into countless love-intrigues. But she was always dissatisfied with the men or women with whom she went to bed, because her Russian strength and vigor surpassed the ability and appetites of her bedfellows. She indulged in utter sentimentality or brutal orgies. More than once she came into conflict with the police when she had aroused the neighborhood in a drunken frenzy or beaten up her maids in true Russian style.

The whip was at that time in use all over the civilized world, but the Italian girls who now served her had a finer constitution than the Russian farmer-girls, and often fainted under her reckless tortures. Her good rubles, however, got her out of every scrape and "the wild Russian girl" was soon a familiar figure in the by-ways of old Rome.

Drinking and gambling and whoring soon exhausted her purse. She took the ancient way out taken by all Eves; became a kept woman, ruining her lovers in a short time with her recklessness. Working for a procurer who catered to strangers of the upper class, she again came into conflict with the authorities. As a result she fled to Nuremberg, which at that time had a flourishing Italian colony. But there she could find neither the customers nor the money which she had been accustomed to in Rome. She therefore married a humble German master-baker, but ran away from him without a divorce when his prick became exhausted after the honeymoon.

Meanwhile her longing to return to Russia had never ceased, and now—she was twenty-seven years of age—she made up her mind to go back. Her affair with Mihail, whom she still carried in her heart, would certainly be forgotten by both him and his father. She resolved to open up a modiste shop in Moscow—one like Mme. Laura had. She was adventuress enough now not to care where the money came from to start such an enterprise. Thus she stole what she could from her German husband, fitted herself out with an elegant traveling dress and, made up as a woman of the world, soon crossed the Russian border. To give herself a good front she carried many a big trunk, although they were filled only with stones. When she reached the gates of Moscow in a public stage coach, she got out and kissed the walls of the huge gateway. So happy was she to be back home.

CHAPTER XV.

The fat little innkeeper indulged in many bows as he showed Grushenka to his "best room." With many delicious phrases he praised Madame's beauty, admired her new Western travelling dress, humbled himself at the honor to be host to such a great lady. But his chatter was intermingled with hidden questions as to the private business of his new guest. Who were her family and relatives in the city, what was her status or occupation? The superficial answers he received were not to his liking. His curiosity had its origin in no personal dislike, nor did it come from anxiety as to whether he would be able to collect his bills. It originated in a very severe ukase of the police to have an eye on lonely women and to report them at once to the authorities. This ukase had been created by pressure of the church in one of the clean-up actions which periodically befall all moral institutions.

Grushenka of course knew nothing about this. As she took her first stroll through Moscow's elegant streets and earned many appraising glances from the promenading gentlemen, she had every hope for a good harvest. At the same time friend innkeeper sneaked into her room and inspected her belongings with knowing eyes. A locksmith soon notified him as to the contents of her trunks, and he crossed himself with a sigh. She seemed a nice lady all right but he did not care to go to Siberia for her sake. Harboring an adventuress? No sir, better advise the police. This he did early the next morning.

Two big dirty policemen broke into Grushenka's room, while she was still soundly asleep. They did not listen to her protests, made her dress hurriedly, and not even allowing her to make up with care, drove her to the prison. A matron six feet tall and tough as the devil, suggested that Madame take her "nice clean dress" off before she went to the dirty cell. She grabbed her garments with undue haste and slammed the door. There sat Grushenka in the half-dark cubicle, listening to the shuffle of feet in the busy corridors and the occasional yelling and crying of protesting women. What was its meaning, why did they lock her up? What had she done? She shivered in her bodice and petticoats and her unkempt hair fell down over her nude shoulders.

After hours of waiting two beadles called for her and led her before the district captain. He was a short man, with a round face and small piercing eyes, impatient to get through with his duties. He hardly looked at her passport and asked what the charge was. "She's a whore," said one of the constables, "that's all." Grushenka had not expected that. She had no story ready to answer this charge and being at a loss for an answer she sputtered out a lot of words to deny the accusation. The sharp question of the captain as to how she was living received the answer, "on my money." But she could not prove that she had any. When she said that she had just returned from foreign countries his suspicion arose even more.

"Maybe there is more about her than whoring," he said. "Maybe she is a spy or a member of one of those secret societies who wants to throw over our beloved Czar. Anyway, make her talk. Put her on the horse. She'll tell us all about it in an hour."

The policemen dragged her away in spite of her shrieks and protests. They took her back to the prison and into the torture chamber. They beat and kicked her viciously. She found it better not to fight them and to keep still. "That's better," remarked one of them. "Behave like a lamb and we will not bite you like wolves"—a joke which both of them greatly enjoyed. But they took no chances with her. They took her bodice off, removed her stays, tore the ribbon from her petticoat, which fell down by itself, and roughly removed her long trousers. They then tied her arms to her back with a strong cord. After that they took it easy and looked her over.

Grushenka's figure had changed greatly during her stay in Western Europe. Her fine, gracious form had filled out; she was plump and firm. Her bust, now moved sharply forward because her arms were forced back, was still of a marvelous firmness. The breasts stuck out without drooping, the waist-line was full and plump, the Venus Hill seemed enlarged and was covered with thick black hair, the legs were rather fat and soft. The most remarkable change, however, was in Grushenka's bottom. This used to be boyish but was now plump, full and womanly, and swung out from underneath the hips in two blooming buttocks. A woman in her prime stood between the two constables, her long black hair floating down over her shoulders, her blue eyes anxiously looking from one to the other and her full mouth imploring them to spare her. One of them, in a matter of fact way, took her full breasts and fondled them; she could not protect herself from his dirty hands with her arms painfully bound to her back.

"I think I am going to fuck her before we mount her up," said he. "She is the fairest of today's newcomers anyway."

"Go ahead," recommended the other one. "Later on I'll take the small blond in cell nine. I like the way she screams when I get her between me and her cot."

"We can't dispute that," was the answer. "You like the young ones when they haven't got hair yet around the hole. I prefer the plump ones, like this"—and he slapped Grushenka between the legs over her wooly spot.

"I'll do anything you want," wailed Grushenka. "Everything! But please don't hurt me, I can't stand it."

"We'll see to that later on," replied the constable. "Turn around now and bend over."

She did as she was told. The other man, to help his comrade, went in front of her, took hold of her head, put it between his legs and closed his thighs, at the same time holding her up by the hips. The first constable had taken his big shaft out of his trousers. He grasped her big buttocks by their soft, thick flesh and moved them apart. He had no difficulty sticking his big prick into her love-nest. The entrance, once so small, was now wide open. Her cunt was juicy but the air of mystery was no more around it. Too many visitors had found pleasure in it and Grushenka's own passionate nature had helped to enlarge it. The constable took his time; there was nothing specially exciting in fucking a prisoner, especially one who was apparently a whore, and the men chatted while he worked away on her.

"Pretty big mouse trap," said the one holding her between his legs. "I hope you don't get drowned in it."

"Better than a crack in the door anyway," muttered the pushing man.

"Dust every nook and corner of it, will you, so that she'll remember you for a long time."

"She'll do that anyway. There are no pricks where she is bound for." Meaning the detention house where whores were sent.

"At least if you give her a brat they won't hang her," —referring to the ancient law that a pregnant woman could not be executed.

While these and other remarks were heard in the room, Grushenka had her head buried between the high boots of the constable. The smell of grease and leather penetrated her nostrils. The dirt rubbed against her cheeks, and in her bent position the blood ran into her head. This was the first poke she received on Russian soil.

How different she had expected it to be; Perhaps as the mistress of an aristocrat in a bed with silk sheets, or perhaps taking a young strong Russian into her own bed to be in the arms of a countryman again! Meanwhile one constable kneaded her full waist-line while the other one clamped his hands in the upper part of her thighs and fucked her with might. She remembered of a sudden that she needed the good graces of these men and she began to counter his pushes, to wiggle her ass with apt swinging and to embrace his love-shaft tightly. Just as she started, he came. She clasped her hands bound on her back, she tried to glue her pussy to his prick. But he took his instrument out in a matter-of-fact way.

Both men agreed she had a fine, softly upholstered bottom, better for the leather whip than for the knout.

They slapped her soundly and let go of her. She straightened herself slowly, her face crimson and soiled with black from the boots. She implored them again not to hurt her. The men did not listen. Orders were orders. They had to put her on the horse.

The horse was one of the oldest of torture instruments. Invented in oriental countries, it had been taken over by the Inquisition and thus spread all over Europe, it being one of the least expensive but most effective machines to be used on female captives. It consisted simply of a board nailed between four high legs in such a way that the narrow edge of the board was uppermost. The constables made her move towards it, forced her to step onto a little footstool and to swing one leg over the board into a sitting position. While one man held her from behind around the waist, the other one chained her feet together and put a weight on the chain. She sat now with her cleft over the sharp wood, the iron weight drawing the weight of her own body down. Placed as she was, she sat on her pussy and on her ass hole, which were the lowest spots on her body, and the sharp narrow edge of the lumber cut into her most sensitive parts. In addition, her jailors fastened a rope which hung from the ceiling through the cords which held her arms to her back. This made it impossible for her to throw herself forward or backward and thus relieve the pain of the pressure. Having arranged things properly, the men strolled out of the room, slamming the door without listening to her pleas that she would tell them all.

The first few moments it hurt her terribly, but she felt she could stand the pain. Then, of a sudden, a roaring pain shot through her loins and she began to scream in agony. She closed and opened her eyes, which rolled wildly. She cramped her hands together, piercing the nails into the palms. She tried to find another position which would take the weight from her tortured pussy. In vain. The weight on her feet and the rope at her back did not allow a change of position, and the more she moved the deeper the edge of the board intruded into her unprotected cleft.

She did not know how long she had been sitting in this cleaving, terrible position. Her screams became howls, the howling diminished to faint sobs. She was ready to lose consciousness, but the excruciating pain would not permit it. The police captain entered and, disregarding her sobbing pleas, took up a leather whip. The blows fell over her thighs, over her belly, over her breasts. They provided a climax of suffering; as the whip cut into her flesh, she jerked her body, thus adding to the horrible pains in her cunt. Yes, she was ready to tell everything—the truth, nothing but the truth.

The captain took the weight off her legs without removing the shackles, and tossed the footstool under her feet. She got onto it and stood with her sore spot only a few inches away from the terrible board; a push against the footstool would have brought her back to her former position. She told all; her whole life story.

The fat little police captain sat on a whipping block and listened. He scratched his head. This was a complicated case. He understood from her story that she was a liberated and free person all right, but on the other hand a runaway slave from the Sokolow estate. To whom did she belong now? To the Sokolows, to Mme. Sophia, or was the later liberation in force and was she to be considered a free person? He would not make a hasty decision on so complicated a question. In any event, for the present she belonged to the State, or better, to himself. Hence he would hold her until some enlightenment should come to him.

He left her standing over the board and went out. After a while, the huge prison matron came in. She took off Grushenka's chains and dragged her back to her semi-dark cell. The woman refused to give her back her finely made undergarments and left her entirely nude. Grushenka's protests were mild; while the pain had somewhat subsided, she felt so weak and sore that she could hardly walk.

Days went by in her dirty cell. The uncertainty of her fate weighed heavily on her, the noise and the screams throughout the busy prison got on her nerves, and the filth crept into her skin. One day the matron dragged her out, gave her a quick cleaning all over, dressed her in an old prison garb and turned her over to a waiting constable. He led her over many hallways and stairs, finally pushing her into the private room of the police captain. She paused, surprised, on the threshold. On the big table in the middle of the room sat a young whore. She was not older than eighteen, but one could see that she had been through much and was tough as leather. She was in her underwear and was engaged in a squabble with the undersized head of the almighty police department. He had no shirt on but was still in his trousers and made a ludicrous impression. Apparently he was as much pleased as annoyed with the impudence of the little creature who treated him like the dirt on her shoe.

"Hey you," she addressed Grushenka, "can you imagine that this big brute here claims that he is too good to kiss my pussy, my sweet little pussy mind you"—and she opened the slit of her trousers and brazenly held her hole open with both hands. "I told him I wouldn't give him a thing unless it was thoroughly licked all over. He sent for you and claims that you ought to understand that job, at least if you don't lie to him—"

"All right," grumbled the fat full moon, slightly annoyed, "give her a Frenching. Perhaps that will make her keep still, brazen hussy that she is. But don't suck her until she comes or I'll beat hell out of both of you. I don't want to fuck a corpse."

Grushenka stepped up and got busy on the vixen. Here was an opportunity to get her own fate decided; better make herself agreeable. She had learned to love to lick a cunt. Down in Italy she had often enticed young girls to come to her apartment, and she had gotten a thrill out of making them wiggle and scream under her tongue treatment. Often her maids had to hold them by force when they wouldn't give in. But she disliked this little whore and she could find no pleasure in sucking off her stinking hole, which, in spite of her youth seemed to be well fucked out. She stooped down and opened her up in order to give herself a comfortable working position. The impudent street-trotter rested her body on the table and sent a triumphant look at the sturdy lover who fumbled about the room, and Grushenka's tongue began the operation.

This tongue had become broad and alert and knew its tricks from A to Z. The pussy, feeling that a master was at work, at once became intensely interested. The blonde creature had started this whole comedy only to tease her lover, but she discovered that—to her own surprise—a treat was in store for her and she decided to allow herself to come to a climax. Grushenka felt how her clitoris, having swollen to hardness, suddenly fell together again. But she kept on licking so as not to have the police captain know that his love-partner was doing what he had forbidden: giving herself out before he put it in.

"Enough of this nonsense," he interrupted Grushenka, and pushed her away. "I'll give it to her now, whether she likes it or not." With that, he shoved his short stub into the wet love-channel. Grushenka turned around, found a washbasin and cleaned her face. Then, looking at the couple, she decided she would not leave the room before she had cleared her own state of affairs with the captain. She saw him bent over the girl, his trousers around his ankles on the floor, his muscular buttocks busy with crafty pushes. An idea came to her. Swiftly she knelt down behind him, opened up his rim and glued her mouth to his back-hole. This had never been done to him. Surprised, he stopped his movements, and standing in front of his sweetheart, gave himself to this enjoyment. The girl, not knowing what was going on, called to him.

"Hey you, what's the matter? Getting lazy? Fuck me, you bastard! Fuck your sweet pussy!" And she heaved her bottom to get him working again.

He pulled the hair over her cunt roughly and his tone was so imperative that she listened in wonder. "Hold still, you swine, and don't move, or I'll beat hell out of you—"

Grushenka caressed his balls with her fingers, tickled his dark hole with her tongue, and then inserted it. His legs trembled, he crushed himself against the young whore's thighs, groaned, and spent rapturously. Getting up to dress, the whore still wondered what had happened, but she guessed the connection when she saw Grushenka cleaning her lips with a wet towel, while her captain gave his testicles some gushes in the washstand. Grushenka found time now to plead her case with him. He kept thinking about it as a ticklish case. He told her to send the matron to him and with this decision, which meant nothing to her, she was led back to her cell by the waiting constable.

That evening the matron brought her his wise decision: as she did not belong to any private person at present, and apparently was not a free girl on the other hand, she belonged from now on to the State and was made herewith assistant to the matron. The deep thought of it was, of course, that he wanted her for his future pleasure and did not want her to die in that filthy cell.

The matron was very dissatisfied with this turn of affairs. She was, as Grushenka would soon find out, greedy to a horrible degree, and she was afraid that Grushenka might be an impediment to her doings. But she had to obey; had to give her some clothes, a living room next to her own, and had to put her to all kinds of tasks. Grushenka found herself busy preparing food—mostly a thin soup of nondescript contents—supervising the prisoners as they cleaned up their cells, and helping around in general

Grushenka soon learned that there existed in the mind of the matron four classes of prisoners. First, those who had outside influence and were to be released soon and were not to be bothered. Secondly, those who had money and could get more from the outside. They were maltreated, but just enough to get more and more out of them. Thirdly, those who had money but did not want to part with it. They were mercilessly tortured. Finally, there were those who had no money or influence and were just left to rot away. She made no distinction in the age or state of health of the women she had under her thumb. She did not care at all whether they were criminals, thieves, whores, or poisoners, or whether they were innocent or picked up by mistake or on false and malicious accusations. They were only objects from whom to extort money, and she put the screws on them mercilessly.

As soon as they were delivered to her ward, she would take all clothes away from them and all money, jewelry, and other valuables. If it was an elderly whore or a woman who had been in the jail before, she would not hesitate to search even their cunts for hidden treasure. Then she would have them send messages through one of the constables to their outside friends demanding cash. If the money was forthcoming, the prisoner received a few days respite in the form of food and clothes and fresh air, the constable received a good tip, and the matron added more booty to her store. But woe if the message was unsuccessful! She would then give the unlucky one torture and Grushenka more than once had to assist her.

The torture chamber was there to extort confessions, as it was up to the middle of the 19th century in all countries of the world—although torture was officially abolished in most countries at the end of the 18th century. The matron, however, used the tortures to get her prey to come through. Furthermore, she did the job herself, and seemed delighted with it.

There was, for example, a big blonde woman about thirty years of age and apparently of means, judging from her wardrobe. She was brought in on a charge of shoplifting, but it was patently a trumped-up charge because she was not brought before the captain for sentence. There was something mysterious about this woman. She refused to communicate with the outer world at all, and this was usually the one and only thought of other captives. She sat in her cell in dirty rags and moped without uttering a word. The matron dragged her to the black chamber, tore the rags from her body, and stretched her over the whipping block. The woman had a full, nice behind, a very light skin and shapely legs which instantly became the field of operation for her huge tormentor. Grushenka, who was supposed to help the matron, just stood around. The old and hardened jailer had not needed any help to tie her victim down, her strong muscular arms and her expertness in fastening the one strap over the middle of the victim's back, did not call for assistance.

"First I'll beat the shit out of you," she shouted at the blonde woman, "then we'll have a little chat."

She made her word good. She began over the knees and hit the tightly stretched legs with all her strength with a switching cane. She went up one leg until she reached the cleft, beat the other leg the same way, and then let out all her rage over the buttocks. The woman was not muscular; she was of the finer type, well made and of soft flesh. She screamed in pain and swung her arms wildly, but was unable to shield her suffering backside with her hands. Blood-blue welts appeared on her body. She wailed and promised to do everything. The huge matron stopped, but she dug her muscular fingers into the smarting behind.

"Will you write a letter to a friend or to your family asking for one hundred rubles to be given to the bearer?" Of course the woman consented.

She was led back to her cell and given time to sob to her heart's content, until Grushenka brought her a quill, ink and paper. The letter was duly sent away with a constable, but he came back saying that at that address there was no one of the name written on the letter. The matron got into a white heat. She did not say or do a thing that day. The next morning when she was through with her routine work, she again took matters into her brutal hands. This time Grushenka had to help carry the woman to the black chamber. She fought like a tigress and swore that the matron would be sorry, that she'd be beaten to death herself when she, the prisoner, should be set free.

Neither threats nor fighting helped her. The matron bound her hands to her back and pulled her up on a rope which was fastened to her wrists. This dislocated the shoulders, and the weight of the body, hanging on the twisted muscles of the arm, caused unbearable pain. The woman screamed that they were murdering her. Grushenka, who herself was no longer soft hearted, felt pity. But the matron did not seem to hear nor to have the slightest compassion. She tied the woman's ankles in a far-outstretched position to some rings in the floor, thus bringing still greater pain to the shoulders.

Grushenka looked at the hanging figure. The twitching face was not beautiful, but still had good-looking features. The breasts, too large and too full, drooped, but the belly was flat and without fat. The best parts were, without doubt, the firm, shapely thighs. Grushenka could not help stepping close up to the woman and studying her, even feeling the cunt which was wide open, due to the out-stretched position of the legs. It was a cunt and not a pussy all right, which means that the hole was large as to entrance and sheath. The woman was strung up so high that the vulva was exactly at the height of Grushenka's mouth, and she could not help making a sarcastic remark. While fumbling around with her fingers, she said to the matron, "I guess she has opened her legs so wide for a sucking, don't you think so?" But the matron, who had meanwhile carefully looked for a knout, pushed her rudely away.

"You'll see what I'll give her, and as you call my attention to her spot, it's a good suggestion. I'll let her have it there."

The knout, a short wooden handle to which were fastened eight or ten short leather straps, began its work. Standing alongside and at an angle to her victim, the matron began slowly and with precision to beat her. She directed the end of the leather straps at the cunt and at the surrounding flesh on the inside of the thighs. She did not count the strokes, she did not hurry. She took good aim, swung her arm out and—swish—the blow crashed into the most tender parts of the hysterical, screaming woman. Not so many blows, only ten or twelve, because suddenly the woman became pale and her head dropped down. She had fainted.

The matron released her leisurely, slung her over her shoulder as if she were a bundle of clothes, and threw her roughly on the cot in her cell. When weeping was heard from that cell, the matron looked after the prisoner again. The woman consented to write another letter, but the outcome was far from what the matron had expected. The constable stayed unusually long and when he came back there was a distinguished-looking man with him who had a release for the prisoner. He swore by heaven and hell that he would get even with the matron when he saw the state the woman was in, and left with her in a hurry. The matron only shrugged a shoulder. Let them complain. Nothing would come of it, even if the Czar was their cousin—and she was right.

Punishments were not usually so cruel, unless the object was to make a prisoner speak. Very often, however, the captain, sitting as judge and gaoler at the same time, ordered a beating on general principles when a woman had to stay in prison only a few days for a minor offense. These minor offenders were not sent to the State prison nor brought before a jury, but did their time, mostly less than a week in the police prison. Such cases were handled similarly to the following, which was entrusted to Grushenka.

Two young whores, hardly sixteen years of age, had been picked up soliciting in the streets. Women were permitted to do that, but only during certain hours of the

evening and on certain avenues. Perhaps these girls, who
were friends, had sought to make a better haul in the
lighter main-streets; anyway, they had become the prey of
the law and were each sentenced to five days in jail. As an
added punishment, they had to sit every morning for one
hour in the stocks and to receive twelve strokes with the
switch.

The girls had no money and were turned over by the
matron to Grushenka. At first they cried bitterly, but having a cell together, they began to make plans for the future
almost before they had started to do their time. They were
more curious than afraid when Grushenka led them to the
black chamber. They took their clothes off meekly and
climbed by themselves into the stocks. Grushenka used
only the hand and foot stocks on them, not the head
stocks, and she saw to it that the boards did not crush their
skin. They sat next to each other on the floor, hands and
feet close together through the boards. They did not seem
to mind that their bare behinds rested on the hard stone
floor. They were good-looking girls, joking with each
other and teasing each other that their lean asses had to
carry their whole weight. They had small, round breasts
and there was something young and fresh about them.

Grushenka, who for a long time had not had a good
party for her pussy, got slightly hot. She bent down and
teased the girls' nipples and was curious about their pussies.
But they pressed their thighs close together and said, "No,
Madame, it costs fifty copeckas to make us open up;
that's our price." Grushenka suggested that they suck her
pussy a little; they claimed that they did that to each other
and could not be untrue to each other. But if she would
promise not to give them the switch—. Grushenka said she
would have to beat them a little in order to make some

marks lest the matron should interfere, and they agreed on that.

Grushenka let them out of the stocks, sat herself on the whipping block, and had one girl kissing her pussy while she got hold of the other one. Kissing her with rising passion on the mouth, she licked her teeth and tongue, and began to feel her up. Moving her hands down to the girl's behind, Grushenka first fingered the pussy a little. This the girl did not mind. Then with passion she began to feel around the little dirt-hole. But to this the girl did not agree. She moved her behind out of reach of Grushenka's hands, which so much more wanted to feel the perversely erotic little spot. Grushenka, however, spent before she succeeded. But she kept it in mind.

She had the girls hold each other in turn over the other's back and laid some six strokes over each behind, just stinging the skin a little. When she was through the girls laughed and protested that they could stand more than that.

The next morning Grushenka used the head-stocks on them. In these the prisoner stood erect and had to put his head and his hands through openings, which were closed by boards laid on top of them. Having secured them that way, Grushenka went leisurely around the stocks and began to pinch and fondle their naked bodies. Finally she shoved a finger of her left hand into the pussy of one of the girls and took possession of her back-hole with the index finger of her right hand. The girl kicked and shouted and moved around uneasily, but was, of course, unable to avoid this treatment.

"You must get used to it someday," smiled Grushenka. "You will soon enough feel bigger things than that move in and out—some men like it only that way." And she gave the girl a long finger-fucking while she thought of the many Italian men, handsome too, who had taught her to come with the same ease whether the prick was in the front or in the back entrance. But the girl disliked the rubbing finger thoroughly and protested that she never, never would stand for that. When Grushenka applied the same playful method to the other girl she had a surprise. This girl was seemingly satisfied with it.

"You see," explained the girl, "it is this way. Next to my father's store there was a cobbler, who was the first man to make love to me. At first I had only to take his shaft in my hands, but then he wanted better things. He was afraid to make me pregnant. I was only fifteen then, mind you, and he did not dare to put his machine into the right place. So he fucked me in the back. That was the first time I ever had a prick in me. I screamed a bit, not too much because I was afraid of detection, and then got used to it. So rub me there a bit, I don't mind—" which of course made Grushenka desist from doing so.

While this and other things went on, the captain made use of Grushenka for his purposes quite often. Any time his impudent sweetheart came to see him, he had Grushenka go down on his back. But he did not allow her to suck off the little whore again, and she in turn was angry at Grushenka's presence. A few weeks passed by, until one day she openly rebelled and refused to let him have her as long as Grushenka was around. He swore at her and beat her, but she answered with not less flowery words and hit back. All the while his prick stood at attention.

Grushenka, seeing the row, had an inspiration. Tearing her clothes off, she got a sudden hold of the captain, encircled him in her arms, and threw him and herself to the carpet. Before the astonished man knew what it was all about, she had her thighs around him, his prick in her

pussy, and she was fucking him with the circling movements of her hips. He was really worked up and soon
answered her thrusts. An amazing encounter started. The
girl, first believing Grushenka was going to help her, then
suddenly realizing that she was fucking her own lover
before her eyes, got enraged and tried to pull the two away
from each other. She rolled them over the carpet, kicked
and pushed them, tore at their limbs, pinched their backs
and kicked them in the behinds. But they were so hotly
involved that they continued fucking in the face of this
bodily aggression—were even stimulated by it. They groaned
in the climax. It was a magnificent experience.

The captain got up first, while Grushenka lay with
closed eyes, exhausted on the floor. The captain was now
really furious with his former bed-fellow. He let her have
it in words and blows, and threw her out, never to come
back. Grushenka got up slowly, softly embraced the man,
whose rage was just ebbing away, and kissed him tenderly
on both cheeks. The fat little captain, who had not been
kissed in this way in years, and who had just detected what
a rare poke Grushenka was, softened to a degree which
was unusual with him.

"No use," he muttered, "to have you out in the ward
all the time. I'll tell you what we'll do. You become my
housekeeper from now on."

He lived in comfortable quarters in a wing of the prison,
and Grushenka moved in. She was more like a dutiful wife
than a housekeeper and lover. She cleaned and cooked for
him, made his private life comfortable, satisfied his sexual
desires with prudence, never overworking him, and saw to
it that he always wanted her. He in turn treated her quite
like a human being. He took her out with him in his
carriage, introduced her to his friends, never beat her, and

was satisfied to be henpecked. Months went by and Grushenka was undecided whether she should make him marry her. Why not? He had plenty of money and a position of a kind, and she would have a certain security. But finally she abandoned this idea.

CHAPTER XVI.

The reason Grushenka did not want to be coupled for her lifetime with the captain of the police was, no doubt, inspired by her physical aversion against him. He was round and fat, his arms, backside, legs; everything about him was stupidly rounded and unpleasantly self-satisfied. He was not a good lover and when, once or twice a week, he put his short and stubby shaft into her sheath and gave himself a good rubbing in her, without considering her desires, he felt well pleased with himself. He snored in bed, he did not believe in keeping himself clean, and he spit in the room as one might have done in a pig-stye. He exercised his duties brutally, and his means to justice was the whip. Even his jokes were vile, so why stay with him?

In order to break away, Grushenka needed money and she had none. The captain, however, had plenty. In the evening his pockets were always bulging with gold and silver; yet he left in the morning without a cent. The bribes he received were enormous. But what did he do with his money? Grushenka found out quickly enough. He had a big iron cash-box, standing on the floor, about three feet high and five long. There was no lock on this box but it would not open for Grushenka. She watched him and saw him move a little handle on the back of it. The next morning she lifted the lid and was amazed. The box was filled almost to the top with thousands of coins; gold, silver and copper. He had thrown them in carelessly, as they came his way.

Grushenka did some thinking. She then proceeded to rifle his pile of wealth systematically. Every day, while he was away, she helped herself to a few hundred rubles in gold. Of these she changed one or two pieces into silver and coppers and threw them back into the box so as not to leave any holes. The rest she kept. Soon she had accumulated many thousand rubles, without the pile of coins having become smaller. She transferred her treasure one fine day to a banker—it was enough for a good start.

All that was now left was to get away from the man. This she accomplished through weeks of careful manipulation. First she became apparently moody and sickly and wailed about her failing health. Then she refused to have him when she felt that way. Of course he would not stand for that, but mounted her against her protests. While he worked away on her, she would start a conversation with him, annoying him all the time by talk. She would ask him to come quickly or, out of a blue sky—when he was ready to come—would ask him what he wanted for dinner the next day.

Of course he in turn did not treat her too kindly. Often he would give her a sound slap, providing her with a good excuse for sulking. Once or twice he turned her over and spanked her bare behind with his hands. She stood it because she knew he would soon want her to leave him.

He began to fuck his prisoners again, as he had been in the habit of doing when he had no whore who enticed him. She would hear, of course, that he was untrue to her, and would make scenes about it.

Simultaneously she spoke with him about the disorderly houses in Moscow, how excellent that business was, and how little the bribes were that he collected from them. Soon she approached him directly as to whether it would not be a good idea for him to run a whore-house himself, give it his whole protection, close all the other ones and— put her in charge of it. He would not listen to it, because he was not interested in money after all. But when she painted, in the brightest colors, how he would be master of it, how she would always provide him with very young girls who would put on great parties for him, he succumbed to her wiles and told her to go ahead and do what she liked. But she was to understand that he had no money whatsoever and that she would have to put the house on its feet by herself. She almost loved him for that and got busy at once.

Grushenka acquired a house in the best neighborhood, where without the captain's protection, nobody would have dared to open an establishment of this kind. The house, surrounded by a small garden in the front and by a large one in the back, consisted of three floors. The upper floors contained about a dozen rooms each, while the groundfloor had a magnificent dining room and four or five very spacious drawing rooms, all leading to a big front hall. Grushenka modelled the whole mansion after the layout of the best whore-house in Rome, which she had visited quite often to get her pussy kissed.

She resolved that it would be best for her to employ only serf girls, who she could train for her purposes without having to consider their wishes. She prepared all this without the captain's knowledge. And she had to make more loots on his cash-box, because she furnished her establishment with the best. There were a colorful carriage and four horses, a few stable men, an old housekeeper, and six sturdy peasant maids, lovely furniture, and of course, a well-selected choice of four-poster beds with canopies and silk sheets. All this assembled, she left the captain, settled down in the big house and began leisurely to buy her girls.

We see her now, going in her own carriage, to all parts of Moscow, looking over features and shapes the way Katerina had done about ten years before, in order to buy her for Nelidowa. But she had it easier than Katerina because she did not have to look for any special type of girl; she needed girls of all types and shapes to satisfy the taste of her prospective customers. The hunger in the poor sections of Moscow was responsible for her best finds. Not only foster-parents, but also parents, would flock to her with their daughters. The girls, on their part, were delighted to enter the services of so fine and elegant a lady, where they would be safe from starvation.

Grushenka would send word through her housekeeper to one of the poorer streets that she was willing to buy a few young girls, between fifteen and twenty years of age, for her private service. She would be told where, for example, in the backroom of a certain inn, she could look over the merchandise. When her elegant carriage rolled into the street, there would be great excitement, the mothers flocking around her, kissing the hem of her garments and imploring her to take their daughters. After the near-riot of her arrival was over, Grushenka would be led into a large room, filled with twenty to thirty girls, all in rags, dirty and smelly. The chatter and shouting of the parents, anxious to sell, would make it impossible for her to select at ease. The first few times she was so helpless against all this, that she left without making an attempt to look the girls over. Throwing alms on the ground for which the mob scrambled gave her the opportunity to leave quickly. But then she found a better way; she removed all the parents from the room, resolutely locked the door from the inside, and went about her task in a business-like way.

The girls had to throw off their rags. Those she disliked she sent from the room, keeping the three or four who seemed likely. She submitted these to the most rigorous examination. Long hair, beautiful features, perfect teeth, well-formed bust, and small juicy cunts were not the only requirements. She wanted girls who showed vitality and strong resistance. She took them over her lap, she had them open up, she played with the tickler and watched the reaction. She pinched them with sharp nails on the inside of the thighs, and when they showed any softness she gave them a couple of coins and sent them away. For those she selected, she made a hard bargain, clothed them in garments she had brought for that purpose, and took them right away with her.

After a meal and bath in her mansion, she administered the first whipping herself. She took this very seriously. It was a further try-out as to whether the girl was to make good. She did not take them down to the black-chamber, which she had found in the house when she had bought it from an aristocrat. Nor did she tie them. She put them on the elegant bed which would be theirs for the love-business later on, and under the threat of sending them back, made them expose those parts of their bodies she wanted to hurt with the whip.

All of the girls had been beaten before, but they had mostly received rough blows and kicks and few of them had been submitted to a skillful whipping by the leather whip. After laying stinging blows on their buttocks and between their thighs, she would make them get up, stand erect, and order them to hold their breasts from underneath ready to receive punishment. Those who complied were not touched at all, but these who were not ready to follow this order, would feel the whip again and again on their backs, until complete submission was affected. Grushenka had lost her softness; she had forgotten the fear and terror of her own youth. And this made her a success.

When she had collected in this way about fifteen girls, she began careful instructions on how to keep the body clean, the nails in perfect shape, how to smile and to walk, how to eat and to talk. She succeeded quickly, especially because she had the most magnificent clothes made for her charges, and fine clothes inspire every woman to refined behavior. Satisfied with this she also gave them special and delicate instructions in how to handle and satisfy the men, instructions which, if repeated here, would make a whole chapter by itself. She spoke to attentive but bewildered girls. They heard the words but did not get the meaning in full, for it turned out that one-third of her fifteen girls were still virgins. If they had been fucked previously at all, they had just lain still when the rough men of their sections were working in their pussies. They did not understand yet how there can be a great difference between an expert courtesan and a peasant girl who just holds her legs open. They should know better soon.

When Grushenka felt she was ready, she held the great and boisterous opening of her establishment. According to the custom of her time, she had an invitation printed which was quite a document, prettily lithographed and adorned with vignettes displaying love scenes. Here you could read that the famous Madame Grushenka Pawlowks, just returned from an extensive tour over Europe in search of new and never-dreamed-of sex excitements, was inviting the Honorable Dukes, Counts and Barons for the great opening of her establishment. Here the customer, from the moment that he passed the threshold, would be drowned in an ocean of pleasure. etc . . . etc . . . followed by the most startling announcement, namely, that for the opening gala banquet, no charge would be made! On this night, every one of the famous beauties would satisfy every whim free of charge, and a free lottery would be played, the prizes being five virgins to be raped by the winners!

Here—according to the style of the time—a special specification was also made, that the winners could deflower their prizes either in private chambers or "in state". It must be known that most marriages of that time started with deflowering "in state", which means that the bridegroom put his prick into the little pussy in the presence of all the near relatives, often all the wedding guests, in order to give a proof by witness that the marriage had been consummated. This habit flourished in the families of reigning houses of Russia right through the better part of the 19th century.

The opening part turned out to be a riotous bacchanal. It lasted not only one day and one night, but more than three days and nights, until it was finally disbanded by the discreet and quiet interference of the police. Grushenka received the guests in a gorgeous gown, very audacious, as was becoming for this occasion. From the waist down she wore a purple brocade skirt with a long train which encircled her in gracious swirls wherever she went. From the

245

waist up she had on only a thin silver veil, which left her magnificent breasts and full rounded back bare to the view of the admiring men. She wore a large white wig with many curls which, because she had no diamonds at that time, was adorned with dark red roses. Her girls wore smart evening gowns which just left the nipples free and which were close-fitting in the waist but wide around the hips and behind. They had no undergarments on whatsoever and while the men were eating, Grushenka introduced them on a platform, one after the other, lifting their gowns up in front and in the back, displaying and covering up their undercarriages from every angle.

Grushenka had counted on about seventy visitors. Over two hundred came. Two oxen had been slaughtered and had been roasted in the garden over an open fire, but she soon had to send out for more food. The battalion of bottles of wine and vodka drunk during those days will never be known. A small army of hired lackeys were busy opening bottles and piling empty ones in the corners.

The first feature after the dinner was the lottery for the virgins. After long, and more rowdy than witty speeches, the men decided between themselves that anyone who would not "fuck in state" should be excluded from participation. The men were all from the aristocratic class, mostly landowners or their offspring, officers of regiments, government officials, and so on. But they were drunk and found that this was one occasion to break down barriers.

They cleared a space in the middle of the great dining hall and herded the five young girls into the middle, where they stood sheepishly. Numbers were hung around their necks, and every man received a numbered card, the winners being those who held numbers corresponding with those of the girls. The girls were now told to slip out of their dresses, while the winners proudly stood next to them. The rest of the crowd lay, sat or stood all around the room in a circle. Some had climbed to the window sills to see better. The girls were frightened and began to cry. The crowd answered with cheers and boos.

Grushenka stepped into the circle and got her wards close together. She spoke to them with quiet determination, but threatening them if they did not cheerfully obey. They slipped out of their gowns and lay meekly down on the carpet, closed their eyes and kept a hand on their pussies. But their ravishers found themselves also in a predicament. Two, it is true, had nice hard shafts when they opened their trousers. The other three could not so quickly find the trick of how to raise an erection in this noisy crowd. They discarded their coats and opened their trousers and lay on top of their girls all right, but good intentions don't mean a job accomplished.

Mme. Grushenka stepped into the breach. She devoted her services at first to those two who had their guns ready to fire. Soon enough a piercing cry came from one of the girls and the struggling of her bottom announced that Mme. Grushenka had, with her apt fingers, put the prick of her first customer into a love-nest. The second outcry came soon afterwards. With the third one—the shaft belonged to a young lieutenant of the cavalry—she had more difficulty. While her left hand tickled his cleft, her right hand massaged his balls and sword so cleverly that she soon inserted it into the sheath.

Number four proved a futile attempt. The gentlemen in question was more than anxious, his prick full but flappy. As soon as Grushenka touched him he gushed into the air and over the hairy Venus Hill of the little bitch underneath. When he got up, crimson in face and ashamed of his misfortune, the watching crowd did not at first understand what had happened. When they finally did, a bedlam broke loose. Of course, a substitute was quickly found and the maidenhead of numbers four and five were duly pierced.

For a moment the half-clothed men lay heavily breathing on top of the nude white forms of the girls whom they covered. The heavy air in the room was filled with rankness. Each fellow, after the climax, got up and proudly exhibited his throbbing prick covered with blood. Grushenka had a devilish time getting the freshly deflowered girls safely out of the room. She had to fight through the crowd of men who clutched and pawed the scared girls on whose thighs were smeared the blood of their rape. Grushenka turned them all over to the old housekeeper who administered to them in a room on the third floor.

When Grushenka came back, she got into another melee with the excited men. They wanted to auction off the other girls also. A suggestion came from some corner demanding another maidenhead, namely that of the backhole. Grushenka did not want to hear anything about that and tried to joke them out of it. They started to manhandle her and as she was about to leave the room, tore the thin veil, even her wide skirt, from her, so that she was left only in her lace pants. They crowded in on her, half good-heartedly and joking, half threatening. She became frightened and promised everything.

She reached her ten remaining girls who were waiting in a room upstairs to hear what was demanded of them. She made a resolution to bundle them all in a carriage and to hustle them out of the house, leaving the drunken men to get sober and to disperse. But on second thought she remembered how dependent she was on the success of this event. Her very last money had gone, even the house having been mortgaged to provide the food and the wine. Furthermore, it might be good to let the girls get some rough treatment from the start. They would not be the worse thereafter. She had them take their gowns off before she marched them into the room where the men waited impatiently. She did not care that her wig was crooked on her head and that she had only her trousers left to cover her body. She was now all energy, resolved to play the game, and to do it in great style.

The men behaved well when she brought the girls in nude. They had put ten chairs in a circle in the middle of the room and had arranged for a complete lottery which took some time to carry out. Meanwhile they stared at the ten naked beauties in their midst. Many randy comments and jests flew through the air. The girls in turn, stimulated by Madame and not knowing what was in store for them, answered the men with no less cheery remarks. They threw them kisses, touching their lips, and then their breasts or cunts in salutation to the fellows who, they said, they would like to win and get poked by.

The winners decided on, Grushenka picked out for every group two helpers who should stand by and give assistance. The girls were told to kneel down on the chairs and to hold their asses in the air ready for aggression. They did so laughingly and opened up their knees, for of course they thought they were going to be poked in the pussy. It was a wise move of Madame's that she had selected those helpers. They now stood alongside each couple, held the girls' heads down, played with their nipples and made excursions towards their ticklers. It was lucky because every one of these simple girls, as soon as she felt that the prick tried to force her backdoor, howled and began fighting. They jumped from the chairs, rolled over the carpet, kicked with their legs, and were utterly inclined to put up a good fight.

And how the watching crowd enjoyed it! Bets were made on who would be the first man to succeed and who would be the last girl to be ass-fucked. None of the men had ever seen such a spectacle and the party became a huge success. The gladiators took their pricks in their hands and rubbed them quite openly. Self-restraint or shame was by now entirely lost. Grushenka herself, standing in the middle of the circle, was caught by the atmosphere and. if the men had demanded that the girls should first be whipped, she would have agreed to it gladly—for her own pleasure as well as that of her guests.

The girls were overpowered in different positions: some lying on the floor on their belly, others with their heads between the legs of a helper bending over them, one in such a way that the man sat on a chair while the two helpers put the girl on his lap, holding her in the air by her knees so that she could not stave off the attack.

Only one girl was still fighting on the floor; a small young girl, very blonde, her long hair loosened and dishevelled over her bust and shoulders. Grushenka stepped in and settled that matter herself. She waved away the man whom the girl had each time skillfully shaken off at the moment when he thought he was about to succeed.

Grushenka made the girl get up and took hold of her by the hair between her legs and by one breast. Hypnotizing her by putting the whole weight of her personality into a few commanding words, she subdued the girl completely.

She made her kneel on the chair and bend very low. Then she opened up the cleft and cleverly fingered the tight ass-hole for a few moments. She now invited the winning man to come and take what was his. The girl did not stir and did not dare to make an outcry when she felt her back-entrance filled with a big love-instrument. She was, incidentally, the only girl who got fucked kneeling on a chair in the way the men had intended it for all of them. But none the less, every one of them lost the innocence of their back-parts.

When this spectacle was over, Grushenka ordered every girl to go to her room and to wait for visitors. She invited the men, after the girls had left, to go into the rooms and to have a good time with the girls. She computed that every girl would have to take care of about ten men, which they could do very well.

The men did not ask for a second invitation, and went not alone but in groups, friends and strangers together, just as it happened. For the next few hours some fellows were sitting in every girl's room. While one man lay on top of a beauty who wiggled her bottom strenuously in order to get through as quickly as possible, others were waiting their turn.

If the men had gone home afterwards, as Grushenka had planned, everything would have been fine. But after shooting their sperm, they returned downstairs and lay and sat around, drinking. Songs filled the air, jokes were told, glasses were emptied, food was devoured. Some slumbered for a while only to wake up ready to begin again. After they had beguiled themselves enough downstairs, they would explore the whole house again watching the fucking and mixing in it themselves.

Many scenes of lust and depravity took place in the girls' chambers. One group of fellows, for example, remembering the deflowered virgins, broke into their rooms and let them have some ass-fucking, in spite of their tears and protests.

Grushenka was everywhere and anywhere, first animated and cheery, then weary and tired. She slumbered in an easy chair, took a drink or two again, comforted her girls, or got drunken men out of the way. Finally she sent a lackey to her captain, who tactfully succeeded in getting the drunken guests out. The mansion was in a state of disorder and dirt. The tired-out whores and their mistress slumbered in a deathlike sleep for forty-eight hours.

But the excitement, costs, and lasciviousness of the strenuous task had not been for nothing. Madame Grushenka Pawlowks had put her establishment on the map, and she handled it afterwards in a spirit very much to the advantage of her purse. She became rich and famous. In fact, so much so that after her death and after her famous salon had long been closed, anyone in Moscow could point out her house, just as in Paris is still pointed out the famous establishment of Madame Gourdan, who one hundred and fifty years ago was known all over Europe as the best Madame in the world, under the pet name, "the little Countess."

How Madame Grushenka ended up her own love life is not known. It might be that she found her satisfaction through the aid of the friendly tongues of her girls; maybe she married a solid young man to whom she clung quietly without the public's knowledge. The last time that we hear of her is in the official document of the police, of which we told in the preface to this story, where she is described as "a distinguished lady in her prime, well formed, and refined, with bold blue eyes and a full, smiling mouth, which is able to talk adroitly and to the point". May this description of her have been fitting to her until her

END.

SECRET
LIVES

Contents

RANDIANA

(Excitable Tales)

Chapter 1

A FIRST EXPERIENCE

Those of my readers who peruse the following pages and expect to find a pretty tale of surpassing interest, embellished with all the spice which fiction can suggest and a clever pen supply, will be egregiously mistaken, and had better close the volume at once. I am a plain matter-of-fact man, and relate only that which is strictly true, so that no matter how singular some of my statements may appear to those who have never passed through a similar experience, the avouchment that it is a compendium of pure fact may serve to increase the zest with which I hope it may be read.

I was born some fifty years ago in the little town of H—, about seven miles from the sea, and was educated at the grammar school, an old foundation institute, almost as old as the town itself.

Up to the age of twelve I had remained in perfect ignorance of all those little matters which careful parents are so anxious to conceal from their children, nor, indeed, should I then have had my mind enlarged had it not been for the playful instincts of my mother's housemaid, Emma, a strapping but comely wench of nineteen, who, confined to the house all the week, and only allowed out for a few hours on Sunday, could find no vent for those passionate impulses which a well-fed, full-blooded girl of her years is bound to be subject to occasionally, and more especially after the menstrual period.

It was, I remember well, at one of these times that I was called early by my mother one morning and told to go and wake Emma up, as she had overslept herself, and the impression produced upon me as barefooted and in my nightshirt I stepped into the girl's room and caught her changing the linen bandage she had been wearing round her fanny was electrical.

"Good gracious, Emma," I said, "what is the matter? You will bleed to death." And in my anxiety to be of assistance, I tried to get hold of the rag where the dark crimson flood had saturated it worst.

In my haste my finger slipped in, rag and all, and my alarm was so great that had it not been for Emma laughing I believe I should have rushed downstairs and awakened the whole house.

"Don't you be a little fool, Master Jimmy," said Emma, "but come up tonight when your father and mother are both gone to bed, and I'll show you how it all occurred. I see you're quite ready to take a lesson," she added, grinning, for my natural instinct had supervened on my first panic, and my nightshirt was standing out as though a good old-fashioned tent pole were underneath.

I had been frequently chafed at school about the size of my penis, which was unnaturally large for a boy of my years, but I have since found that it was an hereditary gift in our family, my father and younger brothers all boasting instruments of enormous build.

I turned reluctantly to leave the bedroom, but found it impossible to analyze my feelings, which were tumultuous and strange.

I had caught sight of a little bush of hair on the bottom of Emma's belly, and it perplexed me exceedingly.

Impelled by an impulse I could not then comprehend, but which is understandable enough now, I threw myself into Emma's arms and kissed her with fond ardor, my hands resting on two milk-white globes which just peeped above the edge of her chemise, when I heard my mother's voice—

"James, what are you doing up there?"

"Nothing, mamma; I was only waking Emma up." And I came downstairs hurriedly, with my boy's brain on fire and longing for the night, which might, I thought, make plain to me all this mystery.

That day at school appeared a dream and the time hung heavily; I went mechanically through my lessons, but seemed dazed and thoughtful; indeed so much so that I was the subject of general remark.

One of the boys, Thompson, the dull boy of the class, who was nearly fifteen, came to me after school was over and inquired what was the matter.

I suddenly resolved to ask Thompson; he was three years my senior and might know.

"Can you tell me," I said, "the difference between a boy and a girl?"

This was too much for Thompson, who began to split with uncontrollable laughter.

"Good God, Clinton," he said (he swore horribly), "what a question, but I forgot you have only one sister, and she's in long clothes."

"Well," I replied, "but what has that to do with it?"

"Why, everything," said Thompson, "if you'd been brought up among girls you'd have seen all they've got, and then you'd be as wise as other boys. Look here," suddenly stopping and taking out a piece of slate pencil, "you see this?" And he drew a very good imitation of a man's prick upon his slate. "Do you know what that is?"

"Of course I do," I said, "haven't I got one!"

"I hope so," replied Thompson with a smartness I hadn't up to that time thought him to possess.

"Well, now look at this." And he drew what appeared to me at the time to be a lenghty slit. "Do you know what *that* is?"

After what I had seen in the morning I could form a shrewd guess, but I feigned complete ignorance to draw Thompson out.

"Why, that's a woman's cunt, you simpleton," observed my schoolmate, "and if you ever have a chance of getting hold of one, grab it, my boy, and don't be long before you fill it with what God Almighty has given you," and he ran away and left me.

I was more astonished than ever. I had lived twelve

years in the world and had learned more since six o'clock that morning than in all the preceding time.

The reader may be assured that, although I had to go to bed tolerably early, I kept awake until I heard my father and mother safely in their room.

My mother always made it a special point to come and see that I had not thrown the covers off, as I was a restless sleeper, and on this occasion I impatiently awaited the usual scrutiny.

After carefully tucking me in I watched her final departure with beating heart, and heard her say to my father as the door closed—

"He was covered tonight; last evening he was a perfect sight, his prick standing up as stiff and straight as yours ever did—and such a size, too: I can't imagine where my boys get them from. You are no pigmy, dear, it is true, but I'm sure my brothers as boys were—" And I lost the rest of the sentence as the door closed.

Now, I thought, is about the right moment, and I slid softly out of bed and across the landing to the staircase which was to lead me to heaven.

How often since then have I likened that happy staircase to the ladder which Jacob dreamed of. I've always considered that dream an allegory: Jacob's angels must have worn petticoats or some Eastern equivalent, and the Patriarch doubtless moistened the sands of Bethel thinking about it in his sleep.

Chapter 2

I ASCERTAIN THE MEANING OF "REAL JAM"

I reached her bedroom door without mishap and found her safely ensconced in bed, but with the candle still burning.

"Come here, dear," she said, throwing back the covers, and for the first time in my life I saw a perfectly naked woman. She had purposely left off her chemise and was stretched out there, a repast for the Gods.

I do not know that, with all my experience of Paphian delicacies since, I ever have viewed any skin more closely resembling the soft peach bloom which is the acme of cutaneous beauty.

Her plump breasts stood out as though chiseled by some cunning sculptor, but my eyes were not enchained by them. They wandered lower to that spot which to me was such a curious problem, and I said—

"May I look?"

She laughed, and opening her legs, answered me without saying a word.

I examined it closely, and was more and more puzzled.

Her menses had passed and she had carefully washed away the stains.

"Put your finger in," she said, "it won't bite you; but haven't you really, Master Jimmy, ever seen one of these things before?"

I assured her that I had not.

"Then in that case," said Emma, "I shall have some virgin spoil tonight." And passing her hand under my nightshirt, she took hold of my prick with a quick movement that surprised me, and although it was proudly erect and seemed ready to burst, she worked it up and down between her thumb and forefinger till I was fairly maddened.

"Oh! for God's sake," I murmured, "don't do that, I shall die."

"Not yet, my darling," she said, taking hold of me and lifting me, for she was a girl of enormous muscular power, on top of her. "Not until I have eased my own pain and yours too."

Emma called passion pain, and I have since proved her to be some sort of a philosopher. I have carefully analyzed that terrible feeling which immediately precedes the act of emission, and find pain the only proper word to express it.

I struggled with her at first, for in my innocence I scarcely knew what to make of her rapid action, but I had not long to remain in doubt.

Holding my prick in her left hand and gently easing back the prepuce, which had long since broken its ligature, though through no self-indulgence on my part, she brought it within the lips of her orifice, and then with a quick jerk which I have since thought was almost professional, I found myself buried to the extreme hilt in a sea of bliss.

I instinctively found myself moving up and down with the regular see-saw motion that friction will unconsciously compel, but I need not have moved, for Emma could have managed the whole business herself.

The movement of her hips and her hands, which firmly grasped the cheeks of my fat young arse, soon produced the desired result, and in my ecstasy I nearly fainted.

At first I thought that blood in a large quantity had passed from me and I whispered to Emma that the sheets would be stained red, and then Mamma would know, but she soon quieted my fears.

"What an extraordinary prick you have, Master James, for one so young. Why it's bigger than your father's."

"How do you know that?" I asked, surprised more than ever.

"Well, my dear, that would be telling," she said, "but now that you have tried what a woman is like, what do you think of it?"

"I think it's simply splendid," was my response; and indeed, although long years of varied experience may have dulled the wild ardor of youth, and a fuck is hardly the mad excitement which it had been, I should find it difficult to improve upon the answer I gave to Emma.

Twice more I essayed to valiantly escalade the fortress of my *inamorata*, and each time she expressed astonishment to think a mere child should have such "grit" in him.

All at once I heard a slight noise on the stairs, and thinking it was my mother, hastily slunk under the bed; the candle was still burning.

"Are you asleep, Emma?" whispered a low voice. It was my father's.

"Lor', sir," she said, "I hope the missus didn't hear you coming up. I thought you said it was to be tomorrow."

"I did," replied my father, "but to tell you the truth I couldn't wait. I put a drop of laudanum in your mistress' glass of grog just before retiring, so she's safe enough."

And this man called himself my father. I need scarcely say I lost all my respect for him from that moment.

Not another word was passed, but peeping from my hiding-place I saw by the shadow on the wall that my father was preparing for immediate action, yet he went about it a very different way from me.

He insisted upon her taking his penis into her mouth, which at first she refused, but after some little solicitation and a promise that she should go to the "fairing" which was to be held on the following Friday, she finally consented, and to see my father's shadow wriggling about on the wall while his arse described all manner of strange and to me unnatural contortions, was a sight that even at this distance of time never fails to raise a smile whenever I think of it.

Presently the old man shouted out, "Hold on, Emma, that's enough, let's put it in now."

But Emma was shrewd; she knew what a frightfully drowned-out condition her fanny was in and felt sure my father, with his experience, would smell a rat, so she held on to his tool with her teeth and refused to let go till my father, between passion and pain, forced it away from her.

But judge of his disgust when he found himself spending before he could reach the seat of bliss.

His curses took my breath away.

"You silly bitch," he said, "you might have known I couldn't stand that long," and still muttering despondent oaths, he got out of bed to make water.

Now unfortunately the chamber pot was close to my head, and Emma's exhaustion after the quadruple performance was so great that for the moment she forgot me.

The exclamation of my father as he stooped down and caught sight of his eldest boy recalled her to herself.

I would rather draw a veil over the scene that ensued. Suffice it to say that Emma received a month's wages in the morning, and I was packed off to a boarding school.

My mother had *not* slept so soundly as my father had fondly hoped. Whether the laudanum was not of first-rate quality, or her instincts were preternaturally sharp, I have never been able to determine, but I do know that before my father had dragged me from underneath Emma's bed on that eventful night he was saluted from behind with a blow from a little bedroom poker, which would have sent many a weaker constitutioned man to an untimely grave.

Chapter 3

MORAL AND DIDACTIC THOUGHTS

Having in the last two chapters related my first boyhood experience in love, I think it will equal any to be found in works of greater fame, but I do not intend to weary you with any further relations of my early successes on the Venusian war path.

I pass over the period of my youth and very early manhood, leaving you to imagine that my first lesson with Emma and my father as joint instructors was by no means thrown away.

Yet I found at the age of thirty that I was only on the threshold of mysteries far more entrancing. I had up to that time been a mere man of pleasure, whose ample fortune (for my father, who had grown rich, did not disinherit me when he died) sufficed to procure any of those amorous delights without which the world would be a blank to me.

But further than the ordinary pleasures of the bed I had not penetrated.

"The moment was, however, approaching when all these would sink into insignificance before those greater sensual joys which wholesome and well applied flagellation will always confer upon its devotees."

I quote the last sentence from a well-known author, but I'm far from agreeing with it in theory or principle.

I was emerging one summer's evening from the Café Royal, in Regent Street, with De Vaux, a friend of long standing, when he nodded to a gentleman passing in a "hansom" who at once stopped the cab and got out.

"Who is it?" I said, for I felt a sudden and inexplicable interest in his large lustrous eyes, eyes such as I have never before seen in any human being.

"That is Father Peter, of St. Martha of the Angels. He is a bircher, my boy, and one of the best in London."

At this moment we were joined by the Father and a formal introduction took place.

I had frequently seen admirable *cartes* of Father Peter, or rather, as he preferred to be called, Monsignor Peter, in the shop windows of the leading photographers, and at once accused myself of being a doll not to have recognized him at first sight.

Descriptions are wearisome at the best, yet were I a clever novelist given to the art, I think I might even interest those of the sterner sex in Monsignor Peter, but although in the following paragraph I faithfully delineate him, I humbly ask his pardon if he should perchance in the years to come glance over these pages and think I have not painted his portrait in colors sufficiently glowing, for I must assure my readers that Father Peter is no imaginary Apollo, but one who in the present year of grace, 1883, lives, moves, eats, drinks, fucks, and flagellates with all the *verve* and dash he possessed at the date I met him first, now twenty-five years ago.

Slightly above the middle height and about my own age, or possibly a year my senior, with finely chiseled features and exquisite profile, Father Peter was what the world would term an exceedingly handsome man. It is true that perfectionists have pronounced the mouth a trifle too sensual and the cheeks a thought too plump for a standard of perfection, but the women would have deemed otherwise for the grand dreamy Oriental eyes, which would have outrivaled those of Byron's Gazelle, made up for any shortcoming.

The tonsure had been sparing in its dealings with his hair, which hung in thick but well-trimmed masses round a classic head, and as the slight summer breeze blew aside one lap of his long clerical coat, I noticed the elegant shape of his cods which, in spite of the tailor's art, would display their proportions to the evident admiration of one or two ladies who, pretending to look in at the windows of a draper near which we were standing seemed riveted to the spot, as the zephyrs revealed the tantalizing picture.

"I am pleased to make your acquaintance, Mr. Clinton," said Father Peter, shaking me cordially by the hand. "Any friend of Mr. De Vaux is a friend of mine. May I ask if either of you have dined yet?"

We replied in the negative.

"Then in that case, unless you have something better to do, I shall be glad if you will join me at my own home. I dine at seven, and am already rather late. I feel half-famished and was proceeding to Kensington, where my humble quarters are, when the sight of De Vaux compelled me to discharge the cab. What say you?''

''With all my heart,'' replied De Vaux, and since I knew him to be a perfect sybarite at the table, and that his answer was based on a knowledge of Monsignor's resources, I readily followed suit.

To hail a four-wheeler and get to the doors of Father Peter's handsome but somewhat secluded dwelling, which was not very far from the south end of the long walk in Kensington Gardens, did not occupy more than twenty minutes.

En route I discovered that Father Peter possessed a further charm which, added to those I have already mentioned, must have made him (as I thought even then and I know now) perfectly invincible among womankind. He was the most fascinating conversationalist I had ever listened to. It was not so much the easy winning way in which he framed his sentences, but the rich musical intonation, and the luscious laughing method he had of suggesting an infinity of things without, as a respectable member of an eminently respectable church, committing himself in words.

No one, save at exceptional intervals, could ever repeat any actual phrase of Monsignor's which might not pass in a drawing room, yet there was an instinctive craving on the part of his audience to hear more because they imagined he meant something which was going to lead up to something further, yet the something further never came.

Father Peter was wont to say when questioned upon this annoying peculiarity—

"Am I to be held answerable for other people's imaginations?"

But then Father Peter was a sophist of the first water, and a clever reasoner could have proved that his innuendos had created the imaginings in the first place.

Daudet, Belot, and other leaders of the French fictional school, have at times carefully analyzed those fine *nuances* which distinguish profligate talk from delicate suggestiveness. Monsignor had read these works, and adapted their ideas with success.

"My *chef*," said Monsignor as we entered the courtyard of his residence, "tyrannizes over me worse than any Nero. I am only five minutes behind and yet I dare not ask him for an instant's grace. You are both dressed. I suppose if I hadn't met you it would have been the 'Royalty' front row; Florina, they say, has taken to forgetting her unmentionables lately."

We both denied the soft impeachment and assured him that information about Florina was news to us.

Monsignor professed to be surprised at this, and rushed off to his dressing room to make himself presentable.

Chapter 4

A SNUG DINNER PARTY

Before many minutes he rejoined us, and leading the way, we followed him into one of the most lovely bijou *salons* it had ever been my lot to enter. There were seats for eight at the table, four of which were occupied, and the *chef* not waiting for his lord and master, had already sent up the soup, which was being handed round by a plump, rosy-cheeked boy about fifteen years old, who I afterwards found acted in the double capacity of page to Monsignor and chorister at St. Martha of the Angels, to say nothing of a tertiary occupation which, not to put too fine a point upon it, might go excessively near to buggery without being very wide of the mark.

I was briefly introduced, and De Vaux, who knew them all, had shaken himself into his seat before I found time to properly note the appearance of my neighbors.

276

Immediately on my left sat a complete counterpart of Monsignor himself, save that he was a much older man; his name, as casually mentioned to me, was Father Boniface, and although sparer in his proportions than Father Peter, his proclivities as a trencher-man belied his meagerness. He never missed a single course, and when anything particular tickled his gustatory sense, he had two or even more helpings.

Next to him sat a little short apoplectic man, a Doctor of Medicine, who was more of an epicure.

A sylphlike girl of sixteen occupied the next seat. Her fair hair, rather flaxen than golden-hued, hung in profusion down her back, while black lashes gave her violet eyes that shade which Greuze, the finest eye painter the world has ever seen, wept to think he could never exactly reproduce. I was charmed with her ladylike manner, her neatness of dress, virgin white, and above all, with the modest and unpretending way she replied to the questions put to her.

If ever there was a maid at sixteen under the blue vault of heaven, she sits there, was my involuntary thought, to which I nearly gave verbal expression, but was fortunately saved from such a frightful lapse by the page who, placing some appetizing salmon and lobster sauce before me, dispelled for the nonce my half visionary condition.

Monsignor P. sat near this young divinity, and ever and anon between the courses passed his soft white hands through her wavy hair.

I must admit I didn't half like it, and began to feel a jealous pang, but the knowledge that it was only the caressing hand of a Father of the Romish Church quieted me.

I was rapidly getting maudlin, and as I ate my salmon the smell of the lobster sauce suggested other thoughts till I found the tablecloth gradually rising, and I was obliged to drop my napkin on the floor to give myself the opportunity of adjusting my prick so that it would not be observed by the company.

I have omitted to mention the charmer who was placed between De Vaux and Father Peter. She was a lady of far maturer years than the sylph, and might be, as near as one could judge in the pale incandescent light which the pure filtered gas shed round with voluptuous radiance, about twenty-seven. She was a strange contrast to Lucy, for so my sylph was called. Tall, and with a singularly clear complexion for a brunette, her bust was beautifully rounded with that fullness of contour which, just avoiding the gross, charms without disgusting. Madeline, in short, was in every inch a woman to chain a lover to her side.

I had patrolled the Continent in search of goods; I had overhauled every shape and make of cunt between Constantinople and Calcutta; but as I caught the liquid expression of Madeline's large sensuous eyes, I confessed myself a fool.

Here in Kensington, right under a London clubman's was the *beau idéal* I had vainly traveled ten thousand miles to find. She was sprightliness itself in conversation, and I could not sufficiently thank De Vaux for having introduced me into such an Eden.

Lamb cutlets and cucumbers once more broke in upon my dream, and I was not at all sorry, for I found the violence of my thought had burst one of the buttons of my fly, a mishap I knew from past experience would be followed by the collapse of the others unless I turned my erratic brain wanderings into another channel, so that I kept my eyes fixed on my plate, absolutely afraid to gaze upon these two constellations again.

"As I observed just now," said the somewhat fussy little Doctor, "cucumber or cowcumber, it matters not much which, if philologists differ in the pronunciation surely we may."

"The pronunciation," said Father Peter, with a naïve look at Madeline, "is very immaterial, provided one does not eat too much of them. They are a dangerous plant, sir, they heat the blood, and we poor churchmen, who have to chastise the lusts of the flesh, should avoid them *in toto*; yet I would fain have some more." And suiting the action to the word, he helped himself to a large quantity.

I should mention that I was sitting nearly opposite Lucy, and seeing her titter at the paradoxical method the worthy Father had of assisting himself to cucumber against his own argument, I thought it a favorable opportunity to show her that I sympathized with her mirth, so, stretching out my foot, I gently pressed her toe, and to my unspeakable joy she did not take her foot away, but rather, indeed, pushed it further in my direction.

I then, on the pretense of adjusting my chair, brought it a little nearer the table, and was in ecstasies when I perceived that Lucy not only guessed what my maneuvers meant, but actually in a very sly puss-like way brought her chair nearer too.

Then balancing my arse on the edge of my seat as far as

I could without being noticed, with my prick only covered with the table napkin, for it had with one wild bound burst all the remaining buttons on my breeches, I reached forward my foot, from which I had slid off my boot with the other toe, and in less than a minute I had worked it up so that I could just feel the heat of her fanny.

I will say this for her, she tried all she could to help me, but her cursed drawers were an insuperable obstacle, and I was foiled. I knew if I proceeded another inch I should inevitably come a cropper, and this knowledge, coupled with the fact that Lucy was turning wild with excitement, now red, now white, warned me to desist for the time being.

I now foresaw a rich conquest—something worth waiting for—and my blood coursed through my veins at the thought of the sweet little bower nestling within those throbbing thighs, for I could tell from the way her whole frame trembled how thoroughly mad she was at the trammels which society imposed. Not only that, the moisture on my stocking told me that it was something more than the dampness of perspiration, and I felt half sorry to think that I had "jewgaged" her. At the same time, to parody the words of the poet laureate—

Tis better frigging with one's toe,
Than never to have frigged at all.

Some braised ham and roast fowls now came on, and I was astonished to find a poor priest of the Church of Rome launching out in this fashion. The sauterne with the salmon had been simply excellent, and the Mumms, clear and sparkling, which accompanied the latter courses had fairly electrified me.

By the way, as this little dinner party may serve as a lesson to some of those whose experience is limited, I will mention one strange circumstance which may account for much of what is to come.

Monsignor, when the champagne had been poured out for the first time, before any one had tasted it, went to a little liqueur stand, and taking from it a bottle of a most peculiar shape, added to each glass a few drops of the cordial.

"That is Pinero Balsam," he said to me, "you and one of the ladies have not dined at my table before, and, therefore, you may possibly never have tasted it, as it is but little known in England. It is compounded by one Italian firm only, whose ancestors, the Sagas of Venice, were the holders of the original recipe. Its properties are wondrous and manifold, but amongst others it rejuvenates senility, and those among us who have traveled *up and down* in the world a good deal and found the motion rather tiring as the years go on, have cause to bless its recuperative qualities."

The cunning cleric by the inflection of his voice had sufficiently indicated his meaning and although the cordial was, so far as interfering with the champagne went, apparently tasteless, its effect upon the company soon began to be noticeable.

A course of ducklings, removed by Nesselrode pudding and Noyeau jelly, ended the repast, and after one of the shortest graces in Latin I had ever heard in my life, the ladies curtsied themselves out of the apartment, and soon the strains of a piano indicated that they had reached the drawing room, while we rose from the table to give the domestics an opportunity for clearing away.

My trousers were my chief thought at this moment, but I skillfully concealed the evidence of my passion with a careless pocket handkerchief, and my boot I accounted for by a casual reference to a corn of long standing.

Chapter 5

THE HISTORY OF FLAGELLATION CONDENSED

"Gentlemen," said Monsignor, lighting an exquisitely aromatized cigarette, for all priests, through the constant use of the senser, like the perfume of spices, "first of all permit me to hope that you have enjoyed your dinner, and now I presume, De Vaux, your friend will not be shocked if we initiate him into some of the mysteries with which we solace the few hours of relaxation our priestly employment permits us to enjoy. Eh, Boniface?"

The latter, who was coarser than his superior, laughed boisterously.

"I expect, Monsignor, that Mr. Clinton knows just as much about birching as we do ourselves."

"I know absolutely nothing of it," I said, "and must even plead ignorance of the merest rudiments."

"Well, sir," said Monsignor, leaning back in his chair,

"the art of birching is one on which I pride myself that I can speak with greater authority than any man in Europe, and you may judge that I do not aver this from any self-conceit when I tell you that I have, during the last ten years, assisted by a handsome subsidy from the Holy Consistory at Rome, ransacked the known world for evidence in support of its history. In that escritoire," he said, "there are sixteen octavo volumes, the compilation of laborious research, in which I have been assisted by brethren of all the holy orders affiliated to Mother Church, and I may mention in passing that worthy Dr. Prince here, and Father Boniface have both contributed largely from their wide store of experience in correcting and annotating many of the chapters which deal with recent discoveries, for, Mr. Clinton, flagellation as an art is not only daily gaining fresh pupils and adherents, but scarcely a month passes without some new feature being added to our already huge stock of information."

I lighted a cigar and said I should like to hear something more about it.

"To begin with," began Father Peter, "we have indubitable proof from the Canaanitish Stones found in the Plain of Shinar, in 1748, and unearthed by Professor Bannister, that the Priests of Baal, more than three thousand years ago, not only practiced flagellation in a crude form with hempen cords, but inculcated the practice on those who came to worship at the shrine of their God, and these are the unclean mysteries which are spoken of by Moses and Joshua, but which the Hebrew tongue had no word for, therefore it could not be translated."

"You astonish me," I said, "but what proof have you of this?"

"Simply this, it was the age of hieroglyphics, and on the Shinar Stone was found, exquisitely carved, a figure of the God Baal gloating over a young girl whose virgin nakedness was being assailed by several stout priests with rough cords. I have a facsimile in volume 7, page 343—hand it to Mr. Clinton, Boniface."

Boniface did so, and sure enough there was the Canaanitish presentment of a young maiden with her lovely rounded arse turned up to the sky, and her hands tied to the enormous prick of the God Baal, being soundly flogged by two stout-looking men in loose but evidently priestly vestments.

"The fact that the Israelites and Men of Judah were constantly leaving their own worship, enticed away by the allurements of the Baalite priests, is another proof of the superior fascination which flagellation even in those days had over such unholy rites as sodomy."

"Your deductions interest me as a matter of history," I said, "but nothing more."

"Oh, I think I could interest you in another way presently," said Dr. Price.

Monsignor continued: "The races all, more or less, have indulged in a love of the art, and it is well known that so far as Aryan lore will permit us to dive into the subject, both in Babylon and Nineveh, and even in later times in India also (which is surely something more than a mere coincidence), flagellation has not only thrived, but has been the fashionable recreation of all recorded time."

"I really cannot see," I interrupted, "where you get your authorities from."

"Well, so far as Nineveh goes, I simply ask you to take a walk through the Assyrian Hall of the British Museum, where in several places you will see the monarchs of that vast kingdom sitting on their thrones and watching intently some performance which seems to interest them greatly. In the foreground you will perceive a man with a whip of knotted thongs, as much like our cat-o'-nine-tails as anything, on the point of belaboring something, and—then the stone ends, or in other words, where the naked-arsed Assyrian damsel would be, is *nil*. Of course this has been chipped off by the authorities as being likely to demoralize young children, who would begin to practice on their own posteriors, and end by fucking themselves into an early grave."

"Well," I said, in unbounded surprise, "your research is certainly too much for me."

"I thought we should teach you something presently," laughed Dr. Price.

"I have thousands of examples in those sixteen volumes, from the Aborigines of Australia and the Maoris of New Zealand to the Esquimaux in their icy homes, the latter of whom may be said to have acquired the art by instinct, the cold temperature of the frozen zone suggesting flagellation as a means of warmth, and indeed, in a lecture read by Mr. Wimwam to the Geographical Society, he proved that the frigidity of Greenland prevented the women from procreating unless flagellation, and vigorous flagellation, too, had been previously applied.

"The patristic Latin in which the books of the Holy

Fathers are written,'' went on Monsignor, ''contain numerous hints and examples, but although Clement of Alexandria quotes some startling theories, and both Lactantius and Tertullian back him to some extent, I cannot help thinking that so far as practical bum-tickling is concerned, we are a long way ahead of all the ancients.''

''But,'' observed Dr. Price mildly, ''Ambrose and Jerome knew a thing or two.''

''They had studied,'' replied the imperturbable Father Peter, ''but were not cultured as we moderns are; for example, their birches grew in the hills of Illyria and Styria, and in that part of Austria we now call the Tyrol. Canada, with its glorious forests of birch, was unknown. Why, sir,'' said Monsignor, turning to me, his eyes lit up with the lambent flame of enthusiasm, ''do you know the King birch of Manitoba will execute more enchantment on a girl's backside in five minutes than these old contrivances of our forefathers could have managed in half an hour? My fingers tingle when I think of it. Show him a specimen of our latest consignment, Boniface.'' And the latter worthy rushed off to do his master's bidding.

To tell the truth I scarcely appreciated all this, and felt a good deal more inclined to get upstairs to the drawing room, when just at this moment an incident occurred which gave me my opportunity.

The bonny brunette, Madeline, looked in at the door furtively and apologized, but reminded Monsignor that he was already late for vespers.

''My dear girl,'' said the cleric, ''run over to the sacristy, and ask Brother Michael to officiate in my absence— the usual headache—and don't stay quite so long as you generally do, and if you should come back with your hair disheveled and your dress in disorder, make up a better tale than you did last time.''

Or else your own may smart, I thought, for at this moment Father Boniface came in to ask Monsignor for another key to get the rods, as it appeared he had given him the wrong one.

Now is my time, I reflected, so making somewhat ostentatious inquiries as to the exact whereabouts of the lavatory, I quitted the apartment, promising to return in a few minutes.

I should not omit to mention that from the moment I drank the sparkling cordial that Father Peter had mixed with the champagne, my spirits had received an unwonted exhilaration, which I could not ascribe to natural causes.

I will not go so far as to assert that the augmentation of force which I found my prick to possess was entirely due to the Pinero Balsam, but this I will confidently maintain against all comers, that never had I felt so equal to any amorous exploit. It may have been the effect of a generous repast, it might have been the result of the toe-frigging I had indulged in; but as I stepped into the brilliantly lighted hall, and hastily passed upstairs to the luxurious drawing room, I could not help congratulating myself on the stubborn bar of iron which my unfortunately dismantled trousers could scarcely keep from popping out.

Chapter 6

VENI, VIDI, VICI!

Fearing to frighten Lucy if I entered suddenly in a state of *déshabillé*, and feeling certain that a prick exhibition might tend to shock her inexperienced eye, I readjusted my bollocks, and peeped through the crack of the drawing-room door, which had been left temptingly half open.

There was Lucy reclining on the sofa in that *dolce far niente* condition which is a sure sign that a good dinner has agreed with one, and that digestion is waiting upon appetite like an agreeable and good-tempered handmaid should.

She looked so arch, and with such a charming pout upon her lips, that I stood there watching, half disinclined to disturb her dream.

It may be, I thought, that she is given to frigging herself, and being all alone she might possibly—but I speedily banished that thought, for Lucy's clear complexion and vigorous blue eyes forbade the suggestion.

At this instant something occurred which for the moment again led me to think that my frigging conjecture was about to be realized, for she reached her hand deliberately under her skirt, and lifting up her petticoats, dragged down the full length of her chemise, which she closely examined.

I divined it all at a glance: when I toe-frigged her in the dining room she had spent a trifle, and being her first experience of the kind, could not understand.

So she really is a maid after all, I thought, and as I saw a pair of shapely lady-like calves encased in lovely pearl silk stockings of a light blue color, I could retain myself no longer, and with a couple of bounds was at her side before she could recover herself.

"Oh! Mr. Clinton. Oh! Mr. Clinton; how could you," was all she found breath or thought to ejaculate.

I simply threw my arms around her and kissed her flushed face, *on the cheeks*, for I feared to frighten her too much at first.

At last, finding she lay prone and yielding, I imprinted a kiss upon her mouth, and found it returned with ardor.

Allowing my tongue to gently insinuate itself into her half-open mouth and touch hers, I immediately discovered that her excitement, as I fully expected, became doubled, and without saying a word I guided her disengaged hand to my prick, which she clutched with the tenacity of a drowning man catching at a floating spar.

"My own darling," I said, and waiting for no further encouragement, I pushed my right hand softly up between her thighs, which mechanically opened to give it passage.

To say that I was in the seventh heaven of delight, as my warm fingers found a firm plump cunt with a rosebud hymen as yet unbroken, is but faintly to picture my ecstasy.

To pull her a little way further down on the couch so that her rounded arse would rise in the middle and make the business a more convenient one, was the work of a second; the next I had withdrawn my prick from her grasp and placed it against the lips of her quim, at the same time easing them back with a quick movement of my thumb and forefinger. I gave one desperate lunge, which made Lucy cry out "Oh God," and the joyful deed was consummated.

As I have hinted before, my prick was no joke in the matter of size, and upon this occasion, so intense was the excitement that had led up to the fray, it was rather bigger than usual; but thanks to the heat the sweet virgin was in, the sperm particles of her vagina were already resolved into grease, which, mixing with the few drops of blood caused by the violent separation of the hymeneal cord, resulted in making the friction natural and painless. Not only that, once inside I found Lucy's fanny was internally framed on a very free-and-easy scale, and here permit me to digress and point out the ways of Nature.

Some women She frames with an orifice like an exaggerated horse collar, but with a passage more fitted for a tin whistle than a man's prick, while in others the opening itself is like the tiniest wedding ring, though if you once get inside your prick is in the same condition as the poor devil who floundered up the biggest cunt on record and found another bugger looking for his hat. Others again— but why should I go on in this prosy fashion, when Lucy has only received half-a-dozen strokes, and is on the point of coming.

What a delicious process we went through; even to recall it after all these years, now that Lucy is a staid matron, the wife of a church rector, and the mother of two youths verging on manhood, is bliss, and will in my most depressed moments always suffice to give me a certain and prolonged erection.

The beseeching blue eyes that glanced up at Monsignor's drawing-room ceiling, as though in silent adoration and heartfelt praise at the warm stream I seemed to be spurting into her very vitals. The quick nervous shifting of her fleshy buttocks, as she strove to ease herself of her own pent-up store of liquid; and then the heartfelt sigh of joy and relief that escaped her ruby lips as I withdrew my tongue and she discharged the *sang de la vie* at the same moment.

Oh! there is no language copious enough to do justice to the acme of a first fuck, nor is there under God's sun a nation which has yet invented a term sufficiently comprehensive to picture the emotions of a man's mind as he mounts a girl he knows from digital proof to be a maid as pure in person, and as innocent of prick, dildo, or candle as arctic snow.

Scarcely had I dismounted and reassured Lucy with a serious kiss that it was all right, and that she need not alarm herself, when Madeline came running in.

"Oh! Lucy," she cried, "such fun—" Then, seeing me, she abruptly broke off with—"I beg your pardon, Mr. Clinton, I did not see you were here."

Lucy, who was now in a sitting posture, joined in the

conversation, and I saw by the ease of her manner that she had entirely recovered her self-possession, and that I could rejoin the gentlemen downstairs.

"Do tell those stupid men not to stay there over their cigars all day. It is paying us no great compliment," was Madeline's parting shot.

In another moment I was in my seat again, and prepared for a resumption of Monsignor's lecture on birch rods.

"Where the Devil have you been to, Clinton?" said De Vaux.

"Where it would have been quite impossible for you to have acted as my substitute," I unhesitatingly replied.

My answer made them all laugh, for they thought I referred to the water closet, whereas I was of course alluding to Lucy, and I knew I was stating a truism in that case as regarded De Vaux, for he was scarcely yet convalescent from a bad attack of Spanish glanders, which was always his happy method of expressing the clap.

Chapter 7

A VICTIM FOR THE EXPERIMENT

"Now my dear Mr. Clinton, I wish you particularly to observe the tough fiber of these rods," said Monsignor Peter, as he handed me a bundle so perfectly and symmetrically arranged that I could not help remarking on it.

"Ah!" exclaimed Monsignor, "that is a further proof of how popular the flagellating art has become. So large a trade is being done, sir, in specially picked birch of the flagellating kind, that they are hand-sorted by children and put up in bundles by machinery, as they appear here, and my own impression is that if the Canadian Government were to impose an extra duty on these articles, for they almost come under the heading of manufactures and not produce, a large revenue would accrue; but enough of this," said the reverend gentleman, seeing his audience was becoming somewhat impatient.

"You saw at the dinner table the young lady I addressed as Lucy."

I reflected for a moment to throw them off their guard, and then said, suddenly, "Oh, yes, the sweet thing in white."

"Well," continued Monsignor Peter, "her father is a long time dead, and her mother is in very straitened circumstances; the young girl herself is a virgin, and I have this morning paid to her mother a hundred pounds to allow her to remain in my house for a month or so with the object of initiating her."

"Initiating her into the Church?" I inquired, laughing to myself, for I knew that her initiation in other respects was fairly well accomplished.

"No," smiled Monsignor, touching the rods significantly, "this is the initiation to which I refer."

"What," I cried, aghast, "are you going to birch her?"

"We are," put in Dr. Price. "Her first flagellation will be tonight, but this is merely an experimental one. A few strokes well administered, and a quick fuck after to determine my work on corpuscular action of the blood particles; tomorrow she will be in better form to receive second class instruction, and we hope by the end of the month—"

"To have a perfect pupil," put in Father, who did not relish Dr. Pierce taking the lead on a flagellation subject, "but let us proceed to the drawing room. Boniface, put that bundle in the birch box and bring it upstairs."

So saying, the chief exponent of flagellation in the known world led the way upstairs to the drawing room, and we followed, though I must confess that in my case it was with no slight trepidation, for I felt somehow as though I were about to assist at a sacrifice.

As we entered the room we found Lucy in tears, and Madeline consoling her, but she no sooner saw us than, breaking from her friend, she threw herself at Monsignor's feet, and clinging to his knees, sobbed out—

"Oh, Father Peter, you have always been a kind friend to my mother and myself, do say that the odious tale of shame that girl has poured into my ears is not true."

"Good God!" I muttered, "they have actually chosen Madeline as the instrument to explain what they are about to do."

"Rise, my child," said Monsignor, "do not distress yourself but listen to me." Half bearing the form of the really terrified young thing to the couch, we gathered round in a circle and listened.

"You doubtless know, my sweet daughter," began the wily and accomplished priest, "that the votaries of science spare neither friends nor selves in their efforts to unravel the secrets of nature. Time and pain are no object to them, so that the end be accomplished."

To this ominous introduction Lucy made no response.

"You have read much, daughter of mine," said Monsignor, stroking her silken hair, "and when I tell you that your dead father devoted you to the fold of Mother Church, and that your mother and I both think you will best be serving Her ends and purposes by submitting yourself to those tests which will be skillfully carried out without pain, but on the contrary, with an amount of pleasure such as you cannot even guess at, you will probably acquiesce."

Lucy's eyes here caught mine, and although I strove to reassure her with a look that plainly intimated no harm should come to her, she was some time before she at last put her hand in the cleric's and said—

"Holy Father, I do not think you would allow anything very dreadful; I will submit, for my mother, when I left her this morning, told me above all else to be obedient to you in everything and to trust you implicitly."

"That is my own trump of a girl," said Monsignor, surprised for the first time during the entire evening into a slang expression, but I saw his large round orbs gloating over his victim, and his whole frame trembled with excitement as he led Lucy into the adjoining apartment and left her alone with Madeline.

"Now, gentlemen," said Monsignor, "the moment approaches, and you will forgive me, Mr. Clinton, if I have to indulge in a slight coarseness of language, but time presses, and plain Saxon is the quickest method of expression. Personally, I do not feel inclined to fuck Lucy myself, as a matter of fact I had connection with her mother the night previous to her marriage, and as Lucy was born exactly nine months afterwards, I am rather in doubt as to the paternity."

"In other words," I said, astounded, "you think it possible that you may be her father."

"Precisely," said Monsignor. "You see that the instant the flagellation is ended, somebody must necessarily fuck her, and personally my objection prevents me. Boniface, here, prefers boys to women, and Dr. Price will be too busy taking notes, so that it rests between you and De Vaux, who had better toss up."

De Vaux, who was stark mad to think that his little gonorrheal disturbance was an insuperable obstacle, pleaded an engagement later on, which he was bound to fulfill, and therefore, Monsignor Peter told me to be sure to be ready the instant I was wanted.

Madeline entered at this moment and informed us that all was ready, but gave us to understand that she had experienced the greatest difficulty in overcoming poor Lucy's natural scruples at being exposed in all her virgin nakedness to the gaze of so many of the male sex.

"She made a very strange observation, too," continued Madeline, looking at me with a drollery I could not understand, "she said, if it had been only Mr. Clinton, I don't think I should have minded quite so much."

"Oh! all the better," said Father Peter, "for it is Mr. Clinton who will have to relieve her at the finish."

With these words we proceeded to the birching room, which it appears had been furnished by these professors of flagellation with a nicety of detail, and an eye to everything accessory to the art that was calculated to inspire a neophyte like myself with the utmost astonishment.

On a framework of green velvet was a soft down bed, and reclined on this length was the blushing Lucy.

Large bands of velvet, securely buckled at the sides, held her in position, while her legs, brought well together and fastened in the same way, slightly elevated her soft shapely arse.

The elevation was further aided by an extra cushion, which had been judiciously placed under the lower portion of her belly.

Monsignor bent over her and whispered a few soothing words into her ear, but she only buried her delicate head deeper into the down of the bed, while the reverend Father proceeded to analyze the points of her arse.

Chapter 8

THE EXPERIMENT PROCEEDS

Having all of them felt her arse in turn, pinching it as though to test its condition, much as a connoisseur in horseflesh would walk around an animal he was about to buy, Monsignor at length said—

"What a superb picture." His eyes were nearly bursting from their sockets. "You must really excuse me, gentlemen, but my feelings overcome me," and taking his comely prick out of his breeches, he deliberately walked up to Madeline, and before that fair damsel had guessed his intentions, he had thrown her down on the companion couch to Lucy's and had fucked her heart out in a shorter space of time than it takes me to write it.

To witness this was unutterably maddening. I scarcely knew what to be at, my heart beat wildly, and I should then and there have put it into Lucy myself had I not been restrained by Father Boniface who, arch-vagabond that he was, took the whole business as a matter of course and merely observed to Monsignor that it would be as well to get it over as soon as possible, since Mr. Clinton was in a devil of a hurry.

Poor Lucy was deriving some consolation from Dr. Price in the shape of a few drops of Pinero Balsam in champagne, while as for De Vaux, he was groaning audibly, and when the worthy Father Peter came to the short strokes De Vaux's chordee became so unbearable that he ran violently out into Monsignor's bedroom, as he afterwards informed me, to bathe his balls in ice water.

To me there was something rather low and shocking in a fuck before witnesses, but that is a squeamishness that I have long since got the better of.

Madeline, having wiped Monsignor's prick with a piece of *mousseline de laine*, a secret known only to the sybarite in love's perfect secrets, retired, presumably to syringe her fanny, and Monsignor buttoned up and approached his self-imposed task.

Taking off his coat he turned up his short cuffs and, Boniface handing him the birch rods, the bum-warming began.

At the first keen swish poor Lucy shrieked out, but before half a dozen had descended with that quick tearing sound which betokens that there is no lack of elbow grease in the application, her groans subsided, and she spoke in a quick strained voice, begging for mercy.

"For the love of God," she said, "do not, pray do not lay it on so strong."

By this time her lovely arse had assumed a flushed,

vermilion tinge, which appeared to darken with every stroke, and at this point Dr. Price interposed.

"Enough, Monsignor, now my duty begins." And quick as thought he placed upon her bottom a piece of linen, which was smeared with an unguent, and stuck it at the sides with a small modicum of tar plaster to prevent it from coming off.

"Oh!" cried Lucy, "I feel so funny. Oh! Mr. Clinton, if you are there, pray relieve me, and make haste."

In an instant my trousers were down, the straps were unbuckled, and Lucy was gently turned over on her back.

I saw a delicate bush of curly hair, a pair of glorious thighs, and the sight impelled me to thrust my prick into that divine Eden I had visited but a short time before with an ardor that for a man who had lived a fairly knockabout life was inexplicable.

I had scarcely got it thoroughly planted, and had certainly not made a dozen well-sustained though rapid strokes, before the gush of sperm which she emitted drew me at the same instant, and I must own that I actually thought the end of the world had come.

"Now," said Dr. Price, rapidly writing in his pocketbook, "you see that my theory was correct. Here is a maid who has never known a man and she spends within ten seconds of the entrance being effected. Do you suppose that without the birching she could have performed such a miracle?"

"Yes," I said, "I do, and I can prove that all your surmises are but conjecture, and that even your conjecture is based upon a fallacy."

"Bravo," said Father Peter, "I like to see Price fairly collared. Nothing flabbergasts him like facts. Dear me, how damnation slangy I am getting tonight. Lucy, dear, don't stand shivering there, slip on your things and join Madeline in my snuggery; we shall all be there presently. Go on, Clinton.''

"Well," I said, "it is easy enough to refute the learned Doctor. In the first place Lucy was not a maid."

"That be damned for a tale," said Father Boniface. "I got her mother to let me examine her myself last night while she was asleep, previous to handing over the hundred pounds."

"Yes, that I can verify," said Monsignor, "though I must admit that you have a prick like a kitchen poker, for you got into her as easy as though she'd been on a Regent Street round for twenty years."

"I will bet anyone here 50 to 1," I said, quietly taking out my pocketbook, "that she was not a maid before I pocked her just now."

"Done," said the Doctor who, upon receiving a knowing wink from Father Peter, felt sure he was going to bag two ponies, "and now how are we to prove it?"

"Ah, that will be difficult," said Monsignor.

"Not at all," I observed, "let the young lady be sent for and questioned on the spot where you assume she was first deflowered of her virginity."

"Yes, that's fair," said De Vaux, and accordingly he called her in.

"My dear Lucy," said Monsignor, "I wish you to tell me the truth in answer to a particular question I am about to put to you."

"I certainly will," said Lucy, "for God knows I have literally nothing now to conceal from you."

303

"Well, that's not bad for a *double entente*," said the Father, laughing, "but now tell us candidly, before Mr. Clinton was intimate with you in our presence just now, had you ever before had a similar experience?"

"Once," said Lucy, simpering, and examining the pattern of the carpet.

"Good God," said the astonished Churchman, as with deathlike silence he waited for an answer to his next question.

"When was it and with whom?"

"With Mr. Clinton himself, in the drawing room here, about an hour ago."

I refused the money of course, but had the laugh on all of them, and as we rolled home to De Vaux's chambers in a hansom about an hour later I could not help admitting to him that I considered the evening we had passed through the most agreeable I had ever known.

"You will soon forget it in the midst of other pleasures."

"Never," I said. "If Calais was graven on Mary's heart I am quite sure that this date will be found inscribed on mine if ever they should hold an inquest upon my remains."

Chapter 9

A BACHELOR'S SUPPER PARTY

Having become a frequent visitor at "The Priory," the name Monsignor's hospitable mansion was generally known by, I had numberless opportunities for fucking Lucy, Madeline, and two of the domestics, but somehow I never properly took to flagellation in its true sense.

There *was* a housemaid of Monsignor's, a pretty and intelligent girl called Martha, the sight of whose large, fleshy bum, with an outline which would have crushed Hogarth's line of beauty out of time, used to excite me beyond measure, but I was not an enthusiast, and when Monsignor recognized this, and found that as a birch performer I laid it on far too sparingly, his invitations were less pressing, and gradually my visits became few and far between.

De Vaux, on the other hand, had become a qualified

practitioner, and would dilate for hours on the celestial pleasures to be derived from skillful bum-scoring. In fact so perfect a disciple of Monsignor's did he get to be that the pupil in some peculiar phases has outstripped the master, and his work now in the press, entitled *The Glory of the Birch, or Heaven on Earth*, may fairly claim, from an original point of view, to be catalogued with the more abstruse volumes penned by the Fathers, and collated and enlarged by Messrs. Peter, Price, and Boniface upon the same subject.

As I stated before, I could not enter so thoroughly into the felicity of birching. I saw that, physically speaking, it was productive of forced emission, but I preferred cunt more *au naturel*. The easy transition from a kiss to a feel, from a feel to a finger frig, and eventually to a more natural sequence of a gentle insertion of the jock, were a series of gradations more suited to my unimaginative temperament, and I, therefore, to quote the regretful vale-diction of De Vaux, relapsed into that condition of paphian barbarism in which he found me.

But I was by no means idle. My income, which was nearly £7,000 per annum, was utilized in one direction only, and as you shall hear, I employed it judiciously in the gratification of my taste.

In the next suite of chambers to mine lived a young barrister, Sydney Mitchell, a daredevil dog, and one whose *penchant* for the fair sex was only equalled by his impecuniosity, for he was one of that many-headed legion who are known as briefless.

I had occasionally, when he had been pounced upon by a bailiff, which occurred on an average of about once a month, rescued him by a small advance, which he had gratefully repaid by keeping me company in my lonely rooms, drinking my claret and smoking my best Havanas.

But this was to me sufficient repayment, for Sydney had an inexhaustible store of comic anecdotes, and his smartly told stories were always so happily related that they never offended the ear, while they did not fail to tickle the erective organs.

One morning Sydney came to me in a devil of a stew.

"My very dear Clinton," he said, "I'm in a hell of a scrape again; can you help me out of it?"

"Is it much?" I said, remembering that I had paid £25 for him a few days before.

"Listen, and you may judge for yourself. I was at my Buffalo lodge last night, got drunk, and invited about half-a-dozen fellows to my chambers this evening to dinner."

"Well," I remarked, "there's nothing very dreadful about that."

"Yes, there is, for I have to appear as substitute for a chum in the Queen's Bench in an hour, and my wig is at the dresser's, who won't part with it until I've paid up what I owe, which will swallow up every penny I had intended for the dinner."

"Oh, that's easily got over," I said. "Ask them to dine here instead, say you quite forgot you were engaged to me, and that I won't let you off, but desire they accompany you."

"I'm your eternal debtor once more," cried Sydney, and he rushed off to plead as happy as a butterfly.

I ordered a slap-up dinner for eight from the neighboring

restaurant, and as my "Inn dinners" were well known by repute, not one of the *invités* was missing.

We had a capital dinner, and as Sydney's companions were a jolly set, I made up my mind for a glorious evening. Little did I know then how much more glorious it was to wind up than ever I had anticipated.

When the cigars and the O. P. came on, and the meeting was beginning to assume a rather uproarious character, Sydney proposed that his friend Wheeler should oblige with a song, and after that gentleman had inquired whether my fastidiousness would be shocked at anything *ultra* drawing-room, and had been assured that nothing would give me greater pleasure, he began in a rich clear voice the following:

As Mary, dear Mary, one day was a-lying
As Mary, sweet Mary, one day was
   a-lying,
She spotted her John, at the door he was
   spying,
With his tol de riddle, tol de riddle,
   lol de rol lay.

And then came the chorus, rolled out by the whole company, for the refrain was so catching that I found myself unconsciously joining in with—

His tol de riddle, tol de riddle, lol de rol lay.
Oh Johnny, dear Johnny, now do not
   come to me,

Oh Johnny, pray Johnny, oh do not come
    to me,
Or else I'm quite certain that you will
    undo me,
With your tol de riddle, tol de riddle, lol
    de rol lay.
    Chorus—With your tol de riddle, etc.

But Johnny, dear Johnny, not liking to
    look shady,
But Johnny, sweet Johnny, not liking to
    seem shady,
Why he downed with his breeches and
    treated his lady
To his tol de riddle, tol de riddle, lol de
    rol lay.
    Chorus—To his tol de riddle, etc.

Oh, Johnny, dear Johnny, you'll make me
    cry murder.
Oh Johnny, pray cease this, you'll make
    me scream murder.
But she soon changed her note, and she
    murmured "in further"
With your tol de riddle, tol de riddle, lol
    de rol lay.
    Chorus—With your tol de riddle, etc.

Now Mary, dear Mary, grew fatter and
    fatter,

Now Mary's, sweet Mary's plump belly
   grew fatter,
Which plainly did prove that her John had
   been at her,
With his tol de riddle, tol de riddle, lol
   de rol lay.
   Chorus—With his tol de riddle, etc.

MORAL

Now all you young ladies take warning
   had better,
Now amorous damsels take warning you'd
   better,
When you treat a John make him wear a
   French letter,
On his tol de riddle, tol de riddle, lol de
   rol lay.
   Chorus—On his tol de riddle, etc.

The singing of this song, which I was assured was quite original, was greeted with loud plaudits, then one of the young gentlemen volunteered a recitation, which ran as follows:

On the banks of a silvery river,
   A youth and a maiden reclined;
The youth could be scarce twenty summers,
   The maiden some two years behind.
Full up and a neck well developed,
   That youth's ardent nature bespoke,

310

And he gazed on that virtuous maiden
  With a look she could hardly mistake.
But the innocent glance of that virgin.
  Betokened that no guile she knew,
Though he begged in bold tones of entreaty,
  She still wouldn't take up the cue.
He kissed her and prayed and beseeched her,
  No answer received in reply,
Till his fingers were placed on her bosom,
  And he crossed his leg over her thigh.
Then she said, "I can never, no never,
  "Consent to such deeds until wed;
"You may try though the digital process,"
  That maiden so virtuous said.
And he drew her still closer and closer,
  His hand quick placed under her clothes,
And her clitoris youthful he tickled,
  Till that maiden excited arose.
"Fuck me now, dear, oh, fuck me," she shouted,
  "Fuck me now, fuck me now, or I die."
"I can't, I have spent in my breeches,"
  Was that youth's disappointing reply.

Monsignor Peter had, after an infinite amount of persuasion, given me the address where Pinero Balsam was to be obtained, and I had laid in a decent stock of it, for though each small bottle cost a sovereign, I felt morally sure that it was the nearest approximation to the mythical *elixir vitae* of the ancients that we moderns had invented. Some of this I had secretly dropped into the port wine, and the effect upon my guests had already become very pronounced.

"I say, Clinton," said the Junior of the party, who had only "passed" a month before, and who might be just turned twenty, "your dinner was splendid, your tipple has a bouquet such as my inexperience has never suggested. Have you anything in the shape of petticoats about half so good? If so, give me a look in."

The youth was rapidly getting maudlin and randy; just then came a faint rap at the door. It was the old woman who swept and garnished the "diggings."

"I thought I might find Mr. Mitchell here, sir," she said apologetically, "here's a telegram come for him." And curtsying, the old girl vanished, glad to escape the fumes of wine and weed which must have nearly choked her.

"No bad news, I hope," I said.

"Not at all," said Sydney. "What's the time?"

"Nearly 8:30," I replied, consulting my chronometer.

"Then I shall have to leave you fellows at nine; my married sister Fanny arrives at Euston from the north on the 9:30."

"What a pity!" said the callow Junior, "if it were a sweetheart now one might be overjoyed at your good fortune—but a sister!"

"Is it the handsome one?" put in Wheeler.

"Yes," said Sydney, showing us the face in a locket, the only piece of jewelry, by the way, he boasted.

There was a silence as all clustered around the likeness.

"By Jove," said Tom Mallow, the *roué* of the party, "if I had a sister like that I should go clean staring mad to think she wasn't some other fellow's sister, so that I might have a fair and reasonable chance."

I said nothing, but I fell in love with that face to such an extent that I felt there was nothing I would not do to possess the owner.

I, of course, presented a calm exterior, and under the guise of a host who knew his duty, plied them with a rare old port, and proposed toast after toast and health after health, until I had the satisfaction of seeing in less than three-quarters of an hour, every member of the crew so dead drunk that I felt I could afford to leave the chambers without any fear of a mishap; then rolling the recumbent Sydney over, for he was extended prone upon the hearth-rug, I subtracted the wire from his pocket and saw that his sister's name was Lady Fanny Twisser.

"Oh," I said, a light breaking in upon me, "this then is the girl Sydney's plotting mother married to a rich Baronet, old enough to be her grandfather; this doubles my chances," and locking the door I made my way into the street. It was 9:19, and I was a mile and a quarter from the station.

"Hansom!"

"Yes, sir."

"A guinea if you can drive me to Euston Station in ten minutes."

That man earned his guinea.

Chapter 10

THE EFFECTS OF SHELL-FISH

From the booking office I emerged onto the arrival platform, and hailing a superior-looking porter, placed a sovereign in his hand, whispering in his ear—

"The train coming in the distance contains a Lady Twisser; engage a good cab, put all her luggage on it, and if I should happen to miss the lady, as I might do in this crowd, conduct me to her."

He obeyed my instructions *au pied de la lettre*, and in less than two minutes I was shaking hands on the strength of a self-introduction to Lady Fanny.

I explained that her brother was engaged in consultation with a senior counsel at the bar, and that, had it not been a very important case, he would have met her in person, but my instructions were that she was to come to his chambers, where he would probably be by the time we arrived.

Lady Fanny's portrait had by no means exaggerated her loveliness.

A stately Grecian nose and finely cut lips suggested to me that she was a mare that might shy, but then her soft, brown, dreamy eyes told a sweeter tale, and I leaned back in the cab and almost wished I had not touched the Pinero cordial, for I was in momentary fear of spending in my trousers.

"This, I think, is your first visit to London."

"Scarcely," she replied, in a voice whose gentle music made my heart bound, "I came up with my husband six months ago to be 'presented,' but we only stayed the day."

"London is a splendid city," I rejoined, "so full of life and gaiety, and then the shops and bazaars are always replete with every knickknack, that for ladies it must seem a veritable paradise."

Lady Fanny only sighed, which I thought strange, but before my cogitations could take form we were at my chambers.

"Had not my boxes better be sent to some hotel?" said Lady Fanny. "I am, of course, only going to make a call here."

"Yes," I returned, "that is all arranged," and tipping the cabman handsomely, I directed him to take them to a quiet hotel in Norfolk Street, Strand, and conducted her ladyship to her brother's rooms.

Here I left her for a few moments to see after my drunken guests, but found them all snoring peacefully, some on the floor, others on chairs and sofas, but all evidently settled for the night.

After knocking at Sydney's door I again entered his sitting room, and found it empty.

Damn it, I thought to myself, the bird hasn't flown, I hope.

My ears were at this moment saluted with the gurgling which signaled that her ladyship was relieving herself in the adjoining apartment, and I quietly sat down and awaited her return.

On seeing me she started and turned as red as a full-blown peony, the flower being a simile suggested by the situation, and said, "I had no idea, Mr. Clinton, that—"

"Pray, Lady Fanny, do not mention it; I know exactly what you were about to say."

"Indeed?"

"Yes, you as a matter of fact didn't know what to say, because you thought I heard you—a-hem—in the next room—but, my dear Lady Fanny, in London we are not so particular as the hoydenish country folks, and as an old friend of your brother's you will pardon my saying that I do not think you have treated me overly well."

"Treated you—really, Mr. Clinton, you amaze me; pray what have I done?"

"Rather, my dear Lady Fanny, what have you left undone."

"Nothing, I hope," she said hastily, looking down as though she expected to see a petticoat or a garter falling off.

"No, I don't mean anything like that," I said, coming closer to her, until the flame which shot from my eyes appeared to terrify her, and she moved towards the bedroom, as if to take refuge there.

Now this was the very height of my ambition; I knew once in that apartment all struggles and cries would be of little avail, for the walls were thick, the windows high, and there was no other door save the one she was gradually backing into.

"What does this conduct mean, Mr. Clinton?" said the lovely girl. "I surely am in my brother's chambers, and with his friend, for he has often written and told me of your kindness to him. You are not an impostor, one of those dreadful men of whom one reads in romances, who would harm a woman?"

"No," I said. "Lady Fanny, do not mistake the ardor of devotion for any sinister motive, but sit down, after your fatiguing journey, while I order in some refreshment."

Doubly locking the door, on the principle of safe bind, safe find, I gave an order to the restaurateur around the corner which astonished that gentleman, and in less than ten minutes I had overcome Fanny's scruples, got her to take off her Moiré mantle and coquettish bonnet, and had placed before her a *bijou* supper in five courses such as I knew would make a country demoiselle open her eyes.

"Good gracious me," said Lady Fanny, "does my brother always live like this? If so, I am not at all surprised at his frequent requisitions on my purse."

"Yes," I said nonchalantly, "this is generally our supper. Permit me." And I poured out a glass of champagne, taking care, however, that six drops of Pinero had been placed in the glass.

Chapter 11

A DISAPPOINTED WIFE'S FIRST TASTE OF BLISS

The effect was really magical, for her conversation, hitherto so constrained, became gay and lively, and as this vivacity added to her other charms, I grew more and more enamored of her.

"What capital oysters these are," she said, swallowing her ninth "native."

"Yes," I said, "in your Cheshire home you would find it difficult to procure such real beauties."

"We should, indeed," she replied, "and for the matter of that it is perhaps better that shell-fish are so scarce with us," and she heaved another sigh.

This beautiful woman is decidedly a conundrum, I thought, but determined to probe the puzzle, I inquired the meaning of her last remark.

She blushed and simpered, then fixing her eyes on her

plate said, "I have always understood that shell-fish are exciting, and stimulate the passions."

"That is perfectly correct," I retorted, "and therefore all the more reason why a married lady should patronize them."

She sighed again, and then at last I guessed the reason. Fool that I was not to have divined it before this time. Hope now was succeeded by a certainty.

After disposing of some chicken and another glass of champagne, into which I dropped some more balsam, she sank back into the armchair and murmured—

"How long do you think my brother's consultation is likely to last?"

"Pray heaven," I ejaculated fervently, "that it may last all the night through."

"Why do you say that, Mr. Clinton?"

"Because to see you and to listen to your voice is ravishing delight, which to dispel would seem to me the precursor of death." And I flung myself upon my knees before her, and seizing her hand pressed it to my lips and covered it with burning kisses.

She gently tried to withdraw it, and pointing to her wedding ring, said—

"Dear Mr. Clinton, I am a wife, have pity on me, I am but a weak woman and—"

But I caught her in my arms, and stifled the rest of the sentence with a long and ardent embrace, which, repulsed at first, was at length returned.

Two seconds afterwards, my finger had softly insinuated itself into her willing cunt, and as it encountered the clitoris I found that it was as stiff as my own penis, which was now at the bursting point.

"Oh, Mr. Clinton, for God's sake forbear. If my brother should come in there would be blood spilled, I should be lost."

"Fear nothing, my darling," I said, rubbing her vagina with the point of my finger, and feeling the beginning of the pearly trickle exuding all over my hand.

"Come this way." And leading her ladyship by the hand, never, however, leaving hold of her sweet cunt the while, I placed her on her own brother's bed, and, oh, how can I write further, since to say that she was superb is but faintly to describe the joy I felt as straightening my throbbing prick, I gently slipped it into her.

She gave one loud sigh, then lifted her strong country arse, and I plunged in up to the hilt. At each thrust I gave her ladyship she responded with a promptitude which showed how fresh and spunky her vigorous constitution was.

"Go on, my own precious," she whispered, as I put my tongue into her panting hot mouth.

"Faster, for Christ's sake, faster." And as she said the words I shot into her a discharge which must have clean emptied my cods, for although Fanny still faintly struggled to elicit some more, the last lingering spark of vitality appeared to have flown from me.

I did not seem to have even the strength left to take it out, but lay there on her rounded breasts (for she had undone her clothes before commencing), supine and nerveless.

"Do try again, love," she murmured, toying with my hair. "You will never guess, dear Mr. Clinton, what this has been to me, my old husband never did such a thing, he always uses a beastly machine, shaped like that which is in me now, but made of gutta percha, and filled with warm oil and milk.''

"You mean a dildo, dear?''

"I have never heard its name,'' said Fanny, "but it is nothing near so nice as this dear sweet thing of yours. Oh! I never knew what real happiness was before; could you manage it once more?'' And again her ladyship wriggled her bottom.

In my waistcoat pocket I had a *petite* flask of Pinero.

I took this out, and removing the stopper, drank about half a teaspoonful; the result was electrical.

Drawing my prick nearly out of my lady's passage I found it swelling again, and just giving the potent charm time to work, I softly began once more.

It may almost seem romantic, but I can assure my readers that the second fuck was more enjoyable than the first.

For having made coition a long study, I have always found that, given a cool brain, I can get more pleasure out of a slow connection than a gallopade, where the excitement gets the business over before you can absolutely realize the details.

I revel in slow friction, gradually warming up to fever heat, and quite agree with that exquisite stanza of the immortal native of Natal—

"Who was poking a Hottentot gal,''

and who, upon being remonstrated with, or in the words of the bard—

321

"Said she, oh! you sluggard,"
replied most correctly—

"You be buggered,
I like fucking slow, and I shall."

To resume, we both seemed to be so *au courant* of each other's little ways and modes of action as though we had mutually performed the "fandango de pokum" for years, instead of only a few short minutes.

Presently, to vary the bliss, and to give her ladyship a few wrinkles, I suggested her mounting me, à la St. George.

But she begged of me not to take it out, and on my assuring her that was by no means a necessary concomitant, she agreed.

I have always been distinguished as particularly *au fait* at the St. George, so I managed to roll over very gradually, first one leg and then the other, till I had got Fanny fairly planted on top of me.

But I had gauged her ladyship's cunt power at too low an estimate, for she no sooner found herself mistress of the situation than she took in the position at a glance, and ravished me with such terrible lunges that I fairly cried a "go."

But nothing daunted, Fanny held on, and I stood no more chance of getting my poor used-up "torch" out of her vagina than if it had been wedged into a vise.

At last I felt the hot *crème de la crème* pouring down over my balls, and with a last despairing gasp of mingled pleasure and regret to think she could hold out no longer, Fanny once more sank into my arms about as thoroughly spent as a woman should be who has been most damnably twice fucked in a quarter of an hour.

Hastily putting on her things, and making herself shipshape, I drove with her to the hotel, where her boxes had arrived safely, and in the morning informed her brother, as I had previously arranged with Fanny, that she had sent a messenger to his chambers overnight, saying where she was to be found.

I also told him how I had excused him in a return message by the hotel porter, and his gratitude to me knew no bounds.

I deemed it prudent not to see her ladyship during her stay in town, though she sent me three pressing letters, but I feared we should be bowled out, and wrote her so.

Twelve months after this I heard she had separated from her husband, having presented him, nine months from that blissful evening, with a son and heir, which the old man, not believing in miracles, could scarcely altogether credit the dildo with.

Chapter 12

THE INFLUENCE OF FINERY

Now my next essay was of a totally different character, and may, perhaps, be stigmatized by the fastidious reader as an escapade, degrading to one whose last liaison had been with the wife of a baronet, but to tell the truth, and judging cunt from a strictly philosophical standpoint, there is so little difference between a chambermaid and a countess, that it would take a very astute individual indeed to define it.

It is, perhaps, true, that the countess' opening may be, by frequent ablutions, kept sweeter, and the frangipanni on her ladyship's fine cambric chemisette may possibly make the entrance more odoriferous for a tongue lick, but Dr. Johnson's admirable impromptu definition will apply to the vagina of a Malayan or a Chinese girl equally with that of our own countrywomen. He said, if you remember, on the occasion when poor Oliver Goldsmith was troubled with the venereal, and came to him for sympathy—

> "Cunt, and what of it?—
> A nasty, slimy, slobbery slit,
> Half-an-inch between arse and it;
> If the bridge were to break, would be
>   covered with—"

I have already in the course of this narrative mentioned the duenna who cleaned my chambers. She was a cast-off mistress of one of the old sergeants of the Inn, who had procured her this situation for life, and supplemented it with a small allowance, which enabled her to live in comparative comfort.

Two of her bastard daughters were married, and a younger one, the pretty one as she called her, had just returned home from boarding school, whither the old woman by dint of careful frugality had managed to send her.

She was barely turned sixteen, as upright as a dart, had a fine full face, with plenty of color in it, and a form so shapely that I scarcely gave credence to the mother's statement that she was only sixteen. The old woman was very garrulous, annoyingly so sometimes, but on the subject of her darling daughter I used to let her tongue run on till further orders.

"She's a fine, strapping wench, sir, just the kind of girl I was at her age, though I think if anything she's a trifle more plump than I was."

"Yes, by God, and so should I," was my involuntary

exclamation, as I looked at the aged frump's wizened features.

"I don't know what I shall do with her," muttered her mother. "I shall have to send her to service; this place won't keep two of us, and not only that, sir, I've been thinking that it's hardly the thing for a giddy girl like her to be brought into contact with gentlemen like you."

Of course the mother was thinking of her own youthful transgressions with the sergeant, so I merely remarked that I was surprised such thoughts should run in her head, but I inwardly resolved that come what might I would see if a girl of sixteen with such a full fleshy face had got a cunt to match.

Noticing that the daughter was fond of dress, I bought a small parcel of ribbons one day at the draper's, and had them addressed to her without saying a word as to my having sent them.

The following morning I met her on the stairs, gaily decked out, and I asked her where she was going.

"Only for a walk in this silly old inn," she replied. "I have a beau, sir, an unknown beau, who has sent me all these beautiful ribbons, and a lot more besides, and I thought by going out he might see that I had appreciated his gift, that is if he were watching for me," she added, with an arch smile.

"That's right, my girl, perhaps he will send you something else; by the way, what is your name?"

"Gerty," said the young lady, smiling.

"Well, Gerty, you'll excuse my saying so, but that splendid ribbon with which you have decorated your hat, makes the hat look quite shabby."

"Alas! sir, I know it, but Mother is poor, and I can't afford to buy another one just yet."

"If you'd promise not to tell your mother, promise me sacredly not on any account to tell her, I will take you to a shop where I saw a lovely one yesterday that would suit your style admirably, and I shall be only too happy to purchase it for you."

"Oh! sir, you are very kind, but I could not impose—"

"Tut, child, don't speak like that, but go out into the street and walk to the corner of the Great Turnstile, and I will join you in three minutes."

Of course I did this to avoid observation. Presently I went out myself, and took her to the very draper's where I had bought the ribbon.

"Good morning, sir, I have now got that particular shade of ribbon you wanted yesterday."

The cat was out of the bag; Gerty glanced quickly up at me, and I saw I was discovered.

"So *you* are the unknown beau," she whispered, "well, I am surprised."

"And, I hope, pleased, too, Gerty?"

"Well, I hardly know," she said, "but what about the hat?"

To cut a long story short I rigged her up from top to toe, and before I left the shop I had expended nearly £20 on her.

"How on earth am I to account for having this to Mother?"

"We'll have it sent like the ribbons, and, of course, you can't form a guess where it came from. The shop people must put no address inside." And giving all the necessary instructions, I shook hands with Gertrude and bade her good morning.

In the evening a gentle tap at my door ushered in the young lady herself, who, closing it softly after her, said—

"Those things have come, sir, and Mother went on like anything, but I vowed I didn't know who had sent 'em, so she told me in that case I'd better thank God, and say no more about it."

"Then it's all right," I said, looking intently at her large, rounded bust, which, confined as it was by a tightly-fitting dress, showed itself to singular advantage.

"I'm afraid, sir," she said, "that I didn't thank you sufficiently this morning, and so I thought as mother has gone down to Peckham to see her brother, I'd call in and do it now."

"My dear Gertrude," I said, "there's only one way of showing your gratitude to me, and that way you are as yet I fear too young to understand. Come here, my dear."

I was sitting by a blazing coal fire, and although I had not lit the gas the light was ample; she stepped forward and seemed, as I thought, rather timorous in her manner.

"My dear Gerty," I said, placing my arm around her waist, "you are heartily welcome to what my poor purse can afford. As for those petty matters I purchased today, one kiss from those pouting lips will repay me a thousand-fold." And so saying I lifted her onto my knee and kissed her repeatedly.

At first she tried to disengage herself, but soon I found my caresses were not unwelcome. Presently I began undoing the buttons of her frock, and although she fought against it at first, she gradually allowed herself to be convinced, and as her swelling bubs disclosed themselves to my view I felt transported.

"Oh! Mr. Clinton, you will ruin me, I'm sure you will. Pray stop where you are, and do not go any further."

Her beautiful little nipples, as the firelight threw them into relief on her lily-white breasts, looked like a pair of twin cherries, and before she could prevent me, my mouth had fastened on one, and I sucked it avidly.

"Oh! Mr. Clinton, I shall faint. Do let me go. I never felt anything like this in my life."

"My darling," I said, suddenly placing my prick in her hand, "did you ever feel anything like that?"

Her thumb and fingers clutched it with a nervous clasp, and I felt that her hands were moist with the hot dew of feverish perspiration. Before, however, I could prevent her, or, indeed, fathom her motives, she had slid from my grasp, and was kneeling on the floor between my extended legs.

"What is the matter, Gerty dear?" I said.

I got no answer, but the hand which still held my penis was brought softly forward, her mouth opened, and drawing back my foreskin, she tongued me with a sweet suck that almost drove me frantic.

For at least two minutes I lay back in the armchair, my brain in a delirium of delight, until, unable to bear it any longer, for she had begun to rack me off, I got my prick away, pushed back the armchair, and with mad, and, I may add, stupid haste, broke her maidenhead, and spent in her at the same instant with such force that for the moment I expected (contrary to all anatomical knowledge) to see the sperm spurting out of her mouth.

It would be unjust to Gertrude were I to accuse her of want of reciprocity, for my hearth-rug gave ample good proof that she was by no means wanting in juice, since to say it was swamped would be but mildly to describe its condition.

Hardly had Gertrude wiped out her fanny, and just as I was in the act of pouring her out a glass of brandy and water, to prevent the reaction which in a maid so young might, I thought, possibly set in, when, without announcing her entrance, the mother rushed into the room like a tigress. She had returned to fetch her latchkey.

"So this is what I brought you up for like a lady, is it," she began; "and this is the conduct of a gentleman that I thought was a real gentleman. Don't deny it, you brazen bitch," she continued, seeing that Gertrude was about to try a lame explanation, for she was quick-witted enough. "I've got a nose of my own, and if ever there was a maidenhead cooked it's been done in this room since I've been out. Why, even the staircase smells fishy. I discard you forever. Perhaps the gentleman," laying a sneering stress on the word, "now that he's ruined you, will keep you." And she bounced out of the room.

I took the old woman at her word, and rented a little cottage at Kew, where I kept Gerty in style for about three months, and should have done so to the end of the chapter if I had not caught her one Saturday afternoon *in flagrante delicto* with one of the leading members of the London Rowing Club; so I gave her a check for £100, and she started as a dressmaker, or something of the kind, at which business she has I understand done very well.

Chapter 13

A PARAGON OF VIRTUE

One morning, as the summer was waning, and August warned us to flee from town, De Vaux called upon me at my new chambers, for prudence had suggested my removal from my late quarters, and found me dozing over a prime Cabana, and the latest *chic* book from Mr.—, the renowned smut emporium.

"Glad to see you," said De Vaux. "My friend Leveson has asked me down to Oatlands Hall for a week's shooting, and wishes me to bring a friend. Will you come?"

"Is there anything hot and hollow about," I asked, "for to tell you the truth, my boy, knocking over the grouse is a very pleasant occupation, but unless there is some sport of another kind on as well, the game is not worth the candle."

"Clinton, you are incorrigible. I never remember having met such an incurable cunt-hunter in my life. Well, there may be some stray stuff dropping in while we are there, but I warn you not to try it with Mrs. Leveson, for though she might give you the idea at a first glance that she was fast and frivolous, she's in reality as true as steel to her husband, and I would not give a brass farthing for the chance of the veriest Adonis that ever stood in a pair of patent leather boots."

"I should immensely like to have a slap at this dreadful Diana of yours, De Vaux. Is she a beauty?"

De Vaux sighed heavily.

"I was hard hit myself in that quarter once," he said, "but it was no go. Her eyes are wandering orbs, like a gypsy's. She has the finest set of teeth I ever saw in my life, and a form, well—I'd rather not go into it, for it upsets me."

"I'd rather go into it, for my part," I said, laughing. "Why, you're a very Strephon, De Vaux, in your poetic keep-at-a-distance style of admiring this divinity. Did you seriously try it on now, left no stone unturned, eh?"

"I did, indeed," said De Vaux, "both before and after she was married, but it was love's labor lost. I got my hand on her leg once, and she froze me with a few curt words, and wound up by telling me if I did not instantly go back to town, and foist some lying excuse on Leveson for going, she would expose me mercilessly, and by God, Clinton, I am sufficiently learned in womankind to know when they mean a thing and when they do not."

"Really, I must see this paragon of yours, De Vaux. The more obstacles there are in the way, the better a Philosopher in Cunt enjoys it."

"You can come with me and welcome, Clinton, but I

tell you candidly Mrs. Leveson is beyond your reach or that of any other man. She is simply ice."

"But, my dear De Vaux, ice can be made to thaw!"

"Not the ice of the poles."

"Yes, even that, if you apply sufficient heat. Bah! my friend, I'll wager you twelve dozen of my finest Chateau Margaux to that emerald pin you wear, for which I have often longed, that I will fuck your pearl of chastity before this day week."

The bet was instantly accepted, for although I had previously offered him £50 for his pin, and he didn't want to part with it; still he felt no danger in the present instance, and went home and probably drank in his imagination half of my wine in anticipation.

"Clinton my boy," I said, apostrophizing my prick as I got into bed that evening, "if you don't disturb her ladyship's ice-bound repose before many nights have gone over your proud red head may you be damned to all eternity," and, in response, my noble, and, I may add, learned friend, perked himself up straight, and though he didn't speak, his significant and conceited nod assured me that he at any rate had no misgivings.

Chapter 14

OTHER GAME PREFERRED TO GROUSE

We arrived at Oatlands Hall about five o'clock in the afternoon, after a delightful journey, for it was the 11th of August, and the mellow corn just fully ripened for the sickle greeted our city-worn eyes all along the line. So really picturesque was the view that I lost several opportunities of getting well on with a buxom young chit who wanted fucking worse than anything in petticoats ever did between London and York.

De Vaux slept most of the way, and if without committing murder I could have got the girl's mother out of the carriage window, I should certainly have landed a slice of fifteen, for she could not have been over that age.

Leveson was a very jolly fellow, about thirty-eight or forty, and Mrs. Leveson, a really grand creature, was at least ten to twelve years his junior, but although De Vaux had prepared me for something above the ordinary, I must confess the reality far surpassed my expectations.

Figurez-vous, as our lively neighbors would put it, a sweet smiling Juno, with an oval face, colored prettily by nature's own palette, and a pair of finely arched eyebrows surrounding eyes so dazzling in their lustrous black that I fell a victim to the very first glance.

Poor De Vaux seemed half in doubt, half dread, for this was the first time he had seen her since the *fiasco.* She, however, stretched out her hand and welcomed him cordially.

We had a fine, old-fashioned country dinner, and then Mrs. Leveson proposed a stroll around the grounds. She took great pride in the garden and orchard, and the exquisite fascination of her manner as she described lucidly all the various differences between plants, shrubs, greenery, exotics, and all the thousand and one trifles that interest a botanical student showed me that she was no ordinary woman.

Again I was compelled to silent admiration when we walked through the stables, which Caligula's could scarcely have excelled for cleanliness, and as she patted the horses in their boxes I envied them, for they neighed and whinnied with delight at her very touch.

I was glad when she and her husband had gone into the house, and left De Vaux and me to finish our smoke alone.

"Well," he said, "what do you think of her?"

"Think of her," I muttered, "I'd rather not think of her, she has excited me to such an extent that if I don't get into something in the house I shall really have to go into the village and seek out an ordinary 'pross.' "

"Well, my dear boy, then you'd better do that at once, for unless some of the chambermaids are amenable, I'm perfectly certain that you've no time to lose. You might as well dream of fucking the moon as Mrs. Leveson. She's quite as chaste and just as unattainable."

"That be damned," I said. De Vaux's constant reiteration of this Dulcinea's chastity was gall and wormwood to me.

We were the only guests who had arrived for the 12th, and as grouse shooting meant getting up at dawn, we had one rubber at whist, and retired to bed early.

On the first floor of this large old mansion there were at least a dozen rooms. My own bedroom door immediately faced our host and hostess'; De Vaux slept in the next room to mine.

"How frightfully hot it is," said Leveson. "I should say we're bound to have some rain."

"I hope not," I said, "for it will spoil our morning, though this temperature is simply insufferable." I had been all around the world in my father's yacht, and had spent a considerable time in the tropics, but had never remembered such an intense dry heat.

Taking with me to bed a French novel I had picked out of the library shelves, and getting the servant to bring in a large glass of lemonade, I was soon asleep, in spite of the heat, though I had to forgo sheets, blanket, and counterpane, and simply slept in my nightshirt.

In the gray of the morning I was aroused, and could scarcely believe my eyes. There was a young woman standing by the side of the bed, and I recognized her as a shapely lass who had taken my portmanteau upstairs the previous evening.

I have always had an unpleasant habit in my sleep of twisting and turning until my shirt rucks up under my armpits. Thus it appeared that as this hot night had proved no exception to the rule, Hannah, for such was the filly's name, had knocked at the door to awaken me, but receiving no response, and fearing she should get into trouble if I overslept myself, had opened the door, and the sight of my magnificent prick had simply transfixed her so that she stood there like one bewitched.

I rubbed my eyes once more, then sprang up, and before the girl could, like a frightened fawn, reach the door, I had gently but firmly closed it, and set my back against it.

"Oh! Mr. Clinton, missis would be so angry if she heard me in here."

"Has your mistress been called yet?"

"No sir."

"Have you aroused Mr. De Vaux?"

"Not yet."

"Who knows then of your being here?"

"The cook, sir, and she's a spiteful old thing as hates gentlemen, because they don't never look at her."

"Hannah," I said, "didn't I hear you called by that name last night?"

"Yes sir; please let me go downstairs."

"Hannah, is there light enough for you to see this?" and I quietly raised my nightshirt.

"Oh, Mr. Clinton, how can you be so rude!"

"Now, look here, Hannah, we needn't mince words. Your mistress doesn't know of your being here, but if you cry out she's bound to know it, and of course you'll get sacked for being found in a gentleman's bedroom. I shan't be blamed for trying to get into a girl who actually comes to ask me for it."

"But, my God, I haven't, sir."

"No, but don't you see that is what I should be obliged to say if any awkward questions were put to me."

"Oh! please sir, I'll never come into your bedroom again, sir, indeed I won't."

"My dear Hannah," I said, "I hope you will every night of my stay; but I must have my first taste now."

With a sudden movement I caught her in my arms and threw her down on the bed.

The silly stupid fool struggled with the strength of a giantess, and I saw that it was going to be a fair fight for it.

This is what I enjoy, provided the struggle is not too exhausting, and in this case it was fortunately only of sufficient duration to give the proper zest, for no sooner in the course of her efforts to keep my hand away from her "fanny" and her own touched the top of my splitting jock than she was powerless as a kitten.

I will not dilate upon my fuck with Hannah, for she was in too frightened a state to give me much pleasure at that time.

I have, however, under more favorable conditions, since amused myself with her during a spare half-hour, and although her cunt has not got that tenacity of grip which distinguished Lady Fanny, for example, yet there was that general spunkiness about her final throw-off which places her in the front rank for one in her station of life.

To again quote dear old Sam: "A man's imagination is not so inflamed with a chambermaid as a countess," and besides, Hannah was not a maid, the coachman having settled her hash about six months before.

Chapter 15

CHECKED AT FIRST

After our bout Hannah kissed me and bolted off, and I drank a tumbler of water with a few drops of balsam in it, and felt none the worse for my *affaire par hasard*, but at once joined the shooting party.

I did a fair share of bagging, though the birds were scarcely wild enough to suit my own taste.

I hate the fashionable *battue* business of today, but do not mean to imply that it was anything like that, for I am speaking of more than twenty years ago, but still Leveson's keepers had fed them too well, and they scarcely rose to the tramp of a foot near their cover.

We returned to the hall for lunch, and Mrs. Leveson inquired as to the results of our morning's work.

We told her it had been fair, but I half hinted at my preference for seeing a bit of the country, as I was a fickle sportsman, and one morning's shooting was enough for me. She, without a moment's hesitation, offered to become my *cicerone*, and procuring two horses from the stable I sallied forth with her.

"Now, you must be my mentor in everything, please, Mrs. Leveson. I must admit to being dreadfully ignorant of country matters."

She rode with me fully fifteen miles, and although I felt my way cautiously, I began to see there was an iron bar between us, which would probably prove impassable.

The instant there was the slightest hint or suggestion which implied a *double entente* her cheek flushed, and she looked full in my face with her sparkling eyes, and a gaze of steady searching frankness as if to say, "Do my ears deceive me, or are you trying to insult me?"

"Damn it," I thought, "James Clinton, you've met your match this time." And a still small voice never left off whispering, "See what the balsam will do, try a few drops of it." But I never got the opportunity, and as we cantered down the broad gravel walk that led to the front lawn, she with her face flushed with the excitement of riding, mine flushed also, but with the excitement of a "horn" which I now had the satisfaction of knowing could be relieved without quitting the mansion, De Vaux met us.

"Well," he said in an undertone to me, after he had assisted Mrs. Leveson to dismount, "how does the bet stand?"

"Blast the bet," I said, "I'll give you six dozen to let me off."

He laughed and said he would take one hundred and forty-three bottles, and leave me the other to get drunk upon and drown my disappointment.

Chapter 16

FORTUNE FAVORS THE BRAVE

Hannah did not come up to my room that night, though she had promised to; still the weather was again so damned hot that I was in one sense rather glad of it. About four a.m., however, she came up to call the indefatigable sportsmen, but Leveson had already risen, and had entered my room in his shirt and trousers, so that when Hannah gently opened my door she was petrified at finding her master there trying to persuade me to go with them.

"What the devil do you mean, you minx, by coming into a gentleman's room without knocking first?"

I immediately interposed, and told him what a sound sleeper I was, and spoke of the difficulty the girl had experienced the previous morning.

"Mr. De Vaux is up, so you needn't trouble to call him, and you needn't bring up any coffee to your mistress, for

343

she's as sound asleep as a rock. So you won't come, Clinton?"

"Not this morning, old boy; I'm deuced tired and sleepy."

"Very well, then," he said, "I suppose we must manage without you." And presently I heard both the noble sportsmen quietly taking their departure.

I at first tried to compose myself to sleep, but found it impossible, for my prick had become a cursed encumbrance. The advent of Hannah had excited it to start with, and now there was the tantalizing fact that within a few yards of me was lying the lady of the mansion, yet, in respect to approachability, as far off as if she had been at the Antipodes.

Still the old proverb of "faint heart never winning fair lady" came to my rescue, and I quietly arose and softly opened my door, just to see if there was a ghost of a chance.

As I previously mentioned, my room faced that of Mr. and Mrs. Leveson's. Judge then my delight when I saw that my host had actually, and I presumed by inadvertence, left his door ajar.

Stealthily and silently as a cat I crossed the corridor, scarcely daring to breathe, and pushing the door open, inch by inch, I put my head inside.

There, lying on the bed with nothing but a sheet to cover her splendid form, was the woman for whose possession I so madly longed, but the knowledge that her chastity was an insuperable bar to the ordinary preliminaries of a fair fuck, suggested my attempting the seige in another fashion.

Stooping down and going on all fours, I approached the

bedside, and gently lifting up one end of the sheet I revealed her naked form, for, like me, she had got her night-chemise rolled up as far as her titties. Her legs were lying temptingly open, and, as little by little I worked myself under the sheet, my face drew nearer to the lovely little cunt whose pouting lips looked fit to be kissed.

Gradually, and without sufficient movement to alarm or even awaken my sleeping beauty, I got my head well between her legs.

She did move once, and passed her hand down over my head, murmuring the while—

"Oh George, wait until morning." And as I remained perfectly quiet, she dozed off again.

Presently I got well into position, and putting out my tongue, gave the lips a gentle lick. I could feel that there was a slight tremor, but as that was only the natural effect of the electrobiology, I knew that she was not yet awake.

Another lick, this time a trifle further in, and the next second I plunged my tongue far up, until it touched the clitoris. She was instantly awake.

"Oh George, darling, it is years since you did this. Why, you dog, you haven't thought of such a thing since our honeymoon."

I renewed my licking, thrusting her splendid thighs aside, though, in reality, there was no need to thrust, for she opened them as far as ever she could, until my tongue was in right up to the root, and I found from the rapid up and down movement of her bottom that, unless I speedily withdrew it, she would most certainly come.

In my excitement I muttered "my darling," and she,

hearing a strange voice, threw back the sheet, and I supposed looked down.

She must have seen at a glance that it was not her husband, for she put her hands on my head, and in a low voice, half anguish, half pleasure, said—

"Oh, who are you? How could you?" But the matter had gone too far now to be remedied, and she must have felt this, for the movement of her arse continued, and was getting more violent.

I could stand it no longer, so taking out my tongue, I looked up at her.

"I guessed it was you, Mr. Clinton. You are doing a very wicked thing, but I really must have it now, I can't wait," and pulling me onto her, my prick found the already well-greased hole, which was full of slobber from my own mouth, and with several quick movements, long thrusts, and about half-a-dozen wriggles, we both spent at the same moment.

I believe, had her husband come in at that instant, we could not possibly have disengaged ourselves from each other's arms, for we lay there in a transport of bliss, and I could not help pluming myself on the admirable *savoir faire* I had manifested in my management of the whole business.

"What on earth made you do this, Mr. Clinton?" said Mrs. Leveson, still holding me and keeping me in her, with her legs entwined around my backside, but blushing all the while.

"My darling," I said, "the moment I saw you I felt that if I had to commit a rape I should be obliged to enjoy you, though it cost me my liberty, or indeed, for the matter of that, my life.''

A light movement outside the door attracted our attention, and hiding me under the sheet, Mrs. Leveson inquired who was there; to this there was no response, and we breathed freely again.

"My darling," said Mrs. Leveson, looking at me with beaming eyes, "I am so delighted that although I know we have both committed a great sin, I feel as if the pleasure had not been too dearly bought, but for fear of discovery, hurry back to your own room." And kissing me affectionately, both on mouth and prick, I took my leave of her for the time.

I had no sooner got outside the room and pulled the door to after me when I was suddenly struck dumb with surprise and fear, for I found my own chamber door open, and I felt certain that I had not been such a ninny as to leave it so. I entered the room on tiptoe, in fear and trembling, and found De Vaux standing by the window, looking white and thoughtful.

"Hello," I said, "what, in the devil's name, brings you here?"

"I came back," he replied, "to fetch some large shot which I had in my other shooting pouch."

"Well, you've lost your bet," I said triumphantly.

"I know it," he gloomily made answer, "and what worries me is I cannot understand it. You are not a better looking man than I am. Except in the matter of a few thousands a year and a larger tool, nature, luck and birth have not favored you more than me, yet you absolutely mount a woman you have only known forty-eight hours, while I have for three long years tried in the same direction, and utterly failed. I will let you have the pin tomorrow."

"But you only saw me coming from her room, how do you know that I absolutely won the trick?"

"How do I know? Why, I opened your door quietly to see if you were asleep, and finding you absent I looked around, and saw Mrs. Leveson's door open. I also heard you both hard at it, and could not forbear from peeping in. Oh, what a sight it was; there was she, lovely thing that she is, rising to every stroke, and I could see your long prick actually coming clean out of her, *reculer pour mieux sauter,* and then dashing in again till the sight nearly made a lunatic of me. How in the name of God did you work it, for it seems to me little short of miraculous?"

I didn't satisfy his curiosity, but left him to ponder over it, while I wrapped myself up, for the morning was getting chilly, and fell asleep.

De Vaux proceeded to the *battue,* but if his shooting was not superior to his spirits, the birds must have had a distinctly fine time of it, for if ever there was a man at a country luncheon table possessed by the megrins, De Vaux was that individual, when I met him a few hours later.

Chapter 17

DE VAUX'S CHAGRIN—A PROSTITUTION

During the afternoon, as good luck would have it, a wire from Hull (Oatlands Hall was thirty miles from that town) came to Mr. Leveson, desiring him to repair there to meet an old college chum, who was passing through the seaport en route for Norway. So about five o'clock we had an early dinner, and wished him goodbye until the following day.

Mrs. Leveson had a splendid voice, and as two other musical friends dropped in later on, we had a most harmonious evening.

Towards ten o'clock, while I was turning over Mrs. Leveson's music for her, I seized an opportunity to whisper—

"Shall I come in to you, or will you visit a poor bachelor tonight?"

"The latter," she replied, and blushed up to the roots of her hair. She had not yet learned how to deaden the qualms of conscience, but she was woman enough to intimate, very *sotto voice*—

"We should be observed if we whispered any more.

"Mr. De Vaux, would you mind turning over for me, Mr. Clinton is so very awkward."

This was the cut direct, before three others, too, but I grinned and bore it.

"She did not find you so awkward this morning, Clinton," he whispered, as he leisurely took his stand by the piano, and I passed into the adjoining apartment, where lay a "cut-and-come-again supper," to which I did ample justice.

About eleven o'clock, the guests having gone, Mrs. Leveson bade us both good night in a stately, formal way, and retired, and De Vaux and I proceeded to the billiard room.

"I have a proposition to make you," he said as he was chalking his cue for a game.

I couldn't think what De Vaux's rather serious manner imported, but at first imagined he was sore at losing his pin, and as my intrigue had been so delicious, I told him I knew what he was about to say, and that he might keep the heirloom (for I always believed it was an heirloom); I didn't really want it, and pointed out that he could salve his conscience in not paying the bet, as I had won it under circumstances which savored of unfairness, but De Vaux topped me.

"Let us sit down," he said. "I hardly feel in the

humor for the green cloth tonight. Listen to me a few minutes.''

I sat down, curious to know what was coming next.

''The pin is yours, Clinton,'' he said, ''and I have even forgotten that I ever possessed such a thing, but I wish to speak to you upon another matter.''

''My dear De Vaux,'' I said, ''wait until I have lighted another cigar. Now, fire away.''

''You are, as you justly call yourself, a Cunt Philosopher; lately I have gone in for arse castigation a good deal, and the passion that I once had for the more genuine article I foolishly imagined had died out.''

''What the devil does all this prelude mean, old man?''

''Simply this. Three years ago I was seriously, nay madly, in love with Mrs. Leveson. I would have given my finger tips to possess her, and when I made advances which were spurned, and eventually proceeded to extremes, which resulted in my being politely told to make myself scarce, I was cut up more than I have ever been in my life, either before or since.''

''What damned nonsense you are talking, De Vaux.''

''I'm speaking the sober truth, Clinton. I accepted Leveson's invite down here thinking I had got over my foolish passion, but before I had been in her company ten minutes I had all the old feeling come back again with renewed force, and knowing how hopeless was the endeavor to become possessor of her charms, I made up my mind to cut short my visit.''

''What noble, lofty sentiment is this, my worthy friend; I'll be shot if I can understand it.''

"When I came in and discovered you this morning, the first feeling that predominated was rampant jealousy, and I really believe that, had I not governed myself by walking hastily away from the scene, I should have shot both of you."

"Damn it, man, the bet was of your own making."

"I know it, and I cursed myself as a blasted idiot for having made it, and then calmer thoughts prevailed. Now, as you have enjoyed one of the divinest women that was ever cast in beauty's mold, I want you to do me a good turn. I have, I think, without wishing to remind you of obligations rendered, done you one or two services in the fucking line."

I remembered Lucy, and at once acquiesced.

"Tonight, knowing what I did, I watched you and Mrs. Leveson, and although I heard no words spoken, am quite sure that at the piano you arranged an assignation."

"I did."

"In your bedroom, or hers?"

"In my own."

"Clinton, be a good friend," De Vaux said earnestly, "let me take your place."

"She will find you out," I said, not altogether falling in with his view, for although I had guessed what he was leading up to, I didn't quite relish the situation.

"What if she does, it will not matter once I am well in her; she won't cry out, that I can bargain for."

"Well," I said, "how do you propose to work it?"

"Simply in this way: I take your bed, you take mine."

"Right you are," I said, and I really meant to oblige

poor De Vaux at the time, but I was always a practical joker, and as I knew Hannah, the dread of her master having been removed, would be sure to run up within an hour of my retiring, I looked forward to some fun.

Chapter 18

RINGING THE CHANGES

We wished each other good night, exchanging rooms as agreed, and acting upon my advice, De Vaux extinguished his candle, for fear of Mrs. Leveson coming in too soon. I waited to hear him piddle and get into bed, and then undressing myself, hastily crossed over to my darling.

She was lying propped up by the pillows, reading Ovid's *Art of Love,* a book I had seen in the library, and during the evening had recommended to her.

"Dear Mr. Clinton, I thought I was to come to you."

"No, my precious," I said, "the bed is too narrow, and De Vaux sleeps so lightly he might hear us."

As I said this I lifted the bedclothes lightly off her, and found that with natural bashfulness she had gone to bed in her drawers.

"Off with those appendages, my love," I said.

"Oh, Mr. Clinton, don't be indecent; my modesty forbids."

"Julia," for I had ascertained her name, "take off those stupid hindrances to love's free play, or wait, let me take them off for you." And you would have laughed to have seen me executing this feat, for I lingered so long around her cunt every time I approached it, that it took me a good five minutes.

All this time Julia was fairly on fire, for the sight of my huge prick, as upright as a recruiting sergeant, would have excited Minerva herself.

"Now, my darling," I said, "let us have a little eccentricity. I understand both you and your husband want a youngster; now just tell me, does he ever have connection with you except in the old-fashioned way—belly to belly?"

"Never Mr. Clinton. How can there be any other method?"

"Good God," I said, "what venal innocence. Look here, my pet, kneel down as if you were praying for a family." She did so.

"Now, clutch the iron rail at the foot of the bed, and put the top of your head hard down on this pillow, as if you were going to try to stand on it."

"My dear Mr. Clinton, why all these preliminaries? I'm dying for it."

"You shan't have long to wait, my pretty one." For as she had minutely obeyed my instructions, her fair, round arse towered high in the bed, and I could just see the little seam of her vagina peeping at me from underneath.

Drawing back my foreskin until my best friend's topnut

stood out like a glistening globe, quivering with excitement, I cautiously approached her, for I would have it understood, gentle reader, that tyros in cohabitation should always be cool when engaged in this particular style of sport.

"Straddle your knees slightly, my sweet one," I whispered.

"For God's sake hasten, Mr. Clinton, this delay is killing me."

Drawing back once more to allow the candlelight to play on the spot, so that I could not miss my mark, I bulged forward, and got the tip well placed for the final rush, but Julia anticipated me by suddenly squatting backwards, and for the moment I thought bollocks and all had gone in.

Then commenced one of the most memorable fucks in my life's long record, and certainly one of the most pleasurable.

Every time I felt the inclination to spend I purposely stayed myself on the threshold of bliss in order to prolong.

At last, after Julia had saturated me three times, and was beginning to get pumped out, I brought all my forces to the charge, and giving several decisive lunges, which meant mischief, I fairly bathed her womb in boiling sperm, and the way that solid queen-like cunt closed on my prick, and held it as though we twain were one flesh, convinced me that the estate of Oatlands would in less than a year be *en fête*, and the joybells of the old village steeple would ring out to tell of a birth at the Manor House.

In the meantime, what had been going on in my own bedroom?

It had fallen out precisely as I had predicted.

Hannah had sneaked upstairs, and had slid into my bed, and De Vaux, without speaking, had fucked her with the dash and genuine passion born of a three year's forlorn hope.

Nor did he discover himself even after it was all over, but having in his ecstasy shagged her twice in ten minutes, he allowed her to escape, merely whispering in her ear that he hoped she had enjoyed it.

Hannah, on the contrary, had found out the imposture the moment she got De Vaux's prick in her. She had never felt but two, the coachman's and mine, and De Vaux's, although long and sinewy, was no match for either of ours in point of build; still it was better than not being fucked at all, and as De Vaux's ardent imagination was riding Mrs. Leveson, the servant got all the benefit, and not only prudently preserved her incognito, but lifted her brawny arse in such rare style that De Vaux was more than satisfied.

In the morning I went in to see him before proceeding downstairs; he shook hands with me cordially.

"Did she disappoint you?" I asked, with feigned innocence.

"My dear Clinton, she's a perfect angel, and you're trump."

Leveson came back the next day, and I never got another chance of landing Mrs. Leveson, who had fallen *enceinte* by me, and presented her husband with a son and heir nine months to the day.

De Vaux fondly imagines the kid must be his, and I am quite willing that he should continue to think so, but every time Leveson compares dates he thinks of his night's stay at Hull, shakes his head, and mutters that "It's damned extraordinary," yet he wouldn't consider it at all extraordinary, if he knew as much as we do, reader. What do you think?

Chapter 19

CONCERNING SIXTY-NINE; OR, THE MAGIC INFLUENCE OF THE TONGUE

The "gamahuching" process should only be employed as a preliminary and never should be permitted to go to the extent of more than starting the tap. No woman living is able to stand a moist and well-trained tongue. Even those in whom desire has long been dead have been known to shriek for the relief only an erect penis can afford.

Jack Wilton, the greatest essayist on cunt in an analytical form who ever lived, goes further, and even says—"a judicious tongue can galvanize into life a female corpse." (1)

This, of course, I do not admit, but there is a well authenticated instance of a Somersetshire farmer's wife, who had fallen into a trance, and was believed by all her

---

(1) In *The Horn Book: The Girl's Guide to the Knowledge of Good and Evil.*

359

neighbors to be dead, but who was recalled to life simply through the husband giving her fanny one last loving lick.

It is astonishing how prevalent the habit of gamahuching has become in England, and I would, while touching on it, maintain that there is nothing unnatural in it.

A tongue, soft and fleshy, fits in the vagina as though made for it, and though it can only titillate the clitoris, it serves the useful office of *avant-courier* to the prick. The proof, if proof were wanting, that there is a distinct physical sympathy between the latter and the tongue, is that in the case of syphilis the tongue is affected almost as soon as the penis shows signs of having made a mistake. The proof again of its being natural to animal life is the fact that if one carefully observes the collection in the Zoo, it will be seen that when the beasts are in dalliance with one another the male invariably licks over the vagina of the female before proceeding to business.

This is my own observation, and if my readers doubt the statement, a run up to Regent's Park and a few hours in front of the cages will generally corroborate it.

I think to watch a man "gamahuching" a woman is more exciting than to see her being absolutely poked.

I remember staying at one occasion at a hotel in Paddington where a very pretty chambermaid showed me my room. I had not extinguished my candle more than five minutes before I heard a woman's voice in the next room—

"Are you going to sit up reading all night?"

I couldn't for the life of me understand this, and thought the wall must be very thin, but it arose from the fact that some distance up the oaken partition there was a hole, caused through a good sized knot in the wood falling out, and although this hole had a coat hanging in front of it, I very speedily discovered it. It did not take me very long to remove the coat, and I saw the welcome light gleam through. Then, standing on a chair, I applied my eye to the hole, and saw a man leisurely undressing, and a lady-like woman, about thirty, with a splendid head of hair, lying quietly in bed awaiting him.

Now, I thought, there is going to be some fun, when a slight knock at my own door caused me to get down and open it.

"A telegram came for you two hours ago, sir, and they forgot to give it to you at the bar."

"One moment, my girl," I said, hastily slipping on my trousers, and then opening the door, I lighted my candle. The chambermaid was on the point of bolting.

"Don't go, my girl," I said, "there may be an answer to this; wait until I read it, and listen"—then, lowering my voice to a significant whisper— "if you want to see a sight that will interest and amuse you, get on that chair and peep through the hole."

"I daren't sir, I should lose my situation if anyone were to know I was in a gentleman's bedroom."

"I'll swear I won't harm you," I said, and I really didn't intend to, for although the girl was a perfect little beauty, only sixteen and a half, I had done a long railway journey that day, and felt knocked up.

The girl hesitated for a moment, but as sincerity was prominent in the tones of my voice, and she was burning with curiosity to see what was going on, she quietly stepped into the room, and I helped her onto the chair.

361

"Stay," I whispered. "The candle must be extinguished, or they may see you, if they have put theirs out."

So saying I placed the room in darkness, and there was the light streaming through the hole. Mary, for such the *soubrette* called herself, immediately peeped.

For at least ten seconds she never stirred, then, getting another chair, I placed it by the side of Mary's and stood on it, with one arm around her waist.

What was going on in the next room I could only guess by the palpitation of Mary's heart. At last I said, "May I peep, my dear?"

"Oh sir, wait a moment, I never saw such a thing in my life, do wait a moment."

"Certainly, my angel, if you wish it," I said, then taking her hand, which was trembling all over, I gently allowed it to rest on my prick, over which by this time I had lost complete control.

She clutched it wildly, and passed her hand all around the balls, then pulled the skin back, and so proved to me in less than three seconds that her exclamation just now might be a little bit qualified.

"Oh sir," she said at length as I passed my hands up her petticoats and found her quim quite damp with excitement, "I shall be missed downstairs. I must be going, but I should like to see the end of this."

"You shall feel the end of *this*," I said, "and that's much more to purpose."

So, helping her down, I lifted her neatly on my bed, and planted it with such force that she cried out with the pain.

But, whenever I have a new thing in cunts, I am always

perfectly reckless of consequences, and so I gave no need to her ejaculations, but fucked her to the bitter end.

Yet, although I enjoyed it thoroughly, I question very much whether she did, as the next morning she came to see me in a most disconsolate manner, and said she was afraid she would have to go to the hospital, as I had completely split her cunt, but a "tenner" soon squared that, and I would remark here that I have introduced this incident merely to show that the sight of a woman being "gamahuched" is far more exciting than witnessing an ordinary fuck.

Had it been the latter that Mary had glanced at when she mounted the chair, she might have felt a passing interest, but it would have been no novelty. She would probably have called me a dirty beast, fled the apartment, and had a jolly good laugh over the adventure with the cook, but being a new sensation she was glued to the aperture, got excited, and had the implement put in her hand to quiet her.

It is true that she was a bad judge of size, or she might have hung back, but a split-up cunt is no great misfortune, since once the soreness has passed away it enables a woman to enter upon any amorous encounter without the fear of meeting a foe too big for a fair fight.

Chapter 20

AN ADVENTURE AT FOLKESTONE;
THE YOUNG WIFE AND HER
STEP-DAUGHTER

Generally I have not been considered a very plucky man, but an event that occurred about this time almost caused me to believe in my own courageous qualities. I have since, however, in reviewing the past, come to the conclusion that it was sheer devilry, and the mad obliviousness of consequences which supervenes when an excited prick will not listen to the calmer instincts of reason.

I had run down to Folkestone for a brief holiday, and was staying at a large house on the Lees. I had taken the drawing-room floor, which consisted of the drawing room itself, facing the sea, a large bedroom and a smaller one, which I used as a bath and dressing room.

An old General, who had recently come from India, and who in the days gone by had been accustomed to put up with Mrs. Jordan, the landlady, applied for apartments, but as there were only two rooms to let, and he had a young wife and a growing daughter, it was quite impossible to accommodate him. I learned this accidentally through the landlady's daughter, with whom I was cultivating an intimacy that I hoped would develop into something sultry eventually, and immediately offered to give up my bedroom and sleep in the dressing room.

The General was apprised of this, and was naturally charmed with my good nature.

A friendship was struck up over a weed, and the old nabob, in the course of a few days, settled down with his family, to whom he introduced me.

I did not know which to admire most. The wife, Mrs. Martinet, was a *petite* blonde, with those lovely violet eyes which change to a grey in the sunlight, just the sort of large reflective orbs historians ascribe to that darling Scottish Queen, who was fonder of a fuck than any woman born since the days of Bathsheba.

The daughter, Miss Zoe Martinet, was tall and queenlike, dark with the suns of Hindostan, but with a splendid cast of countenance, which seemed to indicate that her Aryan mother had been one of the high caste women of India, who had lapsed with the gay English General when he was plain Colonel Martinet, twenty years before, and while the Grand Cordon and the Star of India were unknown to his breast.

The General was a confiding old fellow, but at sixty-eight one should not trust a wife of twenty-three with a stranger, especially when the stranger boasts a prick which, fully extended and in form, will touch the tape at eight inches.

Every day we went for long walks. General Martinet was very fond of going over to the officers' quarters at Shorncliffe, but although Eva and I were frequently left alone, her society and conversation were so intellectual and refined that I was in a dilemma how to open the ball.

One day, however, as she sat on the beach sewing, the opportunity occurred.

"What a lovely child," she said, as a little girl of some three summers toddled by with a handful of flowers for some waiting mamma.

"Yes, lovely, indeed," I said. "Some day or another I hope to have the pleasure of seeing one with your face and eyes, and if it should be a boy I should take a delight in him for the sake of his mother. You are very fond of children, are you not?"

"Passionately," she murmured.

"I thought so," I observed. "I have often remarked the absorbing interest you appear to take in babies with their nurses on the beach. How long have you been married?"

"Three years"—this with a sigh.

"Three years, good gracious! What time you have been wasting."

She looked down at her embroidery, and became very interested in a wrong stitch.

"It is too bad of the General," I continued, "much too bad. I don't think I should have allowed you to wait all this time."

"Mr. Clinton, what do you mean?"

"Do not feel angry, Eva, for you will forgive my calling you that dear name once; what I mean is this: that you are a woman fond of children and, therefore, formed to be a mother, and in not obeying the voice of nature and becoming one, you are offending against the Divine law, which teaches one to procreate.''

"I have tried, Mr. Clinton"—this in a whisper, with a deep blush—"and have failed."

"Say, rather," I said, now thoroughly excited, "the General has, and it is not your fault; but, my dear girl, every man is not verging on threescore and ten, and we have not all, thank God, been dessicated on the scorching plains of Hindostan."

"Mr. Clinton, do not tempt me!"

"Eva, it is your duty. If the old General were to have a son, your future would be secured. On the other hand what security have you that at the end of a few years he may not die, leaving all his fortune to his half-breed, ladylike daughter, Zoe."

"That is very true," she said, "but still I don't think I could deceive him."

Our conversation was prolonged for another half-hour, and when I retired to rest that night I had lovely visions, in which the landlady's daughter, Zoe, and Eva were all mixed up higgledy-piggledy, but I had an indistinct idea when I awoke that I had not been idle during the night, for I seemed to remember performing on two of them, and it was only the cold sea-water bath that brought me to my senses, and made me lose that great lump of muscle at the bottom of my belly, till I began to believe that I should have had to pick it out with a pin—perri-winkle fashion.

Chapter 21

WHERE IGNORANCE IS BLISS; OR, HAPPINESS IN AN ARMCHAIR

The General was a great gourmand, fond of sitting over his dinner a long time. The following day, after the conversation related in the last chapter, he invited me to share the repast with him, and after the meal regaled me with long stories of his conflict with the Sepoys and other natives of India.

"Why, sir," he said to me, pointing to a pair of revolvers on the mantelpiece, "Zoe's mother once fell into the hands of three vagabonds, and I shot them all and rescued her with those very weapons. That was how we became acquainted, and I would do as much today, old as I am, to any blackguard who dared insult her daughter."

I cordially agreed with him that such would be only a just retribution, but I inwardly added that Zoe's cunt would be worth running the risk for.

After this we rejoined the ladies in the drawing room as I had insisted on their using that apartment. After sitting there and chatting for about half an hour the General dozed off into a heavy sleep, and Zoe asked her stepmother to come out for a little while.

This Mrs. Martinet declined to do, on the ground that it was slightly chilly, so Zoe, who was a willful specimen of womanhood, wished us *au revoir* and sallied forth.

I then poured out a glass of port, for Eva rather liked that wine, and unobserved by her, dropped out of my waistcoat phial enough Pinero Balsam to have stimulated an anchorite.

"Do have half a glass, I entreat you; it will put life in you. I have remarked that you seemed languid today."

"Well, I will just take a wee drop," said Eva, and she half emptied the glass as she spoke.

"Your husband sleeps soundly, Eva."

"Hush; don't call me that here. Yes, he always sleeps so after dinner for a good half hour."

I was sitting in the armchair during this colloquy; Eva was standing by the window, and I could just reach her skirt by leaning forward. I did so, and with both hands gently, but with adroit force, pulled her backwards, until she sat upon my lap.

"For God's sake," she whispered in an agony of dread, "let me go; if he were to wake he would kill us both."

"But he won't awake. You told me yourself he would be sure to sleep for half an hour, and there is ample time for what we want to do in that space. Come into my bedroom for five minutes, my darling."

"Mr. Clinton, I dare not; think of the exposure."

369

"I can think of nothing but this, my sweet Eva," and suiting the action to the word, I clapped my hand upon her lovely rosebud of a snatchbox before she had the slightest idea that I was anywhere near it.

She proved a game girl; she didn't cry out, for that would have meant death and damnation, but she appealed to my good sense.

"Not now," she said imploringly, "be counseled by me; not now, some other time."

"My darling," I said, "stand up for one moment." She did so, and I instantly lifted all her clothes, having in the meantime brought out my stiff straight cock, which I was mortally afraid would discharge its contents before it was properly positioned.

"Now sit down, dear."

She obeyed me, and as she did so, I opened with the thumb and finger of my left hand the delicate sprouting lips; her arse did the rest, and I went in with a rush that made my very marrow twitter with pleasure.

"Oh God," burst from Eva's lips, "this is heavenly."

The old man turned uneasily on the couch; the back of the armchair was turned to him, so that all he could see was the top of Eva's head.

"Is that you, Eva?" said the General.

"Yes, dear," replied his wife.

"What are you doing, my love?"

"Still embroidering your new smoking cap, dear."

"Where's Clinton?"

"He's gone out for a smoke," said the trembling girl.

"All right, call me in half an hour." And in less than three minutes the dear old soldier was once more in the land of Nod, but during that three minutes we seemed to have lived an age. I would have gladly got out of her and sneaked away, for I could not help thinking of the revolvers, but she had never tasted the exquisite bliss a young man's prick can convey, and was, to use a "servantgalism," rampageous for it. She had never had a fuck before in such a position, but women are quick to learn a lesson when sperm is to be the prize, and in less than a minute she had wriggled out of me more genital juice than had ever rushed up my seminal ducts before. When she found she could draw no more, she quietly rose and walked to the window, leaving me to button up and vanish on tiptoe out of the drawing room.

Chapter 22

THE MYSTERIOUS NOTE AND FRENCH LETTER SEQUEL

The reader knows my character by this time sufficiently well to be fully aware that I did not permit a single opportunity to escape of performing on Eva, till I think that young lady grew to look for it as regularly as a cat watches for the advent of a horseflesh purveyor.

One morning, however, I did not keep my appointment with her as usual, for we generally went out about midday, as I had found a quiet cowshed in a field on the Dover Road, behind which the grass grew thick and long, and there we were free from interruption.

There, too, if there be any truth in the general belief that semen is a great fructifier of the soil, the grass should grow thicker than ever by this time, for I am sure that Eva and I had bathed it with the best essence we possessed.

This particular morning, however, I received a note in a handwriting I did not know; the letter ran thus:

"Sir,

Your *liaison* with Mrs. M—is known, and it depends upon you whether it will be divulged to her husband. Meet me near the spot you *generally* meet her, at two p.m. today.

                                   Yours,
                                   One Who Has Seen All."

It was a woman's hand, and I was puzzled. I dropped a few lines to Eva, saying I could not keep my appointment with her and proceeded to the *rendezvous* to find my fair anonyma.

I arrived at the back of the cowshed and turned the corner, when to my intense surprise Zoe stood there, in her hands a bunch of fresh wild flowers; as she was expecting me, whereas I never dreamed that she had sent the note, she had me at a decided disadvantage.

"Well, sir," she said, "you received my communication?"

"I did," I replied, "and I'm sorry to think you have seen all, for I was hoping to some day afford you the novelty of examining it."

"Mr. Clinton, how could you have been so wicked? My poor old father is not far from the grave; you might have waited until Eva had been left a widow."

If you look at me another moment with those flashing eyes I shall do you over in the same way, my pet, I thought.

"Let us sit down and reason, Miss Martinet; you have

chosen a strange place for a serious conversation, but it will be infinitely better for you to sit down and then the tall grass will conceal you from view, whereas standing up every country yokel who passes by sees us both, puts his own construction on it, and your reputation is irretrievably ruined.''

"You are perfectly right," said Zoe. "I will sit down, especially as I note some uniforms on the road yonder, and they might be officer friends of my father's."

Zoe sat down and put up her parasol, but the two gentlemen she had remarked came around the head of the road at the same time. They were two lieutenants of the —th, at Dover, and I had been to a ball where I had knocked up against them some little time before.

"Hello! Clinton, what the devil are you—Oh, I say—a petticoat. Well, I'm damned—*alfresco*, eh? under the azure dome of heaven. Well, good luck, my boy; but give me a pair of nice clean sheets and native nakedness." And down the road went the pair, humming a godless tune they had picked up in the camp before Sebastopol a few years before.

I turned to Zoe.

"What a fortunate thing you were out of sight, my dear," I said, sitting down beside her.

"Yes, it was, indeed," she said, trying with her short skirt to conceal a shapely ankle, which, in a pair of elegant scarlet stockings, looked simply delicious.

I know it was very rude and ungentlemanly of me, but I could not help remarking aloud what an exquisite *tournure* the stocking gave to her leg, and inquired whether she thought the color had anything to do with it.

"Mr. Clinton, I think we had better go," was all the answer she gave me.

"But, my dear Zoe, I thought you had brought me here to read me a prim lecture on morality?"

"Alas!" she said, sighing, "I could not tell on poor dear mamma, she is so artless, and—"

"And I am so artful, you would say; but, my dear young lady, I admit having made a great mistake in intriguing with the General's wife, I can see it now."

"And I hope," she said, making a pretty bow, "that you are contrite?"

"Yes," I said, "I am, but shall I explain to you the error I committed?"

"If it will not take too long in the telling."

"Well, my mistake was in going for the wife, and not the daughter."

"Mr. Clinton, how can you say such a thing?"

"Zoe, from the moment I first saw your matchless face, your eyes burned into my bosom's core like fire, and now, by heaven, that we are here alone, with none but bright Phoebus as our witness, I must—" Here commenced a struggle in the grass, but it was of short duration.

She threatened to scream, but I hurriedly pointed out that if she accused me of rape I could bring the two young officers as witnesses that I had a lady with me who was sitting on the grass apparently only waiting for it, and besides—but all my entreaties were of no avail, until at length growing desperate, and with a prick on me like a bull's pizzle, I forced her legs apart, and would have ravished her by sheer strength, when she whispered in my ear—

"For God's sake use a French letter; I'm so afraid of falling in the family way."

Now I never slip from home without a letter, but I hate using them when I know the cunt is fresh, and untainted with a *soupçon* of an afterthought, so that although the request coming from one I had supposed a virgin rather astounded me, I was fully equal to the occasion.

Taking one from my waistcoat pocket, and beginning to fit it on, I said, "Then you've had the root before, Zoe."

"Yes," she said, "once, with a young captain in Pa's regiment at Allahabad, but this was when I was seventeen. He always used them for fear of the consequences."

By this time I had fitted it, and Zoe showed her perfect readiness to wait patiently for the operation.

"Let me have one peep, darling," I said.

She laughingly lay back flat on her back, and showed me a large forest of hair, as glossy as a raven's back and as black, while beneath it I saw as neat a little quimbo as one could wish for.

Reader, do you blame me, if after seeing such a sight, I surreptitiously pulled off the letter and let my John Thomas approach his lair *au naturel?* I should have been more than mortal to have refrained. Flesh is cent. per cent. better than a nasty gutta percha cover, and although Zoe was unaware of what I had done, she showed herself fully appreciative of my *premier* thrust, though her action took me completely by surprise.

Whether it was the springiness of the soft green grass on which we lay, I know not, but with all my experience I cannot recall to mind any wench, even one having her first grind, who showed such arse-power as Zoe.

The Hindoo and English cross must be a good fucking breed, I thought, but scarcely had the fleeting idea passed through my brain than one more vigorous push brought on the crisis of delight.

Zoe, at this point, was working her bottom with what the Yankees would call an "all-hell-fire motion," when she suddenly seemed transported with delight, and kissing my neck, bit me in a frenzy till she actually brought forth blood.

Much as I had enjoyed myself, this was a style of emotion I was not enamored of, and I screamed out with the pain.

I got up, leaving Zoe still lying exhausted on the ground, when to my horror I heard a step behind me, and before I could button up found myself confronted by Eva.

I do not know why it should have been so, but although the meteorological record for that year does not return the weather in May as being particularly warm, I found it at least 212° Fahrenheit on that eventful day, in spite of the sea breeze, so not liking tropical heat, I returned to town. I have met Zoe in society since, but poor Eva, after tasting forbidden fruit, and finding it so much sweeter than the withered-up stiff obtainable from the husband's orchard, went wrong again and again, and was finally bowled in the very act, but, luckily for the gay Lothario, the General had left those chased revolvers at home.

Chapter 23

A DISAGREEABLE MISTAKE

Not always have I had the happiness of being fortunate in my amours. It is true that I have managed to escape the dread fate of those poor unfortunate devils whose tools are living witness to the powers of caustic and the lethal weapons of surgery, but I have on occasions been singularly unfortunate, and as the warning voice of my publisher tells me I have little more time or space at my disposal, I will devote the present chapter of this work to detailing a most unpleasant incident, which all people are more or less liable to who go in for promiscuous intercourse to any large extent.

My only sister, Sophy, came up to London with her husband shortly after my return from Folkestone, and although he was a perfect brute of a fellow, and a man I disliked very much, I made myself as agreeable as I could,

378

and took a furnished house for them during their stay, near the Regent's Park.

Frank Vaughan, a young architect, and a rising man, was one I introduced them to, as my sister had brought a friend, Miss Polly White, with her, who lived near our old home in the country; and being anxious to see London, her parents had placed her under my sister's guardian wing to do the "lions" of the metropolis.

Polly was an only daughter, so knowing the old people had a good nest egg, I thought it would be a capital opportunity to throw Frank in her way.

I told him precisely how matters stood, and advised him to make a match of it.

"The old people are rich," I said, "but if they object to you on the score of money, fuck her, my boy, and that will bring them to reason."

"Is she perfectly pure now?" said Frank. "For to tell you the truth I haven't come across a genuine maid since I landed a stripling of thirteen, nearly ten years ago. Are you sure *you* haven't?"

"I'll swear it, if you like," I returned, laughing at the soft impeachment, "but take my advice, Frank, and win her. She'll be worth at least 40,000 when the old folks snuff it."

"I'm on the job," said Frank; and it was easy to see from the immaculate shirt front, the brilliant conversation, and the great attention he paid her, that he meant business.

One night, however, I was puzzled, for I thought Frank was far more assiduous in his manner to my sister than he should have been, considering that the "nugget," for so we had christened Polly, was present.

I could not understand it at all, and determined to watch the development of the situation.

There was, I must tell you, an underplot to all this, for several times I had noted that Polly's regard for me was a trifle too warm, and once or twice in the theatre, and in the brougham, coming home particularly, I had felt the soft pressure of her knees, and returned it with interest—but, to my story:

Frank proposed going to Madame Tussaud's, and as Polly had never been, and my sister knew every model in the show by heart, Frank suggested that he should take the "nugget," "unless you would like to go with us," he said to me.

"Not I, indeed," was my reply. "Besides, Sissy here will be alone, as her beautiful husband has been out all day, and will, I suppose, turn beastly drunk about midnight. No, you go together and enjoy your little selves." So off they went.

When Polly passed me in the hall, she gave me a peculiar look, which I utterly failed to comprehend, and asked me to fasten her glove. As I did so she passed a slip of paper into my hand and when she had gone I read on it these words:

"Be in the study about nine o'clock."

What can the little minx mean? was my first thought. She surely wouldn't go about an intrigue in this bare-faced fashion; she has been brought up in a demure way. Yet what on earth can she mean? At any rate I will do her bidding.

Making an excuse to my sister about eight o'clock, for I was as curious as possible to know what it could all portend, and saying I was going out for a couple of hours, I slammed the hall door behind me, and then quietly crept upstairs to the study.

I found it in darkness, but knowing where the couch was situated, at the far end of the room, I made for it, and I must confess the solitude, the darkness, and a good dinner, all combined, made me forget curiosity, Polly, the warning note, and everything else, and in less than five minutes I was fast asleep.

I was awakened by a scented hand I knew was a woman's touching my face and a low voice whispered in my ear—

"You are here then; I never heard you come in."

Damn it, I thought, it's an intrigue after all; but she's too tall for Polly. Oh, I see it all, she's our prim landlady (who retained one room in the house, and was, I knew, nuts upon my brother-in-law). Polly found out about it, and set me on the track, so without saying a word I laid her unresistingly on the couch, and in a few seconds was busy.

I could not help thinking while wiring in that she displayed much vigor for one of her years, since I judged the lady to be at least forty-five, but her ardor only made me the more fervent, and at the end of a long series of skirmishes the real hot short work began.

It would be impossible to express my horror at this moment when my hand come in contact with a cross she was wearing around her neck, and I found that it was my own sister I was rogering.

I had, unluckily, got to that point where no man or woman could cease firing, but the worst part of the damned unfortunate affair was that I burst out with an ejaculation of dismay, and she, too, recognized my voice. The situation was terrible.

"Good God!" I said. "Sophy, how on earth has this come about?"

Then, sobbingly, she told me that her husband had abstained from her for more than two years because he had contracted a chronic gonorrhoeic disorder and that Vaughan had won her over to make this *rendezvous,* and had intended letting Polly be shown through Tussaud's by a friend he had arranged to meet there. "But," she added, "how was it I found you here?" This I dared not tell her, as it was now evident that Polly was aware of the assignation, and to let my sister know—that would have been death.

Poor girl, she was sufficiently punished for her frailty, and Polly, who had caught a few words of the appointment, was sufficiently revenged.

Polly never forgave my friend Frank for what she always considered his base desertion.

As for Sophy, I got her a divorce from her husband shortly afterwards. I give her an allowance myself, and I believe in my heart, that as women go, she is a very good one. I know that she has never ceased to pray for what she calls her great sin, but which I term my damned misfortune.

Polly married a brewer down in Devonshire, and as I have had several opportunities of testing her quality, I can assure my readers that the brewer has no cause to complain of his draw in the matrimonial lottery.

Chapter 24

REFLECTIONS ON "AULD LANG SYNE," HAPPY MEETINGS, AND CONCLUSION

Fifteen years have now elapsed since I scribbled the former part of my experiences. Times are sadly altered with my best friend now, and I am rapidly approaching the time when all may prove, "Vanity and vexation of spirit," for although I still carry a most formidable outward and visible sign, the inward and spiritual grace so necessary to please the ladies is now almost dormant in my fucked-out nature.

Just now I have been reading a fine little book on rejuvenescence, called *Abishag*, by David II, which I think gives an excellent remedy for such cases as mine. George the Fourth must have thoroughly understood the theory advocated by the writer, for although in early life his motto was "fat, fair, and forty," he afterwards was found frequently engaged in seducing by any means, fair or foul, the youngest and most innocent girls he could find.

The more I study the character of the first gentleman in Europe, as he was called, the more thorough a voluptuarian he seems to have been; his youthful vigor at first delighting in the charms of thoroughly developed and sensual women, and gradually in his later years turning to the worship of Moloch, sacrificing to his lustful God the unfledged virginities his numerous Myrmidons placed in his way.

Years ago I remember how I looked with something like contempt upon the art and science of flagellation as dilated upon by Monsignor Peter; now I am quite converted to his theory.

A most fortunate rencontre has been the means of this conversion; lately sauntering down Regent Street, thinking of the time when I used to do three or four pretty *demimondes* in a day—

"Ah, Gerty, do you know him, too?" in an ever to be remembered voice caused me to suddenly turn and confront the speaker, who proved to be none other than Mrs. Leveson, looking almost as lovely as ever, and incomprehensively in the company of my old flame Gerty, of the Temple.

This was a delightful renewal of old acquaintanceships, and a very few explanations let me thoroughly into the situation.

Leveson had been dead several years, leaving his wife sole guardian of their son (my son, she assured me in a loving whisper. "He is now eighteen—never can I forget the night you made him for me").

Gerty had been persuaded by Mrs. Leveson to give up her dressmaking business, and live with her as a kind of companion housekeeper, the former's Sapphic tastes having attached her to the voluptuous Mrs. L., who discovered it from Gerty's remarks on the women of the day in Paris, who prefer their own sex as lovers, and care very little for the attentions of men.

"My son is abroad with his tutor; will you, Mr. Clinton, come home to dinner, and spend the evening at our quiet little town house? James is such a rake—just like his father—I don't mean Mr. Leveson, poor dear, he was rather too good, and never made a baby for me or anyone else. Gerty knows all about it, but your name was never mentioned, and now I suppose you are the Temple student who seduced her with finery, and took advantage of her young inexperience, although she never mentioned you?"

"Really, this is most charming, but, my dear ladies, I can only accept your hospitality if you promise we shall be a happy family—free from jealousy."

"Make yourself easy, dear Mr. Clinton; as to that, everything is common between us in thought, word, and deed; in fact, with our dearest friend, Lady Twisser, we are three loving communists, each one's secrets as sacred as if our own!"

"Lady Fanny Twisser, who was separated from her husband because he couldn't believe his dildo was the father of her boy!" I exclaimed.

"Good God, Mr. Clinton, there you are again; you must be a universal father. Now I'm sure it's you who did that service for dear Fanny, and we'll wire to her at once to come and join our dinner party."

Highly elated they conducted me to their carriage, which was waiting outside Lewis' and Allenby's, and soon reached Mrs. Leveson's house, in Cromwell-Road, South Kensington.

Gerty showed me to a room to prepare for dinner, and it was arranged we should have a real love *séance* after the servants had gone to bed.

At dinner I saw Lady Fanny, who met me with a most fervent embrace, assuring me, with tears in her eyes, that I was the source of the only happiness she had ever had in her life (her son, now at college at Oxford).

All dinner time—and the long while we sat over dessert talking over old times, while I felt as proud as a barn-door cock with three favorite hens, all glowing with love and anxious for his attentions—the ardent glances of lovely Mrs. Leveson told too plainly the force of her luscious recollections, while Lady Fanny, who sat by my side, every now and then caressed my prick under that table, as he slightly throbbed in response to her touches.

At length coffee was brought in, and the servants told to go to bed.

"At last!" sighed our magnificent hostess, springing up and throwing her arms around my neck, "I have a chance to kiss the father of my boy; what terrible restraint I have had to put on myself before the servants. Dear James, you belong to us all, we all want the consolation of that grand practitioner of yours; have which of us you please first; there's no jealousy!"

"But, darling loves, how can I do you all? I'm not the man I was some years ago!"

"Trust to Gerty's science, for she let us into the Pinero Balsam secret, and we have a little of it in the house for occasions when it might be wanted. It's very curious how you ruined the morals of both Fanny and myself, two such paragons of virtue as we were; we could never forget the lessons of love you taught us, and, now we are both widows, with dear Gerty here, we do enjoy ourselves on the quiet. Fanny's boy has me, and thinks it is an awfully delicious and secret *liaison*; my James returns the kindness to my love's mother; while dear abandoned Gerty is only satisfied sometimes by having both with her at once yet neither of them ever divulges their amour with Fanny and myself. And now, how is the dear jewel? You surely don't require the balsam to start with," she said, taking out my staff of life, and kissing it rapturously.

Lady Fanny did the same, and was followed by Gerty, whose ravishing manner of gamahuching me recalled so vividly my first seduction of her in the Temple.

She would have racked me off, but I restrained myself, and requested them to peel to the buff, setting them the example, my cock never for a moment losing his fine erection.

Having placed an eider-down quilt and some pillows on the hearth-rug, they ranged themselves in front of me in all their naked glories, like the goddesses before Paris disputing for the apple.

"Catch which you can," they exclaimed, laughing, and began capering around me.

I dashed towards Mrs. Leveson, but tumbled over one of the pillows, getting my bottom most unmercifully slapped before I could recover myself. My blood tingled from head to foot. I was made to be into one of those luscious loving women, and in a moment or two caught and pulled down Fanny on top of me; the other two at once settled her, à la

St. George, and held my prick till she was fairly impaled on it. They then stretched themselves at full length on either side, kissing me ardently, while their busy fingers played with prick and balls, as the darling Fanny got quickly into her stride, and rode me with the same fire and dash which characterized her first performance on her brother's bed in the Temple.

My hands were well employed frigging the creamy cunts of Mrs. Leveson and Gerty—what a fuck, how my prick swelled in his agony of delight, as I shot the hot boiling sperm right up to Fanny's heart, and she deluged me in return with the essence of her life as she fell forward with a scream of delight. Her tightly nipping cunt held me enraptured by its loving contractions, but at the suggestion of Gerty, she gently rolled herself aside, and allowed me to mount the darling Leveson before I lost my stiffness.

What a deep-drawn sigh of delight my fresh fuckstress gave, as she heaved up her buttocks and felt my charger rush up to the very extremes of her burning sheath.

"Let me have the very uttermost bit of it! Keep him up to his work, Gerty, darling," she exclaimed excitedly, then gluing her lips to mine she seemed as if she would suck my very life away.

A smart, tingling, swish—swish on my rump now aroused me to the fact that both Fanny and Gerty had taken in hand the flagellation, and gradually putting more force in their cuts, raised such a storm of lustful heat, that I fucked dear Mrs. Leveson till after some minutes spent in such an ecstatic agony of bliss, both of us lost our consciousness for a time, and when we recovered ourselves, declared that no such exquisite sensations had ever before so completely overwhelmed either of us.

Such was the power of the rod to invigorate me, that Gerty soon had her cunt as well-stuffed as the others had been by my grand prick, as it seemed to be bigger and stiffer than ever.

This loving *séance* was kept up to the small hours of the morning before I could think of tearing myself from their seductive delights; but I now often join this community of love in the Cromwell-Road and no pen can by any possibility adequately describe the delights we manage to enjoy under the influence of the birch.

THE END

THE ADVENTURES OF
GRACE AND ANNA

Chapter 1

It was in one of the big amusement parks that I first met Anna. Being alone and out for a good time, I so arranged that I secured the next seat to her on one of the many rides, and an acquaintance was soon struck up and at the close of the festivities I was awarded the privilege of escorting her home.

She lived on the other side of the city, and upon seeing my car, together with Joseph the chauffeur, her eyes grew wide, and at first I thought she was about to refuse to go with me and instead board the street car as she had come there.

It did not, however, take much persuasion on my part to have her enter my car, and once seated on the luxurious cushions I knew that the battle was won. I asked her if she wished to dine, but she informed me that she would have to arise early as she worked in the downtown district, and as she had now overstayed her time, she had better hurry right home and leave it for some other time.

It is now time that I give her the benefit of a short description, in order that the reader may form in his mind the nature of the choice prize that had fallen to my lot on that evening.

Her name, as I have related, was Anna. Her nationality, typically American, an up-to-date flapper. Her hair was bobbed and short, done in the customary style of the day, and she was clad in a short, abbreviated dress that showed off to perfection the full symmetry of her well-formed legs.

Her eyes were of a deep violet hue, with long silken lashes, and a cute pert little nose, and an adorable pouting mouth.

Her age—well that is hard to judge, in these days of modern fashion when granny dons short dresses and bobs her hair—but I judge she was not much over seventeen, although she stoutly maintained she was fully eighteen.

Her thin, almost transparent dress hardly concealed the perfect contour of her two delicately chiseled breasts, held in tight by a slender brassiere, and the sight of these two tempting mounds of girlish flesh almost made me reach forth to squeeze them, but knowing that too much advance might frighten this tender and demure morsel I restrained myself and contented myself in making a covert survey of her girlish attractions.

Her dress, as I have stated, was very short, as was common with all girls, and as she climbed into the machine, a little of her leg above the stocking top showed, and revealed to me a slight expanse of her bare and glistening flesh and I felt my member throb in response as though touched with an electric machine.

Seated beside her in the machine I leaned close to her and felt the magnetism of her person communicate itself to me, and instructing Joseph to drive to the address she had given, I leaned back in the seat and we slowly moved away.

Joseph, my man who had been in my service for years, was an observing and devoted servant, (of this more hereafter) and well knew what was going on in his master's mind, and did not at all exceed the speed limit, in fact proceeded less fast than a walk in order, as he well surmised, to give me plenty of time to carry out whatever projects that I had in mind.

I passed my arm back of her head, and allowing it to fall about her waist encountered not the least resistance, and boldly drawing her close to me I snuggled her in my arms and attempted to kiss her on the lips.

She laughingly repulsed me, and looking significantly at Joseph, whose back was turned to us, although he could see us in the mirror before him, she shook a reproving finger at me.

I immediately reached forward and drew down the shade that obscured Joseph's view, and again passing my arms about her slender waist held her closely to me in a tight embrace and now, without the least resistance on her part, she allowed me to press my lips to hers and with warm kisses I held her tight to me, and her arms went around my neck.

Allowing my hand to fall to the front of her waist, I boldly squeezed and manipulated her breasts, allowing a finger to titillate the dormant nipple to a state of erectile hardness, and then, allowing my hand to fall down on her leg, I dove up under her short skirts and moulded and caressed to the full her bare and electric thighs.

At this she drew back a bit, and made as if to stop me, but now, my yard being like a bar of iron I pulled her back to me, and allowing my hand to dive right up between her thighs, I felt the bare lips of her sex and the crinkly pubic hair.

At this she lay forward on my chest, her arms about my neck, and seeing that her resistance was over, I divided the hot moist lips of her cleft and seeking out the touchstone of her nature, by gentle and successive rubs soon had it standing and hard as if to battle an invader.

I now removed my hand for an instant, and tearing open the front of my pants, allowed my stone-hard sockaldodger to spring forth. I seized her hand and guided it to the throbbing shaft and was gratified to feel her grasp it in a firm embrace and begin to rub it slowly up and down its engorged and burning length.

The sudden magnetic touch of her tender and delicate hand on the seat of my sensations, the twining of the white, soft fingers about my shaft of love, my arrow of desire, together with the sweet, melting softness of her clinging lips, together with the soft compression of her thinly-clad body, strained tightly against my own, all conspired to send the blood leaping through my veins like molten fire, and in an excess of passion I drew her roughly to me and plunged my finger which was at the mouth of her sex, deeply up into her person almost to the second joint, which action caused her to give a little cry of pain and hurriedly draw from me and seat herself on the far side of the car.

Her hand had dropped like a coal of fire my throbbing rod, and as I saw tears rush to her eyes, I knew that I had made a mistake, and cursing myself inwardly, quickly began apologizing and begging her pardon, telling her that she had affected me too much, of my fiery nature, etc., and in a moment or two she was again snuggled to my side and my truncheon was again clasped in the soft, magnetic whiteness of her tendril-like fingers.

This time I did not do as before, but contented myself by kissing and caressing her, gently insinuating my hand again under her skirt and regaining the ground that I had lost.

For some moments I contented myself with delicately moulding and squeezing her bubbies and then parting the moist lips of her little quivering slit and titillating her standing clitoris, and feeling as if the sweet compressions of her hand might cause me to spend all over her, I gently disengaged it, and pulled her astraddle my lap and pushed her dress up about her waist.

She now allowed me to do my will and placing the head of my enlarged member against the lips of her slit, I allowed her to slowly settle down upon it, and held her firmly in my arms while we began the delicious weaving dance of lust.

"Oh, oh, oh, ah, a-h-h!" she breathed, "that is so, s-s-o-o-o n-i-c-e! Oh, oh, oh." She slowly wove about on my penetrating needle. "Oh, how lovely; oh, oh, oh, ah, I'm going . . . O-h-h-h!" And she rained down upon the head of my tempestuous rod a torrent of her vital juices.

I felt myself about to melt, and wishing to pierce her deeper, I lifted her in my arms, and placing her upon her back on the cushions of the car, with a few deep and thrilling drives, I let go my charge and felt it bubble and boil in great soul-stirring spurts within her tender and clinging vagina!

We lay for a moment in this close embrace, enjoying the sweet silent aftermath of a pleasant conjunction, and then, taking a handkerchief, I placed it about my rod and slowly drew out of her, causing her to clasp tightly to me as if to hold me there.

I allowed the handkerchief to remain between her thighs, and drying myself I replaced my staff and pulling down her dress gathered her again in my arms and kissed her tenderly on the lips.

She seemed all aflutter, her pulses beating like mad, and her hand nervously went to the front of my pants, and undoing the buttons she again had my limp pintle in her embrace and she rapidly waggled it to and fro impatiently, giving little cries of irritation at its softness and kissing me frantically as if, through the contact of her lips, she wished to stimulate it to renewed hardness.

It soon grew stiff, and rolling her once more back on the seat, I again plunged it within her, and with little gurgles and cries of joy she began a mad waggling of her loins, which, together with the slow jouncing of the car served to draw forth from me a second charge of my dew which spurted and shot from the head of my prong in tempestuous jets to be greedily swallowed by her greedy womb as though she was jealous of losing even a drop of that fluid that is so all-powerful in its effects on the feminine frame!

By this time we were almost to her house, and repairing our apparel, we sat close in each other's arms, and Joseph, bringing the car to a stop, awaited further orders.

"When will I see you again?" I asked her. "You are indeed a nice little girl, Anna, and I must see more of you. Will you allow me the pleasure of seeing you tomorrow night?"

"Oh, no," she answered, "tomorrow is my night out with my fellow, so I could not see you then. If you wish to make it Thursday night"—this was Tuesday—"I will be able to meet you, but we cannot stay out late as I have to be up early in the morning, so you had better meet me early if you wish to."

"And indeed I do!" I answered, allowing my hand to again run under her short dress and to enclasp the lips of her slit. "I will meet you here at seven thirty, and if you wish it, we will go somewhere where we can have some fun. Now, here"—placing my hand in my pocket and drawing forth a bill—"here is something for yourself and if you wish you may buy yourself something to make you look pretty when I meet you."

"Oh, thanks!" she said, somewhat surprised at my liberality, as she noted the banknote was a rather large one, "I will be here sure, and we will do as you say, but now"—and she held up her lips for a kiss—"I must really hurry away and get up in the house as I must be up early in the morning and off to work, otherwise I may be looking for a job!" So after another long melting kiss I allowed her to depart.

You may be sure that I was anxiously on the spot agreed upon on Thursday night, and having taken the precaution of having Joseph keep the car about half a block away, I was awarded by seeing my dear little girl friend hurrying down the street, and after a hurried greeting we were soon ensconced in the car and were quickly whirled out of her neighborhood.

"Where to?" I asked her gayly, after kissing her several times and finding for myself that she had not at all changed in a certain portion of her body, as I held her close to me in a suffocating embrace.

"Oh, I don't care," she replied, "I will go wherever you wish, and the only stipulation that I make is that you have me home good and early for I sure got the dickens for being out so late the last time!"

"Oh, that will be all right," I said, "you may be sure that I will be careful to have you home at an early hour, but for the present, my dear, I would like to, if you are willing, have an opportunity of enjoying you alone—all by yourself—to love, to possess you, my dear Anna, if that is all right with you."

"Well! I guess yes!" she answered. "That is just what was in my own mind, but I did not want to say so, and if you have some place that we could go to, where we might be alone . . ."

"Enough," I cried. "Joseph!" (This to my man, who had received previous instructions) "You may drive at once to where I have told you!"

He immediately turned the car and we were soon rapidly rolling along towards an apartment that I maintained for just such incidents as these.

It was situated in a rather quiet part of the town, and Joseph, being my confidant, knew all about it and even acted as man-servant in these pleasant little pleasure jousts, and in a few moments the car stopped at the door.

I ushered the fair girl out, and leaving Joseph to park the car, I entered the hallway and with my pass-key opened the hall-door and entered my apartments which were situated on the first landing.

Anna, of course, was all eyes, and upon me ushering her into the front parlour she gave a little gasp of astonishment at the furnishings, which, if I do say it myself, were a little out of the ordinary.

I had, as the place was designed for the purposes of pleasure only, hired the services of a capable decorator and furnisher, and he had done himself well in the task of furnishing up the place, as in the front room, instead of the usual couches, tables and spindly-legged chairs, he had placed a number of the softest and coziest divans, all laid on the floor, and for the exception of several very fine etchings on the wall and a small table to contain cigarettes, lighter and a tray for refreshments, the room was not at all cluttered up as most are.

I closed the door behind me and slipped home the bolt knowing that Joseph would let himself in with his key by the rear, and taking the fair girl in my arms I drew her down to me on one of the soft cushions, and gluing my lips to hers, soon had her in a perfect furor of passion and desire.

Not that this stimulation was needed for Anna to warm herself to any occasion, for by nature she was one of those naturally tempestuous creatures of lust and passion that was always ready to "go," and needed no spur in the least to start her desirous blood shooting through her veins.

"Oh, you hurried old bear!" she panted, gently disengaging herself from my arms. "Why, Mr. Anderson!"—for such was the name that I had given her which you may be sure was a ready and fictitious one—"I am surprised indeed at your actions, that you, a gentleman as you are, would so treat a young lady when she visits you for the first time! Aren't you ashamed of yourself!" And struggling to her feet amidst gales of laughter from us both, she made as if to leave the room, only to be caught tightly in my arms and subjected to a new torrent of kisses, embraces, and fondlings so dear to us both.

Finally, both panting with breath we came to a halt, and I was gratified to hear a slight discreet tapping on the door, and allowing my fair charge an instant to set right her short and hardly concealing frock, I opened the door and found that as I had expected, it was Joseph with a tray with two cocktails of a special brand that I liked very much.

"Oh," said Anna, "it's your man! Why, I did not know what was about to happen, but now that I see that he is the bearer of good news"—this with a cute grimace at the sparkling drink on the tray—"I suppose it is no more than right that we should accept it with good grace." And taking the glass that I proffered her she gently tasted it, and voicing her approval drank almost half of it down at once.

I was glad that she seemed to like these cocktails, as they were quite aphrodisiastic in quality, and two or three given to an impressible girl of her sort, would speedily make her forget whether she was on her head or her heels so I urged her to finish it.

I drank my own, the potent liquor stealing through me and filling me with a pleasant warmth, and indicating to Joseph that he might replenish the glasses, I again seated myself at the side of the desirable girl and engaged her in conversation, deeming it best to allow her to rest a moment from my advances, as I would have plenty of time after the liquor had taken full effect.

"Well, my dear," I said, "I see that you are all 'prettied' up tonight, and I must indeed compliment you upon your taste in dress, as you look simply lovely and sweet, and for a girl of your age you certainly know how to clothe or unclothe yourself."

She laughed merrily at this, and then placing her hand over mine she said, "Why, really, my dear benefactor, you yourself have played a leading part in this; it was you that gave me the money to buy this pretty dress." And she lifted it up for my inspection, exposing her pretty leg almost up to her thigh, the sight of the cool, bare flesh above the rolled silk stocking top causing my pintle to stand up and take notice. "It was you that bought me this, so you may compliment at will, but it is yourself that is the reason for what you term my prettiness upon this festive occasion!"

"Well, well!" I said laughingly, "I am sure, my dear, that I was never aware of this, and now that I have seen the result of my small investment you need not be at all surprised if I repeat the experiment!" And gathering her into my arms I allowed my hands to run riot over her pretty and thinly-clad person.

"Oh, oh," she laughed, "if you are going to act that way, I will never, never in the future say a word about what I buy to you as I see you are all set on finding out for yourself just what your money has purchased. And by the way, that reminds me, this dress is not all that I have new, due to your kind generosity!"

"Oh, there is more," I cried, pretending to be surprised. "Well, my dear, you must tell me all about this, also. What is it, the new hat?" And I gazed admiringly at the chic chapeau that now lay on the small table.

"Oh, no, no!" she laughed, "you are far, far away! But still!"—this with a somewhat serious look at me, which was, however, a mock one—"I am afraid, my dear, if I were to tell you about it, or them, you might want to follow the same tactics that you have done with my dress, and that, I am sure, would be perfectly terrible!" And she held up her hands in mock horror.

At this instant Joseph returned with another of my cocktails, or to be true, a pair of them, and handing Anna the generously-filled glass, I was gratified to see her drain it at once, as the room was rather warm, the windows being tightly closed and the shades drawn.

Joseph discreetly left the room and again seating myself by her side, I passed my arm about her waist and drew her close to me and allowed my roving hand to take possession of one of her budding breasts, the nipple of which stood out strongly under the thin covering, and urged her to proceed.

"Well," she laughed, "just as I told you, if I told you you would want to feel, and the articles that I mention are those that are not for public display, and constitute, to be frank with you, my intimate undercoverings or lingerie. So you see, I could never, never, never . . ." But before she could tantalize me further I had tumbled her on her back on the divan and had pulled up her dress and exposed her person to the waist and was gratified to find that her lower portion was clad in a pair of the cutest, frenchiest, laciest open-work pants that I had ever had the pleasure of looking upon!

"Cheater!" I cried. "You never told me about these!" And I passed my hand over the thin covering, allowing it to rest for an instant on the seat of her sensations, which caused her to writhe and bounce about so I deemed it best to desist till later.

"You are a nice little girl to come here with a pair of panties like that on!" I chided her. "And they are all closed up! Are you afraid of being raped while you are in my company? Is that the reason, Anna?"

"It might be that I was afraid that I might not be!" she giggled, now showing the effects of the cocktail, as she reached to the front of my pants and tore open the buttons and allowed my throbbing charger to leap forth into the confines of her warm little palm. "May I depend upon it, my dear Mr. Anderson, that you are not at all jesting when you mention this terrible thing?"

For an answer I persuaded her to completely remove her scanty dress, and retaining only her very scant panties, her brassiere and her stockings and slippers, I again clasped her into my arms and covered her lips with stormy caresses.

"Off with these!" I cried, dragging at the band of the closed drawers, and they were soon dangling about her ankles, and I drew them off and laid them on the divan beside us.

"Why you rude thing!" she pouted. "Just for that, I think it no more than fair that you also be punished by being made to shed your clothes so that there will be no difference between us!" And she began to undo my waistcoat, etc., and sooner than it takes to write I was in a state as naked as Adam, and she that of Eve.

Our disrobing was no sooner completed, when Joseph's discreet knock disturbed us, and Anna, looking wildly about for something to cover her, acted a little terrified, but upon me telling her that Joseph was an intimate of mine and had been with me for years, she made no further effort to clothe herself and lying back in my arms, all her charms exposed to view, she allowed Joseph to enter and to tender us more refreshments.

Joseph did not betray by the least sign that he was at all surprised at this sight, and Anna, dashing off her drink, gave a little giggle and threw herself in my arms, one of her hands still encircling my standing and throbbing tool.

I could no longer wait, and throwing her roughly upon her back in Joseph's presence, I guided my tool to the entrance of her slit and with one drive buried it within her to the balls, and grasping her about the cheeks of her magnificent posteriors, I plunged in and out of her sweet secret recess, her membranes clinging to my staff in a loving glove-like embrace, till she finally with great cries and sobs sucked every drop of my elixir from the head of my cock and lay back swooning and panting in my arms.

"Oh, oh, oh," she cried, "that is just delightful! Just marvelous! Oh, do it some more!" And she twisted and gyrated her loins about as though to instill renewed life in my staff which was still held tightly in the moist and burning embrace of her cleft, but alas! it was soft and limber, and as it slipped out of the clinging embrace of her sex she gave a little vexed cry of disappointment, and pressing her thighs closely together buried her face in the cushions and almost sobbed forth her unsated lust, her entire naked body quivering and tingling as though from an electric charge, and I gathered her in my arms and endeavoured to console her for the lack of my "staying powers," but she angrily pulled away and refused to be at all consoled.

At this point I raised my eyes to Joseph, who had stood by, an interested spectator to all this violent little love-play, and a plan entering my mind. I bent close to her and whispered in her ear:

"Anna dear! If you will listen a moment I am sure that I will be able to alleviate your distress in full; listen to me for an instant!" And her curiosity aroused, she allowed me to proceed.

"Joseph," I said "as you may well see, is quite excited at present, and a glance at the front of his pants will convince you that the sight of you, with your charms uncovered, has set him all ablaze, and I am sure that if you will allow it he will be very glad to see what he can do towards giving you a charge of what seems, at the present moment, all that you want. Look, Anna, at his pants. Do you see it?"

At this she turned a bit, and noticing the large bulge in the front of Joseph's pants, hid her face again and said,

"Oh, it looks so big that it really might hurt me, but if you really want him to . . ."

I spent no further time in parley, but nodding my head to Joseph, (who had followed every one of our words!) he hastily left the room and I kissed and caressed the dear girl in hopes of another rising of the senses.

"Oh," she said in a somewhat disappointed tone, raising her head and looking about, "oh, where, where did he go to? I thought—I thought that he was going to—going to . . ."

"He is," I laughed at her, "you need not worry at all about him! He is going to do as you wish him to do, but I thought it better that he should retire and remove his outer clothing; it might be more agreeable to both of you that way—but here he is now." At this point the door opened and Joseph, bare to the skin, entered, his long sockaldodger standing out before him like an immense iron rod.

He certainly was a man that was fully gifted in these parts, his prong being fully a foot long and some inches in diameter, and being naked as he was, his huge balls dangling below this horse-like prick, it was enough to startle any girl, and Anna gave a little scream at the sight and again buried her head in the cushions.

"Come, Anna," I coaxed her, "surely you are not at all afraid of that monster! You have just been crying for more and more, and here when I provide you with a real honest-to-goodness one you immediately act as if you were scared to death. Do you want me to send him away? Say so if you do!"

There was no answer, of course, to this, and Joseph lying down beside us, I placed the girl in his arms, and after kissing and hugging her a bit he rolled her flat on her back and climbing on top of her lifted himself up and placed the head of his prong at her slit and began to bore away at her.

Anna assisted him as much as she could, placing her arms and legs about his back and after a few pushes and stabs he finally succeeded in entering her and the dance of love began anew.

Joseph was an ardent cocksman; one who took a real love in his work and who was almost able to satisfy the lust of any ordinary girl, but our dear little Anna, being no ordinary girl, indeed, stood up under two charges of his dew, and then seemed unwilling to allow him to withdraw that sweet plug of love, so effective had been his poundings, but finally it was over and the three of us lay together on the floor.

Joseph arose and prepared fresh refreshments, this time taking one for himself, and we all talked together. Anna told us of her young man, what a fine fellow he was and how she expected to marry him, and while speaking of this I asked her if it were possible that she might bring a girl friend with her the next time that she came, and to this she immediately assented.

"I shall bring Grace," she said. "I am sure that you will like her for she is a very nice girl; about my own age, and she is the girl that I go with all of the time. She is blond, and has a wonderful shape, and likes to go out and have a good time, and I am sure that Joseph here will find a good home for this terrible thing!" And here she seized hold of his joy-stick and gave it a wicked tweak, causing us both to laugh.

"But you must understand, Anna," I said seriously, "there are times when I have Joseph together with us in our bouts, but you must understand that I wish you to secure this girl for me and for me alone, as Joseph fully understands this and I wish you to, also. Is that clear to you, my dear?" And I kissed her full, pouting rosebud lips.

"Oh, yes," she laughed, "if you will have it that way, I suppose it must be, but nevertheless, you shall see her if you wish, and I am sure that she will prove acceptable. As far as I am concerned I would be perfectly willing to go along all by myself . . ."

"That," I said emphatically, "you must let me be the judge of. As long as you are here and I remember you," here I bent a significant glance upon her, "you should be more than satisfied, and you may assure your girl friend that if she conducts herself in accord with my ideas I will treat her as liberally as I do you. Do you think that will please her?"

"Please her?" echoed Anna, her hand still encircled about Joseph's cock and massaging it gently. "I should say it would! Grace, like myself, has ideas of getting married, and I think it will take place right soon, and as the fellow has not a lot of money, she is like a hungry little wolf for money and I think that she will do almost anything for it, so you need not worry about that part of it. When do you want her?"

"At our very next appointment," I told her, "but now, let us confine ourselves to the present. I notice that Joseph here is in a state of appealing hardness and I myself am in no ways soft, so I judge, dear girl, that you are due for another plunging, so roll over on your back and let me see if you can reduce this to a state of shrinkability!'' And I rolled her over and mounted her, and in a moment poured into her womb another charge of my balm, and arising, allowed Joseph to fuck her, which operation lasted for fully twenty minutes till finally, with groans, twists and cries, and scratching of his back, they both drained the reservoirs of their sex, and lay panting on the floor.

I made her the usual ''present'' of a bill, which she was well versed enough to know was to reward her labour in her task of reducing my hardness of feelings, and making another appointment to meet her, I had Joseph drive her back to her neighborhood and dismissed her from my mind for the present at least.

At this portion of my narrative I deem it best that I acquaint the reader with some of the fads and follies of the writer, so that, later on in this sparse history of a sensual life, he may be more familiar with the traits both normal and abnormal that will at times be depicted upon the written page.

As I have stated earlier here, I am a gentleman somewhat on in years, and if I do say it myself, of somewhat pleasing appearance, especially to the opposite sex. Being left fairly well off and having a business that is practically self-operating, I devote the majority of my time to my pleasures, which as the reader has determined by now, are mostly those of the flesh.

I am an ardent admirer of beauty in all of its manifest forms; I am a lover of flowers, paintings and the finer things of life, and like above all things the full well-developed form of the modern girl, the flapper.

Being situated financially in a manner to gratify most of my

411

wishes I sought high and low for complaisant pretty girls, and if they were in accord with my will and desires, I treated them in a courtly fashion and repaid them liberally for their time.

Not that I cared to associate with the demi-monde, the street walkers, the prostitutes and all their ilk; much rather would I caress the clothed knee or thigh of a fair young damsel and be content with that than to lie abed with a hardened old roustabout; I love youth, beauty, and the delicious freshness that was the endowment of modern feminine girlhood.

Joseph, as the reader may well judge, was a confidential servant, indeed, and had assisted me and taken active part in many another little affair of this kind, and I trusted him absolutely, and now with this dear Anna, I was sure that I had secured another active helper.

Her promise of her girl friend, Grace, was indeed a pleasant fillip to my lustful imagination, and I carefully dressed on that evening and was on the corner long before the time set, anxious to catch a glimpse of the girl that had been so warmly described to me.

Sure enough, I saw Anna walking quietly down the street, accompanied by another girl about her size, and in a glance I saw that Anna had not misrepresented the girl's qualities in the least.

She was as Anna had told me, a truly beautiful girl with large blue eyes and a mop of golden hair which was shortly bobbed as is the fashion.

She was perfectly formed, the shape of her youthful body being well put off by the abbreviated dress that she wore, and was without a hat, having evidently left the house on the pretext of going for a short walk.

Introductions were soon over, and I assisted both of them into the car and Joseph started to drive slowly through a number of side streets and I discreetly drew the shades so that we would not be seen by passers-by should the car be halted at the crossings.

"Now, here you are," said the laughing Anna, "here, Mr. Anderson, I have delivered my captive, and I assure you that it was a job, indeed, for Grace is wildly in love with her Charlie, and for a while was at a loss as to whether to come at all, but I told her that I had promised you, and I am sure that once we are together a while she will forget all about her sweetheart, and will have as much fun as any of us! Isn't that right, Grace dear?" she asked, turning to the blushing girl who was seated beside me.

Grace made no answer for a moment and then allowing her head to lie over on my shoulder, passed a hand behind my back and seized that of Anna and laughed nervously and said in a low voice, "Well, you know, Anna, that this is quite—quite irregular for me to go out like this—and Charlie—that is my fellow"—(this to me)—"and he is terribly jealous of me and doesn't allow me to go with anyone—if he should ever know of it, it might ruin our marriage—and I am simply crazy about him and I must watch myself. You know that, Anna."

"Oh, yes," said Anna, "I know you are crazy about your Charlie, and I am the same about Jim, but still, Grace, that is no bar to you and I having a little fun, and who, seeing there is just you and I, is ever going to know anything about it? Then besides, Mr. Anderson is such a wonderful man! I am sure after you know him better you will be just eager and waiting for the time to come to meet him! Isn't that right, Mr. Anderson?'' she said, looking to me for confirmation.

I laughed at this, and passing my arms about the waists of both of the girls, I said to Grace, "I should think my dear, that you, as you are engaged to your dear Charlie and are even getting ready right now to marry him, should be all the more accustomed to the company of men, and the fact that you go with me, and that I might—might even go as far as to treat you like Charlie does—that in itself would in no way flurry or upset you, in fact, I think—.''

"Oh, Mr. Anderson," interrupted Anna, "I forgot altogether to tell you''—and here she laughed as if her heart would break—"I forget to tell you that our dear little Grace, so wild is she about her dear beloved Charlie, that she does not even stay with him or allow him to touch her—she thinks that if a girl does that that a fellow will never, never marry her. Can you imagine that?'' And she laughed again.

Poor Grace blushed redly at this and I immediately set about to put things to rights by saying that in some cases that was the best plan, and was immediately set upon by Anna who evidently conducted herself in an entirely different manner with her own suitor, and a heated debate ensued between us, in which Grace took no part whatever.

By this time we had arrived before the building in which I had my rooms, and Joseph bringing the car to a stop, opened the door and assisted the two girls to alight.

Once within the confines of the apartment, the girls lighted cigarettes and Joseph brought in a tray with three of the cocktails of such aphrodisiastic qualities.

To my surprise, Grace refused to drink with us and

stood the guying of Anna, who taunted her unmercifully, and contented herself with looking about the room. I saw that she was ill at ease and set about to make her feel at home, and flatter myself that I did a bit, for she sat on the cushions and was soon laughing and talking the same as her girl friend.

Knowing that we had not long to spend, I rose to my feet and taking Grace by the hand, asked her to come and see the house with me, and let her into an adjoining chamber furnished like the one we had left, and once within I bolted the door behind me.

Anna had watched us with curious eyes, and seeing that we were to leave her alone made no remark, and Joseph entering at that instant with another drink, I knew that she would be occupied till our return as I had instructed my servant before the rendezvous, and knew that I had the fair Grace to myself for a few moments at least.

She evidently knew what was transpiring in my mind, for she allowed me to gently draw her down on the cushions beside me, and once in my arms, I pressed hot kisses on her lovely lips and allowed my hands to run riot all over her girlish perfection.

I found, however, that she was quite matter-of-fact in regard to terms, for drawing gently back from me, she arranged her dress, and looking about to see that we were alone she said in a low voice, "I understand, Mr. Anderson, that Anna and you have been quite close together—in fact that you know one another quite intimately—that you have possessed her—and when Anna told me that you wished to meet me and to have a party with me, you must understand, Mr. Anderson, that one of the main reasons that I accepted is that you had her understand that I was to receive something in return—that you are to pay me. This, of course, is a rather abrupt way of putting it, but you must understand that I am an engaged girl and am shortly to be married, and I do not accord these favours even to my own intended husband, and if we intend to proceed I wish that clearly understood between us. Is not that right?''

"Oh, yes," I said, relieved to find that she was so materialistic. "I told Anna exactly that, and you may be sure that I meant exactly what I said, and now that I have seen you I have no reason indeed to regret my bargain and assure you that I will do exactly as she outlined to you.'' And I made as if to gather the beautiful girl to me and smother her again with my caresses.

She, however, held me back again, and pulling her short skirt over her knees, held up her finger at me and continued, "Anna also told me that the man that drives your car, that he also is to take part in the bargain, and I wish to know if that is all, because I would not, for any consideration, stand any more, not that I am not able and perhaps willing, but an engaged girl has standards to maintain, and would it not be for the money involved, I would never think of starting in the first place.''

"You have been stayed with?" I asked curiously, puzzled at this girl's strange conversation, so different she was from the exuberant Anna.

"Oh yes," she admitted, "I have been with men quite often, and although I deny myself to others and even to my intended, you may be sure that it is not for any dislike for the act, but the consequences attending it. Pregnancy, etc., have filled my heart with fear, and I am eager for a home

416

and children, and in my marriage with Charlie I am sure that I would realize all of my fondest dreams. This, to me, is merely a means to an end, and I do not consider it wrong at all, but now that we have understood one another, let's get set and get going or I shall have an argument to contend with should I not return in a short space of time.''

"But," I persisted, "supposing—supposing pregnancy should result from this—this occasion? Does that not enter your fears at all? Do you not fear that you would be in a delicate state in a few months should you submit to Joseph and myself?''

"I marry in three weeks," she said simply, "and although Charlie has never possessed me, you may be sure that by that time he will be my husband, and any consequences, as you put them, will be well taken care of, so you may rest easy as to that.''

At this instant I thought it best to bring this matter-of-fact discussion to a close, and pressing a bill of rather large denomination into her hand, I pressed her close to me and abandoned myself to the delightful pleasure of the contact of her fresh, youthful form.

She lay in my arms, allowing me to do my will, and pressing the front of her dress I moulded and caressed her firm young breasts, bare to my fingerings except for the thinness of her silk dress, and passing my hand over her silken-covered legs I allowed one of them to mount to the top of her stocking and reveled in the feel of her bare thighs.

My prick by this time was straining at its bonds, and tearing open the fly of my pants I allowed it to spring forth to be in an instant encompassed by her tiny hand and she submitted it to a delightful and tingling compression that made me feel as if I would shoot right over in her palm and over her bare wrist and forearm.

"Oh, you are lovely," I murmured, and dividing her thighs, I allowed my hand to run up on her belly and then to slip down and play riot with her pubic curls and to squeeze and compress the lips of her sexual slit, till I was almost mad with lust and desire. I sucked her mouth into mine, and passing my arm about her neck drew her to me in a stifling embrace and sought as if to ravish her on the very spot.

"My dress, my dress!" she said, "do not get it wet, I beg you! You may go off and spot me, and I would have to . . ."

"Then off with it," I said, somewhat brutally, I think, and suiting the action to the word, I began to drag it over her head. She drew away and arose, and squirming out of it allowed me to see all of her form, and loosing her panties at the waist allowed them to fall from her and stood naked before me.

I seized her by the hand and drew her down beside me and covered all of her lovely nakedness with kisses of fire, and my cock now in a state of pulsing hardness, I pushed her flat on her back and bestrode her, almost mad with pleasurable desire.

She opened her thighs wide and allowed me to lay within them, and presenting the head of my priapus at the entrance of her slit I thrust away at her, but was agreeably surprised to find that I could not even make the head of it enter, and push as I might the natural dryness of my prong, together with the tightness of her orifice, made connection impossible.

"You—will—never—never—do—it!" she gasped, the breath driven out of her tender young body at the assaults I made upon her. "I—know it—I am too tight. It is a long time—a long time since I had it before!"

I determined that she was right in her surmise, and leaping to my feet I pulled the bell cord for Joseph and stood surveying her as she lay naked on the floor.

"What are you going to do?" she asked, looking up at me, and making as if to arise to her feet, but I again gently pushed her back on her back.

"I am ringing for Joseph" I explained, "and will secure some cold cream, so that I will make my entrance much easier. You need not worry at his entrance, as he is to have you, too, and it will be a pleasant introduction for him."

At this instant Joseph discreetly knocked at the door and I admitted him and made known my wants in this particular direction. He cast a glance at the girl on the floor and she turned her face on the cushions in shame, and from the opened front of his pants I knew that he had been consoling Anna, and he left and soon returned with a jar of the desired unguent.

Placing it on the cushion beside us, I again mounted the form of the prostrate girl, and anointing the head of my staff liberally, I took her again in my arms and again essayed the ravishment of her sexual charms. This time I succeeded in wedging the head within the tightly-closed lips, and settling down full upon her, I pushed forward with my loins and soon had a full inch of my throbbing rod impaled in her vitals.

"O-o-o-o-o-h-h-h" she murmured, thrashing about on the cushions and placing her hands against my chest as though to push me from her, "you are h-u-r-t-i-n-g me! Oh, oh, oh, that is too—too big! Take it out a minute! Just a minute! It stretches me too much! You are . . . wait! Wait!"

But I had gained my point and was in no mood to relinquish it, and passing my hands back of her naked and bouncing posteriors I poised myself high upon her and with one drive sheathed half of the entire length of my dart into its clinging and trembling cove, and she gave a wild scream of pain and fell back trembling and senseless in my arms.

That one cruel plunge must have hurt her, but now seeing that she was insensible I made the most of the opportunity, and with a few more drives soon was in her cove to the hilt and then lay panting upon her till Nature saw fit to restore her to her senses.

I knew that the cry must have startled Anna, but depended upon Joseph and the soothing presence of his kidney tosser to secure me from interruption, and the door being locked, waited with patience for her return to her senses.

She soon began to thrash about, and opening her eyes, moved her loins about and the first pain of the entrance over, I began a slow weaving, rhythmic motion on her body, allowing my prong to glide in and out of the heated moistness of her glove-like membranes.

"Oh, oh, oh," she cried, "you are cruel, cruel indeed! Why could you not be easier with me?"

Then, pain giving way to more passionate sensations,

she allowed her bare arms to steal tightly around my neck and her loins gave me back thrust for thrust and her lips met mine in a clinging embrace and we melted into one, a moving rhythm of lust, and our breath came in pants and bursts as I held her close to me!

"Oh, oh, o-h-h-h-h-h-h-h-h-h!" she sighed, thrusting upwards with all her might to meet the descending charger, "oh, oh, o-h-h-h, there . . . t-h-e-r-e!!!" as her slit opened and closed on my staff with lightning-like loving strokes. "T-h-e-r-e, that, t-h-a-t is it! Oh, ohohohohoh o-o-o-o-o, I'm coming! O-h-h-h-h, lover darling, that is s-o-o-o n-i-c-e!" And her hot flow bathed and sprayed my swelling charger.

Again and again this delightful compression of her tight slit took place, and each time she vented a shower of girlish dew upon me, and feeling that I, also, was about to spend I took her firmly in my arms and whispered in her ear, "Here, here! Here is the child that you fear! I will spout into your womb a living, pulsing life! There, there, there," as I exploded in her, "that is the first fruit of your marriage! Take it and rear it as a gift from me!" And I shot and bubbled in great spurts into her womb the largest charge that I could ever recall, and driving my prong far up into her, sought as if to more firmly embed it within the most secret confines of her being.

She, at the same instant, gave down another charge, and we then lay melting in each other's arms, relaxed and breathless on the cushions.

I lay on her for some time still, my throbbing prick still embedded to the balls within her, and she, as though mad with lust, began another series of wiggles beneath me, and feeling life revive, I again commenced a slow weaving upon her.

This second bout was much longer than the first, and I enjoyed to the full the tight and clinging constrictions of her slit upon the heart of my sex, and after she had vented four or five times I again discharged within her and we again lay still.

I lay for a few minutes and then withdrew, the charge from her fleshy bottle spurting out as I removed the cork onto the cushions and made my toilet. Grace pressed her thighs closely together and rolled on her side as if to hide the damage done to her pretty person, and I noticed that the wetness was stained with red and knew that her maidenhead, or at least the remnants of it had now departed her forever, and felt a strange thrill of pride run through me as I looked at the naked girl.

"Now for Joseph," I said gaily.

At this she turned her tear-stained face to me and held up a restraining hand and said, "Please, please, I beg of you! Wait just a few minutes at least! I will take him as I have agreed to do, but in a moment I will have regained my composure and then, if you will, I will carry out my part of the agreement!"

A wave of pity overcame me, and I thought to myself that this poor girl, in order to arrange for her marriage with her lover, a man that had never known her—that is, sexually—was prostituting herself for the means of possessing her, and here she was, about to submit to the embraces of a perfect stranger, a servant, and my seed soaking in her womb . . . It was too unbearable . . . it must not be. Suddenly it occurred to me . . . what if she was pregnant? With my child pulsing in her womb? Why not wait and see the outcome of it? Joseph would be well satisfied with Anna, and should Grace, as she feared, become with child with me, how novel it would be! I made up my mind instantly that it should be as I planned.

"No," I said to her, "you will not even have to be with Joseph. I have changed my mind, and when you have sufficiently recovered you may dress yourself and leave. Is that agreeable to you, my dear?" And I again lay at her side and covered her face with kisses.

"Oh, yes," she said, "I am glad that you did that. I am willing, as I said, to carry out my part of the bargain, but really, you have hurt me dreadfully, as I have never had one that big, and it opened me up so large that I feel as if I will be unable to even walk! Will you assist me to my feet, please."

I assisted her to arise, the spent charge of our combined balm running in pinken streams down her naked thighs, and finding to her surprise that she was now really dead, I handed her a towel and left her to repair the damage done to her person and opening the door quietly peered out to see what Joseph and Anna were up to.

It just happened that I came just in time, for they were engaged in a terrific sexual combat, tossing about with interlaced limbs: Anna, now bare of all apparel and Joseph stripped to his shorts and drawers. I turned to Grace, and she seeing through the door the delicious act of sexual combat watched with glistening and lustful eyes as the pair melted away in a series of panting sobs and finally lay still and trembling, his dew spouting into the young girl's tender being.

At the sight of us, they grew confused and hastily scrambled to their feet and we both laughed heartily at their actions.

After this, both of the girls dressed and as I signified a desire to hear of their previous love affairs and the bestowal of their maidenheads we again arranged an early date, and conducting them to the neighborhood of their respective homes, left them and repaired to other pleasures.

Of these, the reader may not doubt that there were many channels that served to supply me, and Joseph, in his capacity as personal servant, always had something on tap that was sure to provide me amusement, and tonight had arranged an affair that I was sure would give mê pleasure. But of that more anon as it takes place.

We proceeded to another section of the city, and Joseph parking the car, we went on foot to a somewhat disreputable hotel where Joseph had engaged rooms earlier in the evening under assumed names, and ascending in the elevator we were soon by ourselves.

"Now, Joseph," I said, taking a drink from a pocket flask that he had thoughtfully brought with him in the car, "what is it that you have this evening? I hope it is something new and uncommon, as I am pretty well tired after my bout with Grace, and promise you that you will be well taxed to provide me entertainment now, my good man."

"I thought so, Sir," said Joseph respectfully, "and in view of that I have provided for something that I am sure will meet with your approval. I am sure, in the past, that I have done my best, and I would not now think of anything that would tax your energy, and you will see that my judgment is as good as ever."

And indeed he had! And I admired him for his ingenuity and diplomacy in these matters. No doubt, many a dollar had made their way into his capacious pockets through his master's lustful desires, but that I cared naught of, so long as he provided for my pleasures, and this he really did and was ideal in this respect, and I was now all pins and needles to know what he had on tap.

"What is it, Joseph?" I asked.

"You will see, sir," he said, and made no further revelations and I awaited with curiosity, watching his movements.

He went to the phone and asking for a certain room engaged in a cryptic conversation, and then with a smile replaced the receiver on the hook. In a moment or two a light rap came on the door, and upon Joseph opening it, to my surprise a figure, presumably that of a girl, entered the room—but what a girl!

She was scarcely three feet in height, although perfectly formed in all particulars, but was indeed a miniature girl—indeed a midget! It almost floored me with astonishment at the sight of her, but now being somewhat accustomed to Joseph's surprises, I hurriedly invited her to enter, and closed and fastened the door behind her.

"This," said Joseph, somewhat proudly, "is Mademoiselle Tiny, whom you have doubtless seen at a number of the theatres about town. I have already informed her of the profound admiration that you have for her, and have at last succeeded in persuading her to come here and see you. I am sure that you will find her admirable company and now that you are together hope that you will pardon me, as I wish to step downstairs to keep an appointment that I have made.''

And with this, my estimable servant bowed quite low to us and opened the door and vanished. I asked the little lady to be seated, and she looked curiously about the room and seated herself, not on the chair but on the edge of the bed, looking like a tiny little doll.

"I am certainly glad to have this opportunity of meeting you," I said, "and I must indeed compliment you upon your stage appearance," (although as far as I recollect I had never seen her on the stage, but thought to follow the suggestions so adroitly conveyed me by the invaluable Joseph). And she smiled at this and in a low, quiet voice thanked me, and to my utmost astonishment boldly placed her tiny hands on the front of my pants and in a jiffy unbuttoned my fly and drew out my limber prick and moulded and compressed in a manner that bespoke much previous knowledge in this delectable art!

This, of course, broke the ice, and I discarded all reserve or consideration that I might have had in regard to her, and drawing her over close to me, I sought out her tiny breasts and pulling open her little dress I soon had them out and my lips glued to one of her nipples.

She still continued to pull away at my staff, which by now was assuming a state of agreeable hardness, and allowing one of my hands to dive under her dress I found that she had her stockings rolled to the knee and I rubbed and squeezed the tiny legs and thighs and sought to get up further to her sexual parts. She had, however, a pair of bloomers on, and this in a manner put a stop to my explorations, and laughing and giggling she begged me to stop an instant, and upon me finally releasing her she detached her hands from my prick and springing lightly to the floor began to disrobe.

The sight of this tiny person, a veritable jewel of a woman, disrobing before me caused me to experience a lustful thrill, and as she quickly disrobed, unveiling to me all of her cameo-like charms, I sought to encompass her in my arms.

Her size, however, made it easy for her to avoid me, and seeing that I was only using my precious time I lay back on the bed and allowed her to continue undressing.

Finally she was stripped to her stockings, and standing proudly before me allowed me to survey all of her naked charms, even turning about slowly to allow me to see her miniature back and buttocks, and I could wait no longer; I leaped to the floor and picking her up in my arms, carried her to the bed and throwing her on her back lay beside her and allowed my sensual tongue to run all over her body.

She again regained hold of my standing prick, and with both hands now held it against her tiny breasts, and I pushed back and forth as though already in the sexual embrace, and she bent her head low to it, and to my surprise engulfed the flaming head of it in her tiny mouth and with adroit tongue began to titillate and bang upon the throbbing head in quick jerks with her tongue so that I almost leaped from the bed.

I pressed the back of her head, and settled down to enjoy to the full this lustful abnormal act, and in a moment or two I felt my prick swell and throb to the bursting point in her mouth and pressing it as far as I could down the confines of her throat I let loose my seething boiling load of balm and she choked and tried to back away but all of my essence bubbled and spurted in great spurts down in the confines of her throat, and when at last, exhausted, I fell back on the bed, she pulled away, sputtering and gasping and breathless beside me.

"Oh," she said, after she had regained her breath, "my goodness, what a load you shoot! Why, you nearly strangled me! I thought sure that I was drowned!"

"Then you have done it before?" I asked, curiously, taking her again in my arms and kissing her.

"Oh, yes," she said, laughing, "my husband, who, by the way, was a much larger man than you are, always found an especial delight ın that form of amusement; and I myself formed quite a liking for the 'French' act, as it is called, and there was many a charge of his that found its way down my throat. Besides, when he died—well—there were others, you understand!" And she looked at me and laughed merrily.

"Your husband was much larger than I was?" I echoed. "You mean that he was constituted physically in all ways—?"

"I know exactly what you mean," she laughed. "You are wondering whether his parts were as large as yours are, and I will tell you yes, and even more so. I am so built that it is possible for me to have regular intercourse with men of normal size, and although at first it was rather trying, after living with my husband for a few years I now not only can bear it, but take the keenest enjoyment in the act myself, provided there is mutual desire."

This was quite new to me in spite of all my experience, as I had thought that midgets and others of their ilk could and would only have intercourse with their own kind and build.

The idea that this tiny person was capable of sustaining the assaults of a fully-developed man like myself was indeed intriguing to me, and in an effort to ascertain for myself as to the condition of these parts, I allowed my hand to slip down between her thighs, and dividing the lips of her sexual slit, I found to my surprise that it was just as she had said, and somewhat regretfully I considered the soft shrinking state of my organ and longed for hardness in order that I, too, might possess her.

She evidently was in full accord with my moods, for her tiny hand stole down to my dart and with many sweet compressions and fondlings she sought to bring it to a state of usable hardness, and then, quickly slipping down in the bed, she applied her provocative mouth to the tip of my rod and in a few instants it stood up ready to battle.

"But how?" I asked her, as she held it up for my inspection, planting a last moist kiss on the now throbbing head.

"Why, the same way," she replied, turning on her back and allowing me to mount her. She quickly guided the head of my staff to her eager and receptive slit, and I gently plunged it home, marvelling at her capacity for this giant tool, especially so in regard to her size, but the nervous clasping and unclasping of her hot, burning tissues about the sides of my torrid rod soon sent all other ideas flying from my mind and I commenced to fuck away in earnest.

The little creature pressed her cunt up close to my plunging brick as if she did not want to miss a bit of it, and I, a sadistic mood overcoming me, plunged away at her as if I wished to really split her in twain.

The previous combats that I had indulged in during the day served to prolong my pleasure and I must have bounded up and down upon her for upward of twenty or thirty minutes before Nature saw fit to open the sexual flood gates and allow me to flood her womb with a bounding charge of my manly sap.

We both lay quiet, my prick being squeezed of its last spurting drops by the compressions of her tingling quim, then I gently withdrew, not without a little protest from my charming, diminutive partner who tried to hold me to her, and allowed a flood of our combined juices to flow out, down her bare buttocks onto the counterpane.

I was now quite exhausted and after allowing her to dress, I repaired the damage done to my own apparel, and awaited the return of Joseph, who I knew was nearby watching the outcome of the affair that he had planned. I did not offer her anything for herself as I knew that Joseph had taken care of that end of the matter. He soon entered and after inquiring if the affair had terminated to my satisfaction, we took our leave.

I gave Joseph a substantial tip for himself, as I enjoyed these affairs that he arranged for me, and we then returned to the car and I was driven homewards. I looked forward with great pleasure to a second meeting with Anna and her pretty partner Grace, and thought to myself what new methods I would plan to more thoroughly sate my lust upon the fair bodies of the two young girls who were so willing to accept my gold in return for the divine charms bestowed upon them by Nature.

By this time the reader will have determined, and rightly, too, that my life was mostly devoted to adventures of lust and seduction, and in this he is right and correct. My business being of such a nature that I could very well allow it to be taken care of by trusty subordinates, I had plenty of time and money at my disposal, and to afford me to exercise my sensual pleasures to the full, and as the reader will have seen in the earlier portion of this narrative, I lived only for the gratification of my sensual whimsies.

In a couple of days the time arrived for my appointment with the two charming girls, and I ordered Joseph to have the car at my call, and upon the evening set I was anxiously awaiting at the rendezvous.

After a short wait I saw the pair of girls tripping gaily down the street, and discreetly entering the car, Joseph at once drove up to the apartment.

I had made special arrangements for this affair, at which both of the girls were to detail to me their first experiences in the jousts of love and lust, and had Joseph arrange that a wonderful cold lunch be prepared and champagne placed in convenient coolers.

Both girls gave little cries of delight and satisfaction at the sight of the well-laid table, and Joseph, retiring to the other portions of the house, left us alone for the time being to our own devices.

"Well, well," I said, "you are both certainly all dressed up for the occasion!"

And indeed they were, for both, as I surmised, had made good use of the bills that had been presented them upon their last visit to the place to buy themselves new articles of apparel, and they certainly looked refreshing indeed!

Both girls thanked me for the compliment and Grace, throwing herself back on one of the low lounges that graced the room, lighted herself a cigarette and asked for a drink.

I obligingly secured one for her and Grace, and taking one myself I warned them of the shortness of the time and begged them to proceed at once.

"But which one?" asked Grace. "I am sure that it will not be fair that I start first, for there are many—many—times—"

"Oh, ho!" laughed Anna. "So, my dear Grace, there are many, many other times that I have never heard of! Well, you may be sure that I will be interested in that, for there are many times that I know of, and others that you have told me of, and if there are still others"—and here she significantly shook a reproving finger at the blushing Grace—"you may be sure that they must be indeed terrible! Start, I am waiting!"

"Just a minute," I intervened. "As Grace says, it is not at all fair that one should start before the other, but as it must be done, what do you say if we toss up a coin and let that decide it? I am sure that will be fair and square. What do you say, girls?"

Both girls assented to this and I secured a coin from my waistcoat, and upon them each making their selection, I tossed it into the air, and Anna, much to her dissatisfaction, was chosen as the first to retail to us the loss of her maidenhead.

She was a little bit downcast at this, but soon perked up,

and seating herself between us, crosslegged on the cushions, the whole form of her adorable and scantily-clad lower person almost unveiled to our eyes, began as follows:

"Well, I see, dear Grace, that you, with your usual luck, have succeeded in having me be the first to bore Mr. Anderson, and I hope that my short tale of boys and stiff dickies will at least amuse you. I am sure that it will not at all be thrilling or exciting, but you have wished it, so here it is. Let's see—where shall I begin?" And she pursed her lips and corrugated her brow adorably, placing a finger under her chin as if she was deep in thought, and causing both Grace and myself to burst into peals of merry laughter at her silly antics.

"I shall skip," she said decidedly, "all of the silly acts and thoughts of childhood, the little playings of house, etc.—"

But at this Grace and I both set up a howl, and laughing, she held up a restraining hand and then said, "Well, I see how impatient you both are for all, for everything, so I will see what I can think back to!

"The first I can remember—that is, in a 'sexy' way— was when Doris and I, Doris being a little girl friend of mine—the first I can now remember is when I was about nine or ten years old, and Doris, who was about my own age, used to take me down walking by the river banks and we would try to peek out and see the boys in swimming, whom, as you may well imagine, wore not the least of clothing.

"This, I thought, was quite wrong and exciting to me, and though having no notion of what it was all about, we used to creep up and down amongst the bushes, here and

433

there catching a glimpse of some boy we knew, who, naked to the skin, was poised for a dive off the banks.

"Knowing as I do now, of the powerful stimulus of the naked male form upon a 'sexy' girl, I now can explain to myself the greedy glistening that came into the eyes of my little girl friend, and I suppose into my own, if I must admit it, at the sight of their limp, immature pintles laying lax between their legs.

"Of course, Doris and I had seen these things before, and had even gone so far as to take almost by force her young brother, and despite his roars and screams, to pull out his pecker and handle and fondle it and wonder to ourselves what it was all about.

"I suppose that we were not a whit different than thousands of other girls of our age, and I assure you, that at that age, there was no sensual urge in me, merely an all-impelling curiosity to see these 'things,' and Doris being as curious as I, we made the most of our opportunities whenever we could."

Chapter 2

"Well, nothing of particular interest transpired then for a while, and I guess it must have been when I was about eleven or twelve when I began to attend the usual parties that were held, and where we played postoffice, spin the platter, etc., and other kissing games, and although some of the older boys would hold me rather tight when they 'delivered a letter,' etc., I never noticed anything out of the way, and was too young and silly to look for any especial difference in the sexes.

"Then came the age of change. When my little fanny began to show its little shadow-like hairs, and my breasts began to swell and my legs to fill out, I unconsciously avoided (I knew not why) the rougher of the boys and wished to be by myself.

"During this time I was not fortunate in having Doris as

a counsellor, she having been sent to a boarding school, and had to think for myself. My mother, of course, told me of what was about to happen, and I naturally was extremely curious to see how it would manifest itself, and when, for the first time, I had a monthly bandage pinned tightly between my thighs, at times I felt heated and quite moved, but up to now knew not the least thing in regard to the sexual act.

"At last the unpleasant period being over, I thought that my viewpoint seemed a bit different and I instinctively shied away from some of the boys that I knew and acted in a more discreet and retiring manner.

"At this time, some of the girls in my class at school had, in some way, secured a number of those common smutty pictures, and these, of course being circulated about, came into my hands and you may be sure that I went over them minutely, and the acts portrayed there were indeed a surprise to me and served to arouse my curiosity to such an extent that I appealed to a girl friend for further instruction in these strange things.

"She, of course, knowing no more about it than I did, gave me a luridly coloured recital of the sexual act in all of its phases, and I was now determined to find out for myself just how it all happened and kept my eyes peeled for the purpose.

"It so happened that we had a cook, a buxom young Irish lass, who seemed to be on good terms with the man who delivered our ice, and I noticed, now that my eyes were opened in regard to these things, that they would wander out on the back porch which was an enclosed one, and that Joe—that was the ice-man—would sometimes stay there for probably fifteen or twenty minutes on some days and I thought to myself that something might transpire that might further my education, and made up my mind that on the next day I would be on hand and would see what really did happen.

"It so happened that circumstances favoured me in that respect, for in one corner of the porch was an old box, quite large and never locked, in which a lot of old brooms and mops were stored, and this, I thought to myself, would give me my place of concealment.

"Joe came early in the morning, and this particular day being a Saturday, I had no school and was up betimes and before his arrival was snugly ensconced in the box, my eye applied to a hole in the side so that I could observe everything that transpired.

"I waited for what seemed years, the rough wood of the box scratching my legs, and at times I was forced to lift the lid in order to gain a supply of air, the openings not being sufficient, and I thought he would never appear, but finally I heard the tramp of his rough boots ascending the stairs and a huge piece of ice was dumped on the porch, the ice-box thrown open, and it was flung in.

"You may be sure that by this time my eye was glued closely to the peep-hole and I was tickled to see that Norah, the cook, opened the kitchen door and stepped out on the porch and in an instant she was tightly hugged in the brawny Joe's arms.

"This convinced me that my suspicions were fully justified, and my eye being just on the level with Joe's trousers front I saw his pecker leap up and swell and strain fiercely against the confining clothing.

"I could hear their voices distinctly, and Norah was whispering to him to keep quiet and not say a word as the folks about might hear, and he, being of a rather direct type, as some ice-men are, soon had his hand up under her dresses, exposing to my eyes her well formed and unclothed thighs, and I sensed that his hand sought out her sexual spot and he pressed her close and rubbed against her with his standing cock.

"Then I saw her hand go down to the front of his pants and she unbuttoned his fly and out leaped his standing rod, and to me, unversed as I was in the actual sight of these terrible 'dodgers,' I almost cried in amazement at the sight of his gigantic flaming weapon, so large and hard it was, but Norah seemed not the least afraid of it but moulded and squeezed it in her palm like a magic lodestone of love and even seemed to drag on it as if she wished it inside her.

"All this, of course, happened in a much shorter space of time than it takes me to tell it, and you may imagine that I was now ablaze with curiosity and mayhaps desire, not knowing the meaning of the word at that age, and to my gratification and delight I saw him lean Norah back on a long swing that stood on the porch and throwing her dresses high so that all of her uncovered sexual parts stood out in bold relief for my excited view, he allowed her to guide the head of his torrid and raging tool to the entrance of her pinken and pouting slit and she soon engulfed it within her, writhing about on it like a fish on a hook!

"The regular pumping motions of the strong man's loins as he pushed in and out of her his erect and standing prick, the sighs, the moans, as they both spent on each others parts, all these conspired together to make me break into a perfect fit of frenzy and were it not for their actions which held the attention of both, I was sure that I must be discovered.

"Finally it was over. He let fall her dresses, buttoned up his pants and giving her a parting kiss picked up his ice-tongs and clumped away down the stairs.

"I lay back, half fainting in a swoon inside the hot box, and dared not breathe until Norah had retired to the kitchen. After waiting a while, I cautiously made my escape, and stealing to my room threw myself on the bed and lay there, staring at the ceiling and re-living in my mind the lustful scene that I just witnessed between the cook and the ice-man.

"At that time, my dear friends, I knew nothing at all about the digital method of relieving my excited feelings and even to this day, I would much rather resort to the poorest-made man with a shriveled member than comfort myself with the old maid's method of sex cooling!''

Grace and I both laughed at this, and kissing Anna for her frankness, and not to slight Grace, repeating the same caress with her, I begged her to continue.

"Well,'' she said, "my mind being all taken up with the ice-man, I immediately made plans in my mind to have that standing 'thing' for myself; to have it up in me like he had done to Norah, and early the next morning when he appeared, I secreted myself in the basement that he must pass before going upstairs, and determined to see what would happen.

"I stood just within the door so as I might walk out as he passed me, as though it was entirely accidental, and with heart beating high awaited his arrival. Both of you, of course, will laugh at me for my foolishness, but bear in mind I was a child, and all this was quite new to me, and all that I thought of at the present time was that standing and flaming prick which filled my mind night and day.

"Sure enough I heard him coming, and timing my actions so that I would be just coming out of the door as he ascended the stairs, I confronted him with what I was sure was a winning and seductive smile, and to my surprise and astonishment he pushed me gently aside and proceeded up the stairs!

"I stood still, frozen to the spot with astonishment, never having thought that he would so rudely pass me by, and before I could collect my scattered senses he was up the stairs, and for all I know was engaged in filling Norah's fat and greedy quim with his standing organ!

"I almost cried with vexation at the result of my carefully laid plans, and mentally wished them both dead and in their graves, and was ill-tempered all day, but finally the humorous side of it presented itself to me and I laughed merrily.

"I had, however, not given up my plans for seducing the long-pronged ice-man, as you shall soon hear, and gleaning some ideas out of the novels that I had read on the sly, made new plans for his capture.

"In some of the novels that I had read, the entrancing young heroine had attracted the attention of her admirer by pretending to have been thrown from a horse and spraining her ankle, and not having a horse or even a mule to my disposal I determined to dispense with that part of it and put the latter part of the plan into operation and to see what would result.

"To put this plan into operation, I seated myself on the lower steps where I would be in direct path of the ice-man and upon hearing him ascend the stairs I contorted my face into what I thought was an expression of pain, I lifted my foot up on my knee and held it in both of my hands and waited.

"Ascending the stairs with his ice on his shoulders, his head bent down he almost ran over me before he saw me, and then noticing my attitude and the look on my face, he placed the ice on one of the lower steps and inquired what was the matter.

" 'Oh, oh,' I said, 'I think that I have broken my leg, Joe! Look!' I said, sticking it out for his inspection, as he stood there stupidly looking at me. 'I was coming down stairs and slipped, and it hurts me awfully and I think it is broken! Is it?' And I held it up high almost in his face, and he unconsciously took my tiny ankle in his calloused and perspiring hand.

"This was the moment that I had planned for, for I had on only a pair of very short, abbreviated panties, slit wide open up the middle, which showed most of my lower belly and thighs, and if he cared to look I knew that my hair covered quim must stare right out so that he could not help but see it.

"I even slid down on the step and spread wide my thighs as though inviting him to take out his dart to impale me, but to my surprise and disgust, he concentrated his gaze on my ankle, and rubbing it gently between his palms, laid it gently back on the steps.

" 'There's not much the matter with it,' he said. 'If there was you would holler when I rubbed it. Just bathe it in hot water and it will be all right tomorrow.'

"I was so astounded and surprised that I had not at all noticed the friction that he had applied to my leg, and almost crying with vexation I saw him about to pick up his ice and begin to ascend the stairs.

"At this point I brought up my reserves, and taking another trick from the book, I gave a little cry and slid down a few steps and pretended to faint. You may be sure in the slide that I allowed my dresses to rumple up so that he might have a good sight of my lower body, and peeking out from beneath my eyelids I was gratified to see the lump in his trousers swell up and throb away like mad.

" 'Now,' I exulted, 'here is where I get it!' But outside of this natural action of his prick, he just stupidly stared at me and to my disgust clumped up the stairs.

"I heard him tell Norah that I had fainted on the stairs and hearing her running down, I made haste to pull down my dresses and allowed her to 'revive' me and to escort me, burning with vexation, to my room. You can imagine how I felt at this, and not only that, but I had to act for the family for a whole day, and complain of a perfectly healthy ankle and to remain in my room.

"Still, I do not doubt in the least that the bouncing that he gave to Norah, heatened perhaps by the sight of my young and immature charms, in some way benefitted her, so you see there is some good in everything. It is funny how some men are so dense and so lack understanding, and should be so stupid as Joe was."

Both Grace and myself roared with laughter at this, and

442

when we had subdued and partaken of another drink served by the discreet Joseph, she continued her story.

"Well, the ice-man, as far as he was concerned, passed out of my life, although now and then I like to think of his actions with the cook, and the size of his organ; but I must proceed to the later and more important part of my tale.

"As Doris was away, I was left to myself most of the time, and during the summer used to occupy myself by frequenting a wooden park that was nearby, and sitting on the grass and feeding the swans.

"By this time I had developed in a startling manner and now had breasts indeed to be proud of, and having beguiled mother to allow me to dress as I wished, flattered myself that I was indeed an object of interest for any boy or man, but had not even a sweetheart.

"But to get back to my story. As I have told you I often went to this park, which was quite a large one, and one day, while seated near the edge of a small lake, I noticed that I had attracted the attention of two youths who were seated on the grass a little way from me, and who were glancing at me and evidently discussing my charms with one another.

"I, of course, was tickled to death, and pretending not to notice them in the least, went on with my play of throwing peanuts to the swans, who by now had come to know and look for me, and I was not at all surprised when one of the youths detached himself from the other and slowly approached me.

" 'They are nice,' he said, indicating the graceful swans as they preened themselves and swam about on the placid water and daintily turned their heads.

" 'Oh yes,' I said, in what I thought was a rather worldly manner, 'they are to people who do not see them every day.'

" 'I suppose you do?' he said, seating himself on the grass and taking some peanuts from his own pockets and throwing them to the swans.

" 'Well, not every day,' I confessed, 'but I see them quite often. But if you feed them, they will forget all about me!' And I laughed and looked right into his eyes.

"He was a nice appearing chap, one whom I had never seen before, but this made not a bit of difference to me, so eager was I to know about man's strange tool, and the sensations it inspired in a girl's quim when she had it pushed in her like Norah had filled my mind to the exclusion of everything else, and I could not, to help myself, keep from casting a quick glance at the front of his pants as if I, little fool, expected to see it hanging out on display as it were!

"By this time we had finished all the peanuts we had, and declining his offer to purchase more, we arose and he presented me to his boy friend.

"After we had walked about a bit, one of the boys asked me if I ever went rowing, as they had boats to rent in the park, and upon my agreeing to it (in fact I was willing to agree to anything as long as I might attain the purpose that I had in mind, which was that of feeling in me the prong of a male) we walked to the edge of the small lake and were soon ensconced in one of the boats with Frank at the oars and his friend sitting in the other end of the boat at his back and I facing him.

"It was a wonderful day and the water was like glass

and I cast an admiring glance at the broad shoulders of Frank as he pulled away at the oars and sent the boat spinning ahead of us over the cool and peaceful waves.

"Frank kept up some small talk and his friend contented himself by looking about him at the other rowers, and I, thinking that the time had come when I should disclose to them the purpose of my taking up with them, I allowed my dress, which was rather short to begin with, to rest up to my knees, and widely spread my thighs and made some remark that would cause Frank to observe the view I so impudently laid open for him.

"He turned to talk to me, and almost missed a stroke of the oars so sudden were the charms that I had so suddenly unveiled to him, and the remark that he intended to make died away on his lips and his eyes glued themselves to my silk stockinged legs and the upper bare portion of my thighs that was bared by the reefing up of my skirts.

"My eyes, in turn, were fastened to the front of his pants, and to my satisfaction and delight I saw a huge lump slowly form and he tore his eyes away from the sight of my legs and turned to his friend to speak to him.

"I myself was so excited over this sudden turn of affairs that I did not know in the least what he had said, but in an instant both of their gazes were fixed on my crotch, and I, longing to keep up this admiration of myself, allowed my legs to come together, closing from them this impelling view, and pointed out some of the attractions on the lake.

'It so happened that we were just abreast of a small isle situated in the centre of the lake, and Frank had rowed over close to it under the shelter of some overhanging bushes and pretending he was exhausted, allowed the oars to float idly alongside the boat.

" 'It is a long time since I have rowed a boat,' he said, laughingly, 'and I must rest a while.'

" 'Will you allow me to row for a while?' asked his friend, his eyes still on my legs, and mayhaps perfectly willing to take his partner's place at the oars.

" 'Oh, no, no!' said Frank, hurriedly regaining his hold on the oars, 'I am not—not at all as tired as I thought—and we will go at once!'

"I had to laugh merrily at this unwillingness of Frank to lose his point of vantage, and really taking pity on the boy I said, 'Oh, we have been rowing enough, and I think it better that we stay here for a while, then we can row back. But, by the way, Frank, are you not sure that the sight of me, here in front of you, may be the reason of causing you to tire? Perhaps it might be better if your friend and I change seats and then probably you might be able to row better.'

"Poor Frank! He cast such a pitiful glance at me that I burst into roars of laughter, and his friend bending forward tried to find out what it was all about.

" 'If you—if you—' blurted out Frank, his face red with embarrassment, 'if you—would only keep your legs covered—I would be able to go ahead!'

" 'Oh, Frank!' I said, pretending to be greatly shocked, 'I am indeed surprised at you for speaking that way, and I am sure that if we were back at the landing I would leave you at once! I am indeed!'

" 'Oh, Anna!' said Frank, pitifully, 'you do not—you do not understand! I assure you, Anna, that I had not the least

446

intention of offending you, in fact, quite the reverse, as I think your legs are very, very pretty, and I like them very much—'

" 'Oh, you like them!' I said, pretending to be agreeably surprised. 'Oh, Frank, that makes it altogether different! I thought that you meant that my legs were so ugly that they prevented you rowing! Oh, I thank you, Frank, for the compliment, and that changes the situation quite completely.'

" 'Yes,' said Frank, now having regained his assurance, and speaking in what he thought, I suppose, a bold manner, 'I think, Anna, that you have very pretty and well formed legs, and I assure you that I sure do like the sight of them, especially higher up,' and he nodded significantly, 'and I am sure that my boy friend does, too.'

"I did not pretend to be at all shocked, for, to tell the truth, I was well pleased at this talk, and naturally knowing that I had pretty and well-formed legs, did not think it was at all extraordinary.

" 'I notice,' I said, in just as bold a tone as he had used, 'that they have a charming effect on you!' And at this I fastened my eyes right on the front of his pants where that swelling lump was still bulging. 'You are not at all polite, Frank, to act so in the presence of a lady, and I am indeed surprised at you! I'll wager your boy friend is not at all in the terrible state that you are.'

"This naturally broke the ice, and his boy friend, coming forward to the center, leaned over Frank's shoulders and took part in the joking.

" 'Let's get out and go walking about on the island,' he said, 'I am sure that it will be much better than sitting here talking in the boat!'

"I was perfectly willing to do this, but Frank called our attention to the signs displayed warning everyone off, and saying that we would surely be seen as it was still light all over the lake, said that it would be best to wait for a while until it grew darker and then we would not be noticed.

" 'But you'll go when it is darker?' he asked me, his eyes flashing and his hand unconsciously straying to his hardened prick as though he wished in his own way to relieve the feelings that I had instilled there.

" 'I don't know,' I joked then, 'I think that it might be terrible for a girl to go alone with two boys on that island, and Lord knows what you might do to me, and I think it best, perhaps, that we leave it go altogether. Won't it be all right if we—if we just stay here?' And I leaned back a little in the boat and allowed my legs to open a bit, disclosing to their eyes my scantily-clad lower parts, causing both of the boys to breathe faster and lean forward with distended eyes.

"In fact, Frank made as if to rise in his seat, and make his way in the boat over to me, but a wild rocking of the craft and a cry of alarm from his friend caused him to re-seat himself and to utter a cry of vexation. He looked longingly at the tree-covered isle, but I had again closed my thighs, and he buried his face in his hands for a moment and then said, 'I tell you, Anna, if you keep showing me your legs, and raising your skirts like this, either here or on the island I will come over and fuck you good!' And he tore open the front of his pants and displayed to my startled eyes a whanger of indeed immense proportions, causing me to give a little sham cry of shame and to cover my face with my hands.

"I, however, you may be sure, peeked from between my fingers and saw him slowly frig it up and down and longed to lean forward and replace his frigging hand with my own, but with an approaching boat coming in sight, he quickly replaced this object of my desires and picking up the oars slowly fended off the isle and slowly rowed again.

" 'Why, Frank!' I said, pretending to recover, and keeping my voice low to prevent it carrying over the water, 'what—what was it you said? Did you swear at me?'

" 'I did not!' said Frank, savagely pulling at the oars and sending the boat through the water in great leaps, 'I merely said that I wanted to fuck you, and there is nothing wrong in that! You have had it plenty of times, and you want it now, and if it were dark you would now be on the island getting it in your belly from both of us! And you cannot tell me any different. The way you show yourself shows that! Don't it?' he said, turning to his companion for verification.

"I said nothing at this, but his rough talk thrilled me, and I really did long to have that huge stabber of his within me, and myself was longing for darkness and hoped that they both might have me.

" 'I should say she does,' said Frank's friend, his bold eyes on my person, 'and we will give it to her when it's dark. Row around a bit, Frank, and then we can come back. By that time it will be dark enough.'

" 'Before it gets too dark,' said Frank, sculling the boat about, 'I would like to row back under those trees and have her show me her legs again. It gives me an awful hard on! Will you show us, Anna, if we row back? Then we will fuck you when it is dark. Is it a bet, Anna?'

" 'Sure! I said gayly, my own senses reeling at the smutty language of these boys. 'If you will row back where the trees hide us, I will show you what you want, and then when it is dark we will go on the island and I will fuck you both!'

" 'Hurrah!' said Frank, and spinning the boat back, he brought it to a sudden stop against the bank. He pulled out his prick and told me to show them my legs and thighs.

"I threw my dress up to the waist, and having on only a tiny pair of silken drawers, which were generously slit up the middle, allowed them to look, even opening my thighs for them, and at the sight of me sitting there moving about my arse and showing myself to the boys I thought they were both about to 'shoot' and to preserve this period I laughingly dropped my dress and told them to row some more.

"Both regretfully replaced their pricks and we rowed out again, and moved lazily about the small lake.

" 'Cripes,' said Frank, disgustedly, 'if it were only dark! How I could fuck you now.' And he bent a glance on me that was fiery and thrilling in passion. 'I bet if my prick was in you now, you would be blowing your sap over me! Don't you think so?' he said to his friend.

" 'Oh, oh, oh,' said that party, his hands somewhere in the region of his sexual part, 'don't talk to me about fucking! I am almost off now, and if we do not hurry soon, I will fuck her here and now in the boat.'

" 'Now boys,' I said, consolingly, 'I too am as eager as

you both are, but see,' I said, pointing to the sky, 'darkness is approaching, and in a few minutes we will all be over there, and then you may do it to me as long as you like.'

"True, as I had said, it was growing dark, and soon the lights were turned on, and after holding the boys back so that I was sure we would not be observed from shore or from passing boats, I allowed Frank to row over to the isle, and the darkness now being black I allowed him to cautiously assist me from the boat and I stood on the ground.

"There had been some dispute as to which was to be first, but Frank had settled this, and I was in his hands, leaving his friend to guard the boat.

"He led me willingly into the depths of a dense thicket, and coming to cleared space, wound his arms about me and covered my lips with kisses, his hand running up under my dresses and feeling my now wet sexual parts.

"I, on my own part, allowed my eager hand to seek out his standing rod, and quickly freeing it from its imprisonment, moulded and fondled it, squeezing its hardness into the palm of my hand and flicking my finger over its bulging head.

"The more I pulled and teased it the hotter it seemed to make him, and releasing me for a moment he drew off his coat and placing it on the ground tumbled me upon it and was astride me.

"I felt his prick bang against my bare thighs, and opening my legs for the assault, wove my arms about his body and allowed him to place the head of his rod at my sexual cleft.

"My drawers seemed to bother him and he begged me

451

to remove them, which I accordingly did, and allowing him to run his hands all over my lower bareness I begged him to go ahead and fuck me.

"Little did I know, at that time, of the pain that attended the first attempt of this act, and I thought, silly girl, that it was loaded only with pleasure and ecstacy, and I willingly urged him to possess me.

"Frank, on his part, naturally judged that I was no stranger to this, and getting his prong in place held me tight to him and began the insertion of his member.

"The tightness of my cleft surprised me, and also him, I suppose, but growing frantic with desire he lifted himself high on my body, and with one drive—oh, how can I ever, ever describe it to you!—he drove his rod up into me and deprived me of my maidenhead!

"Oh, the pain of that sudden and unexpected assault! I screamed; I cried; I moaned, but all to no avail, for the animal in him was dominant and he drove away at me like mad and I soon felt his charge spurt and bubble into me in great jets, soothing somewhat the damage done by his tearing prick.

"I seemed paralyzed from the waist downward, and try as I might, could not in the least move about my lower body. Frank gyrated on me to a second bursting of his sexual pods, then abruptly withdrawing, he ran to the boat and I was left crying and moaning on the grass.

"I strove weakly to rise to my feet, only to fall back weakly, and upon my second attempt found I was restrained by the presence of the second boy, who with standing prick was forcing me again on my back on the grass.

"I tried to mumble some excuse or subterfuge to him, but the sudden insertion of his standing rod, reopening and again distending the tiny cleft that had been so sorely assaulted by the brutal Frank, put an end to my complaints and I guess I must have swooned, for when I awoke he was standing beside me drying his penis on his handkerchief.

"He assisted me to my feet, but upon me again collapsing ran for Frank, who returned alone, having evidently left his friend to guard the boat.

" 'What is the matter?' he asked me in a frightened manner. 'Have you hurt yourself, Anna?' And he seated himself beside me, and took me in his arms and kissed me.

" 'Oh, oh, oh,' I cried, 'I am hurt; terribly hurt. You have split me, I know it! I am all bleeding and I feel awful! You tore me, Frank!' And weeping, I buried my head in his arms.

"He attempted to console me, and leaving me for an instant, told his friend to row the boat about for a while alone so as he could stay with me until I had a chance to recover.

"His friend rowed away, and Frank, taking me in his arms, soon had me back to my senses, and I was agreeably surprised as the sense of pain departed my quim, and his kisses and caresses soon had me again seeking out his prick, and finding to my satisfaction that it was in a state of agreeable hardness—shameful as it may be for me to confess—before his friend had returned I had him give me another taste of that charm that had so brutally abused me.

"That, Mr. Anderson and Grace, is the story of my

maidenhead, and now having told you, I beg you, Grace, to detail to us the tale of losing yours."

"Oh, oh," said Grace, suddenly brought to her senses by Anna's remark, "I am . . . am too . . ." And I gently removed my hand from a part of that young lady's person that was just spouting forth its torrent of sexual dew. "I am . . . am . . ."

"You are spending," I laughed. "I am surprised at you, Anna, to ask a girl to tell you of the loss of her maidenhead, when the story you have just told has caused her to wet all over her thighs!"

"With the assistance of your fingers," sniffed Anna. "That's the thanks I get for doing all the work!" And she tossed about as if offended, but we knew her too well to mind her.

Grace gently displaced my fingers, and arranging her dress, kissed her friend warmly and prepared to begin her tale.

My own gorge had been brought to the spending point by Anna's tale, and before allowing her to begin, I drew out my swollen bolus, and throwing Anna flat on her back beside the eager Grace, I opened her thighs and in an instant was within her and almost immediately gave into her spending quim an enormous charge of my boiling balm.

We then both dried ourselves, and setting our apparel to rights, began to listen to Grace's story.

"I am not at all as fortunate as Anna," she said laughingly, "and I did not, in my early youth, have the opportunity of observing all of the things that she saw, and of having instructions in those things that are common knowledge to all girls of these days.

"As you very well know, Anna," she said significantly, "I have never, never told even you of the manner in which I was deprived of my maidenhead, as you term it, and up to this time have kept it a secret to myself."

"But you're going to, now?" asked Anna curiously, looking at her in a startled manner. "Surely, Grace . . ."

"Oh, yes, I am," said Grace, "I am going to tell you all about it. Every bit. When I was a child, I was not in a position to play about like Anna, and my family not having a wealth of money, I was somewhat ashamed to go with the other girls of my set. Clothes, you know, and things. Well, when I was near sixteen, having gone to movies and such, I had occasion to go with a boy friend of mine to a chop suey restaurant, situated at the corner of——and——streets.

"There were a number of girls that used to go there, and this boy I was with, although no particular sweetheart or friend of mine, naturally took me there to eat, and having been in there with other girls and boys at different times, I had never noticed anything out of the way there, and to be frank, neither did I now; that is, with one exception. A Chinaman (or at least that is what I judged him to be) when I had occasion to return from the lavatory, gave me a rather peculiar look, and I, paying no attention to it, returned to my seat.

"Well, nothing happened on this occasion, and one evening, the first one I believe that I had gone there alone, this man went so far as to speak to me. I, of course, did not in the least answer him, having heard tales of the wickedness of these Chinamen, but the manner in which he addressed me was courteous and refined and in reality I had nothing to be offended at.

"Remember, I was still a virgin, and totally ignorant of all things sexual with the exception that I had heard discussed the sexual act, and knew mistily how it was performed, but had never, as yet, had the pleasure or pain of enacting a part in it.

"At that time I thought nothing of his actions, never having it in mind that he may have been attracted to me on account of my looks or appearance, but now knowing what I do, I know that this must have been what was in his mind at the time.

"Perhaps a few weeks passed by, and although I had frequented the place on a number of occasions, he never addressed me, until one day, happening to be there all alone when I came to pay my check, he tendered me a little package and begged me to accept it, saying that it was a present for me.

"I, alive with curiosity, unwrapped it immediately in his presence, and found that it was a beautiful jade ring evidently worth some money.

" 'Oh, how pretty!' I could not help saying. 'But Mr. Mott, (for this was his name) I could never accept this. It would not be right.'

" 'Why not?' he asked in perfect English. 'I like you and would like to have you have it, and no one will ever know where it came from—that is—unless you tell them.'

"I was really struggling with myself as to whether to accept it or not, as you must bear in mind what I have told you about my conditions at home, but once I had slipped it on my finger it was indeed too pretty to take off—so I kept it.

"This was evidently quite pleasing to him, and he beamed upon me with the utmost satisfaction, and leaning over the counter said in a low voice, 'Miss Grace, you are a very nice girl and I like you; like you a whole lot. If ever there is a time that you will let me help you, just let me know and I am sure that you will not be disappointed.'

"This remark, of course, was clear enough even for me to understand, and blushing furiously, I hurried from the place.

"My mind was in a tumult of emotion as I stumbled down the marble stairs, and the thought that a 'Chinaman' had been so bold as to demand the possession of me irritated me so much that I nearly collided with a number of people.

"I say 'irritated,' but in a few minutes my conceit came to the fore, and I thought how sad it was that it was only a yellow man that appreciated me enough to pay attention to me. Of course, it was ridiculous and I would never go there again and I laughed to myself and dismissed it from my mind.

"Well, a few days later when I went in there—"

"Just a minute!" interrupted Anna, who had introduced her hand inside of my trousers and was now subjecting my prong to the sweetest of teasing manipulations in her tender palm, while I flicked the nipple of one of Grace's titties, "I thought that you just said that you were never going back there again, Grace!"

"I did," admitted Grace, "but you know Anna, it would not be fair to him, the poor fellow, to leave him thinking of me; and if it did not entail anything on my part—''

Both Anna and I laughed uproariously at this, and Grace looked from one face to the other in mystified wonderment, and I, controlling my merriment said, "Never mind us, Grace, we know exactly how you felt and how you pitied the poor fellow. Proceed, I beg of you."

"Well," said Grace, "as I said, I went in there again after I had been given the jade ring, and this time there was a strange Chinaman with my friend, Mr. Mott, and I noticed that he gave me a lot of attention, but paid no attention to either of them and finishing my meal, and prepared to depart.

"As I paid my check, Mr. Mott asked me if I minded if he introduced me to the man, and before I had a chance to say 'no' he did so, and that is how I came to know Ki-Ling.

"He was a tall, sallow man, well-built and well-dressed, and he bowed over my hand and acted perfectly charming. I immediately left the place, but soon later Mr. Mott seized a chance to talk to me and told me that Ki-Ling was a very rich man and that I had impressed him very much, and if ever I was in financial difficulties he was sure that he would help me without question.

"By this time I had overcome my resentment to the yellow man, and I laughingly said in a joking manner, 'And I suppose, Mr. Mott, that he will ask for full interest on his investment. Is that what you mean, my friend?'

" 'No man is interested in anything that he does not derive pleasure or gain from,' said Mr. Mott gravely, 'but still, my dear, I think that you may at least bear my remarks in mind.'

"I laughed gayly at him and ran out of the place.and dismissed it instantly from my mind.

"And then—then came Betty Moore's party—I—"

"Oh ho!" cried Anna. "Now I know! I know now why you—"

"Hush! Anna dear!" I said, placing a hand over her excited lips. "Surely you do not wish to spoil Grace's story. She did not do that to you."

Anna remained silent and Grace continued.

"And then came Betty Moore's party. I was of course invited, and having nothing to wear, I had seen a gorgeous gown in a window downtown that I was just crazy to have, but the price, alas, was far, far outside of the means of my purse. A number of times the words of Mr. Mott came to my mind, but I resolutely set it aside, but finally, I decided to go and see, at least, what he would offer. And that was the beginning of the end.

"One day, after school, I went up to his place and no one being present, I told him that I would like to talk to him about Mr. Ling.

"He was instantly all smiles, and opening a little door in back of the counter, asked me to step into a little room that was there.

"I went in, trembling as you may well imagine, and he called to one of his men and after offering me a drink of some stuff out of a bottle asked me what he could do for me.

"I was as nervous as could be, but fixing my mind on the gown and thinking of the hit that I would make, I said in a determined tone, 'How much, Mr. Mott, will Ling pay me if I—I—go to him?'

" 'I do not know,' he said frankly, 'that I would have to see about. Do you wish me to find out for you?'

" 'But,' I said, 'would he want to—to do something to me? To be like boys are with girls? You know what I mean.'

" 'I suppose so,' said Mr. Mott, 'but that you must expect if he pays you. But nothing will happen to hurt you.'

" 'But I might have a baby,' I said. 'That might happen, might it not?'

" 'Oh, no,' he said, 'not with Mr. Ling; he would take care of that. If you wish to, I will see him and ask him and will let you know tomorrow if you are in earnest.'

" 'I am,' I told him, 'and I wish you to find out.' And I rose to leave.

"To my surprise he approached me, and upon me drawing back he stopped and smiled at me.

" 'I will not hurt you,' he said, and still smiled at me.

" 'But that was not in the bargain,' I said. 'I asked you about Mr. Ling.'

" 'But at least a little recompense is due the arranger,' he said. 'I want nothing to do with you, at least in the way that you think. And I assure you that you will leave this room in the same state as you entered. But before I can go ahead and talk to Mr. Ling, it would be necessary that I verify certain facts—facts in relation to yourself that I am sure can in no way harm you.'

" 'But what are they?' I asked, now frightened. 'Tell me and I will let you know. What are they?'

" 'Mr. Ling,' he said simply, 'is not at all interested in soiled flowers, and by that you must know that I, myself, have no desires in that certain direction, but still I must know whether you are a virgin or not. If you are, I will go ahead; if not, dismiss the idea from your mind, as it would be out of the question.'

" 'Do you mean—if I have a maidenhead?' I asked not understanding clearly what he meant.

" 'Yes,' he answered, 'that is it.'

" 'But I have,' I told him, 'I have never, never been with anyone. I can assure you of that.'

"He lifted his hands deprecatingly and leaned back to the wall.

" 'I must see,' he said.

" 'Must see!' I repeated, rather stupidly, I think 'You must—must look at me, there?'

" 'Yes,' he said, 'but if you are bashful I will extinguish the lights.'

" 'Oh, no!' I said, fearing that he was at once going to put the room in darkness. 'Not that, not that!' For I was sure, once the lights were out and me in the dark, he would ravish me to his will.

" 'Well, then,' he said, 'lay up here on the table.' And he lifted the bottle to a side table.

" 'But you might do something?' I said, rather nervously.

" 'I will not,' he answered, and despite my fears I allowed him to assist me to the table, and allowing him to gently push me on my back I felt him drawing up my dresses and pulling my tights wide apart.

" 'Oh, oh, no,' I said, putting my hand down and trying to push him away.

461

Chapter 3

" 'Very well,' he said coolly, 'we shall let it go and I will not call Mr. Ling.'

"The sight of that gown filtered before my eyes, and my hands gently relaxed their hold on my dress and fell lax to my sides and he again resumed his operations.

"You must imagine how I felt! My dress was turned up to the waist, and my pants were unbuttoned and pulled down off over my ankles and the cool breeze of the room kissed my bare lower flesh and caused me to shiver. I hid my face under my arm to hide out the sight, and felt him divide the lips of my slit, and his fingers drew apart the lips and to my intense surprise I felt the most delicious sensation of my funny spot and an electric shock ran through my entire body.

"Wondering what this thrilling sensation could be, I

462

raised my head, and saw Mr. Mott down in between my thighs with his lips applied to my sensitive sheath, and with his hot, hard tongue he was titillating my membranes.

"Oh, what thrills and sensations ran through me! What pleasure I experienced at the touch of this tongue, the hard little sentinel of pleasure. I writhed, I gasped, I moaned, and finally I gave down my spend to be gobbled up by this yellow degenerate who fairly luxuriated in my effusion.

"Twice, thrice, this act was repeated, then, feeling weak and faint, I allowed him to assist me down from the table.

"I almost reeled to the floor and would have, had it not been for his supporting arms, and he handed me my panties and departed from the room. I sat down for a moment to don them, and straightening out my dress, cautiously opened the door and peeked out.

"He was waiting without, and motioned me to come into the dining room, and whispering to me that he had verified himself as to my condition, told me to come in the next day.

"I staggered down the stairs, and gaining the house, went to my room and fell into a deep dreamless sleep. Towards morning I awakened and could no longer sleep, my mind being filled with the thoughts of the actions of the Chinaman, and so powerful were they that I was—well, I was wet when it was over!

"Well, the whole next day I was consumed with curiosity as to what Mr. Ling would say, and right after school I hurried to the restaurant, and seeing a number of people following me, who were strangers to me, I made haste to steal into the little room behind the counter and close the door after me.

"In a few minutes Mr. Mott entered, and his face as grave as before, said to me, 'Mr. Ling begs to inform you through me that he accepts your kind offer and will pay you for your services in this matter, one hundred dollars, and has sent by me'—and here he fumbled in his pocket and drew out an envelope—'twenty-five dollars on account.' And with this he handed me the envelope.

"One hundred dollars! How pleasant that sounded to me! And twenty-five already! I tore open the envelope to verify it, and sure enough within were two tens and a five! The gown cost seventy-five dollars and with this twenty-five I could pay a deposit and have much left over. This was certainly great luck!

"While I was musing thus, I felt Mr. Mott gently urging me to lie down on the table, and I in no way being in discord or dissent with this notion, unhesitating allowed him to do so, and felt him strip off my drawers and again apply his lips to my cleft.

"So sudden was this sweet conjunction, that I almost immediately gave down in his mouth a proof of my feelings and then settled down to real enjoyment. Doubtless, both of you must think that I was a thoroughly degenerate little girl, especially at this age, to be so affected by the feel of this yellow man's tongue, but you must bear in mind that it was all new to me, and to be frank with you it affected me to my toe-nails!

"Well, four or five charges left me, before he was content, and he then told me that he had arranged it for the following Saturday, which was two days away, and that he was to conduct me to Mr. Ling's place.

" 'Oh, isn't he coming here?' I asked him.

" 'Oh, no,' he answered, 'he has a wonderful place of his own over on the south side. You will like it when you get there, and I want you to make some excuse so that you may be away and meet me here at eleven o'clock in the morning on Saturday.'

"I promised him that I would be on time, and leaving the place, I went immediately to the store and paid a deposit on the gown. I did not leave the whole twenty-five dollars, paying only ten, as I intended to spend the rest on some pretty undergarments, stockings, and slippers so that I would make a presentable appearance on Saturday.

"This I accordingly did, and as you will remember, Anna, I left the package at your house, and told you that I was going somewhere Saturday and would stop in for it on Saturday morning.

"Well, Saturday morning came, and I was up early and hurried to your house, after telling my folks that I was going on a 'hike' out of town, and you, sleepy head"—this to the listening Anna—"as you were sound asleep, I secured my package, and going in the bathroom donned all of my new finery and left my old ones neatly wrapped under the bath tub.

"I hurried to the restaurant, and early as it was I found Mr. Mott all ready and waiting for me, and whispering to me to slip downstairs and to wait around the corner, he dismissed me.

"I returned to the street, and turning the corner of . . . . street, which as you know is a quiet one, I stood there for a minute and then a car drew up to the curb and to my surprise I saw Mr. Mott within it.

"He motioned me to enter and I hurriedly cast a glance around and did so and we were quickly driven away by the driver.

"We drove for quite a while, and finally we stopped, and I saw we were in the Chinese quarter and were before a Chinese laundry. Was the dignified Mr. Ling a Chinese laundryman?

"I had not much time to think as Mr. Mott hustled me from the machine and into the shop, and no sooner were we in than we were into the back room out of observation. There was one man in the room, a Chinaman, and he manifested no surprise at our entrance but stood before Mr. Mott.

"Mr Mott said something in Chinese and the man drew a cupboard out from the wall, and to my surprise an opening presented itself and Mr. Mott invited me to enter.

"I hesitated a moment, scared by the darkness of the opening, but thinking that I had come this far, I determined to proceed, and following Mr. Mott, entered the dark passage-way and after walking a few feet we came to an iron door, which he unlocked and then I found we were in what I presumed the adjoining house.

"A few more steps and we came out into a long hallway, and a Chinese servant, a young girl who was evidently awaiting us, smiled at me and bowed, and Mr. Mott, giving me into her care, suddenly took his departure leaving me alone in the quiet hallway.

" 'Come,' said the Chinese girl in perfect English, 'you are to follow me. I am Ling's servant and will conduct you to a room where you may arrange your toilet before meeting my master.'

"I was somewhat confused at the suddenness of all this, but followed the girl up the long winding stairs, and she conducted me into a room that was furnished with all the articles necessary for a careful toilet, and she then left me, gliding out of the room, her soft slippers making no sound on the heavy carpet.

"I gazed into the elegant mirror and arranged a few locks of my hair and dabbed my face with powder and anxiously awaited the return of the servant. In a few minutes she returned, and smiling again she led me out, down the hall, and coming to the door of another room, she whispered to me that she was about to lead me into the presence of Mr. Ling. She threw open the door and motioned me to enter before her.

"The flood of light that came through the suddenly-opened door startled me for an instant, but accustoming my eyes to the new scene I saw that it was a luxuriously-furnished room, set out as a library, and seated in a large chair was Ki-Ling.

"He was attired in what I thought must be a full Chinese costume, wearing a long kimono, and a small cap with a button topping it on his head, and he sat still, his oblique eyes ravishing my form from head to toe.

" 'You may go, Santi,' he said shortly, 'I shall ring for you if I wish you.' And the Chinese girl made a low bow and left the room.

"He regarded me for a moment without a word, then, rising to his feet, he made a low bow and said, 'I am pleased, dear Miss, to again meet you, and according to our dear friend, Mr. Mott, under such favorable circumstances to myself. I trust that the information that you imparted Mr. Mott was right and correct, and that in coming here, you have determined to take advantage of the poor help that I can give you, and in return to offer yourself to my pleasure. Is that right, my dear?' And his eyes glistened with what I was sure was lust and sensuality.

" 'Why, yes, Mr. Ling,' I said, somewhat nervously, I must admit, 'I told Mr. Mott that I would—would be nice to you in the way you wish—and he gave me twenty-five dollars and told me . . .'

" 'That I would give you another seventy-five,' finished Mr. Ling, seeing that I was blushing with embarrassment. 'Well, he is right, my dear, and now that you are here, I will outline in a way the entertainment that I have arranged for your especial benefit.'

" 'Entertainment?' I echoed, not knowing what in the world he meant by this. 'Entertainment for me? I guess, Mr. Ling, that I am somewhat stupid, as I thought that I was to be here for your entertainment . . .'

"He smiled at this, and coming closer to me, motioned me to seat myself on a low couch that stood against the wall, and continued, 'A girl like you, my dear, is worthy of much more than I, in my humble way, could furnish, but I have arranged in our own peculiar way, a slight form of Chinese entertainment that I am sure will in no way prove offensive to you. I suppose you have not as yet dined, and it is a little dinner that I have arranged, and at it I will have a number of my friends, who will, however, have nothing to do with the little matter that you and I have in mind.' And here he bent a significant glance

on me, causing me to blush furiously and to turn my eyes
from him. 'And you may assure yourself, my dear Grace,
that among those present, there are none of them that will
in any way claim your attention, much less your kind
services.'

"As he finished he again walked back to his seat, and
pulling a bell-cord, the silent Chinese girl again entered
the room, and Ling telling me that it was his desire that I
apparel myself in Chinese fashion, he entrusted me into her
care and she again conducted me back to the room that I
had so recently departed.

"Once within, she closed the door, and going to a
closet, opened it and displayed to my eyes a number of
Chinese robes, all wonderful in color and design, and
indicated that I was to select from them the one that I
desired to wear.

"I gave a little cry of surprise, and looking them all
over selected a wonderfully-embroidered one, and she,
laying it on the bed, then pulled open one of the drawers
of a huge chest and unveiled to my eyes the most gorgeous
selection of foamy, silken underclothing and many, many
pairs of sheer spider-work silken stockings.

"Of these I also selected a number of things, and with
the assistance of the girl, completely undressed to the skin
and appareled myself in my new apparel. She then produced a pair of tiny, list slippers, and putting them on my
feet, brought a cute, bespangled hair ornament and then
led me to the glass to observe the results of her labours.

"I gave a little cry of astonishment at the result, and it
certainly did change my appearance a lot, and now that I
was ready she again led me back to the room of Ki-Ling.

"He was walking about the room and at the sight of me in my Chinese clothes, gave a little grunt of approval and dismissed the girl with a wave of his hand.

"I stood there for a moment and he then rang a gong in the room, and after listening a moment offered me his arm, and proceeding through another door that I had not noticed, we walked down a hall to a large dining room in the center of which was a low table decorated with flowers, and silent Chinese attendants standing against the wall.

"To my surprise there were no chairs in the room, the guests seating themselves on huge cushions, and I saw all dressed in Chinese fashion and some wearing medals and decorations. I noticed that there were no other girls present, and upon Ling leading me to the head of the low table, he allowed me to sink on the cushions beside him, and the others sat down and the servants began to place before us a variety of dishes that I had never seen, much less tasted before.

"I was naturally hungry, and set to work at once, and noticing all of the men drinking something from small cups, I asked Ling what it was.

" 'That', he said, sipping a cup, 'is a certain variety of wine that is made only in China, and is very good, I assure you. Try some; I am sure that you will like it.'

" 'But I never drink,' I said, 'and it might make me sick. I might not—'

" 'I wish it', he said simply, 'and I am sure, my dear, that you are not going to start out by opposing my will.' And he tendered me one of the cups.

"I took a tiny sip of it and it ran like fire through my veins, and seeing that they were all drinking freely of it, I thought that it would do no harm for me to finish one cup at least, which I did.

"Well, it would do you both no good to go ahead and tell you all the different kinds of food that were served, and so I will to the conclusion of the dinner, in which I think you will be interested.

"As soon as we had finished, which must have been at least two hours, Ki-Ling conducted me from the dining room, and into another large apartment, in the middle of which was a large sunken pool level with the floor.

"He led me to a soft, wide couch and seating himself beside me, struck a blow on a huge gong that hung beside the couch, and a group of musicians entered and seating themselves behind some shrubbery that was arranged at the other end of the room, began to play on their stringed instruments.

"I allowed Ling to gently lay me back on the couch and to pass his arms about my shoulders and to hold me close to him. I felt him unfastening my kimona, and having on nothing underneath it but the foamy abbreviated panties and stockings that I had selected, he allowed his hands to run riot over every portion of my naked person.

"A young girl, garbed only in a small cloth that covered her loins, leaving her well-formed breasts bare, served us with two tiny cups of liquor on a tray, and this seemed different from the rest, for after drinking, things grew a bit confused to me and I seemed to sink away in a confused dream in which Ki-Ling played a leading part.

"I saw a group of dancers enter the room, both boys and girls, and after they had danced gracefully about the room, the young men seized the girls in their arms and throwing them to the floor took violent possession of their persons, and the wild cries, the grunts of the victors all seemed to impell within me a violent desire to imitate them.

"By this time Ki-Ling had my kimona flung fully open and his hand was now busy with my sexual part, and two of the young girls, coming close to the couch, opened his own covering and allowing a dart of enormous size to fly forth, took my lax hand and placed it about its giant circumference.

"Oh, what a penis that was! I had never seen, much less felt, or even imagined in my wildest dreams a peg of this size, and as I rushed it up and down my palm I thought that indeed it was large enough to split me in twain. Still, I did not seem to fear it, and as one of the girls bent over and applied her lips to it, and then arranged about it some thin little bands with tiny knobs upon it, I did not at all sense their purpose.

"Finally he rolled over on me, and allowing the huge whanger to bang against my bare belly, the tiny knobs that decorated it tickling me furiously, I gave a little cry of fear, and struggled to withdraw, only to be held tightly against the couch by Ki-Ling and the two girls, and the Chinaman, rising upon me, placed the head of his giant priapus at my slit, and bore gently against me.

"The distention of my outer lips brought about by this so unnatural conjunction caused me a little pain, and I thrashed about in an effort to escape, and felt a bare hand and arm dart under my buttocks, and some pungent burning liquid was applied suddenly against my nether parts, causing me to suddenly dash my body violently upward in an effort to escape this burning pain, and at that instant the Chinaman drove into me with all of his might, the huge prong tearing and driving up into me, tearing and rending its way far up into my vagina, the tiny knobs on his phallus causing it to open me more, and with a loud cry of pain I remembered no more but fell back senseless on the couch!

"I do not know how long I remained that way, but coming to my dazed senses, I found that iron dart still impaled within me, the man working with deep steady strokes within me, and at that instant, I felt it stiffen out like a shot and the squirt of his fluid spurt in huge spouts within me, and I again passed into oblivion. I awoke in a dazed condition evidently due to the drink that I had taken, and found myself still in the arms of the cruel Chinese!

"I remember one time, coming to my senses, to find myself entirely nude, destitute of all clothing and lying on the floor. It seemed as if some other man was having me, but of this I am not sure, for finally awakening, I found myself clothed in the clothing that I had worn there, and lying on a bed in the rear of the Chinese laundry.

"An envelope had been placed in my bag, and in it was the seventy-five dollars promised me, and a wonderful laveliere which I have never even worn and which I have now hidden at home. That, my dears, is the story of my seduction, and I never saw Ki-Ling again!"

By this time, I had out my erect staff, and for the last few moments Grace had been fondling and tickling its swollen head.

I immediately upon the conclusion of her tale bore her gently on her back on the floor, and lying over her, placed my prong into the proper receptacle which I found as before pleasantly tight and glove-like, and I gave her the benefit of my surcharged emotions.

Anna was an interested spectator of this, and with Joseph entering at this moment, she made no loss of time in unveiling his staff and impaling herself upon it as he lay under her, and between us we ran a merry race to its wet and sticky conclusion.

"Oh," I said, as Joseph retired for another drink, "I really believe that I enjoyed you more this time, Grace, than I did before! It certainly takes a good stiff story to liven one up to their best. How did you like yours, Anna?"

"All I can say," replied that sensual young miss, as she dried her parts with many a grimace, "is that our young Joseph certainly carries a large meat-roll in his pant and sure does know how to pack it! Oh, golly, I can hardly touch myself!"

"How is it, girls," I said, growing more serious, "that in your tales of your seductions, you have, neither of you, taken part in the delicious French or sodomistic scenes that I am sure must be known to you?"

"Sodomistic?" echoed Grace, looking at me perplexed. "What, Mr. Anderson, do you mean by that? In what way is that done? Is it something new—something—" And as she saw Anna and I laughing at her she stopped with her mouth agape.

"As you see, Anna knows something of it," I said, "and I am sure, dear Grace, that your education has been sadly neglected in this respect, and I am sure that if you once tasted the joys of a stiff pintle thrust forcibly into the confines of your rectum you would never, never be content with any other method."

But the disgusted looks on both of the girls' faces told me that they had never, as yet, been enjoyed in that particular manner, and Grace, especially, placed her tiny hand over my lips as though to stop my speech and Anna placed her fingers in her ears.

"But you simply must listen, girls," I said, "this is of importance to you, and if you like it or not, I will make you my proposition."

At this their natural curiosity to hear what I had to say overcame their prudent scruples and listening eagerly, I said slowly and distinctly, "If either, or both of you, would at any time find yourself willing to submit to me in this manner, without reserve, and allow me to thoroughly and completely sodomize you, I am willing to duplicate the offer of the Chinaman, or to be frank, to give you for yourself the sum of one hundred dollars."

"Never!" said Anna emphatically. "You would never, never persuade me to submit to that! It is true that I have heard of it, and have even known girls who have had it done to them, but as far as I am concerned personally, you will never have occasion to give that sum to me, my dear Mr. Anderson."

"But how—how on earth can it be possible?" asked Grace, her brow corrugated with wonderment. "I do not at all see how it would be earthly possible for a man to put his thing up in a girl back there! Why, I should think that it would kill her!"

"Oh no," said Anna, adopting an air of wisdom, "I do not think, Grace, that a girl would actually die from it, especially if the man used a little care and did not violently assault her, but as far as I am concerned, I do not want any part of it, and will be content with the natural way for the present."

"Oh, I was not thinking of trying it," said the bashful Grace, "I merely wondered about it, for it is the first time that I ever heard of it, and as I know there must be many things that I do not know of, naturally I wanted to find out all about it."

"Well," I said, "my offer still stands, and as you both know where the place is here, and also the phone number, you may let me know at any time and if I am disengaged, I will gladly hold you to the agreement. This, of course, does not in any way change our plans for the future, and now girls, if you are ready, we will drive back to your street."

Anna again emphatically stated her views on this matter, Grace saying not a word, and calling Joseph, I told him to make ready the car and I escorted the girls back to their corner, and making an appointment for a later date left them, and being tired, had Joseph drive me right home and to bed.

To my intense surprise (about noon the next day) I received a phone call and upon answering, the following conversation ensued:

"Hello, is this Mr. Anderson?"

"Yes," I said, wondering who it might be.

"Well," said a laughing voice, "this is Anna. You know."

"Oh, hello!" I greeted her, wondering what in the

world she was calling for at that time of the day. "How are you Anna? Well, I hope?"

"Oh, I'm all right," she said, "but I called you to find out if you are still willing to spend that sum you spoke of when we left the other night. Is it still an offer?"

"Oh, yes, yes!" I said, perfectly befuddled at her words, after her remarks of the other evening when we had been together. "But—but—you know—your views—your ideas on such things—"

"Oh, bunk!" she said snappily. "I did not think in the world that you believed that talk when I said it. Surely you do not think that I would come right out in front of Grace and express myself? It will be all new to me—but still— the consideration—that is what attracts me. Do you wish me to meet you tonight?"

"Well, just a minute," I parried, "you are rushing things rather hurriedly, and I do not know what I have to do—maybe—"

"But this surely is important!" she laughed in the phone. "I am sure that business might wait in view of what I offer you—but still if you wish to postpone it I can—"

"No", I said shortly, "I will meet you in the same place tonight, and I am sure that you understand fully the matter, do you, Anna?"

"Oh, yes," she said, "I will be waiting, but now I must go as I am on my lunch hour. Be there! Good-bye!"

I mechanically replaced the receiver and thought to myself what an ardant hypocrite this young girl was, and then to myself, perhaps this was not the first time, but of that, I was willing to chance it, as experienced or new, it would be a novel experience for me.

But the marvels of the day were not over, for later in the afternoon I received another call, and this time it was from demure Grace, who asked if she might see me by herself as there was something that she wished to tell me.

"So!" I thought to myself. "Both of the fish are nibbling at the bait and here is the second catch!"

I was, however, careful not to mention it directly over the phone, as I knew that Grace was an entirely different girl in a lot of respects than the somewhat bold Anna, and told her that I was going out that night, but if she knew how to reach my apartment that I would be more than glad to see her on the next evening at seven o'clock.

She seemed somewhat disappointed over the fact that she could not see me that evening but consented to meet me as I arranged and after telling her to be punctual, I chortled in great glee at this prospect of a double potion of amusement.

In preparation of the event I sent Joseph to the bank for some currency, and dressing myself with care, I set out that evening to keep my appointment with Anna.

She made early appointments and kept them, and once we were within the confines of the car, she laughed merrily over my bewilderment on the phone and Joseph drove up rapidly to my apartment.

Once within, he prepared some drinks and Anna, having worn a light coat, as the evening was somewhat cool, laid it aside and dashed off the drink of potent liquor at one swallow.

"Why, Anna!" I marvelled. "You must be real thirsty tonight!"

"Considering what is in store for me," she said, "I

478

think it best that I feel rather good before it happens, for in my own senses I do not think that I would ever be able to go through it. Why, Mr. Anderson, can you not be content with the other way, and leave that go for some other time, and I promise you faithfully I will stand by my bargain at any time you ask for it.''

"Now, now," I said, shaking a finger at her, "surely Anna, you did not come here to wheedle me out of the agreement that we made over the phone. If you did so, I will tell you that you are wasting time, and I will have none of it. I am perfectly willing to treat you nice, and to allow you to have all of the fun you want, but this''—and here I produced a roll of small bills to the amount of one hundred dollars, and displayed them to her—''is what I promise to you, and it is yours if you carry out your part of the thing? Do you wish it, or shall I call it off?'' And I pressed the bills into her tiny hand which closed unconsciously over them.

"It is so terrible," she said, making a wry face, "but still, I know that you will be as easy with me as possible and if you will let me drink a few drinks as I know that I will get awfully hot, then I will not notice it so much—and before I know it, it will be all over—or at least I hope so.''

I could not help but laugh at her peculiar method of reasoning, but promised to allow her to drink as much as she wished, and calling Joseph in I told him to bring in a full bottle of liquor and leave it on the small stand beside us.

Upon his retiring, I took the fair girl in my arms and subjected her to a storm of passionate caresses, and upon my suggestion she wriggled out of her short skirt, and

479

clothed only in her short step-ins, stockings, and slippers she abandoned her winsome person to my roving hands.

I thought it best that I also remove my apparel, and stepping into the adjoining room I stripped to the skin, and putting on only a long bath robe and slippers, returned to the room.

Anna had helped herself liberally from the bottle while awaiting me, and upon my return, seeing that I had completely disrobed she gave a little cry of sensual joy and seizing hold of my staff patted and squeezed it between her warm litte magnetic hands till I was forced to gently move them from it lest I spurt my charge on her wrist and elbows.

"No, no Anna," I said, "the first thing that you know you will have me shooting all over you! Be careful with those touchy little hands of yours, Miss Passion."

"The better for me," she said, "when I have to let you do that to me! If I get you to the spending point I am sure that you will not be able to hurt me, so you see, there is method to my madness."

"I shall soon stop that," I said, pushing her over on her back and mounting her perfect nude form and spreading her tights with my knees, "I shall at once give you this charge up into what you term the 'proper place,' and then, Miss Smarty, you may have the second one in the place I have paid for."

Anna made a little grimace of disappointment, but my peg once in her, she forgot all else and wiggled and twisted about it like a worm on a hook and milked from its throbbing length a full charge of my steaming dew and drew it all up into the soft moist confines of her gaping womb.

I always enjoyed the possession of this beautiful girl, and the thought of sodomizing her, of opening this most private of all private orifices of her body, designed by Nature for so different a purpose, had thrilled me all the day with pleasant expectation, and now, the prize in my arms, I did full justice to my sweet and adoring prey.

By reason of the two or three generous drinks that she had taken, combined with her natural hot and burning sensuality when she was once threaded with a sexual worm, all combined to make her a weaving, dancing torrent of lust and I was forced to spill twice before her greedy quim somewhat relaxed its tight compression on my throbbing rod and allowed it to slip out between her feverish thighs.

We both lay there exhausted, and pouring the girl another drink, I allowed her to repair the damage done to her person and we sat for a while talking of many things.

"Do not in the world tell Grace a word of this," she said suddenly. "I would not have her know about this for the world!" she said earnestly. "Have I your word for that, Mr. Anderson?" And she sat up, displaying to me all her adorable nakedness like a young nymph as she poised the half-emptied glass in her hand.

I saw she was growing drunk and assured her that I had no intention of communicating her confidence to her girl friend (which was of course the truth) and she relaxed back in my arms with a contented sigh.

I amused myself for a while toying with the erect nipples of her well-formed breasts, an action that in no way displeased the naturally sensual girl, and allowing my hand to run over her naked back, I slipped it down to her swelling posteriors and slapped her lightly on the elastic cheeks.

This seemed to bring back to her mind the task that lay before her, and passing her bare arms about my neck she kissed me warmly on the lips and again asked me if there was no way that I might like that might dispense with this ultimate sacrifice of her backward quim.

Chapter 4

These efforts of the beautiful girl to seduce me from my intent, to replace for the so-much desired act one that was, although pleasurable to me, in no way compared with the thrill I expected to receive in her abnormal rape, all worked powerfully on my senses, and with difficulty I refrained from possessing her here and now on the spot.

"No, Anna," I said softly, "I will not be turned from my purpose, and all your blandishments, your sweet endearments, your soft and seductive kissings, will in no way prove a substitute for what you have already agreed on. I am determined to possess you in that way, and any artifices or excuses that you might use only strengthen in me my desire to impale you to the full length of my prong—to feel it revel within you—to enjoy your tightness and constriction—in fact, my dear, I doubt if you, even without our agreement, could ever dissuade me from the thought that I now have in mind!''

To my surprise she immediately desisted, and taking a stiff drink myself, I gave her another, and watched her eyes glisten as the fiery liquor coursed through her veins.

I now, however, considered the means at hand to complete my project, as I knew that it would be impossible to bind the girl, and left free, a healthy young animal like she was, was bound to struggle and twist and would make the conjunction hard if not totally impossible once started.

To get her on her stomach and to impale her, especially for the first time, would require some ingenuity, and in this respect I evolved a plan that I was sure would not only meet with success but also with her approval and of this I now spoke.

''Anna, dear,'' I said, kissing her again, and feeling my rod stiffen at the contact of her velvety lips, ''we are now approaching the time when you are to deliver to me your nether maidenhead, and knowing your warm nature, I have devised a plan that I think will meet with your utmost approval.''

''Oh, what is it?'' she cried wonderingly.

''Simply this,'' I answered. ''I know that the act that I intend to perform upon you may at first hurt you, but supposing that at the time you were impaled upon the juicy hardness of my man Joseph's cock; do you not think that that, in itself, would in some way take your mind off what is happening to you in the rear?''

She clapped her hands at this suggestion, and ringing for Joseph, upon his entrance I cast him a significant glance and he immediately began to strip himself of his clothing.

By this time Anna was slightly drunk and lay back in my arms, her sexual charms open for any that might care to look, and Joseph, shedding his last garment, threw himself down beside us.

Anna lost not an instant in capturing in her hand his standing and erect tool, and Joseph, having been fully instructed by me as to what procedure was to take place, allowed her to handle and fondle it until it stood up like an oak tree.

He then lifted Anna to her feet, and throwing her on a low bed that stood alongside the room, seated himself on its edge, his feet on the floor, and I helped seat Anna astride his lap, she lifting the giant throbbing prick up to her quim, and sinking down on it with ecstatic wiggles and gasps she buried it in herself to the roots, and wrapping her arms about Joseph's neck, she gave herself up to the pleasures held in his throbbing prick.

Such, however, was not my intentions, and as I had thoroughly coached Joseph he restrained from moving about, and gently lay back on his back on the bed, bringing the girl down with him on his chest, and spreading his legs wide, allowed me to advance between them and to present my peg in the middle of her dimpled posterior cheeks.

I noticed that he wrapped one of his legs about each of those of the girl, and held her closely wrapped to him, and as she uttered faint panting moans of sensual pleasure, I boldly pulled the elastic cheeks of her posteriors apart, and placing the head of my now iron-hard peg at her diminutive hole, I seized her by the shoulders, and leaning heavily over her I began to shove away to force the tiny citadel.

She stiffened out like a board, her face uplifted in a gesture of pain from Joseph's shoulder in which she had buried it, and wriggling and twisting about in a frenzy of helplessness, she cried and roared at the top of her voice, but Joseph, following my instructions pounded regularly away at her slit, his huge prick gliding in and out of her quivering slit in heavy, soulsearing strokes, and bracing my feet on the floor I drove again and again at the tight hole, and at last—I felt the membranes reluctantly give way—the head of my bolus was slowly engulfed and compressed in the hysterical closures and slowly but surely it relentlessly drove in and in an instant I was buried within her to the very balls!

What screaming! What raving! The nervous tantalizing compressions of this never-entered cove of Nature on my dart-o-love I am sure would have caused me to melt, without any exertion at all on my part, but this, this was not the idea I had in mind, and driving away in this tight little channel I subjected her clinging folds to such a titillating series of movements that I felt Joseph's prick leap, spout and bubble within her through the thin membrane that divided her secret orifices.

At last I vented! Oh, what a charge I distilled within her! It bubbled and boiled, a veritable geyser of hot lasciviousness, leaping and spouting up into her nether cleft, and all three of us lay half fainting on the bed.

I withdrew my peg with a sudden p-l-o-p! that allowed her to leap from the prostrate Joseph, and attempting to run, I doubt if she knew where, she fell in a lifeless mass on the floor.

I feared at first that I had injured her, but the faithful Joseph, his sperm-drenched prick still dripping from the sexual flood, gave her his attention and she soon returned to her senses and allowed him to conduct her to the lavatory.

She did not return for a few minutes, and then, when she did, she seemed perfectly sober, and a little pale, but in no way hurt otherwise from her pleasant or unpleasant experience. I treated her with the utmost kindness and respect, and after talking a while she said that she now felt in no way hurt and was again laughing and chatting as if nothing had happened. This tripe charge of my juices had been a lot for me, and after making sure that she would meet me as agreed with her friend Grace, I gave her an extra present of a large bill and ordered Joseph to drive her home by himself as I wished to retire early.

This Joseph did, and upon his return he told me that on the way to her street, he had stopped in a dark spot and returning to the back of the car, had given her another taste of his peg and that she had enjoyed it with fierce ardour, so in this way I knew that she was back to "normal," as that was a good test for the little sensual beauty. Both Joseph and I laughed over this particular incident, and wishing to be perfectly fit for my engagement with the demure Grace on the following evening (although nothing had been specified) I retired early and did not arise till late the following day.

I had, of course, informed Joseph of my expected appointment with the charming girl and on the stroke of seven she entered the hall and Joseph respectfully ushered her into the room in which I was reading, and retired until called for.

"Well, my dear," I said, "you are certainly charming tonight! I am sure that your husband should be well content with the prize that he has won, for should I be a few years younger, he would have a contest on his hands, I'll warrant you."

She smiled wanly, and coming close to where I sat, she looked about and said in a low voice, "I am sure, Mr. Anderson, that he would not at all think he had a prize if he were conversant of the true character of his wife. Not that I am repining or bewailing what has occured, but—I must tell you—that is why I came—" And she blushed furiously and dropped her azure eyes to the carpet and fumbled about.

"Come, Grace," I said soothingly, "surely it is not at all as terrible as you make it. What is it, my dear, that seems to so upset you? Tell me, I beseech you!"

"Well," she said, rather shamefacedly, "I think that I told you that I am to be married in three days time—and in preparation of that event, I, of course, figured out the time, you know what I mean—my menstrual period—and although I was due 'sick' at least three days ago—I have not come 'round' and I fear that I am indeed pregnant! And you—you are the only one that I had anything to do with!"

"Oh, my!" I said, somewhat startled, but at the same time knowing the girl was too timid and honest to be attempting to blackmail me. "Why, Grace, if you are sure of that—well, it is too late to do anything now—you know what I mean—stop it—and as you will be in your husband's arms in three days, why not—let it—let it go— I am sure that you will not find me at all parsimnious in remembering things—if it does come about!"

"Oh, I am so glad to hear that," she said in a relieved

tone. "Of course, it may sound terrible to say that, but still, as you say, there is no other way, and as I am marrying to have a home, I will keep the secret close to my heart, and none shall know except you and I, and as for Anna—"

"Trust me," I said, drawing her close to me as she stood there. I passed one arm around her waist, and drawing her face down to mine I pressed warm kisses on her fragile and dormant lips.

"Of course I knew that," she said, in no way making a move to stop the bold explorations of my hand as it opened her waist and displayed to my view her tender and budding breasts, "but still, Mr. Anderson, now that that is settled I think I shall go, as you may have something else to do."

"Why, my dear," I said, allowing one hand to glide up her well-shaped leg on her bare and electric thigh, "I thought surely that you might have come here tonight in hopes of winning the prize I have offered for you—and I am sure, my dear, that it would be ample repayment for a few moments of your time. Have you thought of it, dear Grace?"

"Yes, I have," she confessed, "a whole lot—in fact, I thought all day yesterday of it—but still, it seems so unnatural—so obnoxious, so—well, so out of the way— and the disparity in sizes—why it might lead to consequences that are serious—men, you know, in the grip of love—they sometimes overestimate the possibilities of things—and were I more adept in that way of love—"

"Poppycock!" I said to her, pleased to hear that she had given thought to attaining the prize. "I will in no way injure you, you may assure yourself of that, and I am sure

that once performed it will remove from your mind all of
the ideas of pain that you have associated with it.''

"Oh, it would!'' she said. "I know it would.'' But by
this time my hand was between her thighs, and the tiny
knob within her inner lips was hardly moving about under
my forefinger, and she leaned close to me and breathed
faster. "Oh, Mr. Anderson, if I only knew—if I knew it
would not hurt me too—too much—would you really and
truly be careful? Have I your word?''

"Oh yes,'' I promised her, "but still if you wished to
assure yourself of an absence of nearly all of the pain,
there is a little trick that you might resort to, that I am sure
would make the passage much easier.''

"How?'' she queried, now drawing gently away from
me as she felt herself about to melt under the adroit
manipulation of my moving finger.

"By taking it in your mouth for a while and wetting it
good,'' I answered, "the natural slipperiness is augmented,
and if it is performed properly it will greatly lessen the act.
Do you wish to try it?'' And I drew out my standing cock
and wagged it to and fro before her.

"Oh, I did not know that was in the bargain,'' she said,
but in no way abashed at this sudden proposal of mine.

"But here,'' I said, thrusting my hand in my pocket and
bringing to view a roll of bills and pressing them into her
hands, "you have merely to amuse both Joseph and myself
for a short while and you will depart from here without a
word to anyone and so much richer. And I am sure that
you can use the money to advantage, especially in view of
your coming nuptials. Is it a bargain, my dear?'' And I
again kissed her warmly, and titillated the nipples of her

breasts which were standing hard and erect as if to do battle.

This idea of bringing in Joseph on the bargain was sudden with me, but correctly analyzing the natural timidity of the girl, I boldly assumed that she knew that was the bargain and determined to have all or none.

"I must be home by ten," she said, as she still held the bills in her hand, "and I am sure, Mr. Anderson, that you—and Joseph—will retain this affair secret—a secret to us three for all time—as you must consider—"

"Enough!" I cried, driven to a frenzy of desire at the sight of this beautiful timidity of the fair girl. "It shall be as you say! Abandon your person unreservedly to me, and besides the sum you now hold in your hands, I will remember you liberally!" And reaching for the bell-cord I gave it a vigorous yank which was instantly answered by Joseph, who I do not doubt was an interested listener at the outside of the door.

"Joseph," I said, "our young friend here, the adorable Miss Grace, has consented to honour us with the gift of her divine person, and due to one of the visits she made here in the past week she is of the opinion that she now holds within her womb a miniature replica of your Master, and as she is to be married in a few days she is making to us a last disposal of her person to be used in any manner that we see fit! It is unnecessary to inform you that the most profound secrecy is to be preserved by you as to our part in the affair, but on the other hand, at this last bestowal of herself to our sensual senses, Miss Grace makes no restrictions of any kind and in a short while I intend to possess her in the manner of the Greeks, which act she will lighten in a way by thoroughly kissing my cock! Is not that right, Grace?'' I asked her, my hand still up under her short skirt on the knob of her sex.

She made no answer but leaned over on me, her breath coming in short pants, and I felt her love liquor spill on my rubbing finger, and telling Joseph to lock the house, he returned to the room and began to disrobe himself.

He was in a fine state of erection, and with his assistance we soon disrobed Grace to the skin, even removing her stockings and shoes, and I did the same.

This act of being so suddenly disrobed by two naked men, their stiff pricks standing before them, and sometimes brushing her naked form, caused the modest girl to blush like a peony, the crimson loveliness covering her face, shoulders, and breasts, and once disrobed, I had her kneel before me as I sat in the large morris chair, and presenting my standing cock to her lips I told her to suck it.

Joseph, at a nod from me, had taken his place on the floor behind her, in a kneeling position, and introducing his peg into her moist cavern of sex, and as I held her by her short hair close to my standing dart, he drove up in her with all of his might, and as though timed exactly to a second we both vented out juices in the opposite orifices of her body.

Grace choked and gagged over the pulsing cargo, being perhaps at the spending point, and I finally allowed my limp peg to slip out from between her lips.

Joseph had dried her and we now repaired the damage done to our own pegs, and Joseph still being hard, I suggested that she take him in her mouth, and accordingly his peg was held to her lips and I watched her slowly move her head up and down the glistening shaft.

Joseph did not finish in her mouth, but suddenly withdrawing his dart, pushed her on her back and mounting her lay heavily upon her, the cheeks of her posteriors grasped in his hands and weaving about her in a perfect frenzy of lust, his lips glued to hers, he poured into her pregnant quim a second load of his sexual oil.

The sight of this timid girl, in three days to be a bride, being pounded by my servant's massive tool, the sensual gestures, writhings and winding of the panting pair, the stiffening of both bodies as his sperm shot and volleyed within her, affected me so much that I sprang to my feet, my whanger again in a stare of stone-like hardness.

Joseph rose from off her, and in obedience to my instructions drew out a long, narrow piano bench that was in the room, laid Grace on her stomach upon it, and going to her head, he drew her hands out in front of her and held them tightly within his own.

Grace knew not what this was all about, but in a moment was to find out to her full satisfaction, as I mounted her from behind, divided the soft, billowy, trembling cheeks of her well-formed posterior and introduced my prick in the dark hollow and directly against her touch-hole.

Now she knew what it was, and feeling the pressing of the hard head of my bolus in that unaccustomed spot, she thrashed and wiggled about in an attempt to escape, but now it was all too late, and I, mad with lust—thinking nothing of what I wrought, drove away fiercely at the helpless girl and in a few fierce furious drives succeeded in impaling myself within her and almost immediately vented my juices within her.

I lay for a minute upon her, and seeing Joseph's eyes glittering with desire, I withdrew my prong, and taking his place at her head, I allowed him to ride this now almost unconscious charger, stilling her frantic wiggles and cries as Joseph bore far up in her and subjected her person to a series of shoves that almost displaced her from the bench.

Finally he finished, and she lay lax and dispirited, her arms and legs hanging downward from the bench, the combined charges of our juices trickling down from her ravished spot into the lips of her already sodden quim, and pity taking the place of lust, with Joseph's assistance I carried her to the bed and laid her there to recover her senses.

It was an hour or more before she was able to arise and dress herself, and being somewhat timid and nervous, I led her to the front door, and telling Joseph to look out to see no one was around that might observe her, I stood beside her in the hallway.

"I shall see you after I marry?" she asked me, her large, lustrous eyes turned up to mine, as she placed her hands on my arm and prepared to depart.

"Indeed," I said, "I shall see you quite often, my dear." And bending, I kissed her, the complaisant warmness of her lips leading me to again encompass and squeeze her budding breasts.

"Oh," she said, weakly attempting to evade me, "I must go now! You will be started again! I—"

Joseph returned at this instant, and seeing my preoccupation made preparations to efface himself, but I hailed him:

"You may get the car, Joseph," I said, "and as for you Grace, I intend before you leave here, to possess you once more!" And tumbling her back on the carpeted stairs I drew out my peg and was in an instant between her legs, my dart burned to the roots in her delicate grove!

This last and sudden assault of her person, so sudden it was, and so precipitate my charge, that she spent in profusion over me and I rained into her cleft another charge of my boiling dew.

Being rather tired we both got up and dressed. I asked Grace to come back the next evening because Joseph was going out of town on some errand.

Grace arrived early and after pouring a couple of drinks, we were soon undressed and in bed. Fondling each other for several minutes, our passion began to mount, but I was not anxious to bring things to a too rapid conclusion. The keen edge of my desire had been removed by our first embrace and I was now more interested in that ero-without coming to too rapid a conclusion.

For several minutes I gave her a sort of Swedish massage until her entire nervous system must have been tingling with lust. Then, feeling that I had increased her amativeness, I began kissing her; starting at the nape of her neck, I kissed her repeatedly, moving my face down her back. Removing myself from my position astride her hips, I reclined on the couch beside her; my face traveled down her backbone to her glowing rounded buttocks; she was now a quivering mass, her body twisting and straining from side to side.

I gave her no quarter whatever; down the backs of her legs my hot lips traveled, rapid kisses raining on her now

495

heated flesh. Finally I came to the feet, which I would have kissed also, but found that she was too ticklish in that part of her anatomy, so I was forced to forego. However, knowing the celebrated Eastern recipe for arousing passion— that which is said to be capable of melting the most frigid woman who ever lived, which is said to be invincible and which no living woman can resist, no matter how indifferent or cold she may be—taking her great toe between my lips, I began to titillate it with the tip of my tongue. Immediately the girl went into a paroxysm. She flung herself about on the couch, her hands clutched the bed-clothing and she moaned with excitement and pleasure.

A moment of violent sucking of her toe was sufficient; I knew that a little more of it would cause her to spend and I was not ready for that yet—then, grasping her by the ankles I gave her a twist indicating that I wished her to turn over which she did with a violent twist, and lay supine on the couch; her lovely face was flushed and her beautiful body lay before me, the legs wide flung, and her chest heaving with laboring breath.

Had she needed further encouragement, I would have done other things to her, but I was beginning to fear that she would spend before I wished it, so I decided to come to a conclusion.

Lowering my lips to her ankles, I began kissing her again, this time traveling upwards towards her body. I don't think she quite anticipated what I was going to do, so innocent was she, but she lay there quite sprawled out upon the couch, her body quivering and moving from side to side.

Rapidly kissing her knees, her thighs, I came to her

belly; instantly her legs clutched together wildly; my hands seized her thighs and slowly spread them apart and with a sudden movement I buried my face in her red crotch, kissing her hotly upon the lips of her cunt! She uttered a moan which was almost a scream; her hands clutched my hair and she dragged my head up tightly to her body as my tongue inserted itself into the hot crevice of her quim—her body began to shake and shiver, then suddenly with a few wild heaves she approached her climax; I assisted her by tonguing her rapidly and fiercely and with a few moans and a final violent twisting of her body she reached her orgasm, then sunk back in utter collapse after the violent tension she had recently experienced. I raised my face and crept up beside her on the couch; taking her in my arms I held her tightly until she once more found her senses.

For several minutes she lay as though in a stupor; her breath came heavily, with low moans. Then her beautiful eyes slowly opened and she looked up at me with a smile.

"Well, how do you feel now?" I inquired.

"Oh, my goodness!" Grace replied. "I thought I was in heaven. You nearly made a wreck out of me." And her white arms squeezed me ecstatically.

"Well, did you like it? You won't think less of me for what I did to you, will you?"

"Oh, my no! Oh, that was delightful and I love you for it. And now what can I do to give you a thrill?" she said, looking up at me archly. Her hand had stolen down and found my stiffened pecker and was squeezing and manipulating it slowly.

I did not leave her long in the dark. I think she knew pretty well what I wanted; the fact that I had kissed her on that spot would of course have indicated that I might appreciate a return of the compliment. She was so aroused that she cast all reserve to the wind and rising to her knees, she placed herself beside me on the couch and began to handle my now throbbing member.

She gazed at it with considerable interest, her fingers twisting and turning it about; she pulled back the skin over its ruby head, then slipped it up again; she tested its hardness by squeezing; holding it in her fingers she examined the skin closely, noting the veins and hair, then her hands played about with my bollocks for a few moments.

Suddenly she stooped her head and began to kiss his majesty, then her lips opened and she received into her mouth the head of my cock, which throbbed mightily at the soft moist touch of her red lips.

She played with him thus for some moments; slipping him in and out of her mouth, her tongue gliding up and down the rigid shaft and curling itself around his red and swollen head. I lay still trying to control myself; I was not yet ready to spend in this fashion; that would come later, I hoped.

"What do you say if we try some different positions?" I asked.

"Oh, sure!" Grace replied, with considerable interest.

"Well," I remarked, "if you want to give me a thrill, I will tell you what to do."

She was only too willing, so I showed her how to assume that gem of all positions; as I lay flat on my back on the couch, I had her straddle me in a kneeling position, her pussy directly above my cock; settling down, the pin was driven into her hot cunt; she needed no further directions but proceeded to give me the utmost in pleasure, her body twisting from side to/side as the patches of hair on our respective pubes ground together. Then at my direction she started slowly raising and lowering herself, at the same time the muscles of her cunt tightly grasping the stem of my penis, thus grasping my tool as she raised herself, causing a sort of sucking sensation I felt as though I should lose my very soul through my penis, so great was the pleasurable sensation thus engendered.

But I was still not ready for the orgasm. After a few moments of this sort of play, I had her dismount from her position of impalement on my member, to assume a position on the couch on her hands and knees.

Arising, I placed myself behind her; parting the lips of her cunt which had by now become thoroughly moistened with the liquid which lubricates the heated vulva, I slipped between those rosy lips the head of my cock and with a few slow moves pushed it solidly home. My hands clasped her breasts as I thus knelt behind her; the feeling of her soft, rounded buttocks against my belly giving me a tremendous sensual thrill so that for a moment I was tempted to work us into an orgasm, but feeling as I did that this was, in a sense, the lady's party and not mine, I decided to finish the performance in a position which would perhaps be less delightful to myself, but more pleasing to her, so that, after a few moments in the present position, I removed my penis and lay back upon the couch once more.

Grace looked at me expectantly, wondering what was coming next. Holding out my arms I invited her to come on top of me, which she did. Next, securing a pillow from the head of my bed, I placed it beneath my buttocks, thus elevating my belly and groins so that when I had once more placed my cock in her now hot and excited quim, our bellies were tightly pressed together and I could feel my pubic bone pressing tightly against hers and she straddled my prone body, my hands clasped her legs and drew them widely apart, thus bringing our pubes into the tightest possible conjunction.

We were now all set to go, so my hands began manipulating the back of her head and around her ears; my fingers curled through the luxuriant dark red hair and massaged her scalp; then my hands traveled along her shoulders; she was of the type who react immediately to massaging of the shoulder blades and back, so I slowly kneaded and rubbed the flesh of her shoulders and back, up and down, as far as the hips; meanwhile she was twisting and writhing, my stiff, hard prick imbedded to the utmost hilt in her hot, tightly gripping cunt; her arms clutched me tightly about the neck; her eyes were half-closed and turned upwards in a frenzy so that I could see the whites of her eyeballs underneath her up-rolled eyes; her breath coming in short, quick gasps of passion while low moans came from between her tightly clenched teeth.

Impaled as she was upon my hard pecker, she seemed determined to break it off; with violent downward motions of her hips and body she lunged and shook; I could feel the head of my member grinding against what I took to be the entrance of her womb; I felt quite sure that the lady was receiving for the first time in her life a thoroughly satisfying fuck, so I prolonged the operation as long as I possibly could.

Her heat and passion, however, together with her wild

manoeuvers, finally became too much for me and I felt I was approaching my climax. My finger worked in and out of her buttonhole; my left hand massaged her neck and scalp; occasionally I would slip the tip of a finger into her ear; I whispered "What are we doing, Grace?" It seemed to cause her to become even more excited, so sensing that the time was about ripe, I whispered, "Are you ready?" "Oh, yes, yes—oh!" And with a series of moans and sighs, her lips glued themselves to mine in a long kiss—my tongue slipped between her hot lips and into her mouth—violently sucking it, she reached her paroxysm and I my-self felt the long-delayed orgasm arriving, and with a mad heaving of our twisted bodies we reached that state of ineffable bliss together.

They both got up and putting on their clothes, Grace was ready to go feeling well satisfied with the roll of bills I gave her.

VICTORIAN EROTIC CLASSICS
AVAILABLE FROM CARROLL & GRAF

☐ Anonymous / Altar of Venus	4.50
☐ Anonymous / Autobiography of a Flea & Other Tart Tales	5.95
☐ Anonymous / Black Magic	6.95
☐ Anonymous / Careless Passion	5.95
☐ Anonymous / Confessions of an English Maid & Other Delights	5.95
☐ Anonymous / The Consummate Eveline	4.95
☐ Anonymous / Court of Venus	3.95
☐ Anonymous/ Best of Erotic Reader	6.95
☐ Anonymous / Eroticon	4.95
☐ Anonymous / Eroticon II	4.95
☐ Anonymous / Eroticon III	4.50
☐ Anonymous / Fallen Woman	4.50
☐ Anonymous / Harem Nights	4.95
☐ Anonymous / The Intimate Memoirs of an Edwardian Dandy	4.95
☐ Anonymous / The Intimate Memoirs of an Edwardian Dandy, Vol. II	4.95
☐ Anonymous / The Intimate Memoirs of an Edwardian Dandy, Vol. III	4.95
☐ Anonymous / Lay of the Land	4.50
☐ Anonymous / The Libertines	4.50
☐ Anonymous / Maid and Mistress	4.50
☐ Anonymous / A Man with a Maid	5.95
☐ Anonymous / Memoirs of Josephine	4.50
☐ Anonymous / The Merry Menage	4.50
☐ Anonymous / The Oyster	4.50
☐ Anonymous / The Oyster II	3.95
☐ Anonymous / The Oyster III	4.50
☐ Anonymous / The Oyster V	4.50
☐ Anonymous / Pagan Delights	5.95
☐ Anonymous / The Pearl	6.95
☐ Anonymous / Pleasures and Follies	3.95
☐ Anonymous / Romance of Lust	5.95

☐	Anonymous / Rosa Fielding: Victim of Lust	3.95
☐	Anonymous/ Sharing Sisters	4.95
☐	Anonymous / Secret Lives	3.95
☐	Anonymous / Sensual Secrets	4.50
☐	Anonymous / Sweet Confessions	4.50
☐	Anonymous / Sweet Tales	4.50
☐	Anonymous / Tropic of Lust	4.50
☐	Anonymous / Venus Butterfly	3.95
☐	Anonymous / Venus Delights	3.95
☐	Anonymous / Venus Disposes	3.95
☐	Anonymous / Venus in India	3.95
☐	Anonymous / Victorian Fancies	4.50
☐	Anonymous / The Wantons	4.50
☐	Anonymous / White Thighs	4.50
☐	Anonymous / Youthful Indiscretions	4.50
☐	Cleland, John / Fanny Hill	4.95
☐	van Heller, Marcus / Adam and Eve	3.95
☐	van Heller, Marcus / Lusts of the Borgias	4.95
☐	van Heller, Marcus / Seduced	5.95
☐	van Heller, Marcus / Unbound	5.95
☐	van Heller, Marcus / Venus in Lace	3.95
☐	Villefranche, Anne-Marie / Passion d'Amour	5.95
☐	Villefranche, Anne-Marie / Scandale d'Amour	5.95
☐	Villefranche, Anne-Marie / Secrets d'Amour	4.50
☐	Villefranche, Anne-Marie / Souvenir d'Amour	4.50
☐	von Falkensee, Margarete / Blue Angel Confessions	6.95
☐	"Walter"/ My Secret Life	7.95

Peace Be
With You

Presented to:

_____

_____

By:

_____

_____

_____ 19 ____

Peace Be With You

Henry Drummond

Photography by Harold Lambert

BROWNLOW PUBLISHING COMPANY, INC.
P. O. Box 3141
Fort Worth, Texas 76105

Brownlow Gift Books

Flowers That Never Fade

Flowers for You

Flowers for Mother

A Father's World

Flowers of Friendship

The University of Hard Knocks

Longfellow Birthday Book

Better Than Medicine

By His Side

Making the Most of Life

Aesop's Fables

A Time to Laugh
      —or Grandpa Was A Preacher

With the Good Shepherd

Thoughts of Gold
      in Words of Silver

For Love's Sake

The Story of Jesus

The More Years the More Sunshine

Peace Be With You

Daybreak

Windows

Living With the Psalms

Today Is Mine

Contents

The Need for a Remedy

I HEARD the other morning an address by a distinguished preacher upon "Rest." It was full of beautiful thoughts; but when I came to ask myself, "How does he say I can get Rest?" there was no answer. The address was sincerely meant to be practical, yet it contained no experience that seemed to me to be tangible, nor any advice which could help me to find the thing itself. Yet this omission of the *how* was not the fault of the preacher alone. For the whole popular religion is in the twilight here. And when pressed for really working specifics for obtaining these experiences, it falters and seems to lose itself in mist.

● *The want of connection between the great words of religion and everyday life* has bewildered and discouraged all of us. Christianity possesses the noblest words in the language; its literature overflows with terms expressive of the greatest and happiest moods which can fill the soul of man. Rest, Joy, Peace, Faith, Love, Light — these words occur with such persistency in hymns and prayers that an observer might think they formed the staple of Christian experience. But in observing the actual life of most of us, how surely would he be disenchanted! I do not think we ourselves are aware how much our religious life is made up of phrases; how much of what we call Christian experience is only a dialect, a mere religious phraseology with almost nothing behind it in what we really feel and know.

● *To some of us the Christian experiences seem farther away than when we took the first steps in the Christian life.* That life has not opened out as we had hoped; we do not regret our religion, but we are disappointed with it. There are times, perhaps, when wandering notes from a diviner music stray into our hearts; but these experiences come at few and fitful moments. We have no sense of possession in them. When they visit us, it is a surprise. When they leave us, it is without explanation. When we wish their return, we do not know how to secure them.

● *All this points to a religion without solid base, and a poor and flickering life.* It means a great bankruptcy in those feelings which give Christianity its personal solace and make it attractive to the world. It is as if we knew everything about health — except the way to get it.

I am quite sure that the difficulty does not lie in the fact that men are not in earnest. All around us Christians are wearing themselves out in trying to be better. It is not more heat that is needed, but more light; not more force, but a wiser direction to be given to very real energies already there.

● *The thoughts which follow are offered as an humble contribution to this problem,* and in the hope that it may help some who are "seeking Rest and finding none" to a firmer footing on one great, solid, simple principle which underlies all experiences and all life.

What Christians want is method. It is impossible to believe that there is no remedy, or that the remedy is a secret. The idea that some few men, by happy chance or happier temperament, have been given the secret — as if there were some sort of knack or trick of it — is wholly incredible. Religion must ripen its fruit for every temperament; and the way even into its highest heights must be by a gateway through which the peoples of the world may pass. I shall try to lead up to this gateway by a very familiar path.

II

Effects Require Causes

NOTHING that happens in the world happens by chance. God is a God of order. Everything is arranged upon definite principles, and never at random. The world, even the religious world, is governed by law. Character is governed by law. Happiness is governed by law. The Christian experiences are governed by law. Men, forgetting this, expect Rest, Joy, Peace and Faith to drop into their souls from the air like snow or rain. But they do not do so. Rain and snow do drop from the air, but not without a long previous history. They are the mature effects of former causes. Equally so are Rest, and Peace and Joy. They, too, have each a previous history. Storms and winds and calms are not accidents, but are brought about by antecedent circumstances. Rest and Peace are but calms in man's inward nature, and arise through causes, just as definite and as inevitable.

● *Realize it thoroughly: it is a method-ical not an accidental world.* If a housewife turns out a good cake, it is the result of a sound recipe, carefully applied. She cannot mix the assigned ingredients and bake them for the appropriate time without producing the result. But it is not she who has made the cake; it is nature. She brings related things together; sets causes at work; and these causes bring about the result. She does not expect random causes to produce specific effects — random ingredients would only produce random cakes. So it is in the making of Christian experiences. Certain lines are followed; certain effects are the result. But the result can never take place without the previous cause. To expect results without antecedents is to expect cakes without ingredients.

● *Now what I mainly wish to do is to help you firmly to grasp this simple prin-ciple of Cause and Effect in the spiritual world.* And instead of applying the prin-ciple generally to each of the Christian experiences, I shall examine its application to one in some little detail. The one I shall select is Rest.

Take such a sentence as this: Residents in the swamps are subject to fevers which cause restlessness and delirium. *Restlessness has a cause.* Clearly then, any one who wishes to get rid of restlessness would proceed at once to deal with the cause. If that is not removed, a doctor might prescribe a hundred things without producing the least effect. Things are so arranged in the original planning of the world that certain effects must follow certain causes, and certain causes must be abolished before certain effects can be removed. Swamps are inseparably linked with the physical experience called fever; and this fever is infallibly linked with a mental experience called restlessness and delirium. To abolish the mental experience the radical method would be to abolish the physical experience — hence, abolish the swamps, or cease to go there. Now this holds good for all other forms of Restlessness. Every other kind of Restlessness has a definite cause, which can be removed only by removing the allotted cause.

This is also true of Rest. If restlessness has a cause, must not *Rest also have a cause?* Necessarily. If it were a chance world we would not expect this; but, being a method-ical world, it cannot be otherwise. Rest, physical rest, moral rest, spiritual rest, every kind of rest, has a cause as certainly as restlessness. Now there is one kind of cause for every particular effect, and no other; and if one particular effect is desired, the corresponding cause must be set in motion. It is no use proposing finely devised schemes, or going through general pious exercises in the hope that somehow Rest will come. *The Christian life is not casual, but causal.* All nature is a standing protest against the absurdity of expecting to secure spiritual effects, or any effects, without the employment of appropriate causes. The Great Teacher dealt what ought to have been the final blow to this infinite irrelevancy by a single question, "Do men gather grapes of thorns or figs of thistles?"

Why, then, did the Great Teacher not educate His followers fully? Why did He not tell us, for example, how such a thing as Rest might be obtained? The answer is, that *He did.* He assigned Rest to its cause, in words with which each of us has been familiar from his earliest childhood. He states: "Come unto Me, and I will *give* you Rest."

● *Rest, apparently, was a favor to be bestowed;* men had but to come to Him. But the next sentence takes that all back. The *qualification,* indeed, is added instantaneously. For what the first sentence seemed to give was next thing to an impossibility. For how, in a literal sense, can Rest be *given?* One could no more give away Rest than he could give away Laughter. We speak of "causing" laughter, which we can do; but we cannot give it away. When we speak of giving pain, we know perfectly well we cannot give pain away. And when we aim at giving pleasure, all that we do is to arrange a set of circumstances in such a way that these shall cause pleasure. Of course there is a sense, and a very wonderful sense, in which a great personality breathes upon all who come within its influence an abiding peace and trust. Men can be to other men as the shadow of a great rock in a stormy land. Much more Christ! much more Christ as Perfect Man! much more still as Savior of the world! But it is not this of which I speak. When Christ said He would give men rest, He meant simply that He would put them in the way of it. By no act of conveyance would, or could, He make over

His own Rest to them. He could give them
His recipe for it. That was all. But He
would not make it for them: (1) for one
thing, it was not in His plan to make it
for them, (2) for another thing, men were
not so planned that it could be made for
them, (3) and for yet another thing, it was
a thousand times better that they should
make it for themselves.

● *That this is the meaning becomes obvious from the wording of the second sentence:* "Learn of Me and ye shall *find* Rest."
Rest, that is to say, is not a thing that can
be given, but a thing to be *acquired*. It
comes not by an act, but by a process. It
is not to be found in a happy hour, as one
finds a treasure; but slowly, as one finds
knowledge. A soil has to be prepared for
it. Like a fine fruit, it will grow in one
climate and not in another. Like all growths
it will have an orderly development and mature by slow degrees.

● *The nature of this slow process Christ
clearly defines* when He says we are to
achieve Rest by *learning*. "Learn of Me,"
He says, "and ye shall find Rest to your
souls." How novel the connection between

these two words, "Learn" and "Rest"! How few of us have ever associated them — ever thought that Rest was a thing to be learned. Does it not show how entirely new Christ's teaching still is to the world, that so old and threadbare an aphorism should still be so little applied? The last thing most of us would have thought of would have been to associate *Rest* with *Learning*.

• *What is that which if duly learned will bring to the soul of man Rest?* Christ answers without the least hesitation. He specifies two things — Meekness and Lowliness. "Learn of Me," He says "for I am *meek* and *lowly* in heart." Now to these two accomplishments Rest is attached. Learn these, in short, and you have already found Rest. These are direct causes of Rest, which will produce it at once. This is necessarily so, for causes are never arbitrary, and the connection between antecedent and consequent here and everywhere lies deep in the nature of things.

What is the connection, then? I answer by a further question. What are the chief causes of *Unrest?* If you know yourself, you will answer Pride, Selfishness, Ambition. As you look back upon the past years of your life, is it not true that its unhappiness has chiefly come from the succession of personal mortifications and almost trivial disappointments which life has brought you? Great trials come at lengthened intervals, and we rise to breast them; but it is the petty friction of our every day life with one another, the jar of business or of work, the discord of the domestic circle, the collapse of our ambition, the crossing of our will or the taking down of our conceit, which make inward peace impossible. Wounded vanity, disappointed hopes, unsatisfied selfishness — these are the old, vulgar, universal sources of man's unrest.

Now it is obvious why Christ pointed out as the two chief objects for attaining peace the exact opposites of these. To Meekness and Lowliness these things simply do not exist. They cure unrest by making it impossible. These remedies do not trifle with surface symptoms; they strike at once at removing causes. The ceaseless chagrin of a self-centered life can be removed at once by learning Meekness and Lowliness of heart. He who learns them lives henceforth a charmed life. Christianity is a fine inoculation, a transfusion of healthy blood into an anaemic or poisoned soul. No fever can attack a perfectly sound body; no fever of unrest can disturb a soul which has learned the ways of Christ. Men sigh for the wings of a dove that they may fly away and be at rest. But flying away will not help us. We aspire to the top to look for Rest; it lies at the bottom. Water rests only when it gets to the lowest place. So do men. Hence, be lowly. The man who does not think of himself more highly than he should can never be hurt if others do not acknowledge him. Hence, be meek. The lowly man and the meek man are really above all other men, above all other things. They dominate the world because they do not care for it. The miser does not possess gold, gold possesses him. But the meek possess it. "The meek," said Christ, "inherit the earth." They do not buy it; they do not conquer it; but they inherit it.

There are people who go about the world looking out for slights, and they are necessarily miserable, for they find them at every turn — especially the imaginary ones. They have never learned how to live. Few men know how to live. We grow up at random,

carrying into mature life the merely animal methods and motives which we had as little children. And it does not occur to us that all this must be changed; that life is the finest of the Fine Arts and has to be learned with lifelong patience.

• *Yet this is what Christianity is for —to teach men the Art of Life.* And its whole curriculum lies in one statement — "Learn of Me." Unlike most education, this is almost purely personal; it is not to be had from books or lectures or creeds. Christ never said much in mere words about the Christian Graces. He lived them, He was them. Yet we do not merely copy Him. We learn His art by living with Him, like the old apprentices with their masters.

Christ's invitation to the weary and heavy-laden is a call to begin life over again upon a new principle — upon His own principle. "Watch My way of doing things," He says. "Follow Me. Take life as I take it. Be meek and lowly and you will find Rest."

• *I do not say that the Christian life can be a bed of roses.* No educational process can be this. And perhaps if some men knew how much was involved in the simple "learn" of Christ, they would not enter His school with so irresponsible a heart. For there is not only much to learn, but much to unlearn. To learn simply what it is to be meek and lowly may cost one half of what he values most on earth. Do we realize, for instance, that the way of teaching humility is generally by *humiliation*. There is probably no other school for it. When a man enters himself as a pupil in such a school it means a very great thing. There is such Rest there, but there is also much Work.

I should be wrong, even though my theme is the brighter side, to ignore the cross of hardship and minimize the cost. Our platitudes on the "benefits of affliction" are usually about as vague as our theories of Christian Experience. "Somehow," we believe affliction does us good. But it is not a question of "Somehow." The result is definite, calculable, necessary. It is under the strictest law of cause and effect. The first effect of losing one's fortune, for instance, is humiliation; and the effect of humiliation, as we have just seen, is to make one humble; and the effect of being humble is to produce Rest. It is a roundabout way, apparently, of producing Rest; but Nature generally works by circular process. Hence we must all go through the mill. Hence death to the lower self is the nearest gate and the quickest road to life.

* *Yet this is only half the truth — Christ's life outwardly was one of the most troubled lives that was ever lived:* Tempest and tumult, tumult and tempest, the waves breaking over His life all the time till His worn body was laid in the grave. But His inner life was a sea of glass. The great calm was always there. At any moment you might have gone to Him and found Rest. And even when the blood-thirsty men were dogging Him in the streets of Jerusalem, He turned to His disciples and offered them as a last legacy, "My peace." Nothing ever for a moment broke the serenity of Christ's life on earth. Misfortune could not reach Him; He had no fortune. Food, raiment, money — fountain-heads of half the world's weariness — He simply did not care for; He "took no thought" for them. It was impossible to affect Him by lowering His reputation. For He had already made himself of no reputation (Philippians 2:7). He was silent before insult. When He was reviled

He reviled not again. In fact, there was nothing that the world could do to Him that could ruffle His spirit.

Such living is altogether unique. It is only when we see what it was in Him that we can know what the word Rest means. It lies not in emotions, nor in the absence of emotions. It is not a hallowed feeling that comes over us in church. It is not something that the preacher has in his voice. It is not in nature, or in poetry, or in music — though in all these there is soothing. *It is the mind at leisure from itself.* It is the perfect poise of the soul; the absolute adjustment of the inward man to the stress of all outward things; the stability of assured convictions; the eternal calm of an invulnerable faith; the repose of a heart set deep in God. It is the mood of the man who says, with Browning, "God's in His Heaven, all's well with the world."

Two painters each painted a picture to illustrate his conception of rest. The first chose for his scene a still, lone lake among the far-off mountains. The second threw on his canvas a thundering water-fall, with a fragile birch tree bending over the foam;

at the fork of a branch, almost wet with the cataract's spray, a robin sat on its nest. The first was only *Stagnation;* the last was *Rest.* For in Rest there are always two elements — tranquility and energy; silence and turbulence; creation and destruction; fearlessness and fearfulness. This it is in Christ.

It is quite plain that whatever else Christ claimed to be or to do, He at least knew how to live. All this is the perfection of living, of passing through the world in the best way. Hence His wish to communicate His idea of life to others. He came, He said, to give men life, true life, a more abundant life than they were living: "the life," as the Revised Version has it, "that is life indeed." This is what He himself possessed, and offers to all mankind. And hence His direct appeal for all to come to Him who had not made much of life, who were weary and heavy laden. These He would teach His secret. They, also, should know "the life that is life indeed."

What Yokes Are For

THERE is still one doubt to clear up. After the statement, "Learn of Me," Christ throws in the disconcerting qualification, *"Take My Yoke* upon you and learn of Me." Why, if all this be true, does He call it a *yoke?* Why, while professing to give Rest, does He with the next breath whisper *"burden"?* Is the Christian life, after all, what its enemies take it for — an additional weight to the already great woe of life, some heavy restriction and trammelling of all that is joyous and free in the world? Is life not hard and sorrowful enough without being fettered with yet another yoke?

● *It is astounding how so glaring a misunderstanding of this plain sentence should ever have passed into currency.* Did you ever stop to ask what a yoke is really for? Is it to be a burden to the animal which wears it? It is just the opposite. It is to make its burden light. Attached to the oxen in any other way than by a yoke, the plough would be intolerable. Worked by means of a yoke, it is light. A yoke is not an instrument of torture; it is an instrument of mercy. It is not a malicious contrivance for making work hard; it is a gentle device to make hard labor light. It is not meant to give pain, but to save pain.

And yet men speak of the yoke of Christ as if it were a slavery, and look upon those who wear it as objects of compassion. For generations we have had homilies on "The Yoke of Christ," some delighting in portraying its narrow exactions; some seeking in these exactions the marks of its divinity; others apologizing for it, and toning it down; still others assuring us that, although it be very bad, it is not to be compared with the positive blessings of Christianity. Instead of making Christ attractive, it makes Him out a taskmaster, narrowing life by petty restrictions, making misery a virtue under the plea that it is the yoke of Christ, and happiness criminal because it now and then evades it. According to this conception, Christians are at best the victims of a depressing fate; their life is a penance; and their hope for the next world purchased by a slow martydrom in this.

The mistake has arisen from taking the word "yoke" here in the same sense, as in the expressions "under the yoke," or "wear the yoke in his youth." But in Christ's illustration it is not the *jugum* of the Roman soldier, but the simple "harness" or "ox-collar" of the Eastern peasant. It is the literal wooden yoke which He, with His own hands in the carpenter shop, had probably often made. He knew the difference between a smooth yoke and a rough one, a bad fit and a good fit; the difference it made to the patient animal which had to wear it. The rough yoke galled, and the burden was heavy; the smooth yoke caused no pain, and the burden was lightly drawn. The badly-fitted harness was a misery; the well-fitted collar was "easy."

And what was the "burden"? It was what all men bear. It was simply life, the general burden of life which all must carry with them from the cradle to the grave. Christ saw that men took life painfully. To some it was a weariness, to others a failure, to many a tragedy, to all a struggle and a

pain. How to carry this burden of life had been the whole world's problem. *And here is Christ's solution:* "Carry it as I do. Take life as I take it. Look at it from My point of view. Interpret it upon My principles. Take My yoke and learn of Me, and you will find it easy. For My yoke is easy, works easily, and *therefore* My burden is light."

● *There is no suggestion here that religion will absolve any man from bearing burdens.* That would be to absolve him from living. What Christianity does propose is to make it tolerable. Christ's yoke is simply His secret for the alleviation of human life, His prescription for the best and happiest method of living. Men harness themselves to the work and stress of the world in clumsy and unnatural ways. By placing a rough, ill-fitted collar where the neck is most sensitive, they make its strain and friction past enduring; and by mere continuous irritation this sensitiveness increases until the whole nature is quick and sore.

This is the origin, among other things, of a disease called "touchiness" — a disease which, in spite of its innocent name, is one of the gravest sources of restlessness in the world. Touchiness, when it becomes chronic, is a morbid condition of the inward disposition. It is self-love inflamed to the acute point; conceit, *with a hair-trigger*. The cure is to shift the yoke to some other place; to let men and things touch us through some new and perhaps as yet unused part of our nature; to become meek and lowly in heart while the old nature is becoming numb from want of use.

● *It is the beautiful work of Christianity to adjust the burden of life to those who bear it, and them to it*. Without doing any violence to human nature it sets it right with life, harmonizing it with all surrounding things, and restoring those who are jaded with the fatigue and dust of the world to a new grace of living. In the mere matter of altering the perspective of life and changing the proportion of things, its functions in lightening the care of man is altogether its own. The weight of a load depends upon the attraction of the earth. A ton on some other planet, where the attraction of gravity is less, does not weigh half a ton. Now Christianity removes the attraction of the earth, and this is one way in which it diminishes men's burden. It makes them citizens of another world. What was a ton yesterday is not half a ton today. So without changing one's circumstances, merely by offering a wider horizon and a different standard, it alters the whole aspect of the world.

Christianity as Christ taught is the truest philosophy of life ever spoken. But let us be quite sure when we speak of Christianity that we mean Christ's Christianity. Other versions are either caricatures, or exaggerations, or misunderstandings, or shortsighted and surface readings. For the most part their attainment is hopeless and the results wretched. But I care not who the person is, or through what vale of tears he has passed, or is about to pass, there is a new life for him along this path.

How Fruits Grow

The Christian experiences are not the work of magic, but come under the law of Cause and Effect. And I have chosen Rest only as a single illustration of the working of that principle.

I knew a Sunday scholar whose conception of Joy was that it was a thing made in lumps and kept somewhere in Heaven; and that when people prayed for it, pieces were somehow let down and fitted into their souls. Views as gross and material are often held by people who ought to be wiser. For Joy is as much a matter of Cause and Effect as pain. No one can get Joy by merely asking for it. It is one of the ripest fruits of the Christian life, and, like all fruits, must be grown. The world is pretty unanimous now in its belief in the orderliness of Nature. Men may not know how

fruits grow, but they do know that they cannot grow in five minutes.

● *Whence, then, is joy? Christ put His teaching upon this subject into one of the most exquisite of His parables.* It so happens that He has dealt with it in words of unusual fulness. It is the parable of the Vine. It was not simply a statement of the union with Christ. It was that; but it was more. After He had said it, He turned to the disciples and said He would tell them why He had spoken it. It was to tell them how to get joy. "These things have I spoken unto you." He said, "that My joy might remain in you and that your Joy might be full." It was a purposed and deliberate communication of His secret of Happiness.

Go back over these verses, and you will find the Causes of this Effect, the spring, and the only spring, out of which true Happiness comes. *Christ* was "the *true* Vine." Here, then, is the ultimate source of Joy. Through whatever media it reaches us, all true joy and Gladness find their source in Christ. By this, of course, is not meant that the actual Joy experienced is transferred from Christ's nature, or is something passed on from Him to us. What is passed on is His *method* of getting it. There is, indeed, a sense in which we can share another's joy or another's sorrow. But that is another matter. Christ is the source of Joy to men in the sense in which He is the source of Rest. His people share His life, and therefore share its consequences, and one of these is Joy. His method of living is one that in the nature of things produces Joy. When He spoke of His Joy remaining with us, He meant that the causes which produced it should continue to act. His followers, by *repeating* His life would experience its accompaniments.

● *The medium through which this Joy comes is next explained:* "He that abideth in Me, the same bringeth forth much fruit." Fruit first, Joy next; the one the cause or medium of the other. It lay partly in the bearing fruit, partly in the fellowship which made that possible. Partly, Joy lay in mere constant living in Christ's presence, with all that this implied of peace, of shelter and of love; partly in the influence of that Life upon mind and character and will; and partly in the inspiration to live and work for others, with all that this brings of self-riddance and Joy in others' gain. All these, in different ways and at different times, are sources of pure Happiness. Even the simplest of them — to do good to other people — is an instant and infallible specific. There is no mystery about Happiness whatever. Put in the right ingredients and it must come out. He that abideth in Him will bring forth much fruit; and bringing forth much fruit is Happiness. *The infallible recipe for Happiness, then, is to do good; and the infallible recipe for doing good is to abide in Christ.* The surest proof that all this is a plain matter of Cause and Effect is that men may try every other conceivable way of finding Happiness, and they will fail. Only the right cause in each case can produce the right effect.

● *Then the Christian experiences are our own making?* In the same sense in which grapes are our own making, and no more. All fruits *grow* — whether they grow in the soil or in the soul; whether they are the fruits of the wild grape or of the True Vine. No man can *make* things grow. He can *get them to grow* by arranging all the circumstances and fulfilling all the conditions. But the growing is done by God.

Causes and effects are eternal arrangements set in the constitution of the world, fixed beyond man's ordering. What man can do is to place himself in the midst of a chain of sequences. Thus he can get things to grow; thus he himself can grow.

● *What more need I add but this — test the method by experiment.* Do not imagine that you have got these things because you know how to get them. As well try to feed upon a cook book. But I think I can promise that if you try in this simple and natural way, you will not fail. The fruits will come, must come. In times past we have paid immense attention to *effects:* we have described them, extolled them, advised them, prayed for them — done everything but find out what *caused* them. Henceforth let us deal with *causes.* In other methods of living the Christian life there is an uncertainty. In other methods of acquiring the Christian experiences there is a "perhaps." But in so far as this method is the way of nature, it cannot fail. Its guarantee is the laws of the universe, and these are "the Hands of the Living God."

The True Vine

"I AM the true vine, and my Father is the husbandman. Every branch in me that beareth not fruit he taketh away: and every branch that beareth fruit, he purgeth it, that it may bring forth more fruit. Now ye are clean through the word which I have spoken unto you. Abide in me, and I in you. As the branch cannot bear fruit of itself, except it abide in the vine; no more can ye, except ye abide in me. I am the vine, ye are the branches: he that abideth in me, and I in him, the same bringeth forth much fruit: for without me ye can do nothing. If a man abide not in me, he is cast forth as a branch, and is withered; and men gather them, and cast them into the fire, and they are burned. If ye abide in me, and my word abide in you, ye shall ask what ye will, and it shall be done unto you. Herein is my Father glorified, that ye may bear much fruit; so ye shall be my disciples. As the Father hath loved me, so have I loved you: continue ye in my love. If ye keep my commandments, ye shall abide in my love; even as I have kept my Father's commandments, and abide in his love. These things have I spoken unto you, that my joy might remain in you, and that your joy might be full." — John 15:1-11